Also by J.T. Ellison

SO CLOSE THE HAND OF DEATH
THE IMMORTALS
THE COLD ROOM
JUDAS KISS
14
ALL THE PRETTY GIRLS

WHERE ALL THE DEAD LIE

J.T. ELLISON

MIRA®

Recycling programs
for this product may
not exist in your area.

ISBN-13: 978-0-7783-1387-8

WHERE ALL THE DEAD LIE

For questions and comments about the quality of this book please contact us
at Customer_eCare@Harlequin.ca.

www.Harlequin.com

Printed in U.S.A.

This one's for Laura Benedict,
who saved it for me at the eleventh hour,
and my Randy,
who made it come alive.

CHAPTER ONE

Scotland
The Highlands
Dulsie Castle
December 22

Dear Sam,

There is a moment in every life that defines, shapes, transcends your previous spirit, molding you as if from newborn clay. It's come for me. I have changed, and that change is irreversible.

Sam, there's no doubt anymore. I'm losing my mind. The shooting is haunting me. The horror of your loss, of who I've become, all of it is too much. I'm not sure how much longer I can stand to go on like this, trapped under glass, trapped away from everyone. I'm lost.

The walls here speak. Disconcerting at times, but at others, it's a comfort. The ceilings dance in the candlelight, and the floors shimmer and ripple with my every step. I escape out of doors, and when I do, all I find is fog, and mist, and lumbering sheep. Cows with gentle, inquisitive eyes. The dogs have a sense of humor. But you can tell they'd turn on you in a second. I've known people like that. The deer are patient, and sad, resigned to their captive lives. The crows are aggressive. The seagulls act foolish, and there's something so wrong about seeing a soaring gull against the mountainous backdrop. The chickens are huge and fretful, the grouse are in a hurry. The mist settles like a cold shawl across the mountain's shoulders, and the road I walk grows close, like it's planning to share a secret.

Above all, there is no one. And everyone. I feel them all around me. All the missing and the gone. I can't see them, except for late at night, when I'm supposed to be asleep. Then they push in on me from all sides, stealing my breath. The room grows cold and the warnings begin.

It strikes me that I'm surrounded by doctors, yet no one can help. I have to find the strength from within to heal. Isn't that what they always say, Physician, heal thyself? I shall amend it: Lieutenant, command thyself.

Sam, please, forgive me. It's all my fault. I know that now.

In moments of true peace: outside by the statue of Athena, looking over the gardens, watching the animals on the grounds, I feel your sorrow. I finally understand what you've lost. I've lost it, too. I don't think there's any coming back. I don't think there's any room for me in our world anymore.

There's something wrong with this place. Memphis's ancestors are haunting me. They don't like me here.

I did the best I could. I messed everything up, and I don't know if I can fix it.

Hug the twins. Their Fairy Godmother loves them. And I love you. I'm all done.

Taylor

Taylor slammed the laptop shut. Nauseous again. Pain built behind her eyes. A demon's hammering. Her only recourse was to lie down, lids screwed shut, praying for the hurt to pass. Percocet. Another. The pills they provided had stopped working. Nightfall signaled her brain to collapse in on itself, to allow the doubt and pain to rule. Weakness. Mornings brought safety, and courage.

Her mind was made of hinges, pieces that held imaginings she didn't want to acknowledge. If she did, the demons overtook her thoughts.

Defying the headache, she stumbled to the window, stared out at the mountains. Darkness enveloped their gentle curves. Bitter snow reflected the outline of the massive Douglas firs. Completely desolate. Private. Perfect for her to hide away, in the wilds of Scotland, pretending to the world that she was fine, just visiting for a time, on holiday, as the Brits around her liked to say.

She'd run away from the people who knew the truth about her situation—Dr. Sam Loughley, her best friend, and Dr. John Baldwin, her fiancé. She'd even managed to push away Memphis Highsmythe, a friend who wanted more from her than she was willing to give.

She brushed her hair off her shoulders and leaned against the window. The cool glass felt good on her temple. The small, puckered scar, another battle wound, nearly healed. Even the pinkish discoloration was beginning to fade. She no longer bore the blatant stigma of the killer known as the Pretender, at least on the outside. He'd stolen something from within her though. Something precious she didn't know how to retrieve.

Now she was only half a woman, half herself. A crazy little girl shut up in a castle, too tired to play princess anymore.

Movement over the mountains. The storm was changing. Gray clouds billowed down into the valley, nestled up against the loch, and opened. Stinging ice beat a merciless tattoo on the ground.

Her heart beat in time with the sleet, the pounding as insistent as a knock on the door—over and over and over—and the grip of the pain became too much to bear. The migraine overwhelmed her. The heavy Victorian-era furniture in her room was coruscating, beginning its nightly danse macabre.

Defeated, she pulled the curtains, went to the bathroom. Dumped two of the thick white Percocets in her palm and swallowed them with water from the tap. Hoped that they'd help.

Back to the bedroom. She saw her laptop was open. She'd been online? She shouldn't have had so much to drink. She was feeling sick again. The drink, the drugs, the pain, it was all jumbling together.

The truth.

Shadows heavy as blankets swathed her body, nipped

at her bare feet. She made her way to the bed by rote, lay down on the ornate spread, and gave in to the pain, the fear, the gut-wrenching terror that filled her night after night after night. The only things she could see were the dancing lights that shimmered off her brain, and the pearly outline of the ghost who'd come to tuck her in. She closed her eyes against the intrusion. Perhaps it would leave her alone tonight.

No.

It was here.

She felt its chilly caress slide against her cheek, its slim finger moving across her forehead, stopping at last to trace the bullet's entry wound. The scar burned cold. She would not move, would not call out in fear. The thing loved her terror, and this, this moment of abomination, when the ghosts of the past and present mingled in the very air she breathed, this was the one moment when her voice came back full and true. She'd made the mistake of screaming the first time it touched her, and would not give it that joy again.

The chilled path moved lower now, to the long-healed slash across her neck. She wouldn't be so lucky the next time. The touch was a warning. A sign.

And then it was gone. She let the throbbing wash over her and wept silent tears.

BEGINNINGS

One Week Earlier

"Like a broken gong be still, be silent.
Know the stillness of freedom
where there is no more striving."
—THE BUDDHA

CHAPTER TWO

Nashville, Tennessee
December

"Taylor, you're doing great."

Dr. Benedict had the laryngoscope deep down Taylor Jackson's throat. The anesthetic they'd sprayed before the procedure made her tongue curl; it tasted like bitter metal. Who the hell could be a sword swallower? This was ridiculously intrusive. Though she didn't hurt, she could tell they had something threaded into her. The thought made her want to gag. The doctor caught the motion and murmured to her, softly, touching her on the shoulder like he was gentling a horse.

"Shh, it's okay. Almost done. Just another minute."

She was tempted to get him a stopwatch. That was the third time he'd promised he was almost done. She tried to think of something, anything, that would distract her. The panic was starting to rise, the claustrophobic feeling of having her mouth open for too long, the knowledge that there was something…

"Okay, cough for me, Taylor."

Finally.

The metal slithered out of her mouth. She felt like an alien, regurgitating a particularly indigestible meal.

At least she could breathe again.

The examination table was close to the wall. She slumped back for support and watched the doctor set aside his tools. The scope made a thunk against the metal of the tray, discarded, no longer an instrument of healing-by-torture, just an inanimate implement with no intent, no plot.

He patted her shoulder again. "Why don't you get dressed and come on into my office. We'll talk more there."

She tried not to notice that he winced when he said *talk*.

She wasn't doing a lot of that these days.

Taylor dressed, shedding the thin paper gown in a huff. Why she'd needed to get seminude for Dr. Benedict to look down her throat was a mystery to her.

John Baldwin, her fiancé, stood quietly in the doorway, waiting for her. Reading her mind, he smiled. "Because if you'd had a bad reaction to the anesthetic, or had a problem, he wouldn't be able to take the time to get you undressed to stabilize you."

She nodded. That made sense. She knew the logic behind it, but that didn't mean she had to like it.

She watched Baldwin watching her, his green eyes full of concern, his black hair standing on end, the salt at his temples smoothed back. He was tall, six foot four, and broad-shouldered. She'd always thought him beautiful; it wasn't an appropriate adjective for a man, but he was. Well proportioned, a full, teasing mouth, high cheekbones and a sharp jaw. He was her everything.

Was. Had been. She didn't know why she was thinking in past tense—he was still here, she was still here. Together. They were touching, holding hands even. But physical proximity means nothing when your world's been turned upside down.

She was afraid of more than just her visible injuries. She was scared that the invisible ones, especially the brittle crack in her heart, would be what did her in. He'd lied to her about his past. She asked for one thing, loyalty, and he had failed her.

"Let me help you," Baldwin said, and squeezed her hand as they started down the hall. She let him. It had been nearly a month since the shooting, and she was still wobbly. Head shots did that to you. A mantra that had been forced on her for weeks.

She ignored the fact that he was looking at her with that confused gaze, the one that said please, *please,* let me back in. As if he'd known what she was thinking. He did that sometimes, stole her thoughts right out of her head.

Oh, Baldwin. What have you done to us?

Dr. Benedict had left the door open. Baldwin held it for Taylor as she entered the room, then followed behind her. There was a lot of dark wood, a huge desk, a few framed photos and degrees. She sat in one of the two chairs facing the desk and raised an eyebrow expectantly.

Dr. Benedict cleared his throat. "Okay. Good news first. I'm not seeing anything that indicates a permanent condition. The dysphonia responded to the botulinum injections—though your vocal cords are still bowed a bit, they are starting to adduct in the midline and when you cough. There are no signs of polyps or tumors. This is good news, Taylor. Your vocal cords are intact and working. When you were shot, when you fell, you hit your throat on something. That blunt force trauma is what caused the dysphonia. This isn't a result of the bullet track, or the surgery. You were damn lucky. Your voice should come back."

She shook her head and pointed at her throat.

"Taylor, I don't know. All I can say with certainty is that the problem is no longer a purely physical one. The bullet didn't penetrate into the vocal area of the brain, otherwise you'd really have some issues. There's nothing out of the ordinary in your neurological profile, and the wound has healed nicely. Your balance is remarkably good, considering. You're eating all right, sleeping all right, for you at least. The headaches aren't getting any better?"

She shook her head. The pain left her breathless sometimes.

"That's not entirely unexpected. They'll fade in time. Rest, and no stress, that will help. But your voice…"

He broke off, and she braced herself. She was experienced in giving bad news. She got the sense she was about to get a huge dose of it.

"I think you may be experiencing a bit of what we call a conversion disorder."

She shrugged. He bit his lip a couple of times, then continued.

"You've just suffered a major trauma, both physically and emotionally. You're healing well, so I'm inclined to think that this continued dysphonia is non-organic, more of a… psychological disequilibrium, if you will. And as such, it's much more treatable through some form of psychotherapy, combined with antianxiety medication. Which also wouldn't hurt to help get you through the stress of...all this."

Dr. Benedict actually waved his hand around in a circle.

Can you banish it for me, Doctor? Can you wave your magic wand and make me better?

All this. Being shot in the head by a suspect. Spending a week in an induced coma while the swelling on her brain subsided, then, when the medication wore off, scaring everyone to death by not waking up for another week. Opening her eyes to find Baldwin hovering anxiously over her. Not being able to talk...to tell him she loved him, and that she hated him. The Pretender, setting up residence in her brain, invading her dreams, haunting her days. Psychological disequilibrium. What a perfect term for what she was feeling. Pissed off and scared, too. This couldn't all be in her head. Could it?

She grabbed the pad of paper from her pocket, flipped it open and scribbled furiously. She held it up for the doctor to see.

He raised his hands in defense.

"Now, Taylor, I'm not saying you're crazy. Far from it. A conversion disorder fits with your symptoms. And it's fixable."

Baldwin shifted in his chair, faced her, his voice deep and grave. "Taylor, he's right. A conversion disorder does fit. We've talked about you having PTSD. You should hear yourself sleep. You moan and scream and yell. You thrash around all night. It's obvious you're reliving the shooting."

She shook her head vehemently, wrote *That's not true* and showed it to Benedict. She didn't need him to see how weak she'd become. She put her hand on Baldwin's arm and scowled at him. He seemed grimly determined to sabotage her today.

Of course she was reliving it. Every second of every day. It was on loop in her head.

Benedict frowned at her. "Taylor, you need to let me know these things. I prescribed Ativan when you were here last—you're not taking it regularly, are you?"

She shook her head. The Ativan made her logy.

"I keep telling her she needs to take the meds."

She hated when Baldwin sided with the doctor against her. If he could just be on *her* side, and stop being so fucking solicitous and knowledgeable.

Maybe I am just sitting on a head full of crazy. I can't talk. I can't work. I'm communicating with a notepad. Yeah, I'm going to be just fine. Sure.

She missed her life. She missed her team. Her homicide detectives at Metro Nashville: Lincoln Ross, Marcus Wade, Renn McKenzie. Her former sergeant, Pete Fitzgerald. Sam, Forensic Medical, the acrid scent of formalin. Commander Huston. Everyone. Even missed Baldwin, though her fury at his lies hadn't faded, and the hurt was all that was left behind. But she didn't know how to face them. Any of them.

Her breath started to come quicker.

"Taylor?" Baldwin said, jerking her from her thoughts.

She needed to get out. Away. Now. She shot daggers at them both, then stood and marched from the room.

She made it out of the doctor's office and into the vestibule by the elevators. She wasn't going to get far. Baldwin had the car keys.

She tried to say the words aloud that were burning her mouth, her throat. But the images started—the hardwood floor, covered in dust that tickled her nose, the beating of her heart, so loud, so close, the blackness she knew was blood covering her eyes. Her blood. Baldwin screaming, Sam bleeding, the Pretender crumpled in a heap just inches from her, his eyes open, staring into hers as she struggled, and failed, to maintain consciousness.

She was dying again.

She started to hyperventilate. A fucking panic attack, in public, for everyone to see. She glanced about wildly—where could she go?

Strong arms encircled her. She smelled cedar, Baldwin's natural scent.

"Breathe, baby. Just breathe. Deep in through your nose. You're all right."

She was getting tired of people telling her she was all right. Obviously she wasn't. She was far from all right. She was broken.

She sagged against Baldwin, let him take her weight. How many times had they done this in the past few weeks? Four? Ten? Fifty?

She felt herself center, the panic subsiding. The Ativan was supposed to help avoid and alleviate this very problem. Maybe she should try it again. She just hated to admit defeat. She kept hoping she would find a way to handle this.

"Honey, come on back inside. I think Dr. Benedict wants to finish."

She fought to get the words out—*fuck Dr. Benedict*—but they wouldn't come. Instead, she clamped her lips tight together and followed Baldwin back into the office. They took their seats.

Benedict acted like nothing had happened. He just cocked his head and asked, "So?"

I'll do it.

Benedict clapped his hands together. "Good. I'll send word over to Dr. Willig that you'll be making an appointment to see her ASAP. She's well versed in conversion disorder; I can't think of a better doctor to work with on this. I'll see you back here in a couple of weeks. If you have any pain, or problems swallowing, or bleeding, you get in here immediately, all right?"

They stood, and he walked them to the door. He let his hand linger a moment on her back in reassurance.

"Hang in, okay? This will improve. Time heals all wounds, remember that."

God, if only that were true.

"I know this is hard. I know it sucks. Whether you're ready to admit it or not, you've been through an unbelievable trauma, no matter how 'lucky' you got with that shot. The stress of your situation alone is enough to cause the conversion disorder. Listen, I'll throw in some incentive. You see Victoria—regularly, mind you—and I'll talk to Commander Huston about you going back on the job. I see no reason you can't at least handle a non-field post in a few weeks."

How much convincing had Baldwin had to do to talk the doc into that? At least driving a desk would be something. Better than sitting at home waiting. Waiting for her voice to come back, or the anger to fade. For Sam to forgive her. For Baldwin to agree to talk about the search for his son.

"Deal?"

She nodded, and put out her hand to shake.

At this point, she'd do almost anything to get back to normal, even if it meant getting her head shrunk. Working murder was her life, her purpose. Take that away and she felt like a shell of herself. Take away her voice too, and she was slowly locking herself down, inside, where only her demons resided. This was a fitting punishment for her sins, to be sure. A little bit of hell on earth. She just wondered how long it was going to last.

CHAPTER THREE

When they'd arrived at Baptist, Taylor had watched an older couple get out of a car in the handicap space, two tiny, shriveled beings, male and female, showing up for an appointment. It had made her sad, the parallels between them—old and young, both hurt and looking to be fixed. Taylor knew her odds were better, but she couldn't help but feel that this was what she had to look forward to. The romantics of growing old with someone were shattered by the realities of the flesh incrementally dying.

But leaving the hospital, she wasn't feeling as pessimistic. As annoyed as she was, with both Baldwin and the doctor, she couldn't help but feel buoyed by her appointment. Having a plan of attack was eminently preferable to this constant sitting and waiting.

"Hungry?" Baldwin asked.

She nodded. She was starving. She wrote *Prince's*.

"Hot chicken? At 9:00 in the morning?"

Her mouth started to water at the mere thought. When she was coming up on the force, they ate at Prince's almost every night shift, right around

3:00 a.m. Ridiculously hot fried chicken, full of spices and peppers, a true Nashville delicacy. It brought tears to your eyes. She'd seen more than one tough cop use the spices in the chicken to cover real tears after a particularly nasty night.

Baldwin laughed briefly. "Prince's it is." He turned right onto Charlotte. She stared up the hill, wishing she could go straight to the CJC right now, announce herself and jump on the closest case. Commander Huston wouldn't like it. She'd given strict instructions about Taylor's time off. Everyone was coddling her, when in truth a little action might shake things loose. She was mentally stable, the wounds were healed, the headaches were manageable, most of the time. She just couldn't talk. Really, that wasn't much of a handicap, was it?

Unless no one believed that was all that was wrong with her.

Baldwin was playing with the steering wheel.

"So you're cool with seeing Willig?"

Taylor nodded, shrugged.

He took his right hand off the wheel, laid it gently on her wrist. "Honey, remember, I've been there. I know what it feels like to revisit a nightmare. To feel like I somehow failed, even when it wasn't my fault."

She felt tears prick at the corners of her eyes. Solicitousness was bad. She could handle most anything—anger, fear, pain, concern. But pity set her off. She was too strong to be pitied, damn it.

Baldwin just wouldn't let up. Every word from his mouth was like stepping on hot coals. Her teeth clenched.

"We can talk about it anytime you want. I want to help, Taylor. Let me help you."

She responded with a deafening sigh.

Leave. Me. Alone.

They drove on in strained silence until they reached the trailer that housed the restaurant. She was hoping that the spices would loosen things up in her throat, like really hot tea. It hadn't worked yet, but she was willing to try most anything.

Her cell rang as they pulled into the lot. It was Dr. Benedict's office. She opened the phone and handed it to Baldwin. He uh-huh'd for a second, then looked over at Taylor. "Today at one o'clock with Willig sound good?"

She nodded. The sooner the better.

He hung up and handed the phone back to her. They got out of the car, let the chilled air surround them. There was a stream of warmth coming out of the side door to the trailer. It enveloped her so thoroughly she almost forgot it was winter.

They ordered their chicken—extra hot for her, medium for him—then sat at the picnic table with a bundle of napkins, waiting for their food to be ready.

"Wanna talk?" Baldwin asked softly. She turned to him, his clear green eyes full of empathy, and shut down. He was doing it again, that look of sadness, of compassion. Couldn't he just yell and scream like a normal man, get pissed at her for giving him the cold shoulder? He was too understanding. Goddamn it.

How about you go first. A little more detail about your son would be nice. How are things in adoption land?

He flinched as if she'd struck him. Perfect. She'd wounded him right back.

Baldwin stared at her for a second, anger boiling beneath the surface, his lips in a thin, forbidding line. Then he took a deep breath and shook his head, refusing the engagement.

He was so damn patient with her, and she was getting really frustrated with him. They needed to have a knock-down, drag-out fight, clear the air, find a way back to themselves. She'd been poking at him, and he'd been unwilling to react, nor to discuss his side of the issue. It just served to make her more upset. She wanted a fight, even if she couldn't actually yell at him.

She turned her back and watched the steam rise out of a manhole cover, venting thermals from beneath the earth. This was not working. Despite her physical problems and her wild mood swings, hurting Baldwin had become a source of satisfaction for her, and that didn't bode well for their life together. She twisted her engagement ring around her finger, the Asscher-cut diamonds catching the sun and sparkling onto the dirty gray pavement, a symbol of hope. If she'd just let it be. Get the hell out of her own way and allow things to get back to normal.

Taylor had never been in this situation before. Probably because anytime a relationship started to head south, she'd just ended it cleanly and walked away. No sense in struggling to make it work. But this, this was different. Baldwin was different. She needed to decide what she wanted from him. He needed to do the same. They couldn't keep dancing around like this, cutting each other from different angles. One of the cuts was going to bleed too much, and then it would be over. And she didn't think that was what she wanted.

Baldwin handed her a Coke, and she took the opportunity to down a Percocet. Her head was starting to pulse, and she had the whole day in front of her. It would be the first pill of many, she could tell that already.

They ate in silence, then got back in the car and headed home. There was nothing for her to do downtown anyway; her appointment wasn't until 1:00. He pulled into the driveway, into the garage, entered the house, all without saying a word. Inside, he excused himself to go to his office to get some work done. Taylor was left adrift, feeling annoyed with herself for digging at him, sorry that he wasn't near her, glad he wasn't, and confused about what all that meant.

At this rate, she was going to drive herself mad.

She needed to kill some time. She could read, but that would make the headache worse. Exercise, but she'd already done that this morning, before the doctor. She decided to check her email, and was immediately glad that she did.

There was a note from Memphis. Generally a highly diverting event.

James "Memphis" Highsmythe, so dubbed by his classmates at Eton after a trip to Graceland in Tennessee when he was a child, was a friend, a detective inspector with the Metropolitan Police in London. He was also the Viscount Dulsie, and a confirmed rake. He'd worked a case with Baldwin and ended up in Nashville, made a play for Taylor's affections in Italy, and was a source of annoyance, amusement, and lately, comfort to Taylor. Undeniably a friend who wanted to be more. Much, much more.

The email's subject line was blank, as usual. Memphis wasn't one for pith when it wasn't needed. She clicked it open.

Francesco Stradivari just had a birthday. Can you imagine what it must have been like to have a father whose work was respected the world over? Did you know he forged his father's signature on a few of the pieces in late 1730's? Today is also my father's birthday, and I've promised him a night out. I'm catching the train to Edinburgh at four. What sort of brilliance lies ahead for you?

Taylor calculated the time difference. Memphis was six hours ahead of her. He would probably be on the train now. He often wrote to her while traveling. It helped him pass the time.

She hit Reply.

I went to the doctor this morning. Everything is a-okay, just still don't have any voice to speak of. Pun intended. He offered me a deal: if I see Victoria Willig, the department's psychologist, then he'll approve me going back to work on limited duty in a few weeks. I have an appointment with her this afternoon. Where are you taking your father to dinner?

His message came back quickly. She was right, he was on the train.

Open your chat.

She did, and Memphis was there, a default smiley face waiting on her.

Dinner is at The Witchery, of course. The finest meal in Edinburgh. It's divine. I'd love to take you sometime. We'll have Beef Wellington and burnt custard for pudding.

That does sound good. But what, no haggis?

Would YOU eat sheep's stomach stuffed with oats? It's actually not bad. I simply prefer a more refined meal.

Ugh. No thanks. What else will you do tonight?

That's it. Father is taking the car back to the estate, and I'm heading back to London on the late train. This case is getting ready to blow up, I can just feel it. I'll be pulled in by the morning.

Memphis had mentioned the case to her before. Two girls missing, now three, from their London homes. He'd been watching it from afar, wondering what sort of escalation was coming. Taylor knew that feeling. An investigator is only as good as their instincts, and she respected the idea of a hunch.

At least you'll be calling the shots. Your mother won't be joining you for dinner?

The Countess? No, she's in South Africa with my brother. His vineyard is having a wee bit of difficulty, and she offered to go and help.

The Countess is a vintner too?

Her talents know no bounds. Like someone else I'm acquainted with.

Taylor let that slide. She wasn't feeling terribly talented these days. Not having her own case to work, her own show to run, she just wasn't herself.

Memphis wrote again.

I've been thinking: If you have to see a therapist to get clearance to return to work, why don't you make plans to visit? One of my dearest friends is a celebrated psychologist. You can stay at the estate, she can drop in for your visits, and you can get a break. Do some outdoors stuff. I know it's a bit chilly now, but with the proper gear it would be lovely. The house is all done up for Christmas, it's quite beautiful. My father will be joining my mother in South Africa for the holidays, so there's no one around. You can have the run of the place. Get away from those pesky reporters who've been nagging you. What do you think?

Taylor sat back in her chair, the mouse forgotten in her hand. Scotland. For Christmas. An escape from Nashville, from the condemnation of her loved ones, away from the silence that bound her. She wouldn't be expected to speak if she were alone. No one to look over her shoulder, check on her every movement, look at her with doubt. No one to talk about her behind her back. She wouldn't have to keep pretending that she didn't notice that everyone was acting like she was some ticking time bomb.

And she'd been fodder for the Nashville media yet again. They'd done story after story, broadcast her condition, delved into her past and speculated about her future. She didn't go a day without at least one interview request. They filled her email box and took up space on her answering machine. What was she supposed to do, go on air and mime what had happened? No thanks.

Taylor? Are you still here?

She wouldn't be cleared to go back to work for a few weeks anyway. What harm could come of her sneaking away for a bit? If Memphis's doctor friend would check in with Benedict for her, maybe that would suffice to get him to clear her to go back to work.

But what would that mean to Memphis, if she agreed to come stay on his estate? Memphis was forever pushing, purposefully misinterpreting her intentions. Fending him off wasn't always as easy as it should be. The constant attention was flattering. Memphis was different than Baldwin. Baldwin loved her, Memphis wanted her. She had no illusions about the difference.

Things with Memphis would be…simpler. Lust was always easier than love.

She realized he was waiting for an answer.

I'm here. Sorry about that. I don't know, Memphis. I've just promised to see the department shrink. Maybe this isn't the best timing, you know?

Dearest Taylor, you'll go mad being around the office and not allowed to work. It's a travesty that they've even suggested you suffer this indignity. Why don't you wait until you can return fully, unencumbered by this little glitch? We can fix you. Heal you. I know it.

She had an idea of what kind of healing Memphis would like to employ. Would that make things better for her, or worse? And were things so off the rails with Baldwin that she was actually tempted to find solace with another man? Not just another man, but Memphis? She shoved that thought away; she didn't want to go there. Not now. Not after the morning they'd had.

I'm sure Baldwin wouldn't take kindly to me jetting off to the UK. I'd have to ask him along.

No, no, no. That's exactly the point. A getaway, a holiday, means being away from everything and everyone.

Including you?

There was a pause on his end this time.

I wouldn't presume to lurk on your holiday. I'd see you safely ensconced at the estate, introduce you around, maybe give you a tour of the Highlands, then I'd have to return to London for work. Truly, think about it. Relaxation, and being away from your cares, might be just the ticket.

So she really would be alone. That was tempting. So very tempting.

I'll think about it. Promise. I have to go though, my appointment with the shrink is soon. Have a nice dinner. Wish the Earl Happy Birthday for me. Enjoy the grouse.

How did you know that's what I'd be ordering?

Just a guess. See ya, Memphis.

Au revoir, ma chere.

The chat window closed and she was left alone, wondering why she was even entertaining the idea of taking Memphis up on his offer. It was a foolhardy, dangerous thing to do. Baldwin wouldn't agree to it in a million years. But maybe leaving town would help? Distance could make the heart grow fonder.

Or break it cleanly in two.

CHAPTER FOUR

Dr. Samantha Owens Loughley stood poised over the body of an older man who'd passed away on the porch of his home, taking notes. *Slight skin slippage. Facial congestion. Insect activity on legs.* She was relatively certain he'd died of natural causes, but an unattended death meant an autopsy.

The rest of the day's autopsies were lined up on their individual tables, attendants at the ready, waiting for her to stop by and do the external exam before they turned the pristine stainless-and-white autopsy suite into a Technicolor rainbow—the subcutaneous fat gamboge under the skylights, the organs a muddy sinopia, limp inside their dead homes, the blood as vivid and intense as a burning fire. There were four techs but five bodies, so she'd offered to take one of the guests herself to make things go quicker.

She finished her notes, made her rounds.

Everyone was situated now.

"Let's go," she said.

She returned to her table. Consulted the case file one last time. Pulled on her mask and picked up her scalpel.

She was just about to make the Y-incision when the lab phone rang. It startled her; she'd been very much lost in thought, not seeing the body beneath her blade, not mindfully thinking about the possibilities of the apparent cardiac infarction. She'd been watching the sharp tip of a large knife slide into her sweater, then slowly, inexorably, pierce the skin of her lower abdomen.

Son of a bitch.

"You got that, Doc?" Stuart Charisse was her favorite tech. He was handling the body of an overdose on the other side of the wall.

She tossed the scalpel onto the tray to her right with a clatter. The phone rang again.

"Let it go. If they need me, they'll page."

Sam turned away from the autopsy table and took a seat on a stool near the sinks. Though snow was expected in the afternoon, for now the skies were misleadingly sunny, the frosted skylights dropping warm beams onto her shoulders. She breathed in deeply, counted to four, then let her breath out. The phone stopped ringing. Her breath didn't slow. Shoot.

"I'm stepping out. I'll be back in a second."

There were murmurs of assent. Her team understood; she'd had to step out a few times over the past month.

She stripped off her gloves, pushed through the door to the changing area, and sat at the desk in silence, her breath a background noise to the snapping, sawing and clanking behind her.

This had to stop. Her work was her sanity. She'd always had a comfortable level of detachment from her cases. The precision of the human body was fascinating, and she was damn good at her job. She was helping, she knew that. Giving answers. Putting minds at rest. Solving cases. But being lost entirely outside the room while she was cutting wasn't fair to the bodies she worked on. They deserved better.

But damn, would she ever be able to look at her work the same way again?

When Barclay Iles had finessed his way into her life, she hadn't even seen him coming. She'd laughed with him, trained him, worked alongside him, shared meals, late nights, even gave her blessing to his union with her receptionist. When that same man dropped the pretenses and alias, kidnapped her, tied her to a chair, revealed himself as the Pretender and divested her core of the small, innocent life within, she thought she might go insane. It was one thing to miscarry, to have your body make the decision for you. But to lose a child by force, before it was even born, that was too much for her to handle.

The moment replayed itself over and over and over. She could swear she felt the child tear away from the wall of her uterus; the ripping sensation found her in her dreams. The knife wound had been nothing compared to the massive cramp that had seized her midsection. She'd simply wanted to roll into a ball and cry, but with her arms handcuffed behind her, she was forced to make do with a slight bending at the waist. She didn't want him to see her pain, which was a mistake. He liked pain. He liked to inflict it, and loved to see the effects his actions had on her frailty. When she finally admitted to it by crying out, he had stopped.

But the damage was done. Sam was alive. But her child was lost.

My God. If Taylor had just arrived sooner. If she and

Baldwin had figured out who Barclay was earlier. If Taylor had only...

If Sam hadn't trusted him like a fool.

If, if, if.

She wanted to blame Taylor. Wanted to lay the blame at her feet like a dog drops a rolled-up newspaper. *Here, you take it. It's your responsibility. Now I'm going back to my life.*

Her rational brain repeated, over and over, that it didn't work that way. That she was wrong to blame Taylor because a serial killer decided to target her. That it was inevitable that Sam would be caught in the cross fire. That Sam was the one who'd opened their doors to the Pretender instead of helping to catch him.

Sam had sat back and watched her best friend take ever-increasing risks. She should have known better. Taylor had a breaking point, just like all people. She wasn't a superhero, she was just a woman, who'd been pushed too far.

Sam could have done something. She could have seen the madman for who he was, instead of being charmed by him. She could have looked more closely at her friend, paid attention to the cracks in her ever-present armor.

But Taylor didn't have to take things into her own hands, either. If she'd just told someone of her hunch— that she suspected the Pretender had returned to his former lair—someone could have gotten to Sam in time. If Taylor had just let her team in, let them know what she was planning, maybe Sam wouldn't have lost the baby. Maybe Taylor wouldn't have been shot.

Instead, they'd all sat back and let Taylor run off the reservation. Sam thought she was the only one who knew that Taylor wanted to be the one to annihilate the threat. Baldwin had been distracted, worried about his son, and hadn't realized what Taylor planned to do. Had he? Surely he hadn't. He'd never condone murder.

Then again, Sam knew Taylor better than she knew herself. And Sam was the one who was there, locked in that attic, when Taylor had come through the door. She'd seen the look on Taylor's face: for once all the masks pushed aside, all the walls dropped, hate and righteous fury emanating from her…it had frightened Sam. Perhaps her best friend was a better actress than she gave her credit for. She'd always kept the dark side of herself hidden.

Sam pushed her bangs off her forehead and regloved. She went back into the suite, made the rounds, looking at the hearts in situ, then returned to her table, took up the scalpel and made the incision into the dead man's chest a bit harder than absolutely necessary.

She felt so worthless. She could blame no one but herself. She was the one who'd let the monster into their lives. And he'd taken from all of them—her child, Fitz's eye, Taylor's voice.

The man's breastplate was off now, the rhythm of the posts around the room underway. The bone saw whirred to life, a few moments later there was an audible pop and Stuart called out, "Head's ready." Sam dropped her scalpel and went to the body, smoothed her fingers across the young man's brain, saw nothing unusual, then nodded her okay. Stuart took the brain from the cavity with a few quick cuts, set it in the scale to be weighed, and as she went back to her own table again, he shouted, "Brain's ready." It would wait; she'd have to dissect the organs of all five bodies in turn, searching for the clues that would affirm the cause of death. No murders this morning, nothing extraordinary, so no special precautions were being taken. Just another day at the office.

Cutting and sawing and weighing and measuring soothed her tired mind. This was her world, finite, sure, and expected. Unlike Taylor, she had the luxury of being able to work, of finding herself again through her job. To throw herself into the sameness of each day. Every body held its secrets, but inside, they're all alike.

Was she still?

She didn't think so.

Oh, the rational part of her understood that all of her organs were in their proper places. The doctors said there was even a chance she could conceive again. But the thought of losing another child brought her up short. Her grief had been tremendous, but it was the reaction of her husband, Simon, that had been more than she could handle. He *did* blame Taylor, hadn't wrapped his head around the situation yet. They still went to bed stiff and unloving, his back turned to hers. He blamed Sam, too. She knew that. And she agreed with him. She *could* have fought harder, could have seen what was coming. Could have protected their child. She vacillated between understanding his frustration and hating him for blaming her. She hated herself a bit, too. What kind of mother lets her child be murdered?

The haze of the past weeks had finally been lifted by her son's first steps. The twins, Matthew and Madeline, weren't fazed by their mother's inability to pick them up, to look at them. They had each other. They knew, inside, that she loved them, that she was afraid that if she touched them, she'd taint their souls with the rot permeating hers. She saw it in their eyes—the forgiveness, the patience. They would heal her, if she'd let them. For their sakes, she had to come to grips with this.

When she began to bleed yesterday, that's when the rails came off the train again. It was her first period since the miscarriage, and such an open acknowledgement that her life was inextricably altered. She was empty again. No child growing, no soreness in her breasts, no morning sickness. When the child was cut from her, so were the symptoms, with such suddenness that she wondered if it were all a dream.

A nightmare, more likely.

She realized she was standing with both hands on her stomach, her left holding the skin down flat, her right poised at the ready, a scalpel between her fingers, pointed toward her own flesh.

CHAPTER FIVE

Edinburgh

The papers screamed the news, the radio and television repeating the story over and over at ten-minute intervals, making Memphis's head ache. Another girl was gone. Hannah Straithwhite—an eighteen-year-old student. London was up in arms—she was the third girl to go missing in the past three months. No bodies had been found, no signs of foul play. Just a regular girl, from a regular world, disappearing from the streets of her life.

A clear pattern had emerged. All three girls were blonde, eighteen, students, though from different areas of London and wildly different socioeconomic backgrounds. It was a nightmare, and he knew he was going to get dragged in.

Ever since he'd participated in the capture of the Italian serial killer Il Mostro and his literally evil twin, the Conductor, anything that remotely smacked of a serial case was dumped in his lap. His superiors expected a good close. Not that he wasn't willing, of course. More work meant less downtime, less time to think and thus dwell. And around the holidays, that was for the best.

Thank God for the train. An escape. He was looking forward to seeing his father. Being away from New Scotland Yard for a bit. Tomorrow his commander, Toy McQuivey, was sure to pull him into the wet-wool-scented head office and ask him to take charge of the Straithwhite case. But that was tomorrow. He had all night ahead of him.

He stared out the window. Into the darkness, the quickening night.

He couldn't stop thinking about the offer he'd just made to Taylor. It was selfish of him to want her near. He could delude himself into thinking it was about work; she was a damn good investigator. In addition to being the loveliest woman he'd ever set eyes on. He had no business pursuing her, he knew that. But he'd been brought up to take what he wanted, and she presented a challenge. She loved her G-man, no doubt about it, but there was an opportunity. He could feel it. Her catastrophic injuries had changed her, made her…afraid wasn't the right word. Cautious, then. And he knew they weren't getting along. It wasn't very sporting of him to try and separate them, but if there was ever a time….

God would strike him down for this, but he didn't care about eventualities. Not anymore.

Memphis didn't know if he loved Taylor or simply wanted to acquire her, but either way, having that gray-eyed woman in his life made him feel alive for the first time since his wife, Evan, died.

Besides, he wasn't lying about his psychologist friend. Dr. Madeira James was married to one of Memphis's best chums from school, Roland MacDonald, the second son of the Earl of Killicrankie. Roland was content to live the squire's life, not having to work, spending his time hunting, fishing and otherwise engaged outdoors. He'd gone to America in the late '90s and returned with Madeira, already in possession of a doctorate at the tender age of twenty-two, already ripe with his child. Maddee, as she was known, was great fun, a beautiful woman with long, dark hair and a wide smile: a good mother, a good wife, and a good friend to Memphis and Evan. She'd helped pick up the pieces after Evan's death, and Memphis trusted her with his life.

She'd be perfect for Taylor.

If only Taylor would agree to come over. He doubted his money or title impressed her; she'd grown up with largesse and wasn't enamored of its abilities to smooth one's life. It was going to take much more to steal her away from Nashville. It would take compassion, and understanding, and freedom. Freedom most of all. And that he had the ability to give her.

They had so much in common, more than she really knew. Privileged upbringings, yet a desire to eradicate evil, to solve crimes, to put away the bad guys. He knew Taylor was reacting to her father's illegal activities when she decided to become a cop. His path was more direct.

There was a killer, famous in the U.K., who was on a rampage while Memphis was in school. He was known as the Jeweler. He started killing the same year as the infamous Babes in the Woods murders, 1986, and was forever linked to the two young girls found strangled in the woods outside Brighton, even though he wasn't actually responsible for their murders. He'd killed eight women, all by stabbing, then disappeared off the map.

He'd been suspected in the murders of dozens more, women who were lost and never found. Mostly prostitutes, but a few upscale schoolgirls as well.

During the killings, Memphis was just finishing at Eton, on his way to Cambridge, and was convinced that those murders, plus the two lost girls in the woods, with their constant news coverage, instilled the investigative bug into his world. He was captivated by the case in Brighton, followed it in the papers. One night, he and a couple of school chums had gotten legless on whisky and taken a drive up to the woods. He remembered stumbling into the forest, then stopping, certain that the ghosts of the strangled girls were nearby. He nearly pissed himself getting back to the car, his chums in no better shape.

It took more than the idea of a specter to run him off a case now.

He stepped out of the Waverly train station into a spitting cold rain at half six, grabbed a taxi and headed up the Royal Mile.

The rain began falling in earnest. He ducked into the alleyway that led to The Witchery, one of his favorite restaurants in the world. He skipped the main dining room and went to the second door, to what was known as the Secret Garden. The maître d' recognized him, gave him a wide smile.

"My Lord Dulsie, what a pleasure to see you. As always. Our favorite earl is below. Shall I take you to him?"

"Yes, please, Alfred. Lovely to see you as well."

They descended the stairs under the watchful eye of a large elk. The earl was tucked away in the corner, at the best table, his serious brown eyes focused on the menu, though he knew it by heart.

Memphis let Alfred take his coat and slid into the chair opposite. "Happy Birthday, Father. You're looking well."

The earl set his menu down and smiled warmly at his eldest son. "Ah, James, my boy. So good to see you. You've come alone? If I had known I'd have invited Jenny Blakely." He cast an appraising eye over his son.

His father was forever hoping he'd get over the death of Evan and find a new woman to settle down with, and was keen on making the match himself. They'd had a few minor rows about it already, his father proclaiming, "If this was two hundred years ago, I'd have made the match for you and you would have thanked me for it." The earl was full of it. He was about as dedicated to the antiquities of the peerage as Memphis was.

"Jenny Blakely is a pretentious cow and you know it."

The earl spit out a laugh, then shook his head in admonishment. "Now, now, Memphis, that's no way to talk about a lady."

"She's not a lady, Father. Have you seen the mole on her eye? It deserves a title of its own."

They went on like this for an hour, teasing, poking, eating a luscious meal and chasing it with a fine port. The earl grew serious as he signed the bill.

"I know this is a difficult time for you, James. Why don't you come to Johannesburg with us? Get away from here. From the ghost of Evanelle. I can see her haunting you, still. It breaks my heart to see you suffer."

Memphis squeezed his father's arm. "I know it does. I promise, things are better. But no, I won't be able to get away. Work, you know. And I've invited a friend to come stay for the holiday."

"A *friend?*" His father wasn't subtle, he waggled his eyebrows at him lasciviously. Memphis smiled.

"A good friend. The investigator I met in Nashville. I've mentioned her before, I believe. Taylor Jackson."

"You have. Well. I hope that she comes. For your sake. No one should spend Christmas alone."

"No need to worry about me, Father. I have more than enough to keep me busy."

The earl insisted on dropping Memphis at the station, good-naturedly grumbling about him not coming back to the estate. They parted with a hearty handshake, as always, and Memphis boarded the last train back up to London.

Accepting a cup of tea from the trolley girl, he checked his email and sighed. He was in for a long night. The commander hadn't bothered to wait until the morning; he was calling Memphis into the Straithwhite case immediately.

So much for his escape.

Despite his grousing to Taylor, he had to admit this case was intriguing. A challenge. He always did love a challenge.

He put a call in to his detective constable, Penelope Micklebury, known far and wide as Pen. She answered on the first ring, the annoyance clear in her voice.

"Left me to stand in the rain while you had a beautiful dinner with Daddy, eh, Memphis?"

"My repasts are none of your concern, Pen. You eat like a bird anyway, you would have hated it. Tureens of soup and platters overflowing with rich, juicy meat. I can barely move, I'm creakingly full."

Pen was a vegan; she moaned aloud at the thought. "That stuff's going to rot you from the inside, Memphis."

"Perhaps. Where are you?"

He could hear her heels clicking on the pavement, then a door slammed and things quieted down. She must have stepped into her car.

"Victoria. Had a date. Did you get a call from the Boy Toy?" she asked in turn.

"He sent me an email. I've just seen it. And if you keep calling him that, he will find out. And I won't be able to save you."

"It's just a bleeding nickname. You'll be in tomorrow?"

"Unless you need me tonight?"

"No. I've got things covered here. Assembling the files, all that. Go and have a rest."

"Fine, Pen. Until then."

He hung up, watched the lights from the village to his right flash by as the train crossed the countryside. In the daylight, this was a beautiful part of the trip, but in the darkness it became murky and lonely. A fitting scene, really. He *was* feeling rather lonely tonight.

CHAPTER SIX

Taylor and Baldwin were both quiet on the drive downtown. Another indignity—Taylor hadn't been cleared to drive yet. She was dependent on Baldwin, or Sam, to get her around town. She was tempted to get a car service, but stopped when she realized she'd be just like her mother, chauffeured around by relative strangers. Kitty Jackson hadn't been in the front seat of a car for two decades.

She wondered briefly what Kitty was up to. They hadn't spoken since Taylor had arrested her father and sent him to jail. Even though Kitty and Win had been divorced since Taylor was in college, the woman always took his side. Taylor knew it had nothing to do with a soft spot for Win and their once-happy life, and everything to do with the embarrassment of the scandal. Tongues wagged throughout Davidson County's elite when Taylor had sent her own father to prison.

She colored at the memory, anger rising. Typical that the consensus would be that *she'd* acted impetuously rather than that Win deserved condemnation for breaking the law. It was one of the reasons she eschewed her

mother's social set; the values and morals were a bit
askew. In their minds, every family had a blackguard.
It just wasn't seemly to draw attention to such a situation.

She chased the thoughts away as Baldwin pulled in
in front of the Criminal Justice Center. Snow began to
fall in tiny, glittery flakes, making the brown bricks
shimmer. Taylor felt a great sense of contentment run
through her, the same she felt every time she looked at
her office. She was home. And soon she'd be allowed
to get back to her first love: the job.

She smiled at Baldwin, and he grinned back at her.

"Go on. It's noon now. I'll be back to get you at two.
Okay?"

She touched his hand briefly in acquiescence then
got out of the car. Breathed deep lungfuls of chilly,
snowy air. Tried to keep the skip out of her step as she
crossed to the stairs, dug her pass card out of her back
pocket. She swiped it and almost got teary at the noise
of the door unlocking.

The hall smelled like Clorox. The floors had just
been scrubbed, almost as if they'd been sanitized for
her return.

The Homicide offices were full, her elite team—the
murder squad—all in attendance. A full house meant
no active calls, and a chance for everyone to catch up
on their paperwork. They weren't here for her. No one
knew she was coming in today.

She hesitated for a moment in the doorway, but the
room was so small that Renn McKenzie, the newest
team member, and thus the one stuck sitting by the
door, caught movement out of the corner of his eye and
turned toward her.

"LT!" he said, standing so quickly that his papers spilled to the floor. He was joyous, a huge smile on his face, and the general cry went up immediately. Before she could take a breath, she was being hugged and patted, passed around from person to person like a beach ball at a stadium. Marcus Wade was the first to grab her, then Lincoln Ross, then Renn. She was breathless and giddy; damn, it was good to see them all.

To be honest, she'd been avoiding everyone. She was their leader, and she wanted them to see the strong, confident Taylor they were used to. Taylor weak and mewling wasn't helpful.

Despite her lack of voice, she was feeling better, could hide the headache behind the fog of Percocet, could smile without wincing. Her balance had improved to the point where the stupid cane wasn't necessary anymore. Every day she could see the path back becoming shorter. She just wished it would hurry up and end already. Something in her knew that the sooner she got back amongst her people, the sooner she'd heal.

They were all talking at once at her, each finishing the other's sentences, and she felt the most at ease she had in weeks. She made a mental note to send Dr. Benedict a bottle of eighteen-year-old single malt Scotch. He must have known this would be part of the deal, and what she needed as well.

"Heya, Lucky. We didn't know you were coming in today," Lincoln scolded. "You should have told us."

Marcus set his fists on his hips, the left brushing against his Glock. "Yeah, we'd have prepared a little better. Have junior over there make a cake or something."

Renn shot him a bird. "Hugh does all the baking in our house, and you know it."

"Bake this," Marcus said, making a completely obscene gesture with his tongue and cheek. They busted up laughing, and Lincoln hushed them.

"Good grief, y'all need to give it a rest." He turned to Taylor, put his arm around her shoulder, guided her past the guffawing detectives. "They go at it like this all day. It's exhausting." But Lincoln had a wide smile on his face, the gap between his front teeth adding to the merriment. He'd cropped his hair again, the dreadlocks gone. He looked like a very serious Lenny Kravitz, his impeccable Armani dove-gray suit unwrinkled, his tie done in a perfect Windsor knot.

Taylor pointed at the suit; Lincoln was a clotheshorse in the worst way, spent all his spare change and most of his paychecks on the finest materials and cuts available. But the tie was an added touch that he didn't usually worry about unless he had a date he was trying to impress. She had to admit, Lincoln done up in full kit, with his smooth café-au-lait skin and perfect profile, was a sight to behold. She'd always wanted to get him in a tux—she imagined that would be breathtaking.

"Court in an hour," he said.

Ah. That explained it. Marcus and Renn, by contrast, were in jeans and sweaters, comfortable, prepared for the weather. Prepared for anything that might come their way. Her team was unflappable. She'd done everything in her power to make them that way.

She looked into her office, at the empty desk, just waiting for her to return, and decided to stay out in the bullpen. Not enough room in there anyway.

She sat on the edge of McKenzie's desk and smiled

at them. They toned down the jubilation and crowded around her.

"Have you been cleared to come back?" Marcus asked, just as Renn jumped in with "How's the voice?"

She pointed at her throat and shook her head. She pulled out the notepad and wrote *Willig* on it, turned it around and showed them.

There was a collective groan, which completely made her day. Mandated visits with the department shrink were no fun.

She wrote *Condition to return*, which cheered them all up.

"Tell her what she wants to hear, and you'll be back to us before you know it," Marcus said.

She had every intention of doing just that, but not in the way Marcus was suggesting. There was no way, no way in hell, she was going to let anyone inside her head. Especially the shrink who she'd have to pass in the halls and say hello to in the coffee room every day.

The boys didn't need to know that. She smiled and nodded, rolling her eyes for emphasis. They all laughed.

"That's good, because we need you back. We're up to our ears in work. We're catching extras while Special Crimes deals with the Regretful Robber cases. They're all kinds of tied up, have almost all their manpower looking for him."

Over the past several weeks, there had been a spate of bank robberies in the Metro area, all very carefully orchestrated by someone who seemed to know exactly how to cover his tracks. He wore a mask, used stolen cars, and carried a mean .40 Glock 21 that he wasn't afraid to use. A few weeks ago out in Hermitage, he'd shot a hole in the ceiling of a U.S. Bank when the teller took too long getting him his money.

But in a twist worthy of Robin Hood, he returned the stolen vehicles to their rightful owners in the dead of night, with a small cash bonus inside. Hence his name inside the CJC: the Regretful Robber. Thank God that hadn't leaked to the press yet.

McKenzie chimed in. "Without you guiding the ship, things get a little crazy around here. We've got a new sergeant who's a complete dick. Thinks he owns the world. He's always pushing us off in the wrong direction."

Lincoln chimed in, using a dopey voice. "'This isn't an assault, it's a matter of record. Close the case.' We're gonna get creamed in the media if they ever find out. They're trying to cook the numbers again, make it look like the assault rates have dropped. You should see what they're doing in Sex Crimes. Driving us all crazy."

Tell Huston

Lincoln nodded. "We did. She's fighting it for us, but the chief made new guidelines again. Rumor has it he has a job offer. Supposedly, he'll be gone by Christmas, which is going to make an even bigger mess. When someone from the outside starts looking at these figures, we're all going to come under fire."

He shook a sheaf of papers at her, and she shook her head.

I won't let that happen.

Marcus sat back at his desk. "Wish Fitz would come back. Have you talked to him?"

She shook her head. She wanted Fitz back, too, though she didn't see how either of them would manage to lead, between her lack of a voice and his lack of spirit. Fitz had lost too much, and Taylor didn't know if he was going to recover. She'd tried going to see him, but they'd ended up sitting in silence until Fitz's one good eye started to leak, and she knew that when he looked at her, all he could think about was the Pretender, and what he'd taken away from them all. She was waiting for him to reach out; pushing herself on the people whom she loved but who were not thrilled with her had gotten too hard. Between Fitz and Sam, the blame lay squarely at her feet, and right now, forgiveness was too much to ask of them. She understood that completely. She wasn't ready to forgive herself, either.

They chatted a bit more, catching up, until Renn asked, "What time's your sit-down with Victoria?" He was the only one of them who willingly saw the shrink. He had his own battles and demons—coming from the goth world, being gay, losing his fiancée to suicide over his doubts about his sexuality, fighting for respect amongst his peers—all of this had led him to mighty introspection. He and Willig were big buddies.

Taylor glanced at her watch, the gold-and-silver Tag Heuer Baldwin had given her for her birthday. She bolted upright—she was going to be late.

Lincoln grabbed his leather portfolio with his notes. "I'll walk you, I need to get over to the courthouse. Judge Oscar will wring my neck if I don't present my glorious self on time."

Taylor hugged Marcus and Renn goodbye, agreed to dinner soon, and let Lincoln escort her from the room. Just spending some time with the guys made her feel immeasurably better. Lincoln kept up a cheery discourse while they walked, and Taylor felt damn near normal for the first time in weeks. Benedict was right, getting back into the swing of things would help. She could feel the words bubbling in the back of her throat, just ready to spill out.

CHAPTER SEVEN

At the door to Willig's office, Lincoln bussed her on the cheek and left her, poised and ready to embark on yet another journey to regain herself.

She stood there for a minute, staring at the frosted glass. Dr. Willig was a good woman, smart and compassionate. Taylor would have to let her in, at least a little bit, if this was going to work. She took a deep breath and opened the door.

Willig was engrossed in a book, her stocking feet up on the corner of her desk, calmly munching an apple as she read. It took her a second to notice Taylor. She dropped the book onto her desk and sat upright with a smothered exclamation.

"Lieutenant, I'm so sorry. I was reading." She pointed at the book, blushed a bit at stating the obvious. "My little sister's latest book comes out Tuesday, and I'm playing catch-up before I read the new one." She handed the book to Taylor. It was called *The Orchid Affair*, by Lauren Willig.

Pretty cover· I never figured you for a romantic, Victoria·

"Night and day, my mother always called us. I'm much too empirical to be a writer, and she's much too creative to be a doctor."

Taylor smiled. She'd always wanted a sister. Sam had filled the role of surrogate since they were five. Sam had always treated her the same way. Treachery, truly it was, for Taylor to let such a horrid fate befall her best friend. She gulped back a cry of sheer frustration as Willig watched.

"You know, if screaming will help, the office is basically soundproof. I can't imagine anyone would mind."

Taylor gave it serious consideration before dropping into a chair in front of Willig's desk. It wouldn't work anyway. She'd been trying. At home, on the back deck, where only the squirrels and beer bottles were there to hear her, not even there. Nothing. She was stuck with mumbling her *M*s and the occasional laugh.

"Fine. I'll do the talking. Dr. Benedict told me about the deal he made with you. He's a dodgy one, I'd be careful." She said it with a smile. She obviously liked the man.

As Willig talked, she moved around the room, assembling a tray of materials. Taylor watched expectantly. Willig was pretty in an unconventional way, dark tumbling hair that she swept back over her shoulders, eyes spaced too far apart, a thin gold chain with a delicate cross around her slender neck. She wore a subtle perfume and dressed well, in a brown cashmere wrap and green corduroy trousers. Sober and inviting all at the same time, like a forest. Depth and breadth unknown, but on the surface quite striking.

Taylor truly didn't know what to expect, and when Willig locked the door, sat down across from her and showed her the tray, she became even more confused. There was what looked like a Walkman, with a headset and two pods.

"It's for EMDR," Willig said. "We're going to rewire your brain."

EMDR—Eye Movement Desensitization and Reprocessing, Willig explained—was painless. She ran through the procedure. At its most basic, EMDR used several kinds of cognitive therapies to heal the unseen wounds of trauma victims.

"We have a lot of success using this on PTSD. The more we actively utilize the specific methodology, the more we can blur the lines of anxiety in your mind. We'll interlace the moments of fear with moments you control, happy thoughts, and literally desensitize you. It works wonders. I've used it to treat several PTSD patients, with great success."

Taylor started to shake her head, but the doctor cut her off. "Seriously, Lieutenant, you've got classic symptoms of PTSD. There is nothing to be ashamed of. Post-traumatic stress disorder affects millions. It's not reserved for abuse victims or soldiers. Car accidents, intense illness—anything and everything can trigger it. For you, getting shot in the head by a serial killer who'd planned to do much worse, this is rather uncomplicated. You nearly died. It's a miracle you didn't. It's a miracle that your brain seems okay, *physically*. You just can't talk now because you're scared."

Taylor wasn't liking this. She wasn't scared. Hurt, angry, frustrated, yes, but scared? Hell no. She stood up, tossed the pods back onto the tray. They fell with a short bump. She'd missed her target and they sprawled on the floor like black worms.

"Come on, Lieutenant. I thought you wanted to get better. If that's going to happen, we're going to have to be honest with each other." Her voice softened. "There is nothing to be ashamed of."

She searched Taylor's eyes with her own, was apparently satisfied with what she saw. Willig gestured for Taylor to take her seat. Taylor breathed deep, closed her eyes, and sat. Let Willig think what she wanted, all Taylor really cared about was getting back to normal. And if that meant letting Willig think she was afraid, so be it.

"Good. Thank you. I'm going to ask a lot of you today, and over the course of our sessions. We're going to go places you aren't going to want to go, but that's how this works. You'll relive the situation, and using my voice and eye movements coupled with both auditory and tactile sensations, we're going to rework your thought process. There are several steps, and we'll take it gradually. I'm almost one hundred percent convinced that this will work, but you're going to have to let it. Okay?"

Taylor nodded. There were about a million things she'd rather do than relive the *situation*. God, she wished everyone would stop calling it that.

"I've reviewed the details of the case, but there are parts that I don't know. Dr. Baldwin typed up his recollections for me, so I'm there from his perspective. But I'm going to need you to do some homework, too. I need to know everything that happened in that attic. When I can re-create the scene for you, then I'll be able to guide you through it, help you detach and let go. Are you willing to write it all down for me?"

Taylor had already written an account of that afternoon's events. She'd had to explain to Baldwin the few moments that led up to the shooting, try to make him understand how she'd managed to get herself shot.

She had the write-up in her notebook. She pulled it from her back pocket, opened to the right page and handed it over.

"Oh, fantastic. Give me a second here." Willig's eyes moved quickly across the page, moments of recognition showing here and there as Taylor's version matched what she'd read from Baldwin's case notes.

Why wouldn't it? She'd given him what he wanted to hear, too. She'd glossed over some of the details, but no one needed to know that.

After a few minutes, Willig shut the notebook and handed it back, looking thoughtful. Respect and compassion shone in her eyes. "Wow."

Yes, wow. That about summed it up.

"Okay then. Are you ready?" she asked.

As I'll ever be.

Taylor put on the headset, settled the two pods in her palms and grasped them carefully. She felt like an idiot, all wired up like this, but she was willing to do most anything to get herself back up to snuff, so whatever Willig had planned, she was going to try her best to comply.

"This is just a quick test that makes sure everything is running properly."

Taylor jumped a mile as the headset and pods came to life. Her ears were filled with pings, and the pods in her hands pulsed in time. Left, right, left, right, left, right, metronomic, perfectly in time with the ponging in her ears. After the initial sensation, she relaxed.

"Perfect," Willig said. "Everything is in working order. Okay, Taylor. I want you to think of a place that's very safe. A place where you feel completely at home, where you can let your guard down. Someplace that is strictly about you and your happiness. It can be a memory, or a physical spot. That's where you're going to be spending some time, so pick something that's very strong, very immediate for you."

Someplace I feel safe?

Taylor had to think about that for a moment. Home was out, though that normally qualified. Right now it was too intertwined with Baldwin, and that brought mixed emotions. Her cabin in the woods, the place she'd lived before she met Baldwin—that was good. But ruined by the events that forced her to move out. No, neither of those would work.

Unbidden, a memory rose to the surface. She was eight, gangly and awkward, with slightly buck teeth and freckles, her long hair wrestled into submission in a single braid down her back. She was at camp, a whole summer away from home, and while the other campers were sad and lonely for their parents, she felt a kind of freedom she didn't fully understand. She rode horses for the first time, and fished in the lake. Attended bonfires and had a mad crush on a boy much older, thirteen, from the neighboring cabin. Scandalous. Just thinking about it suffused her with joy, and she felt the corners of her lips rise.

Willig nodded. "Excellent, I see you have it. Let it fill you. Let yourself remember the happiness. Focus on how good that feels, to be happy, and safe. Now, we're going to go back to the moment you entered the room and saw Sam tied to the chair. Think about what you saw, how you felt. I want you to rate your emotions on a scale of one to ten. Give a numerical valuation to how you feel right now, thinking about it."

Taylor's mind was shoved back to reality, to the vision of her best friend handcuffed to a chair, tears streaming down her face as blood ran over her stomach and dripped onto her legs. She held up four fingers on each hand. Eight. High enough to reveal her fear, not enough to feel too far out of control.

The pulsing started in her palms.

"What did you feel when you saw her, Taylor?"

Fury. Anger. Hurt. Fear. No, no, no, no. Something else under all that.

She let the emotions wash over her, felt her throat constrict. Willig kept up a soothing instructional flow, having Taylor watch her finger as it moved in front of her face, back and forth. She guided Taylor's thoughts through the attic room, to the chair, looking down on Sam from above, to the actions that allowed her to be freed. As Sam, intact and liberated, left the imaginary room, she glanced back with imploring eyes. Taylor tensed, and Willig told her to shut her eyes and think about her happy place.

The intensity of the ponging increased, wiping out all other noise, and her hands began to tingle. She thought about camp, about that horse she learned to ride on named Tonto, about how ridiculous she thought the name was, but couldn't help herself, his velvety nose was so sweet and he loved carrots....

"Okay, Taylor. Come on back to me now."

Taylor opened her eyes. She was exhausted, and slightly relieved.

"How do you feel? Rate the emotions again, on the one to ten scale," Willig said.

She thought about it. Maybe a six?

"Mmm…mokay." Taylor said. Wow, was her voice working? She tried a few more words, but nothing came. Damn it.

"It's okay, Taylor. You did great. We're already seeing progress. EMDR is a wonder tool, and you're responding to it well. We'll go deeper tomorrow. But think about Sam now. Think about that moment in the attic. Does it hurt as much?"

She thought about it in astonishment. It was still there, the searing, awful pain of her friend's hurt, but the sharp edges that tried to control her were muddled a little bit. Wow. She had to admit, that was impressive. She smiled at Willig, who smiled back.

"We'll go through every step of that afternoon, and I promise you, we'll get you back to normal in no time."

Taylor hoped so. She stood and shook Willig's hand. She couldn't get over the sensation in her palms, and her ears were ringing. She pointed to her left ear and Willig smiled.

"Yeah, it might ring a bit for an hour or so. Just promise me this: if you have flashbacks of the day you were shot, revert yourself to the happy place. Don't go trying to sort things out on your own. I'll help you get through this, Lieutenant."

Willig sounded so earnest Taylor couldn't help but smile. She wrote *How long?* on her notepad, and Willig said, "Give me four sessions, then we'll revisit. We can meet three times a week. Can you come back tomorrow? I like to overload you the first few times. Next visit we'll jump in faster, and go deeper. Okay?"

Taylor grabbed her notebook.

Can anyone provide this kind of treatment?

Willig knit her brows for a moment. "Any qualified therapist who's been trained. It's not as uncommon a therapy as it was several years ago. Why, you thinking about cheating on me already?"

Might be going away for a bit. Just checking.

"Okay. See you tomorrow."

Taylor nodded, and mouthed, "Thank you."

"My pleasure, Lieutenant. This is what I do best."

Taylor left Willig smiling in the middle of her office and went to meet Baldwin at the CJC's entrance. All in all, she felt good about her chances of making it back. The EMDR *had* helped a bit.

She wondered, though, how much Willig would be willing to help if she found out the whole truth about that day.

CHAPTER EIGHT

Sam pulled herself together and finished the afternoon's work. She needed to talk to someone. She didn't have many friends; it was hard to keep folks on her side when they found out she cut up dead people for a living. No matter how politely they tried to incorporate it into conversation, they eventually came to see her as a ghoul. She was used to it now. She tended to have people around who understood why she'd chosen to become a pathologist.

She and Taylor came from the same world: wealth and privilege. But unlike Taylor's incendiary home life, Sam's parents had loved her to the point of smothering. They were gone now, both dead much too soon, her father of liver cancer, her mother, Sam was fully convinced, of a broken heart, less than four months later. She missed them—their enthusiastic encouragement, their grounding force.

Her father had been an inventor, with an engineering degree under his belt and multiple patents, though he rarely would discuss what they were. He'd had something to do with the modern electrical plug and some little gadget Sam barely understood. Her mother used to have a glass of wine at parties and intimate that his inventions were in every house in the world. It had made him millions on top of his already hefty trust fund.

He'd been a quirky man, lively in a way Sam rarely saw from scientists. Jovial. Outgoing. Her mother had adored him. Sam's mom liked to joke she was at Vanderbilt getting her MRS degree when she met Stan Owens.

Despite her parents' social conditioning of their only daughter, Sam always felt apart. An outsider, distant from those around her. She was a quiet girl, fascinated with science, biology and genetics, and determined to be a doctor. She'd decided on her course when she was five. Right around the time she met Taylor.

Sam was a better debutante than Taylor, more interested in the niceties, the responsibilities that came with affluence. But where Taylor was tall and elegant and heedless of her own beauty, Sam had to work on hers, learning how to do makeup to enhance her looks, forever fighting her too-limp hair, carefully managing her diet and exercise regimen. She envied Taylor her effortlessness, wished she could go out without makeup and her hair tossed in a lazy ponytail. Oh, she probably could, but her mother's face popped up just as she was walking out the door in her moments of cultural defiance—*honey, just a little lipstick, maybe some blush. And why don't you let your hair down? You look like a skinned rabbit with it pulled back so tight.*

She was better off with people who couldn't talk back. There were no awkward moments with the lifeless. No worry about how they perceived her.

Sam loved Nashville, and she loved Taylor. She

looked at their relationship as a partnership on several levels—best friends, sisters and responsible for the city's people. Taylor protected the living inhabitants of Nashville; Sam uncovered the secrets of its dead.

Right now, Sam just wanted to talk to Taylor. They were family. Families found ways to put the past behind them, to forgive.

And Taylor couldn't talk back right now. Sam could vent her frustrations on the phone, and Taylor would have to listen. She always had been a good listener. Sam's favorite confidante.

She closed the door to her office and dialed Taylor's cell. It rang three times, then Taylor answered, said, "Mmm," so Sam would know it was her.

"Want to get a drink?" Sam asked.

"Mmmm-hmm."

"You at home?"

The phone disconnected, then her text dinged.

So glad you called. I'm downtown at the office. Baldwin's supposed to pick me up. Why don't you grab me and we'll go somewhere?

Ten minutes, Sam texted back, then stowed the phone in her bag. She was mad at Taylor, sad for Taylor, and sad for herself, but she couldn't not see her best friend. At least Sam was getting a chance to heal; her wounds were hidden, on the inside. Taylor had to parade around town with her scars, and without her voice.

They had to find a way to lean on each other. No one else could understand exactly what it had been like in that attic.

It took her five minutes to get out of the office. She

snuck out the morgue doors into the loading bay, walked around the back of the building to her car in the lot up front. She just didn't feel like facing anyone. It was embarrassing not to have control of her emotions. Even though she wasn't pregnant anymore, her body was still laden with crazy hormones. She was mortified by her outburst this afternoon. She didn't like people to see her cry, and she certainly didn't like to step out of an autopsy because she was on the verge of exploding.

The snow had begun to fall in earnest. Sam drove downtown carefully, mindful of the slick roads.

Sam saw Taylor sitting on the steps outside the CJC. Her bottom must be frozen; she only had on jeans and a short leather jacket. Sam snuggled deeper into her red down coat, chilled at the mere thought. But Taylor seemed completely unfazed. Lost in thought, actually.

She spied Sam's car and stood up, graceful and tall, started down the stairs like a gazelle. She was in a good mood; Sam could see that from a hundred paces. She even waved and smiled. Sam waved back, felt a grin spread across her face. She'd never been able to stay mad at Taylor. She wanted to fix things between them.

She heard a car horn's frustrated beep, then saw a low green Jaguar out of the corner of her eye. It was coming up fast, flying, actually. James Robertson Parkway was a busy street, especially with all the people parking in the garage and making their way across to the courts and the CJC. A group of people were crossing the road, but the Jaguar didn't slow.

Sam watched in horror as the car sped through the intersection, ignoring the red light, and clipped the last person trailing across the street. A Hispanic woman, probably forty years old, took the brunt of the impact.

She cartwheeled into the road, upended, a scream frozen on her lips. She hadn't even seen the car that hit her.

Taylor took off toward the woman. Sam slammed her car into Park and got out. They made it to her at the same time. Blood spilled from her mouth and head. She needed treatment immediately. People were shouting and screaming, rushing around, and Sam flipped open her phone and dialed 911, despite the fact that she was standing outside police headquarters.

Taylor had her coat off and began CPR, though on closer inspection Sam could tell it was all a moot point. The woman had landed forehead first. Her eyes were already rolled far back in her head. The thick, ripe scent of urine and waste rose as her body gave up its fight.

Squashed her noggin, as her mom used to say.

Taylor stopped the chest compressions, wiped her mouth with the back of her hand, stood up and looked east, up the street. Sam followed her gaze. The green Jaguar was long gone.

The scene was swarmed immediately. EMTs came screeching around the corner. The people who had been with the woman crowded around, their wailing cries mingling with the sirens and shouts.

Taylor stepped back with blood on her hands. Snow dusted the hair around her forehead like a silver halo.

Sam reached for Taylor's hands and wiped the blood off with a tissue, then handed her a bottle of antiseptic gel from her purse. Taylor rubbed her palms together vigorously, then grabbed her coat from the asphalt and shrugged back into it, settling the warmth around her in consolation.

Death surrounded them. Again.

Taylor's eyes met hers and Sam could read the thoughts of her best friend clearly.

That was no accident, the look said.

CHAPTER NINE

It took two full hours to get the scene under control. Taylor had remembered the license plate on the Jag, but a quick search revealed that the plates had been stolen off a truck that had been left out on Eastland Avenue overnight. East Nashville—half beautifully gentrified, half crime-ridden and dangerous. Taylor knew who'd win in the end. The stubborn landowners would force the drug dealers and prostitutes and ruffians out and be left with a quiet little oasis with excellent restaurants and cool shops. They were probably sixty percent there already.

The family of the woman, if that's who they were, had clammed up. They wouldn't say why they were coming to the courts, or who the woman was. Their faces were pinched, eyes darting, tawny skin white with fear, and Taylor knew without asking that they were probably all illegal. A search of the afternoon's court docket revealed nothing that would explain the woman's presence; no outstanding warrants matched her description, and no one had a Hispanic woman her age on their current case lists. She wasn't on the rolls for jury duty. She was a mystery, and Taylor felt the stirrings of life at the idea of figuring out the story. But she wasn't allowed. Without batting an eyelash, Huston gave the case to Marcus.

Dejected, Taylor let Sam drive her home.

They didn't talk on the way. The horror of watching a woman die in front of them was enough to steal Sam's tongue as well.

Taylor's head was pounding. She palmed a Percocet from the bottle in her pocket. Sam usually had a juice box or two lying around in the backseat, but there was nothing today. She dry swallowed the pill, hoping it started to work quickly.

When they were close to Taylor's neighborhood, she put a hand out and signaled to the side of the road. As Sam pulled to the curb, Taylor wrote her a note.

Memphis invited me to Scotland.

Sam took one glance at it and turned to her in horror. "Surely you're not thinking of going? That's insanity!"

Taylor shook her head.

I just think a break would be good.

Sam put the BMW into Park and adopted her most exasperated tone.

"Taylor Bethany Jackson, you are a first-class fool if you think that running into the arms of the Viscount of what's-its-name will solve anything."

Dulsie.

"Fuck Dulsie. Don't fuck Memphis. *That* will ruin your life, I guarantee it."

*I'm not planning to fuck him. I'm thinking a little
time apart would be good. Baldwin and I aren't
exactly getting along.*

"So you run off to Scotland, to the man who's desperate to make you his own? Girl, are you out of your
mind? Are the drugs they're giving you addling your
brains?"

Sam's voice was going up an octave with each dec-
laration. Her face was turning red, and Taylor had to
fight not to laugh.

He won't be there. I'll be alone at the estate.

"Ooh, the 'estate.' Don't you mean his *castle?* He is
the son of an *earl,* isn't he? They do have a *castle,* don't
they? You can go play Rapunzel."

*Cobwebby. Hard to heat. At least that's what
he said.*

Sam slapped the steering wheel. "Don't get smart
with me, girl. And don't pretend like you've never
looked it up online, either. Taylor, this is a mistake. A
huge, huge mistake."

*I haven't looked it up. What's the point in that?
Besides, I'll ask Baldwin to come.*

"Brilliant, kiddo."
Sam took three deep breaths through her nose, shut
her eyes for a moment. Taylor waited her out.
"Good grief. I called you for an escape, and now look

at me, yelling at you. And you can't yell back. That's not fair."

Sure it is. I deserve it. Sam, I'm so sorry.

That did the trick. Sam burst into tears, and Taylor took her in her arms.

She couldn't say the words aloud, so she stroked Sam's hair and thought hard at her, hoping she could at least feel the energy.

I'm so sorry, Sam. I failed you. I won't let that happen again. I think I should go away. I have to get my head straight, too. I think this might fix me. Please be happy again, Sam. It breaks my heart to see you cry.

Sam started to snuffle and regain control. She pulled a tissue out of the box in her dash and wiped her eyes.

"You've already decided?"

Taylor nodded, realizing as she did that, yes, she had. She wanted to go. She wanted to get away from everyone, everything. To escape into a world that wasn't her own, just for a little while.

"Just don't do anything stupid, okay? Memphis can be dangerous, on too many levels to count. I love you too much to see you fall apart again."

Taylor wrote *I promise* then opened the car door.

"You want to walk in?" Sam asked. "It's freezing out there."

Taylor nodded again. She needed to stretch her legs and try to get the smell of death out of her head.

"Don't stay out in the cold too long, okay?" She touched Taylor on the cheek, a butterfly caress. Taylor got out of the warm car and breathed deeply. She felt so much better. They'd needed to have that fight. Things weren't fixed, not by a long shot, but at least she knew Sam still cared.

And now, she needed a few minutes alone to figure out what to tell Baldwin.

Taylor walked in the cold, chilled to the bone. She didn't want to capitulate to the weather and head inside, not just yet. One foot in front of the other. Again and again and again.

She'd always been stubborn, a true Taurus, bull-headed, as her mother would pointedly say. She knew deep inside that it was her stubbornness that would get her out of this mess and back to normal, even though she barely believed the small voice inside her who promised all would be well.

It was a blessing that she lived in Nashville, where many people's livelihoods depended on their supple voice box, and all the hospitals have occupational thera-pists that specialize in voice therapy on staff. As she walked, as each step unfolded, her mind spinning, she did the basic exercises they'd given her at the hospital: strengthening her vocal cords by letting her tongue lie flat against the bottom of her mouth, then rolling the edges together, sounding out a single syllable. Having found that Mmm was easiest, for some unknown reason, she'd been going about her days humming the Camp-bell's soup song.

"Mmm, Mmm Good."

"Mmm, Mmm Good."

On her friend Ariadne's advice, she approached her recovery from the holistic side as well, with herbs meant to soothe and relax her throat. She drank green tea with honey. She took the Percocet to relieve the pain. Sometimes, she even took her Ativan. Dutifully exercised and followed most of the doctor's instructions.

She had felt like an idiot, getting Botox in her throat. It had helped, but only temporarily. The minute she started to talk again, during a conversation with Baldwin about the shooting, she clammed up. Literally felt her throat close. She'd had a cat once who would have coughing fits—almost as if it couldn't breathe and began to choke. That's exactly how she felt, constricted, no air, no way to scream.

The nightmares were the worst. They were fever dreams, which amplified and grew simple situations far beyond their proportions—a dark room turning into a cold grave with dirt thrown on her head, figurines who came to life and threatened to strangle her, Sam's baby talking to her, though it wasn't bigger than a speck of dust. She'd wake in the night, body rigid, hair clinging to her head, chest covered in sweat, mouth open, nothing coming out. She couldn't scream in her dreams, either, and she couldn't help but think if she could just let loose there, this would all stop. She'd get her voice back.

But the dreams were worsening.

She knew she needed this change. She'd been clinging to the thought that work would be the solution, but she'd felt so…helpless this afternoon.

The accident, the woman being run down right in front of her—she'd tried so hard to call for help, and nothing had come.

She'd seen the doubt in Huston's eyes. One of the guys must have reported in about her visit that afternoon. It was readily apparent that she wasn't ready to go back to fieldwork. If she wouldn't be allowed to do anything but drive a desk, that would make her stir-crazy.

Getting away, being alone, appealed so much. She was tired of people trying to help. Of being babysat, and chauffeured, and looked at with pity. And suspicion. She couldn't help but read the subtext of her day—*Taylor, we love you, but you're just not ready*. Maybe they had a point. And face it, people got hurt when she was around, whether they were strangers, friends or lovers.

Some time alone might help her find a way to forgive herself. And maybe, find a way to forgive Baldwin. At this point, she was prepared to try most anything.

How to tell Baldwin that she wanted to go to Scotland without him—that was the problem. She didn't feel right about it. She knew Memphis was interested in more than friendship, and that was the biggest thorn in the plan.

Memphis. With his ridiculously blue eyes and obvious hunger for her.

If she could just let go of the idea of them together, none of this would matter. She could go to Scotland, conscience clear, and get some much-needed away time from her life.

Memphis was the only one who treated her like she was still Taylor, not some shell of a being. It was…nice.

He'd be a gentleman. She'd make sure of it. Besides, she was a big girl. She knew how to handle herself. If Memphis got frisky, she'd knee him in the balls.

The thought made her laugh.

She was shivering now. Reluctantly, she about-faced and headed for the house. Back to reality. Baldwin would be waiting, a hopeful expression on his face. He would make her food, ply her with wine. He had gotten her drunk one night and made love to her, and she'd said his name at the end, softly, but there, full in her mouth, and he'd held her so tight she could barely breathe.

Things weren't right between them, not at all, but she needed him. He was a part of her soul, as important to her as her hands. But she needed him to understand her hurt, to understand her desire for a little time apart. She loved him desperately, but looking at him just reminded her of his betrayal. If she hadn't been shot, hadn't been through the horror of the surgeries and the dysphonia, she would have cut off her nose to spite her face and stopped talking to him. This seemed a better punishment, forcing him to watch her struggle.

She had faced the abyss, and turned away, not accepting its lure, and yet here she was, still being penalized.

Two words. That's all she really needed to hear from him. Two words that he danced around.

God, if he would just say I'm sorry.

CHAPTER TEN

Baldwin watched Taylor walking down the street toward the drive. Why she was on foot, he didn't know, unless she and Sam had words and Taylor bolted from the car. Which was entirely possible. Taylor was a cactus with everyone these days.

He thoughtfully chewed the end of a pencil. She was truly struggling, and he'd tried everything. She wasn't letting him in, and after four weeks of begging and pleading to let him help her, he was still getting the big brush-off. He was getting tired of her obstinacy, but didn't know what else to do. And he had his own demons to wrestle.

He watched her stop and glance up at the window. He waved and she waved back. She looked almost happy for the first time in weeks. Maybe things would be all right tonight. He smiled at her, then went back to his desk. Felt like he was turning his back on her. Maybe he was.

His chest was heavy. He was losing her. And after watching her get shot, going down on the floor in a bloody heap, then praying for days that she'd wake up, that she'd be normal, then the constant fighting...all the tension had drained him. She wasn't exactly giving him a lot to work with—the occasional smile, a laugh here or there. Some emails and handwritten notes.

She'd pulled into herself, shut him out. He knew she was angry and upset. Hell, he didn't blame her. But he also felt like she was being unfair. She was fighting her own battle, and not giving him any consideration. He was beginning to have his doubts that she loved him enough to forgive him. He should have told her, yes. But she was carrying the grudge like a mantle, swinging it from end to end with bull's horns.

She couldn't experience the emotions he was feeling. How could she? It was his son that was missing.

His son. He'd only found out about him last year, when the child had just turned four years old. The boy's mother, Charlotte Douglas, was dead. Their affair was a momentary fling during a high-pressure case, and when she'd gotten pregnant, she told him she'd aborted their child.

And he, damn himself, had believed her. Stopped speaking to her, fled to Nashville. He hadn't seen her in years.

Charlotte had carried and delivered the child in secret, gotten him adopted out, and never told Baldwin of the boy's existence. All Baldwin wanted was to find his son and bring him home.

Charlotte hadn't named the boy on the birth certificate. Another slap. Baldwin knew he shouldn't be getting so emotionally involved—this was the kind of situation that often ended badly, but he couldn't help himself. He'd never wanted kids, but suddenly felt the need for family. For permanence. For marriage. Three kids and a dog, no. But something to anchor him to an otherwise elusive world.

He thought Taylor wanted that, too, but the shooting seemed to shake something loose inside her.

Baldwin needed to let that all go for the time being. He had an emergency meeting to attend. Atlantic had sent word that he needed Baldwin, immediately.

His contact was currently eight hours ahead of him, and an early riser. He got into his address book and started dialing numbers. Getting in touch with his handler was a process—phone calls, codes, paging services, emails—all designed to bounce off multiple servers and systems and be nigh on impossible to track.

Atlantic wasn't CIA, or MI-6, or Mossad, or any other official agency. Atlantic ran people from them all from behind the scenes, an agent here, an agent there. Covert missions that were performed by operatives from all branches of the intelligence services across the world on a need-to-know basis. Missions that were so top secret that they simply didn't exist.

Baldwin finished dialing, then sat back and listened to the bells and beeps and whirrs that told him he was being routed through a secure line. The computer screen came to life, and Atlantic popped up like the Wizard of Oz, his disembodied bald head pixilated into submission.

"Good evening, M," Baldwin said.

"Being a smart-ass will get you nowhere, my boy."

Atlantic's gaze was as cold and frigid as the ocean, a genetic anomaly that made his blue eyes abnormally light, like a Siberian Husky. Baldwin had finally figured out Atlantic's heritage: he'd thought the man Belgian for a time, but moving farther east into Eurasia gave him what he was looking for. Baldwin was convinced Atlantic was a full-blood Ainu, the indigenous Japanese, who are often mistaken for Caucasians. The blue eyes were the giveaway; they couldn't belong to any creature that wasn't half-tied to the beginnings of the earth. Atlantic was a big man, broad through the shoulders and torso. His fingers were like sausages, with precisely trimmed and buffed square nails. Baldwin had no doubt that Atlantic could choke the life from a man with one hand while examining the other for hangnails. He was ice.

"We have a problem. One of our specialists has gone off the grid. Julius. I need you to look into it, let us know where he may be headed."

Baldwin was a reluctant member of one of Atlantic's more covert groups, known as Operation Angelmaker. He profiled the men and women Atlantic had on call to do wet work, the assassins tasked with keeping the world a safer place. Atlantic's world, at least. Baldwin was responsible for determining their mental status using thorough psychological examinations and his own special talent for profiling. When one started acting up, Baldwin's job was to predict just how bad the situation might get.

The problem was he had to immerse himself in the case, and he wasn't sure that taking on a job of this proportion, with Taylor so strung out, was such a good idea.

"I assume you've already cleared this through Garrett?"

Garrett Woods was Baldwin's boss at Quantico. He was the one who'd gotten Baldwin wrapped up with Atlantic in the first place.

"Yes. You're teaching at a private enterprise for the

week. Substituting for another profiler who got sick at the last minute. The cover is secure."

"Fine. I'll do it. But Taylor...if I have to travel, I'm worried about leaving her alone."

"You have to stop worrying about that girl. She's tough as nails. Now get to work. The files have been sent to you. I expect a briefing Wednesday morning."

The screen went black. Atlantic was gone.

Well. Dinner was certainly going to be interesting.

CHAPTER ELEVEN

Taylor went around to the back of the house, through the gate, so she could steal one last moment of peace before she went inside. She stopped midway through the yard and stood looking out over the woods. She'd seen a deer the other night, and the damn owl that had taken up residence in their river birch had hooted in alarm. The doe, soft-footed and sweet, seemed utterly unconcerned with the frantic owl and nibbled delicately at a dried corncob Taylor had thrown out for her.

To have that calm confidence back, that was what Taylor wanted.

She smiled at the memory, said, "Mmm, Mmm," twice more for good measure, then took a deep breath and entered the house. The downstairs was deserted. Baldwin must still be up in his office.

The answering machine was blinking, so she grabbed the notepad they kept next to the phone and hit Play.

Three messages.

The first was from a reporter at Channel Four, after her for a comprehensive sit-down exclusive interview.

She deleted it before the girl stopped talking. No way, no how, was she going to do that.

The second was Dr. Benedict's office, needing some arcane insurance detail. She wrote down the information and deleted the message.

The last one shook her.

A voice at once familiar and alien emanated from the speaker.

"Um, hi, Taylor. This is your dad. Listen, um, I'm getting out today. Yeah, I know what you're thinking. It's early. Good behavior. This place has been getting crowded, so they sprang a few of us that weren't considered a 'threat to society.' I'm heading down to Nashville and I thought that we could, I don't know, talk. I'll be at the house. Call me."

He rattled off a number and the machine went dead.

Taylor stood frozen, staring at the phone as if it had sprouted a mouth and started talking. Win. Winthrop Thomas Stewart Jackson IV. Her illustrious father, getting out of the federal penitentiary early for good behavior? Son of a bitch. Really, this day was just getting better and better.

Barely able to contain her annoyance, Taylor wrote a note about her dad's release and mounted the stairs. Baldwin was sitting at his desk, fingers flying over the keyboard. The wide-screen monitor was on. She got a quick glance of what looked like a sumptuous office before Baldwin realized she was there and hit the screen saver. More secrets. She almost turned around, but she honestly couldn't face the idea of her father alone.

"What's up?" Baldwin asked, leaning back in his chair, all nonchalance.

She thrust the note at him. Baldwin read it, then simply stared at Taylor with his mouth open for half a second. Shaking his head, he pushed back from the desk.

"Wine. Food. Let's go make dinner. The rest comes later."

That sounded good to her.

Silent steps down into the kitchen. Baldwin disappeared into the basement for a few moments then returned with two bottles of wine.

"Zinfandel or Nero d'Avola?" he asked. She raised two fingers.

"Nero it is." He popped the cork on the wine, inserted the aerator, poured them each a glass. She took a sip. The wine was rich and thick, and she felt herself relax a bit. She took her Ativan, let Baldwin see her do it. She was going to be a good little girl. She also snuck another Percocet, just a little something to keep the edge of the headache at bay for a while. Maybe she'd actually be able to talk tonight. She kept hoping that her voice would suddenly start working.

Carbonara was on the menu for the evening, and Taylor sautéed pancetta while Baldwin got the pasta boiling and whisked the eggs and cheese together. She adored the dish. Really—how could you go wrong with Italian bacon and eggs?

The meal was ready in ten minutes and they sat together at the table, grinding pepper, sipping wine, both trapped in their own thoughts. Between the salt, the wine and the drugs, the thoughts of her happy place, Taylor felt her throat relax. She recognized this sensation. It generally preceded her actually speaking a few words aloud.

"My dad," she managed to get out before everything tightened up again.

Shit.

"Hey—that was great." Baldwin said. "I can only

imagine what you must be feeling right now. I can make some calls, but it sounds like he's already been released. Do you want to see him?"

Taylor had thought about that while she cooked. She shook her head, mouthed no.

"Okay. Listen, Atlantic called. I have to handle a case for him. It might mean some travel, and you know how this goes—it might be overseas. But I'm not thrilled about leaving you here by yourself, especially going into Christmas. So what do you think? If I have to go, do you want to come with me?"

The thoughts came fast and furious. Seriously? Had he been looking at her chat history? That was awfully convenient timing. She'd already been prepared to accept Memphis's offer; hell, she was going to broach the subject as soon as they finished eating. The phone call from her dad had fully cemented it. Getting over four thousand miles away from her father wasn't just a super idea, it was an absolute necessity. The sessions with Willig could be put on hold for a few days, especially if Memphis had a friend she could work with. There was just one little hiccup. How was Baldwin going to react to *her* news?

"Mmm…Mmmemphis," she said, then stopped, uncertain of how to explain the situation properly.

Baldwin sat back in his chair, searched her face. He finally shrugged. "I was afraid you'd say that. But hey, at least you said it. The consonant practice is helping, yes?"

An olive branch. She could tell he was fighting an internal battle; his face was smiling, but his eyes were cold. Baldwin was not a fan of Memphis Highsmythe.

She hadn't mentioned that she and Memphis had

been communicating by email or iChat almost daily for the past few weeks. It hadn't seemed necessary at the time; it was harmless stuff. Mostly harmless. But would Baldwin see it that way? Well, hell, did Baldwin have any right to dictate who she did or didn't talk to? No. She melted and got her back up at the same time— being upset with Baldwin took so much energy. She just didn't know how to make things right.

Honestly was the only path she had right now. If it cost her everything, so be it.

Taylor grabbed the notepad.

We've been chatting online. He's been a big help. He's offered to have me come to Scotland, work with a psychologist friend of his. This sounds like good timing all around, don't you think? You can work on your case and I can work on getting this resolved once and for all. Now that we know about the EMDR and its promise, maybe I can turn things around.

She slid the note to Baldwin, watched his face turn four shades of red before he sighed, then smiled and looked up.

"Hell, I don't blame you for reaching out to Memphis. I haven't exactly been easy to talk to these past few weeks." He grabbed her hand, knocking over the pepper mill in his vehemence. "I'm sorry, darling. I'm sorry on so many levels. I'm not sure what I can do to make this up to you. Please, please, will you forgive me?"

Taylor felt the tightly banded chain on her heart crack a bit. This was what she wanted, right? For him to apologize. To offer to make things right. They were better as a team. Together they could conquer anything. But apart, they were two lonely icebergs, drifting silently toward a certain doom. She pushed Memphis's face from her mind. Later. She'd worry about him later. She just missed Baldwin so much, even though he was right there with her.

She stood and signaled for Baldwin. Took him in her arms, and let him kiss her. She kissed him back. Felt all the earlier animosity slide away when his tongue touched hers. They were like vinegar and baking soda, a child's science project. Mix the ingredients, put them together and boom, a volcano. Maybe she was softening, maybe she was just tired of fighting it so hard. But there was nothing, nothing in her world that could make her feel like this.

"I love you," he whispered, and she said it back, surprised when the words slid from her mouth without a moment of hesitation. Baldwin walked her backward into the living room, to the couch. They didn't bother with the niceties, simply shed the necessary garments and joined as quickly as they could, finding solace in each other.

They lay breathless, the food forgotten. She felt good. Stronger. More in control. She could handle this.

She must have fallen asleep for a moment, because she came to and realized Baldwin was playing with her hair. He looked down at her with serious eyes.

"Hey, sleepyhead."

She smiled at him, hugged his body closer. God, she missed this most of all.

Baldwin shifted his weight a bit. "Taylor, you weren't really serious about going to Scotland, were you?"

She took a deep breath and blew it out. Sat up, found her jeans and pulled them on. Her notepad was on the table. She looked over her shoulder at Baldwin, lying on the living room floor, an arm crooked behind his head. He read something in her glance, sat up and wrapped his arms around his knees.

I want to go, Baldwin. I need to. I can't take it here right now. Everyone staring and pointing, talking about me behind my back. It's mortifying.

"But Taylor, you're fighting hard. You're nearly there. Another week with Willig and I bet you have your voice back."

He scrambled up off the floor and came to join her at the table.

This is just something I need to do.

"So you're leaving me?"

No no no. No! Not at all. I just think I need some time to myself to get better.

"And where will Memphis be?"

He's working a case. He'll get me up there, then head back to London. I'll be alone, with his shrink friend. Understand, Baldwin, please. I can't do this, therapy, whatever you want to call it, with people who know me. It's just too much to ask.

He didn't say anything. She watched his hand grasping the stem of his wineglass, could see the tension in his fingers. She hated hurting him like this, but it was for the best. She needed some space. No one was giving her any space.

He finished off his wine.

"Fine, Taylor. If this is what you want. Go to Scotland. I give you my blessing."

I wasn't asking permission, she thought, but refrained from writing it down. No sense in upsetting him more than he already was.

He stared at her for a moment, then stood and threw his wineglass at the sink. It exploded into shards, and he walked out of the room without a second glance.

So it was decided.

She was going to Scotland.

Taylor waited until Baldwin was asleep to send a message to Memphis. It was late in Nashville, past two in the morning, and her head was pounding, but she was wide-awake. She and insomnia were back on speaking terms after a disastrous bout with Ambien left her incoherent. She never responded well to sleeping pills, had the opposite reaction from most people. The Ambien made her frazzled and jumpy all night, then she crashed for ten hours once the sun came up. Turning into a vampire wasn't really an option, even though the doctors said more sleep would help her throat heal faster. She'd managed for all these years already, so she rebuffed their attempts to drug her, stuck with the pain meds and her pool table.

She didn't open her chat. She didn't want to get into a discussion. Coming from sex and fighting with Baldwin to Memphis felt wrong. She just wanted to let him know what she'd decided. She realized she was smiling as she typed the words.

Hey, I hope dinner was great. Baldwin and I talked, and I've decided to come over. He has a case to attend to, so he won't be joining me. I looked at flights; it's simplest for me to fly into Heathrow. Can you meet me in London, then take me up to the Highlands? I'd love to meet your friend, too, and I really want to keep working on getting my voice back. If you can get me her info, I'll have Willig send her notes.

This is going to be great, Memphis. Thank you for asking me. You knew just what I needed. You're the best.
XOXO,
Taylor

MIDDLES

"Be silent in that solitude,
Which is not loneliness—for then
The spirits of the dead who stood
In life before thee are again
In death around thee—and their will
Shall overshadow thee—be still."
SPIRITS OF THE DEAD
—EDGAR ALLEN POE

CHAPTER TWELVE

Taylor was usually a good flier. She was in first class on British Airways, the red-eye, cuddled into the full-length seat, a glass of champagne at her elbow. She couldn't get settled though. This whole trip had her anxious. She fidgeted, played with her hair, annoyed she couldn't put it up—her normal ponytail seemed to make the headaches worse. It started that way. Now she kept it down to cover the scar on her temple.

Baldwin had seen her off at the airport with a bitter kiss. That had been enough to set her off, make her second-guess her decision. She'd never seen him so withdrawn.

But she had to do this. She had to get away. She was sick and tired of being the victim of the story. She was ready to get back to herself, and she truly believed some time alone, away from everyone, would help.

Her voice wasn't coming back, but little bits and pieces of words seemed to find their way out. It gave her hope. She was horribly raspy, even in a soft whisper, her usually huskiness even more so, but somehow things felt...better.

She could have started healing a hell of a lot faster if she'd just given in and forgiven Baldwin sooner. The stress and pressure of being mad at him was certainly a culprit. She'd done one more quick session with Victoria Willig, too, which seemed to help. The horrors from November felt like they were fading a bit. She would get herself back all the way after her stint in Scotland.

For nontherapeutic reasons, she was looking forward to the week ahead. She'd been to the U.K. on a school trip in high school, a ten-day whirlwind around Scotland, Wales, Ireland and England. She'd been entranced by two places: the Lake District—she'd been deep into her Wordsworth stage—and all of Scotland. Wales had fared well in her memory, a late night at a pub in the wilderness, but it was Scotland that always came to mind when she thought back. The barren green-and-brown hills, the rocky crags, the lochs, nestled valley-like into the surrounding mountains, misty and fittingly mysterious, like they held the answer to a millennia of secrets. No wonder the legend of Loch Ness persevered. It was easy to believe that the still waters were a part of the land that time forgot.

Memphis had warned her that he wouldn't be able to stay long. He'd been assigned to the case he mentioned: three missing girls. He could do some work from the estate, but the brass was the brass, which meant he would only be able to sneak away from London for a bit.

Taylor nursed a tiny bit of jealousy after hearing the stress in his voice. She never felt so alive as when she was working a breaking case. She could hear the worry and excitement in his words, feel his distraction, his desire to solve the mystery. She loved that feeling. She missed it.

The champagne had dulled the headache, but she took a pain pill just in case. She let her eyes close. One thing she knew for sure—she was going to be very careful around Memphis Highsmythe.

Taylor woke as the plane landed, the jolt and reek of the tires immediate in her nose. She was shocked at how rested she felt. Even just a couple of hours of shut-eye could rejuvenate her completely. She fluffed her hair, over the scar, allowing it to hang over her shoulders, then gathered her bags and wandered off the plane, stretching and yawning. Customs was bogged down, the line winding around the building in serpentine circles, sleepy, unkempt people being herded into their pens. It was going to take her forever to circumnavigate.

"Welcome to England!"

Taylor jumped a mile. Memphis was standing three feet away, his face partially hidden behind a massive bouquet of fat roses. White ones, not red. Red would have been too inappropriate. He was waiting for her.

She smiled wide and waved. She went to Memphis, accepted the beautiful cabbage roses, and let him kiss her on both cheeks. He smelled good, like wind and rain and man. She felt that familiar tick in her heart that she'd thought she was done with, which made her mad. She scowled, and Memphis looked hurt. She stepped back from him, confused.

"My schedule shifted and I thought I'd walk you through customs, free up some time for you. The weather may turn and interrupt our travels. You don't mind, do you?"

She shook her head. Pointed at her throat, a reminder that she couldn't talk.

"Ah, well. I'd hoped seeing me would bring it all rushing back."

Memphis picked up her bag, started off toward the customs sign. He looked good, blond and tight, strolling through Heathrow. Women turned to look at him, but he was unaware of the attention. Completely oblivious to his effect. Baldwin was like that. Only had eyes for her. She couldn't help the comparisons—Baldwin, dark and tall and lean and chiseled, Memphis shorter, more compact, but just as pretty. Two very pretty men.

They were two sides of a coin. Both good, she had no doubts about that. But there the similarities stopped. Baldwin was rational, whereas Memphis was unreasonable. Violence hid just underneath his polished surface. Memphis didn't look like a brawler, more like a cobra swaying in the breeze. His whole countenance sent off distinct signals—you knew to leave well enough alone or get bitten.

Both smart, both educated, both in love with her. She stopped herself. Comparing them wasn't smart.

Memphis looked back over his shoulder and winked at her. No, all would be well. She had a feeling Baldwin may have had a chat with Memphis, told him to behave. She didn't blame him. Memphis wasn't good at playing with his own toys. And just in case it became necessary, Taylor had written up a stern letter explaining the ground rules. She was hoping it wouldn't be needed, but she found it entirely impossible to predict Memphis's behavior. He could swing between Lothario and Lancelot at a moment's notice. And she, fickle beast, seemed to get caught in his ebb and flow as if he were the moon and she the tides. She wasn't quite sure what to make of that sensation.

Memphis was prattling on as he led her to the front of the line, making small talk.

"I hope you won't be too jet-lagged, but I've set up a breakfast meeting tomorrow with Madeira James, the doctor friend that I mentioned. I believe you'll enjoy her company, Taylor. She is a smart, lovely woman. She's taken good care of me since…well, you know."

Since Evan died. I know, Memphis. I know. No one should have to go through losing a spouse. And a child.

"Yes," Taylor said, the word nearly guttural.

Memphis pulled up short. "Oh, my. That sounds like it hurts. Can you do more?"

She shook her head. It wasn't the pain that stopped her from talking, just the memories. Now that she was starting to be able to vocalize again, she was suddenly shy, every word measured for worth, for impact. She hoped that would go away before too long as well.

They were up to the customs agent now, who asked them business or pleasure in a bored voice.

Memphis answered for her.

"Both."

The man stamped her passport and handed it back. And just like that, she was free.

CHAPTER THIRTEEN

It was chilly outside the terminal, low gray skies and a lingering threat of rain. Taylor pulled her shearling jacket close around her, adjusted her scarf. She breathed deeply, the grit of canned plane air replaced by brisk, cool city smog. It smelled wonderful.

Memphis had a car waiting, low and sleek and black, with a driver who held the door. Taylor raised an eyebrow at him. He just smiled and bowed with a flourish.

"My father sends his best wishes to the lady."

She slid onto the smooth leather, smelling the tiniest hint of cigar smoke wafting up from the seats. Many a deal had been done in the back of this car. She could feel that immediately. Memphis sat across from her, riding backward. The car slid from the curb.

Taylor pulled out her notebook.

Tell him thank you. This is lovely.

Memphis winced at seeing her having to write rather than speak, but covered his dismay quickly. "I thought I could do a quick drive through town for you, give you a taste of London. It's been a while since you were here last, correct?"

She nodded.

"Good. Then we can head to King's Cross. I've booked us seats on the noon train. We could have flown, but it's only three hours, and the countryside is pretty. I thought it would give you a chance to catch up on your rest."

"Thank you, Mmmmemphis," Taylor whispered, then put her hand on her throat. The plane's dry, recirculated air had made it tight and itchy, she was better off not talking. She needed some cough drops. When she wasn't speaking, her throat hadn't hurt at all.

"Oh, goodness, apologies. You must be thirsty. I've got a bit of tea. Would that help?"

She nodded, and he produced a stainless steel thermos and poured her a cup. Earl Grey, with milk and sugar, just the way she liked it. Already prepared, ready to go. She couldn't help but see the quiet smirk on his face. She narrowed her eyes at him but he avoided her gaze, started pointing out landmarks.

London was overwhelming. The sheer size of it, for starters. Taylor was shocked by how much it had changed since she'd been there as a teenager—she remembered Old World architecture and history brimming from the cups on every corner. This new London was spread and steel and glass and fast. It lacked the romanticism she remembered.

But it had a sense of excitement, of glamour and sly humor, hidden just beneath the uptight modern exterior. She craned her neck for a street sign and saw they were on Victoria, which meant they were traveling into the city following the winding Thames. Once she saw the Tower of London, and the gaily-decorated Tower Bridge looming large and blue to her left, the city reasserted itself. A few minutes later Big Ben came into view and she felt more at home, despite the London Eye soaring into the gray sky. The Thames was as murky and gossamer as she remembered, the spires of Parliament and Westminster Abbey gothic and foreboding.

Welcome to England, indeed.

They drove up to Buckingham Palace, the black wrought-iron-and-gold gates glowing in the meager daylight, and she had the same sense of disappointment as she'd had when she saw the palace as a girl. It was a giant box. Elegant and huge, with unbelievably luxurious touches, but a fortress. Taylor was a little girl when it came to kings and queens and princes and princesses. Castles were meant to be gray stone with turrets and moats and crenulated battlements. Balmoral, the Queen's summer residence, in Scotland, was much more in keeping with Taylor's romantic view of proper royal residences. Baronial and tower architecture in castles, that's what really appealed to her. Glamis Castle was another. Of course, Glamis was haunted, by a white lady, a gray lady, a possible vampire child, a monster, the devil—the works. She wondered if Memphis's castle was haunted. Surely he'd have mentioned something like that, knowing her predilections. Ghosts didn't scare her; it was more the living evil she had nightmares about. But she really didn't like the idea of being haunted.

Taylor caught a quick glance into St. James Park, the view at this angle like a glimpse into a Monet painting, lush and green even this late in the season. For some reason, the vision reminded her of her father. She hadn't returned his call, and when he arrived in Nashville and came looking for her, she was going to be nowhere to be found. He'd go to Sam, but Sam had strict instructions. Under no circumstance was she to reveal Taylor's whereabouts, nor any other details about the recent troubles. He was not allowed to be a part of her life. Never again.

Running away from her dad was childish. She'd have to face him sooner or later. Later seemed much preferable, though God knew what sort of trouble he'd manage to get himself into by the time she returned. If Win were a self-destructive drunk, he'd be as trouble-prone as a raging alcoholic with his fourth thirty-day chip and an unopened bottle of cheap brandy. As it was, his excesses ranged to quieter issues. He'd be into something, some scheme, some plan, guaranteed to be illegal, by the time she returned.

The car was turning back now, toward Mayfair. A motorcycle whizzed past them on the right, screaming around the car and cutting it off. The driver slammed on the brakes, and Taylor reeled back in her seat. Her heart began to pound, and she felt a familiar moment of panic. Her breath started to come faster, and she got that strange carsick feeling that preceded one of her attacks. *Oh no, not now. Not in front of Memphis.*

She closed her eyes and tried to force her mind away, but the red wash of blood covered her face, and her head throbbed in sympathetic pain. She looked into Sam's eyes, saw her friend's streaming tears, felt the anger and hate build in her, felt the slick metal of the gun in her hand...

Think about your safe place, Taylor. Camp. The horse. Breathe.

She took sips of air through her nose until her racing heart slowed.

She cracked her eyelids. Memphis was cursing the motorcycle rider. He hadn't noticed. Thank God. She buried her face in her teacup, managed a full, deep breath.

She'd had just about enough serial killers to last her a lifetime.

"Are you okay?" Memphis asked. "You're white as a sheet."

Crap. He *had* noticed.

Yeah. One of the side effects. Flashbacks. Joy.

"So with all the issues you're still having, how did you talk Baldwin into letting you come alone?"

Bribery.

"In other words, you two are getting along better," Memphis said. His tone was neutral—not questioning or beseeching. Just asking.

She turned away from the window and back to Memphis. She took a sip of her tea.

We made up. Things are good again.

"And is it fixing things? Your voice, for instance?"

Let's not do this, Memphis. Okay?

She wasn't kidding, she didn't feel like talking about her relationship with him. It was one thing to talk on the computer, but in person, it felt like a betrayal. And she wasn't here to betray Baldwin. Away simply meant away, a little time, a little space. Less pressure on her to keep up her strong facade. She could be herself here.

She couldn't read his look. He gave her a small smile.

Seriously, Memphis. It's not like that.

"Ah, Taylor. Young love has its ups and downs. Oh, look—there's my place."

For a moment she was confused. Memphis lived in Chelsea, and they were nowhere near his posh neighborhood. But then she saw the great silver-and-blue revolving sign. New Scotland Yard on one side, Metropolitan Police: Working together for a safer London on the other. The entire judicial system of Nashville could fit into its shiny corridors. The building was massive, glass and steel and concrete; she could see the reflection of the stunning redbrick St. Ermin's Hotel in its gleaming windows.

A lone female bobby stood guard at the front entrance, but Taylor had a trained eye. There were layers upon layers of security—a bulletproof glass barrier, cameras and tri-level turnstiles and revolving doors and electronic card readers. A surface-mounted spike system with wicked angled teeth allowed cars to pull into the garage below, but not back up lest they shred their tires. She saw submerged concrete barriers that could be raised at a moment's notice to trap people inside, or stop people from entering.

"Like it?" Memphis asked, and she nodded. It was

fiercely beautiful, very much the new London look that she was starting to get used to. The sun peeked out from behind a cloud for the briefest of moments and set the building to flashing.

"Fancy," she said.

"Wave to Pen. She'll be mad I didn't bring you by. Unless you want to go in?"

She shook her head—that would be too much. Maybe on her way back out of town. She didn't want that feeling of despair and loneliness that she felt every time she thought about work to invade her here. She was here to get away from police work, from her job, her life, her mistakes. All she wanted was a quiet place to heal. And hide.

Memphis's mobile rang and he excused himself, murmuring into the headset. Taylor watched the people of London. It felt like New York, but with bigger smiles and a British accent. Everyone looked cold; they were hurrying about, scurrying, really. It was a blustery winter day, chilly and cloudy with heavy rain expected later in the evening.

Everyone they drove past looked so nonchalant and buttoned-down. It made her feel flashy and childish. Too enthusiastic. She'd have to remember to be more subdued—physically, at least. She had the mousy quiet thing down already.

The drive to King's Cross Station took another five minutes. The driver deposited them and their luggage at the entrance, and Memphis produced two tickets.

"We're in first class, and we've got seats on the right side of the train. It's lovely once we get up toward the border."

The seats weren't crazy luxurious, as Taylor expected

when thinking first class and train. They were roomier than the regular seats, only four across instead of six, a few with completely separate single two-top tables. The food was better, the drinks higher quality. And less crowded; she could see into the train car behind them at the seething mass of people crowding in. One small boy caught her eye—he stuck out his tongue at her and turned into the car with his frazzled mother scooting along right behind.

The last time she'd been on a train was the Caledonian Sleeper from Inverness to London, after a rousing tour of Loch Ness with a gaggle of rowdy teenagers. She remembered purple bunk beds, stainless steel washbasins, tea and toast to soak up their evening's excess. They'd gotten plowed on the train (thrilled to be able to say they were appropriately pissed, in the local lingo) and disembarked with legs that wouldn't hold them properly, giggling and swaying through the train station like a mustering of newborn storks.

Things were more seemly now that she was an adult. Their seats were reserved with a small piece of paper stuck to the top. They faced one another, with a tan plastic table in the middle.

"Forward or back?" he asked.

She motioned to the forward seat. The idea of riding backward made her nauseous.

They took their places. Taylor turned her phone on so she could check her messages, was relieved to see she had none.

And sad, at the same time. It used to be she couldn't go five minutes without a call, but now her phone sat silent and unused. Unloved. She sent Baldwin a quick, needless text that they were on their way, and stowed the phone.

The train's doors closed. The cabin around them was full. The movement began with a gentle tug, then built into a rhythm. Quickly, a girl with a trolley came by. Taylor followed Memphis's suggestion and ordered tea, fruit salad and a bacon sandwich. She was delighted when it showed up—the bacon was crisp, the wheat toast warm and crunchy, and the side was a large dollop of what she first thought was barbeque sauce, but quickly discovered was HP Sauce, similar, but more peppery than what she knew. It was delicious, and she immediately felt at home. Bacon and barbeque sauce in first class on a northbound train to Edinburgh. She could get used to this.

CHAPTER FOURTEEN

Taylor watched the green fields roll by, surprised by their verdancy, considering it was so late in the year. Wintertime, but at sea level, the constant wet kept things lush. The villages along the way were charming, even the smallest, poorest close elegant in its barrenness. She was surprised by the cypress trees, which were so reminiscent of the Italian countryside she loved. The beautiful trees brought up fond memories, memories Memphis seemed determined to ruin with his inopportunely timed interruptions. She'd forgotten what a blue jay he could be. Of course, after being trapped in silence for the past month, most of the people close to her had grown quiet as well. She had to remember that. He was simply being friendly.

"You'll be pleased to know the weather will be fine tomorrow. A brief storm tonight, some snow, but nothing you won't be able to handle. It might liven up a bit later in the week. You did pack your warm boots....

"May I get you some more tea? The trolley should be coming back through any moment....

"You're much too thin, you need a proper fattening

up. Cook will be thrilled to have a project. She gets terribly dejected when my parents decide to spend the holidays away...."

And finally, "Are you ignoring me on purpose, or have you simply lapsed into a travel coma?"

She mentally shook herself. She was being awfully rude.

She held up a finger to make him wait a minute, then retrieved her laptop from her bag. If they were going to have a conversation, it was easier and quicker for her to type.

She opened to a blank page in Word and typed her answer.

Not ignoring. Just used to quiet. Sorry. Where are we now?

"Just north of York."

The trolley arrived again, momentarily saving her from more conversation. She was full of tea, accepted a glass of wine instead. Outside, the clouds turned from white to gray, and small bits of blue tried to peek through. The vistas were changing, growing wider, with more farmland visible. The landscape was dotted with the cotton of lambs.

With the alcohol on board, things became easier. She dropped her walls a bit and allowed herself to enjoy the ride. She and Memphis settled into a comfortable rhythm of chatter and writing. She watched his blue eyes light up when he saw something outside the train windows he thought she should know about. He was full of stories and memories.

"See the cathedral at Durham? One of Britain's most famous serial killers is housed in the prison here....

"We call this the Angel of the North....

"This is still the Thames, all the way up in Newcastle, famous for their bridges. The Tweed River is at the border between England and Scotland...."

They chugged past an undulating concert hall that looked like a roly-poly, one of the insects Taylor had treasured as a child. She'd combed the ground for them, picked them up with her grubby hands, thrilled to watch them curl into tiny balls that made them impervious to her incessant poking.

Trees that looked like miniature Italian Stone pines puffed their tops into umbrella shapes—yet another reminder of her time in Italy. She wondered whether the conquerors brought them or if they migrated naturally.

A murder of crows stood watch in a field. She imagined their caws, overlaid with the delicate notes of the fine songbirds in Nashville. *They'd gathered in the branches at the Snow White's house, their Siren call pulling her in, where the Pretender lay in wait for her...*

God, she had to stop flashing back like this. It was disturbing in the extreme, this inability to divorce the most mundane sights and sounds from the shooting.

She had the most absurd thought, which pulled her back to the present. She knew it would make Memphis laugh. She hoped his mirth would be catching.

Do the crows have a British accent?

"What?"

The crows. The animals in general. Do they have some sort of accent, like you do?

"I haven't an accent. Besides, I would think it's the American animals with the inflections, don't you? A drawl here, a twang there. It's all the Queen's English, after all."

They shared a smile, then were quiet for a bit.

The sun was growing low in the sky. She burrowed into her jacket, suddenly chilled. She was here, she was committed to getting all the way back to herself. So why did she have such a sense of foreboding about the whole venture?

Memphis caught her shiver. "Do you want to talk about it?" he asked, gently taking her hand. She let him, she was chilled, and the warmth felt good.

She knew exactly what he meant. The shooting. The Pretender. Her fall from grace. Her life falling apart before everyone's eyes.

Not really. There's no more to tell. It's over. I just need to let it go. I'm trying, so hard, to let it go. Why don't you tell me about your case instead? I'll live vicariously through you.

He stared into her eyes for a few moments, as if trying to ascertain if she was trying to get him to push harder, or if she really wanted him to back away and distract her. Apparently deciding on the latter, he filled her in.

"All right, then. At best, we have a trio of girls who've run away, joined a cult or some such nonsense. At worst, we'll start finding bodies. The pattern is quite evident, and the victimology is coming together nicely. They all attended different schools, didn't work together, but all three had gone to a 'church' over on the East End. For one it was in her neighborhood, for the others, a tube ride. Out of their way.

"They call it a church, but they don't ascribe to any God I've ever heard of. It's run by a very charismatic young man who is known as Urq. His father is quite rich. I think he's probably a schizophrenic, but seems to be much beloved amongst his flock.

"It's probably a serial, but if that were the case, I'd expect to see bodies by now. I just don't have a handle on it yet. Give me a stabbing in a Mayfair pub any day."

You should talk to Baldwin. He might have an idea of how to approach it. He's good at that sort of thing.

The moment she turned the screen around and saw Memphis's eyebrow rise in response, she realized how it must look. She pulled the computer back and tried again.

I didn't mean it like that. You and I, we're the same. We understand crime. We understand how criminals think. But serial killers have a different mind-set, and Baldwin knows them. Their motivations aren't the same. I keep telling him he needs to write a book, something that investigators like us can use as a handbook of sorts.

Memphis drummed his fingers on the table. "I might just do that. Speak with him, that is. I'm not above asking for help when lives are at stake. Because something isn't right with this case. I just can't put my finger— Oh, look."

Memphis directed her gaze to the window, and the North Sea appeared, rough and choppy even in the relatively calm weather. Taylor could swear she smelled the salt in the air.

"We're getting close now," he said.

And then suddenly they were in Edinburgh, the Waverly station welcoming in its homely concreteness. They disembarked, her legs wobbly on the pavement, the wine adding to her discomfiture, like she was trying to balance atop a very angry rocking chair.

Memphis took her arm and tucked it into the crook of his elbow, holding her upright. She was suddenly exhausted. It was just morning in Nashville, but the time difference, the overnight flight, the wine, the stress of being with Memphis, waiting for the next volley of flirtations, all of it was catching up to her.

Memphis used one hand to wrangle Taylor's bag and the other to steer her around to the stairs. They were met at the bottom by a homely man, mid-thirties, hair longer than his collar and swept back with some sort of gel. He stood in front of a battered Range Rover. Memphis introduced him as Jacques, who promptly showered Taylor in a transformative smile showing hugely white Chiclet teeth that had to be dentures, and spoke a few flowery sentences in rapid French that she translated to "Welcome, I'm your driver, if there's anything you need let me know."

"Merci," she managed to say, in a pretty little croak, which earned her another heavenly smile. She watched him turn to open the door, noticed the small lump under

his arm. Driver *and* bodyguard? Why in the world would Memphis have an armed driver? It wouldn't be unheard of among public figures and high royals, but it seemed like overkill. Memphis was New Scotland Yard, after all. Another of the strange things she would get to ask him about eventually.

She climbed into the back of the truck, happy they weren't in a fancy car, but again struck by the similarities to her mother's escapades. Traveling all over Europe, chauffeured by servants. Hypocrisy had its claws in Taylor's back.

As they pulled out of Waverly and started the trek out of Edinburgh, Taylor was struck by the differences, and the similarities, to her Tennessee hometown. On the surface it was so different: Nashville was slower, a languorous little hamlet in comparison to the hustle and bustle of Edinburgh. Constant slowing at roundabouts and signs that needed a moment's mental translations, dual carriageways and pull-offs for takeaway curry and crisps, tiny one-laned streets that gave way to super-highways: these were all foreign.

But the trees, and the hills, the smiles and the sense of purpose, all reminded her of home.

She knew Memphis was watching her. Watching her take measure of her surroundings. Imagining her driving these roads, shopping in these stores, eating in these restaurants. Hoping she liked what she saw.

Fitting in.

She was never so glad to be mute as this moment. Her voice would have betrayed her.

She saw water up ahead, a wide river. The bridge

looked like the Golden Gate, with a huge railroad trestle off to the right.

"We're fording the Firth of Forth now," Memphis said.

Say that three times fast.

He laughed.

"Live here long enough and it becomes second nature."

The thought brought her up short. Is that was she was doing? Testing the waters to see which parts of her were comfortable with Scotland, and all that it held, and which weren't? Riding along in the car with Memphis by her side instead of Baldwin, and not minding?

The car was warm, and she was suddenly exhausted. Before she could delve too deeply into those thoughts, her eyes closed of their own volition, and she fell asleep.

CHAPTER FIFTEEN

Memphis watched Taylor sleep. She was an angel in repose, cheeks rosily flushed, her mouth slightly open. He wanted to take his thumb and run it along the bottom of her lip, just where it was full to the point of spilling over. He had to sit on his hand to stop the urge. He wanted to wake her and watch those mismatched gray eyes focus fully on him, the pupils dilating in welcome. He wanted to crawl into her hair and pull it around him like a blanket. He wanted to shower her with roses, whisper words that would make her laugh. He wanted to feel her skin warm to his touch. The thought of taking her to his bed, flushed with desire, nearly drove him mad.

God, he wanted to rut with her until his balls ached.

He hadn't felt so strongly about a woman since he met Evan, and being forced to compare the two, to seek out the sameness and the differences, almost made him ill. He was certainly not over Evan. Her death left a gaping hole inside him. The only thing that seemed to fill in the edges was thoughts of Taylor. Having her so near was intoxicating.

But to win her away from her chap was proving more difficult than he ever expected. He hoped that showing her how accommodating he could be, how much freedom she would have with him, no pressure, no fighting, would show her it wouldn't be so bad being the wife of a viscount. He hoped that her outings with his friend Maddee would help Taylor find herself again.

He knew he shouldn't be thinking this way. Taylor wasn't his to take. If he could whip out a knife and cut her away from the uptight Fed, that would make life easier. Or he could just give up, find someone else. Maddee had been encouraging him to find another, more suitable woman for months, ever since he came back from his trip to the States heart-struck.

He'd gotten the feeling that Maddee would like for him to move on with *her,* but that would never happen. Not only was she married to one of his oldest friends, she wasn't his type. Too dark-complected, too brash and forward. Too American. She'd made a move on him once at a party in Inverness, before Evan's death. They'd been seated around a formal dining table and he'd felt a small, creeping hand slide up his leg and settle onto his cock. Maddee, resplendent in a low-cut emerald dress, kept up her conversation with the gentleman on her right while she fondled Memphis.

At first he was too surprised to stop her, and for a moment, he gave in to the pleasure of her illicit dexterity, but a quick glance across the table at his lovely bride had finished the matter. He'd delicately removed her hand and they'd never spoken of it.

That lapse didn't diminish her abilities as a doctor,

nor as a friend. Since then, she'd kept her physical distance, and their friendship continued unabated.

She'd been with him when he got the news about Evan.

Maddee and Roland had come up to London that day, were staying at his flat in Chelsea. The three of them went shopping, saw a show. Went to dinner. And all the while, Evan had been dead, her car plunged into the icy waters, the baby...

Oh, he had to stop this. Evan was gone. Gone forever. He wasn't to blame. He knew that. Maddee had reassured him, over and over, that he wasn't to blame. But he carried the guilt with him anyway. If he hadn't left her alone...

Taylor shifted a bit in her sleep, pulling Memphis back to the now, and he glanced out the window to see they were at the Killicrankie roundabout, which exited to the grounds of the estate.

He roused Taylor from her slumber. She came awake immediately, eyes wide and distant.

"Nightmare?" he asked.

She cleared her throat and whispered, "Yes." Honest and simple, which made him feel more connected to her than before. If she wouldn't let him in, he didn't have a chance; by admitting her fears, showing him her weakness, she was opening the door a bit.

She yawned and her jaw cracked. She opened her ever-present notebook to a fresh page.

Where are we?

"Almost there. We've just taken the roundabout into Dulsie."

She looked around and smiled, and he could tell she

was charmed. The farmland turned into rolling hills of
heather, then a sudden forest, huge fir trees placed so
closely together that getting a hand between the trunks
would be a challenge. When things spread out a bit,
larches, transplanted sequoias, oak, birch and aspen
abounded.

The road twisted into the woods for thirteen miles
before it opened into a glen, tucked into the base of the
mountains, with a small loch that fed the burns throughout the estate. The entry was stone, forty feet high, a
massive archway with steel gates that could be closed
against entrants.

A chicken, flushed from the heather on the side of
the road, burst across the drive. Taylor giggled. Memphis did his best not to cringe at the sound; it wasn't the
open, carefree laugh he was used to hearing from her.

It's huge. I've never seen such a big chicken.

"They're Buff Orpingtons. Free-range, at that. Heavenly eating."

The car drove on, the span of three more heartbeats.
He watched her face as the house came into view, almost
laughed aloud at the surprise he saw there. She turned
to him, eyes shining in delight, and he simply placed
his arm around her shoulder and squeezed.

"Welcome home," he said.

CHAPTER SIXTEEN

Taylor knew her jaw was on the floor, but she couldn't help herself. Memphis had assured her that the house in Scotland was "a cobwebby old thing." Impossible to heat. That's what she'd quoted Sam, too, thinking he was telling at least part of the truth. He'd always downplayed his status in the aristocracy, and she'd felt a connection to him because of that—the desire to make it on your own, to alter your past, to force your parents' aspirations away and lead your own life, free of the encumbrances that came with wealth.

What a lying sack of shit he was. Freaking viscount.

The "house" was a full-fledged castle, right out of her wildest imagination. Complete with towers and turrets and crenellations, and what used to be a moat, now filled with grass and gravel. There was even a portcullis, topped with leering gargoyles. It was almost as if Memphis had a checklist and was mining about in her head, looking for all the things she dreamed about as a girl, then making sure they were incorporated into his home. The exterior was whitewashed stucco instead of stone, with dark brown timbers and a gray slate roof that gave it the look of a Tudor mansion mated with a French château. It was monstrous.

Just how big is this place?

He scuffed his foot in the gravel of the forecourt like a little boy, obviously uncomfortable. She knew the British didn't approach things like size and luxury the way Americans did.

"Well, you know, Dulsie Castle is no bigger than most country houses of this period. We've added on this century, a public tearoom and expanded banquet hall, so it can be used for tours and weddings and such. And the grounds are extensive. There's a great deal of sport round here, history, that lot. People come caravanning, or stay in the village below."

Come on· Spill·

He ducked his head, she didn't know if it was shame or sheer pleasure in surprising her. "It's not that large, truly. We only have seventeen bedrooms."

She did some mental calculating based on her own parents' home, with its six bedrooms and eight baths, and came up with something in the range of about 50,000 square feet. She tried to be nonchalant.

I can see why it would be hard to heat·

He barked out a laugh and she felt absurdly pleased for amusing him.

"I wasn't kidding, you know. It *is* hard to heat, and the taxes truly are crippling. That's why we offset with public tours. But they only get into the first two floors, and access to the attics on Samhain for ghost stories, and we close from the fifteenth of November until the Ides of March. The top floors are all private quarters, and the grounds are segmented as well. Plenty of privacy. And plenty of places to lounge about, if you choose. Or, if you're feeling up to it, you can get your hands dirty. This is a working estate—you saw the chickens. We also have sheep, Highland cattle, gardens and a deer park. Whatever my princess wants, my princess shall have."

She rolled her eyes, but inside couldn't help but feel excited. In addition to the crazy-fabulous castle, she was surrounded by natural beauty, and itched to start exploring.

They exited the Range Rover, Jacques holding the door and bestowing another happy smile, and she could smell the unique scents that went along with a mountain farm. Clean, cool air and sparkling water, fallen leaves, manure and hay, the vanilla and chocolate scents of the evergreen trees, the softly aromatic heather. Cinnamon and yeast and garlic, too. Her stomach growled unceremoniously.

Memphis could smell it as well. She watched his nose twitching.

"Cook's gone and outdone herself now, that smells like venison stew. And there will be apple frushie for pudding." He looked like an eight-year-old boy who'd just found out he gets to eat with the adults for the first time.

She wondered briefly if he'd brought other women here, to charm and shock with his largesse, but decided against it. Memphis may be a cad, but she couldn't imagine him dragging just anyone home. She got the distinct impression that this display was uniquely for her benefit.

"Let me show you round, get you settled. You can freshen up and rest before we eat."

She craned her neck to look up at the tower above the keep, framed in dark storm clouds, the sky coated in amber from the sun setting early this far north, all the while cursing herself. This was Memphis's plan all along, letting her see just what she might have a chance to be a part of. And like Elizabeth Bennet, upon seeing Mr. Darcy's Pemberley for the first time and realizing what she passed up, she felt momentarily foolish.

She heard Sam's disgusted snort in her ear, like she was sitting on the good angel side of things, and nearly laughed aloud. Even from four thousand miles away, her best friend had sway. Taylor could just hear her now: *This isn't your life. This isn't your world. This is just an escape. You don't belong here. You'd do best to remember that.*

Practical Sam. Who'd been in love with the same man since she was fifteen.

Memphis was standing at the top of the stairs, waiting for her. She mentally shoved Sam off her shoulder, tossed him a smile, blushing slightly because she knew he'd been watching the awed thoughts scroll across her face. It took a lot to surprise her, and she was quite surprised.

The inside of the castle was as opulent and impressive as she could expect, all done up for Christmas: fresh wreaths and trees and garlands everywhere, with centuries-old furniture, weapons, decor, impossibly thick stone walls and wide stairwells lined with elegant polished wood balustrades. Chandeliers and antlers and rugs and priceless oils; oversize family portraits showed the ancestral facial structure that was clearly stamped on Memphis's features, an echo of his past. He belonged here. It was actually the first time she'd ever seen him so very much at home.

An older woman met them in the open hallway. Memphis introduced her to Taylor. "This is Trixie. She's been with the family longer than I have. She's mistress of this domain, make no doubt."

Her name was ridiculously incongruous with her being. The woman didn't smile, just turned the corners of her mouth up like she was used to Memphis's teasing and found it very boring indeed. Her hair was iron-gray and pulled back into a severe bun, her eyes a weak blue. She wore a thick wool skirt and a plain wool sweater, and, oddly, men's laced brogues on her feet. Taylor assumed she was in her sixties at least. Her carriage was remarkable for a woman her age: her back was straight, neck long and elegant.

She nodded to Taylor and spoke, her voice higher and softer than Taylor expected. "It's nice to meet you, mum. I'm head housekeeper for the castle. If you're needin' anything, you ring the bell." She pointed out a small doorbell on the wall near the banister. Next to it was a silver bell attached to a pulley. "You'll find 'em throughout the house." Her accent was patently Scots; *house* came out *hoose.*

Memphis saw her looking at the two systems, one new, one antiquated. "We left behind the old pull bells some time ago. The electronic system works wonderfully. Every room is wired to its own ringer on the board downstairs. Yes, Trixie can handle anything you might need when I leave. She's good company, aren't you, old girl?"

Trixie finally gave in to Memphis's charm and gave him a dimply smile. Taylor saw why she didn't do it much. Her teeth were brown and visibly decayed.

"I'd be happy to show the lady to her room," she said.

Memphis shook his head. "No, that's fine. Jacques has her bag. I'm going to give her a quick tour."

"I'll leave you, then," Trixie said. Taylor watched her walk away, wondered if perhaps she'd had scoliosis as a child and been forced to wear a brace. It was rare to see such good posture. Her glance went down the length of the woman's body, and then she saw the reason. The left shoe's sole was four times thicker than the right. Her left leg was dramatically short. To make up for it, Trixie had developed the carriage of a queen. Taylor could only imagine the pain she'd experienced growing up.

As if she knew Taylor was watching her, Trixie looked back over her shoulder for a moment, casting a dark glance at the new interloper standing in her entrance hall. Taylor was a bit taken aback. While not overtly friendly, Trixie hadn't seemed hostile until that moment. Taylor made a note to be wary around her.

Memphis watched Taylor, and he'd obviously seen Trixie's angry glance. He sought to reassure her, spoke quietly.

"Trixie's a good woman. She has been with the family forever, since well before I was born. She was our governess when we were growing up, frightened us all into submission. She has no one, no family, nothing. So when we were grown, Mother took her as her personal maid. She took over running the whole place from the housekeeper several years ago. She's very protective of the family, just doesn't take to strangers. She'll come round. I'm not here very much, but it looks like she has things well in hand. Let's see the rest of the place."

He gave her a brief tour of the downstairs—the dining room, the armory, the public viewing rooms with the history of the castle carefully imprinted on each, then they walked to the back of the castle, down a long hallway lined with deer skulls and antlers. Taylor wasn't against hunting, per se, just wasn't an aficionado herself.

Did you shoot all of these?

"Oh no. See the plaques?"

Taylor looked closer. To the right of each skull was a handwritten note. She traced the line up the hall—Meek age 3, Meek age 4, Meek age 5.

A pet?

"Of sorts. The deer drop their antlers every year. It's always been tradition to gather them up and place them on the wall, attached to the skulls of deer that have passed or been shot. You see how big he got—Meek sired half the herd."

Meek had grown to a fine twelve-point buck before his death at the ripe old age of fifteen.

"Some people collect plates," he said with a shrug.

My mother collects Limoges teacups. She started when she was a girl. The display cases are ridiculous.

She paused and looked back up at the remnants of Meek.

I think I like the antlers better· More character·

He smiled and led her to a set of stone stairs. This took them up a flight to a quiet wooden door with a coded lock. He gave her the code; this would be her path into and out of the castle.

The family rooms were no less opulent, but much more modern and comfortable than the public rooms of the castle. While still traditional, with wooden panels on the walls and elegant plasterwork on the ceilings, there was leather and glass and dark wood, with more contemporary paintings and cornice-work, with tiny feminine touches that set the private rooms apart.

The whole aspect was decidedly uncobwebby. She had to laugh. Her parents' huge house in Nashville, long empty but still theirs, just waiting for Taylor to come to her senses and accept her fortune, would fit twice into the private rooms of Dulsie Castle.

"What's so funny?" Memphis asked.

With a smile, she wrote *Humility.*

"Humility? I thought you liked the place." He pretended to be hurt.

It's lovely, Memphis· A bit grander than I'm used to, but lovely· Where do I sleep?

"Ah, I've been saving the best for last. Come and see."

He held out a hand, which she accepted, and he pulled her along down a hallway, up another flight of stairs to another long hallway. The ancient oak, wide planked floors, glossy with a patina befitting their age, were covered by a thick gorgeous yellow-and-red wool and silk runner that she wanted to lie down on.

"Your chamber, my lady," Memphis said, stopping in front of a large wooden door. It was arched, the handle wrought iron, with a square wooden peephole traversed by a tiny iron fence. She'd seen less grand front entrances on some of the stately Belle Meade mansions at home.

Memphis pushed the door open, and Taylor was, quite simply, blown away. She'd grown up with the trappings of wealth, but this was far beyond what she'd ever been privy to. It was everything a castle room should be.

On closer inspection, they were actually in a suite of rooms, all gorgeously, sumptuously decorated. The ceilings were twenty feet high, paneled, covered in elegantly detailed roundels. The plasterwork was ornate and intricate, bordering on rococo, with draped silk and paintings of cherubs on clouds, a mini Sistine Chapel. The walls were soft golden oak, also in panels that were interspersed with silk tapestries. She could get lost in the stories they portrayed.

The front area held a sitting room. A couch faced a television, but she barely glanced at it after the rest of the room caught her eye. Warm butter-colored leather chairs with a small table and reading lamp faced a virtual library of books surrounding a large stone fireplace, a fire already crackling and putting out warmth. There was a ladder to reach the uppermost shelves.

She went to the tomes immediately, running her fingers over the spines. All of her favorites were there, all the books she and Memphis had discussed over the past several months.

She had a flash of emotion, both affection and sympathy, for all his trouble. This was seduction at its highest—the simple act of memory. When someone remembers what you've said, has actually taken the time to listen and stow away the information for recall later, well, that was beyond flattery. That's what a real relationship was about.

She saw that there was a small theater section as well, with all of her favorite movies on DVD. To her right, there was a large casement window, the sheer curtain drawn. She walked to it and spread the drape back, her breath catching in her throat. The view was stunning—if warped a bit by the glazed glass. She had a complete panorama of the mountains, the valley, the river, the deer park, the sheep, the incoming storm. If she looked far to her right she could see the estate's grass tennis courts. She shivered and pulled her sweater closer around her. If she could have designed a view to be perfect, this would fit the bill.

It was the most romantic place she'd ever seen.

She turned to Memphis, saw he was waiting anxiously for her to say something. Anything.

Without thinking, she went to him and hugged him, hard. He slipped his arms around her back and held her. Not like a drowning man, the way he had in the past, but gently, suitably. She could feel how happy he was that he had pleased her.

"Thank you," she managed to say, and kissed him on the cheek. He stared into her eyes. They were of a height and matched together well. He swallowed hard, and she knew she needed to move away, right now, before things went to a place she wasn't willing to travel.

She stepped back and rasped, "Thank you," again.

He pulled himself together, the pain shooting through his eyes and across his face plainly before he stowed it away and grew cheerful again.

"But you haven't even seen your bedroom or the en suite. Come, I'll show you the rest."

The rest was fit for a princess. A duchess. A queen. And this was just a guest suite; she couldn't imagine what the real aristocracy got. Her wooden bed was king-size on a platform with a pale yellow silk canopy, the bathroom travertine, limestone and glass, with a dual-head shower and separate massive soaking tub, actually long enough for her to lie down. The closet held more surprises, these more practical—a pair of shearling-lined bottle-green Wellies and a hip-length gray North Face down jacket.

"I wouldn't want you to ruin your best coat. This will do for you to play on the estate, should you choose. It's a bit muddy out there, and the weather is unpredictable at best."

You've done too much, Memphis. Too much.

She sat on the edge of the tub to try on the boots.

"It could never be enough, Taylor. You deserve the world. If I could give you that, were it in my power, I would. Instead, I present you with rubbers."

His blue eyes were sparkling. The teasing, flirting Memphis was back. She almost sighed in relief. That she could handle. Thoughtful, tender Memphis was too much for her to bear.

He turned to leave. "Dinner will be at seven. Things can get a bit draughty, so bring a sweater. I'll see you in an hour."

The door closed quietly behind him.

Leaving her sitting alone in an opulent castle bathroom, one boot on, one off, staring after him like the sun had gone out of the room.

Taylor didn't bother unpacking, decided the best use of her hour alone was to warm her feet at the fireplace, reveling in the smoky smell. She knew they used to burn coal here, tribute from the cottars who were forced to dig and burn peat for their own fires—slow, smoldering and smoky—that would last for hours. The timbers above her fireplace had a coating of black that wouldn't come off. She assumed the family left it to stay true to their roots, or maybe they were load-bearing. But this was a crackling wood fire—pine, from the scent of it. The wood sizzled and popped, the flames danced, making her feel completely at home.

Her throat hurt, and her head was aching. She went to her bag and retrieved the pills she needed. Percocet if the headache was horrible. Fioricet if it was only mild. Ativan for the panic. Found a fresh pitcher of water and swallowed the pills. She had a small bar to herself, with multiple variants of amber liquor in crystal decanters, handmade labels placed in front to identify the contents. Dalwhinnie. Oban. Glenmorangie. Bunnahabhain 18. Macallan 21. Laphroaig 12. Scotch. She hated Scotch. Beer. Where was a beer when you need it? She pulled open the cabinets. Of course, a concealed refrigerator, fully stocked with Diet Coke, bottled still water and Heineken. She knew she shouldn't mix the meds with alcohol, but was more worried about showing up to dinner with liquor on her breath. Thinking caffeine might just help the pills' efficacy, she grabbed the Diet Coke instead.

She sat back in front of the fire, her head angled so she could see both the rain begin to fall outside and the flames leaping into the flue. Sipped on the soda. Realized she hadn't checked in with Baldwin. Realized that for the first time in a month, she felt like she could breathe.

CHAPTER SEVENTEEN

Sam Loughley was patiently waiting for Stuart Charisse to finish his lunch so they could get back to work. She didn't have much of an appetite, had settled for a bag of chips out of the vending machine. Salt and fat, that matched her mood.

They had three bodies to post this afternoon, one of whom was the hit-and-run victim from yesterday. Sam might have thought to recuse herself had the lab been staffed to capacity, but as it was, she was two doctors and one death investigator short. The remaining MEs were all sharing duties in order to allow them some actual time off. Which meant Sam got stuck with double shifts five days a week until she got some budget work cleared up and another couple of MEs hired. Sometimes she wondered if she should turn the shop over to someone else, an administrator, but the idea of giving that level of control to a stranger made her numb with worry.

Marcus Wade was planning to attend the post. Sam liked all of the players on Taylor's team, but she had a soft spot for Marcus. He hadn't gotten jaded yet. She hoped that would never change, that he could keep part of himself innocent, separate from all of the horrors they saw on a daily basis.

Plus, he laughed at her jokes.

The Jaguar, an older model XJ6, hadn't been found. It was probably sitting in someone's garage, groaning from the beating it took. Cars don't like to hit people almost as much as people don't like to be hit by cars.

She went to the computer and started reviewing the case details. A late entry by the death investigator, Keri McGee—whom she'd stolen away from Metro's crime lab a month earlier when her favorite 'gator took a bigger and better job in Alabama—caught her eye.

Victim has $1,000 in cash in her pocket, in a plain white envelope. Ten brand-new one hundred dollar bills. One bill seems to have a stain on it, blue, as yet unidentifiable. Sent to lab for testing.

Now that was weird. The woman had been dressed in nice but utilitarian clothes, designer-label slacks and a blouse, both with the label cut, indicating she'd bought them at a steep discount from an outlet store. Her wool coat had a Macy's label, but it was threadbare, lived in, and about five years out of style. She wore black sneakers, the soles nearly worn through but with brand-new cushioned sports inserts inside, which screamed that she was on her feet all day.

Walking around with a spare thousand bucks in her pocket? No way.

Sam went back to the woman's body, looked at her feet. Sure enough, they were covered with calluses. Her hands were also rough and cracked, the nails short and neatly filed. Menial labor then, maybe in a restaurant kitchen. Hard way for a middle-aged woman to live. Especially if she was undocumented. The simple fact that her family had clammed up was a clue that she wasn't in the States legally.

Not a huge surprise. Though the laws were stringent now, for a time, Tennessee had possessed the most lax immigration regulations in the country, to the point of allowing thousands of undocumented workers to get driver's licenses with just a pay stub and water or electric bill to "prove" residency. They'd come from all over the United States, and south of the border, to purchase that little piece of plastic that said they belonged. No more; the laws had changed and were practically draconian in comparison. Proof of citizenship was required now.

But in its wake, the initial freedoms had left behind a massive gang problem. Mainly members of MS-13. Not a nice bunch of folks. Sam saw the vestiges of their march for primacy almost daily.

She heard whistling from the corridor, and a few moments later, Marcus appeared, his floppy brown hair under a University of Tennessee baseball cap, Stuart hot on his heels.

"Sorry I'm late," Marcus said. "Crazy morning. Did you hear about it?"

Sam shook her head. She'd been well lost in her own thoughts. "No, what happened? You catch a break on our hit-and-run?"

Marcus glanced at the naked body of their Jane Doe. "No, not her. Though I do have a name, Marias González. Guatemalan. Undocumented. She lives over in South Nashville, Antioch area, near Nolensville. I'm heading there after the post. No, the big excitement was we got the guy who left that jump drive at Café Coco, the one with all the kiddie porn on it? Remember?"

Sam did remember. What sort of idiot went to public computers, popped in a jump drive and looked at pornographic pictures of children, then managed to leave the jump drive behind? That was beyond her comprehension. Metro had been trying to make an arrest in the case for almost two months. Taylor had told her the man was a true sociopath and extremely dangerous—trying to get away with such a personal act in public was indicative of his narcissism.

"Yeah, he's a grad student at Vanderbilt. Looks like an Abercrombie and Fitch model, all square jawed and handsome. He wasn't so pretty crying his eyes out, I'll tell you that. Stupid fool. We're going to wrap up a whole ring of local and national pedophiles with the information on his computer. Lincoln's combing through the hard drive for Sex Crimes right now."

"That's wonderful news. One less creep on the street."

"You said it, sister. He's a piece of work. So let's talk about Marias here. What's her story?"

Sam gestured toward the computer, where the file was still open. "Did you see the note Keri left about the $1,000 in her pocket?"

"Yeah, I was there when they found it. The stain? Looks like it came from a dye pack to me."

Sam stopped and looked at Marcus. "You mean from a bank robbery?"

"Exactly."

"Ah," she said.

"Ah is right. So you can imagine what's going through my head."

She could do exactly that. In addition to phantom kiddie diddlers romancing their twisted psyches in the coffee shops, the Regretful Robber continued to wreak havoc all over Metro.

"You think she's in on the robberies?" Sam asked, pulling on her gloves and signaling to Stuart to prep for Ms. González. Sam went to look at the X-rays. "Typical crush injuries on the X-rays, compound fractures of the tibia and fibula on both legs, the femurs also cracked. Skull fracture. The jackpot will be her brain. I'm expecting a large subdural hematoma. All that pressure and nowhere to go."

"I suppose it's possible she was the robber. Though the guys in Special Crimes have been working under the assumption that it's a man."

"You know what happens when you assume."

"Ass. You. Me. Got it."

"But if she's involved, why come to the CJC? With your family in tow?"

"They were going to force her to confess?" Marcus said.

"Maybe. Or maybe she saw something she wasn't supposed to, or her car was one of the ones that had been stolen. The $1,000 could have been remuneration—that *is* this guy's M.O."

"Also possible. But I think it was something more. Did you see the fibers they collected from her pocket?"

As they talked, Sam did her external on the victim, looking carefully for anything that wasn't consistent with the accident. She made notes of cuts and bruises, saw nothing out of the ordinary, and signaled to Stuart, who took up his scalpel and opened the woman like he was pulling down a zipper. Marcus took an involuntary step back to avoid the splash of blood that welled over the edges of the incision.

"What fibers?" Sam asked. "I didn't see it in the report."

"Sloppy of them not to include it. There was a wad of something synthetic, almost like a tangle of fishing line, but much more delicate. I thought it was hair, but Keri said no, it wasn't organic. I have no idea what it could be."

"I want to see it," Sam said. "Keri wouldn't have made that mistake, I probably just didn't read far enough along in her report."

Stuart was making quick work of Marias's post; she could step out for a moment. She and Marcus crossed the autopsy suite to the evidence room. The door was hermetically sealed; there was blood evidence in here that needed special attention. She set her finger on the new biometric scanner. All evidence was now kept under lock and key after one of her MEs had been caught stealing marijuana from the evidence lockers. He'd been fired immediately, and new security measures put into place, including cameras and the fingerprint scanner. It helped her keep track of who went where in the morgue.

Keri had left everything for the case right where it was supposed to be. Sam smiled. She liked having a tightly run ship. No searching, no wasted time and effort. She opened the evidence locker, found the bags that matched her case, then went through smaller envelopes until she located the one labeled *Left Pocket*.

Using tweezers, she teased out the wad of fibers. It only took her a second to identify them.

"Wig hair. This is from a wig."

"Was she wearing a wig?"

"No."

"Does the Regretful Robber wear a wig?"

"That I can't answer."

"All right. But why would she have wig hair in her pocket?"

Sam thought about it for a minute. "Maybe she's got a family member with cancer. They lost their hair, she buys them a wig. She obviously doesn't have much money. She might not be able to afford the real-hair ones they're making now, those are surprisingly expensive."

"That's solid. But in her pocket?"

"Locard's theory. Plain old transference. She touched the wig, the strands came away, and either she didn't realize it, or she didn't want to drop them on the floor so she just tucked them in her pocket."

"Head's ready," Stuart called out.

They tidied up the evidence and went back to the body. The hematoma was visible on the brain, right where Sam expected it to be.

"Okay, go ahead," she said to Stuart, who proceeded to remove the brain from its cavity. There was a large squelch as it came away. Sam watched Marcus pale. She'd had seasoned detectives drop at autopsy plenty of times, but Marcus had always been unflinching.

He shook his head. "Never have gotten used to that sound. The pop when the skull comes free, either."

Stuart placed the brain gently on the dissection tray. "Brain's ready," he said.

Sam punched Marcus lightly on the arm. "The body

is a temple of noises, my friend. You want to stick around for the dissection?"

Sam's cart was all assembled with her knives, ready for the afternoon's work. She was very particular about her knives. She had a set of stainless steel Henckels. They were no different than the set she had in her kitchen, except for her workhorse: the twelve-inch blade she used for hearts and livers. She had a regular eight-inch chef's knife, two smaller slicing blades, a set of forceps and a pair of long, delicate, gold-tipped Metzenbaum scissors. Her tools were her pride and joy. She carried them in a large black leather knife case, like a chef. She didn't trust anyone else's tools. She even had a brand-new Dremel that she was itching to try out. Simon had given it to her for her birthday. Love between scientists at its best.

Marcus shook his head. "I think you have it under control. Let me know the final findings, okay? I need to get down to her house, see if I can figure out what her life was about."

"Good luck," Sam said, making a long slice along the woman's liver.

"You too," Marcus replied, a smile on his face. "Don't have too much fun with the organs."

"I'll try," she said. Every body had a story to tell. It was her job to read them right.

She had a moment of guilt—she could use her work to heal. Despite the random flashbacks to the kidnapping, she was healing.

But Taylor was forced to run away. Sam couldn't help but think that work would have been a better fix for her as well.

CHAPTER EIGHTEEN

Memphis knocked on Taylor's door at five minutes to seven. She'd rested up, washed her face, and changed into black wool slacks and a cream cashmere turtleneck. At the last minute, she put on her grandmother's pearls. Memphis said they dressed for dinner, and the pearls were original Mikimotos—a beautiful, graduated, princess-length strand with a delicately scrolled platinum clasp that had a tiny, perfect pearl on it. She hoped that would be dressed enough.

She opened the door, and Memphis looked on her with approval.

"Very nice. Shall we?" He extended his arm, and she accepted it. They started down the hall. "I talked Cook out of serving downstairs in the main dining room. I didn't feel like giving the radiators a workout. We'll be eating in my parents' dining room, the second dining room, we call it, instead. Be prepared, she's gone a bit all out."

They went down a flight of stairs, not the same ones she'd been on earlier, and entered another wide, open passageway. Delicious smells wafted out of the room at the end of the hall.

Goodness, Memphis· Just how many stairways are there in the castle?

He stopped, brows knitted. "You know…I've no idea."

She shook her head. How very Memphis.

She was no longer a stranger to the castle's opulence, but the second dining room, as Memphis called it, was as fine as the finest restaurants she'd ever been in. A fire crackled in the grate; she could have stood, only slightly stooped, in its cavity if she chose. The mahogany table could comfortably seat fourteen. Above it floated a crystal chandelier, each drop pendant reflecting the glow of the ten white pillar candles she counted. Crystal goblets, delicate china on engraved chargers, four sterling forks, three knives. Intimate dining. Yeah, right.

All out?

He just smiled.

At least they weren't sitting at opposite ends of the table—she would have felt like a fool. She'd have to shout pass the salt, and the room would echo in return.

Memphis grandly held her chair for her, then tucked himself in on her right side. He'd remembered that she ate continental-style, with her left, and hated to bump the person next to her. Goodness, he wasn't playing games. He wanted her to know that he remembered every little detail. The momentary flush of flattery was replaced with a tiny touch of concern. Fantasy could easily turn into obsession. She'd seen it happen time and again, with poor results.

She dismissed the thought. *He's trying to woo you,
stupid girl. Not own you.*

No one else joining us?

"Of course not. The servants take their meals in the
kitchen—some traditions aren't easily changed. Trixie
will see to them. That's her job."

Soundlessly, two young girls appeared with the first
of the seven courses Cook had planned for them.

They started with a thick fish soup Memphis said
was called Cullen Skink, then moved into more tradi-
tionally French fare. The venison stew must have been
for the servants.

Memphis explained that Mary, Queen of Scots, was
responsible for the French inflection to their cooking,
having brought a passel of countrymen back from
France when she returned. There was delicate Dover
sole, beef Wellington, venison, fresh veg, carrots and
peas and mashed potatoes, a dizzying array of cheeses,
then burnt cream—she knew it as crème brûlée—and
apple frushie, a delicious open-faced tart, for dessert.
Memphis had also opened a bottle of Châeau Latour
'54. She couldn't help herself; she was impressed, and
said so.

"I'll show you the wine cellar later. You'll love it.
Father is quite the oenophile. He's been adding to the
collection for years, through auctions, estate sales, the
works. He has over 50,000 bottles down there."

"Wow," she managed to say. That *was* quite a collection.

Taylor ate until she was uncomfortably full, succeeding in eating only two bites of the apple frushie before she couldn't handle another bit.

She pushed her plate away and picked up her pen.

My God, that was amazing. Thank you.

"It was, wasn't it? Shall we repair to the drawing room and have some port? It will help you digest."
Good Lord, Memphis, you're making me feel like I've stepped onto the page of a Victorian novel.

"Oh, no. If this were Victorian times, I'd head off for port and cigars and whist and you'd be stuck with the ladies, nannering on about…whatever it is you women nanner on about."

"Ha," she said, punching him lightly on the arm, then scribbled in her notebook.

Besides, you know exactly what we women talk about when we get together.

"Length, breadth and depth, I assume. What else is there to discuss?"

Memphis, you are extremely naughty.

It was so comfortable. She was so comfortable. Even her head hurt less. That was the wine and pills and jet lag talking, she was sure of it.

The room Memphis took her to next was more her speed, subtly decorated while still lavish, but not overdone. The walls were paneled in dark wood. Two leather club chairs faced a leather sofa with a table in between.

The fire was off to the right. Half the room was another library, with floor-to-ceiling bookcases, the other half an office centered around a stunning oak rolltop desk. Very masculine, very posh, but eminently comfortable.

"Nice," she said.

"This is part of my suite of rooms," he said. "My office, when I'm here. I like to have a bit of privacy. Why don't you try talking some more? I know you need to practice. It sounds like your voice is working."

"I…" Nothing else came. Her throat constricted. Damn it. She wasn't ready. She just wasn't ready. The pressure of being asked to speak was too much for the tenuous hold she had on her voice.

Memphis took a step toward her. He traced her jaw-line with his forefinger, then slowly moved his hand down until his palm cupped her throat. Her traitorous heart responded by speeding up. She could feel her pulse fluttering under his thumb. His eyes met hers, desire plain in his gaze.

"Try now."

She shook her head.

"Poor darling. I wish I could fix you myself. Take away the last month, take away your pain."

They stood there, face-to-face, transfixed. She felt oddly vulnerable, in this position of supplication before him, his hand wrapped around her neck.

Memphis was a strong man. All he had to do was squeeze. Cut off her air supply. It *would* stop her pain. No more struggling, no more looks. No more people talking about her behind her back—well, that wasn't true. Tongues never cease, even in death. She just wouldn't be around to hear it. She'd drift away without a care in the world, the scent of Memphis strong in her nose.

Good grief, Taylor. Get hold of yourself.

He meant what he said. No pity, no coddling. Just a statement of fact. He wished she didn't have to go through this. No one else had said that to her.

Interminable moments passed. His eyes spoke to her, questioning. She didn't know how to answer. He finally began to lean his head in and she went rigid. He stopped immediately, dropped his hand and turned away.

"Don't worry about it. Your voice will come back in time." He went to a small drinks cabinet, poured the port into snifters.

"I do hope you like vintage."

He handed her a glass as if nothing had just happened.

Her heart was still pounding. She dragged a breath into her lungs, fought for composure. Wished for that stiff upper lip all Brits seemed to possess. Took a sip of her port, then grabbed her notebook.

Of course I do. Tawny and ruby aren't my thing, I'm glad that's what you have. It's delicious.

He'd made a lucky guess on that one, she wasn't sure she'd ever discussed port with him before. Of course, vintage was more expensive. She recognized that Memphis, while quite understated about his heritage, did enjoy the trappings that came with it.

She started to sit, then felt the strangest sensation down her back, accompanied by a draft of cool air across her shoulders. Her senses went on alert immediately. She'd been a cop long enough to recognize the feeling. They were being watched.

She angled her head to look behind her, assuming one of the servants had entered the room. There was no one there.

Her spine grew cold. She hadn't imagined it. Had she?

She looked back to Memphis, who was whistling slightly as he poured himself another little bit of port. Topping off, her father always called it. He'd done that every time he'd poured a drink—taken a healthy swallow, then filled his glass again. Maybe she'd just had a little too much.

Memphis turned and caught her looking at him. Her face must have registered her distress.

"What's wrong?" He crossed the room to her, set his glass on the table and sat on the sofa next to her. Took her hands in his. "Jesus, your hands are like ice. I told you this place was hard to heat."

She pulled her right hand away.

I just had the strangest sensation that someone was watching us. One of the servants...?

Memphis leaned back, keeping her hands securely tucked in his. "Ah. Not the servants. No, in this part of the castle, that was probably the Lady in Red. She's one of our more famous ghosts."

CHAPTER NINETEEN

Taylor shivered. She didn't believe in ghosts. But the thought that the feeling she'd just had was caused by the otherworld was all too real. She was still overwhelmingly chilly, and suddenly on edge. She pulled her hands from his, grabbed her notebook.

Don't mock me. It's not funny.

Memphis waited a moment, then gently took her left hand back, rubbed it between his to warm them.

"I'm not mocking you, dearest. Dulsie Castle is haunted. Several times over."

Please. It is not haunted. You're just trying to scare me.

"Not at all. It is haunted, just like most of the castles in the Highlands. Battles were fought over these lands, brother against brother. Enemies tried to plunder the castles for their contents. Most were built on sorrow and death, vaults for the overlord's treasures. With all that enmity, it's not at all unusual to have multiple ghosts wandering about."

Come on. That's silly.

"Taylor, it's not silly at all. People pay good money to stay at haunted castles. That's why we opened the attics for Samhain. Let the public in, have a few delicious ghost stories at the ready. One of our best is the Lady in Red."

Okay. I'll bite. Tell me.

Memphis sat back into the cushions. "According to my family lore, she's the ghost of Lady Isabella Bruce, a relation of good King Robert, sold as a child bride to Colin Highsmythe, the fourth Earl of Dulsie. He was forty-eight, widowed, with seven bairns, some of which were older than Isabella. She was fourteen, ripe as a peach, headstrong and unwilling to marry such a disgustingly old creature. She was overruled, of course. It was an advantageous match. Her father recovered most of the lands he'd lost to Longshanks—you'd know him as Edward the First—when Scotland and England were at war in the 1300s."

He settled in closer to her, put his arm around her shoulder. They were touching now, rib to rib. She let him. She was still cold. And despite her interest in Memphis's history, ghost stories weren't her thing.

"She moved to the castle, and they married in a ceremony befitting a queen. Colin doted on her like she was a doll, buying her anything she wanted, throwing the most lavish of parties in her honor. He, being an honorable sort who disliked the idea of bedding a child, promised the girl they could wait until her sixteenth birthday."

Taylor could see the woman-child, promised off, unwilling to devalue herself for the sake of her parents and their ever-amassing fortunes. She liked Isabella immediately.

"But the stupid girl played Colin for a fool. She had an affair with the youngest of the Highsmythe sons at the time, the dashing Oliver, and of course got with child. She hid it for as long as she could, but Colin eventually found out. He had Oliver killed, locked Isabella up in the tower above us for the rest of her confinement. When she had the baby, he took it away and murdered it as well. Then he bedded Isabella as many times as it took to plant his own seed in her belly."

That's hideous!

"Quite. As you can imagine, Isabella was terribly distraught. She'd lost her lover, her child by him, and all the freedom she'd been accustomed to, for Colin kept her in the tower and would allow her no visitors. She was subjected to what amounted to no more than rape on a regular basis. So she hatched a plan. She figured if she could get Colin out of the way, she could have everything back the way it was. She'd find a new lover to mend her broken heart, would dispose of the child she was carrying. She planned to leave it out in the wild, let the faeries take it for their own."

Faeries?

"Oh, yes," Memphis replied. "Faeries all over the land round here. The *auld folk*. You're in the Scottish Highlands, remember. We live for myth."

He brushed a stray hair back from her forehead, gently, then continued.

"Anyway, the lady Isabella kept back a knife from one of her meals, and when Colin came for his nightly assignation, she waited until he was in the throes of passion and stabbed him. Did a good job of it, too. He, mortally wounded, fought with her for the knife, managed to get it away from her and cut her throat, but he was too weak to injure her properly. He died; she lived. But the earl, ever prescient and distrustful of his child bride, had left strict instructions in his will that if anything were to happen to him before the child was born, the doctor was to take it by force from her womb."

Held a grudge, did he?

"Oh, yes. We Highsmythes are known for it." He said it lightly, or attempted to. She wondered who had been fool enough to cross Memphis in the past.

"The doctor kept Isabella alive long enough to give birth. She carried twins, two boys. It's said she traced an *O* in blood on the forehead of the first one, who was named Oliver, after her lover, the child's dead uncle. She died before naming the second, so the family took it upon themselves to call him Colin. As you can imagine, theirs was a contentious life."

Memphis was staring into the fire now. "Young Oliver ended up with the title, oddly enough. Through battles and changes of allegiance and illnesses, the elder Colin's sons from his first marriage died soon after their father. Isabella's son, Oliver, firstborn of the twins, truly in the prime of his life, was legally heir.

"He banished his brother from the area, sent him to England, to Bristol, to the Highsmythe properties there. Where he would be well out of the way. Young Colin worked as a cleric, then rose in the Church's esteem until eventually becoming a very powerful bishop. He made quite a name for himself.

"So the family was permanently split, half propagating in Southern England, the rest of us in the North. I'm directly descended from Isabella and Oliver the younger, by the way. And as such, the legend says that the first son, the Dulsie heir, is the only one who can see Isabella. She appears in the night to impart great wisdom, so we're told."

Taylor knew she was staring at him. What a creepy, odd story.

Do you see her?

"Do I see Isabella?" Memphis flexed his hand a few times, balling the strong fingers into a fist, then stared into the fire. He took his arm from around her shoulders. His tone changed, no longer imparting a delicious ghost story, now more subdued.

"Well, I can't rightly say. May have done a few times, especially when I was a boy. She's supposed to be much more partial to young boys. Once they pass the age of twenty, which was Oliver's age when he died, she loses interest. But I've definitely seen something that could be her, many times. More of a feeling, really, that chill in the air, the sense that someone's watching, an awareness of the color red. Almost like having a bout of synesthesia. I've gotten used to it now."

He was holding back, she could tell.

What is it? What's the matter?

He met her eyes then. "I can't help but wonder, if Evan had carried to term, whether *my* son would have seen Isabella."

Oh, God. Taylor felt terrible, she'd forgotten. It was easy to; Memphis rarely spoke of Evan, and even more rarely mentioned the child she'd been carrying when she died.

"Another dead Highsmythe bride."

He played with Taylor's engagement ring. After a second, she instinctively pulled her hand away. It felt profane to have Memphis touching the physical expression of Baldwin's love. He didn't seem to notice.

"I never got to see her, you know. After the accident. Father wouldn't let me. He said it would be a very bad idea indeed. She'd gone through the windscreen, was cut to ribbons. He thought I would carry the image with me forever. Though honestly, I can't comprehend it could have been any worse than what my imagination conjures up, late at night."

That she understood.

You're right. I tell victims' families the same thing, but I'd want to know. I'd want to see. The mind can play terrible tricks.

"That it can."

He was lost to her, there in the room physically, but

mentally in another world, another time. Grief did that to a person, snuck up on cat's feet when you were most unawares. He must have realized, because he cleared his throat and looked at her.

"We buried them on the estate, you know. Together, of course. In the graveyard up by the kirk. It broke my heart. I don't know which was worse, losing her, or never having a chance to see him grow up."

Oh, Memphis. I'm so sorry. It's just not fair.

They sat quietly for a few minutes, companionable in their silence. Taylor couldn't help but think of Sam, and the child she'd lost. Of her face when Taylor found her, bloodied and tied, the sheer agony of what had happened etched in eloquence across her features. She sighed. Baldwin had lost a child as well, though she was having a hard time equating his loss with Sam's, or Memphis's. His child was most likely still alive. Regardless, they were all surrounded by too much sadness.

Memphis finally roused himself. "I'm sorry. I've gone and properly cocked up our lovely evening."

She sought to distract him, and herself.

No, it's fine. Tell me more. Why is Isabella called the Lady in Red?

He met her eyes then. "Oh, that's simple. She appears drenched in blood."

They'd stayed in his office a bit longer, on safe topics—her plans for the next day, which included the early-morning visit with Dr. James and a little side trip he'd like to take her on, how the weather was expected to behave, what time she'd like to take breakfast—then drank the rest of the port and called it a night. She wasn't tired, but she knew she needed to get some sort of rest.

He left her at the door to her room with a chaste kiss on the top of her hand, in classic French style, and departed without a backward glance. After that moment in his office, she'd expected to have to fight him off, to set the ground rules, but the conversation's turn had put a damper on his mood. It had the same effect on hers.

Upon returning, the rooms seemed slightly changed, which alarmed her for half a second until she realized it must have been one of the maids turning things down for the evening. Straightening up after her like she was an untidy child. No wonder everything in the castle looked so lovely. Unseen hands followed behind the family members, restoring order in their wakes. In defiance, she went and pulled a book at random from the shelves and dropped it on the chair, where it spilled open. There. It looked like someone was staying here now.

A bath sounded heavenly. She started the tub to fill, and took another Percocet. It had worked wonders tonight; the headache had been at a dull simmer in the back of her head for the past few hours. She could continue to keep it at bay if she took the meds now instead of waiting the prescribed six hours. Deciding she felt like reading, she went back in the sitting room to gather the book.

The hardcover she'd so carelessly plucked from the shelves and tossed on the chair was now closed, sitting squarely in the middle of the cushion. Good grief. She went to the door to make sure it was locked. She didn't like the idea of the maids being able to come in and out as they pleased. Memphis had probably told them to tend to her every need, but this was ridiculous.

But the door was locked. And the interior latch bolt had been thrown as well. Which meant no one could come into the room without her knowledge.

She glanced back at the book, sitting so pristinely front and center on the chair, and a little frisson of fear went down her spine.

Oh, don't be ridiculous, Taylor. There is no such thing as ghosts.

She scooped up the book from the chair and headed back to the bath, stripping off her clothes as she went, dropping them willy-nilly on the floor. When she got into the tub, she opened the novel, and nearly laughed out loud. She'd chosen Daphne du Maurier's *Rebecca* from the shelves.

She allowed herself to get lost in the nameless second Mrs. de Winter's world for thirty minutes, until her eyes started to ache and her heart throbbed in her temples, then climbed from the tub. Her room was as she left it. Despite herself, she sighed in relief.

She got dressed for bed, snuggled under the covers, found the bed was equipped with an electric blanket, turned it on and texted Baldwin.

He wrote back immediately. His presence chased away all the ghosts.

How are you?

Fine. Full as a tick, warm from my bath. Going to sleep, just wanted to touch base. How are you? How's the case?

Just fine. I might have to be out of touch for a few days.
Immersion. So don't worry if you don't hear from me.

Ah. She was being punished. She had a feeling this
might happen. She clung to the hope that when she
saw him next, she'd have her voice back, her head on
straight, and could give herself to him again. Either that
or she'd be handing back the ring. The thought filled
her with sadness.

Don't react, Taylor. Be nice. Be sweet.

Atlantic is sending you somewhere warm, I hope.
Maybe you can get a break.

That would be nice. How's the voice?

She tried to ignore the fact that he'd just held back
from telling her the truth. Again. Why he didn't feel
he could confide in her, she didn't know. But it set her
teeth on edge. She didn't feel like a fight now, though.

Scattered and unreliable. It's easier to just
write things down.

You have to practice. Keep doing your exercises.

I will.

Okay, sweetheart. You get a good night's sleep then.

Good luck.

Thanks. I love you. Please, text me when you finish your
session with the new doctor. I'd like to hear how it goes.

I thought you were going to be out of touch.

Maybe. But not until tomorrow night. Don't worry about me. I'll be fine. Sweet dreams.

When she put the phone away, she felt strangely empty. Everything was changing. And she didn't like change.

She turned off the light and tried to sleep. After two hours, she finally drifted off, the lost children of strangers heavy on her mind.

CHAPTER TWENTY

Baldwin hated not being able to share everything that was happening with Taylor. It was better that way, safer for her. She didn't need the details. After the debacle last year, when one of Atlantic's premier assassins had decided to come after Baldwin through Taylor, he'd become adamant about keeping his personal life out of his professional life. He didn't make a lot of friends when he worked with Atlantic. He was fairly certain that would be the case tonight.

One of those nonfriends was the next call he made.

He put the phone to his ear, let it ring once, twice, three times, before a heavy voice answered. Baldwin could tell the man had been drinking. He didn't know if that would work in his favor, or against.

"She's safe in bed. Unmolested, I might add. Surely you don't think I'm that much of a heel," the cultured, lackadaisical voice of Memphis Highsmythe said.

"That's not what I was calling about. I need your help."

"Oh. Quite. Whatever can I do for you, Baldwin?"

"Who do you know at MI-6?"

"Goodness. Planning on giving up all the state se-crets? A fresh Wikileak from the FBI?"

"Seriously, Memphis. I need a favor."

Memphis's voice lost its jocular sarcasm. "What level of favor are we talking about?"

"One from the very top."

Memphis sighed. "That would be Nigel then."

Sir Nigel Ainsley was just the man he wanted to speak with. Knighted in his forties, subsequently in-volved in the arms-to-Iraq deal, Ainsley had been outed as an agent, then retired, so to speak, to MI-6, where he ran the men and women he'd previously been a peer of. He was an exemplary spy, well known for his genial manner and first-rate discretion.

Discretion Sir Nigel applied when arranging to use members of Atlantic's Angelmakers. He'd been the last to engage the now-errant Julius's services. Memphis didn't need to know that.

"Good. That's who I was hoping for. Can you ask if he'd be willing to speak with me?"

"I can. But why? What sort of scheming is the FBI up to? Speaking of which, I'm a bit chafed at you. Get-ting me pulled back to New Scotland Yard last month wasn't necessary."

"Wasn't me. I swear it." He was telling the truth, too, he hadn't been the one to pull the trigger. There had been concern about Memphis from other quarters. Granted, Baldwin had cheered silently when Memphis had been pulled off the Quantico counterterrorism detail, but it had come from within his own service, not from Baldwin's end.

"Ah. Interesting. Why, exactly, can't you call him yourself?"

"Classified."

"Right."

"I'm available by phone for the next hour if he can spare me five minutes."

"Fine. I'll call him. But I'm going to need a favor in return, then."

"Anything within reason."

"My case. I'm probably dealing with a religious zealot who is schizophrenic. I make this call, you give me some guidance on how to approach him. Deal?"

Hardly a big price to pay. "Deal."

"Thank you. Have a pleasant evening, Baldwin."

"Memphis, wait."

"Yes?"

"How is she?"

There was a pause. "You were right. She's exceptionally fragile. But stubborn. The essential spark of her is still there. She has a pure heart. She will get through this."

Baldwin breathed a sigh of relief.

"I'm glad to hear you say that. Please, let me know if anything changes."

"I will. Good night."

"You as well, Memphis."

Keep your grubby paws off my woman, he added silently.

Memphis hung up the phone and stared at it a few minutes. John Baldwin, profiler extraordinaire, in need of a private chat with Sir Nigel Ainsley. The call was a ruse; Baldwin could get through to Ainsley anytime he wanted. He just wanted to check on Taylor.

He couldn't say that he blamed him.

He placed the call, had Nigel's assistant cum body-guard roust the man from his nightly game of dominoes. It was late, but Nigel would be up, in his library, an untouched Macallan 18 at his elbow, engrossed in his game. He sounded slightly annoyed when he answered, though years of interruptions tempered his aggravation. Especially since the disruption came from the son of one of his oldest friends.

"Sir Nigel. A pleasure."

"Ah, Lord Dulsie. It's been too long. How is your father?"

"Just headed to South Africa as we speak. We celebrated his birthday yesterday."

"I hope he received the Benelli 20-bore. I had that stock hand engraved by a company called A&A, in South Dakota. The real Wild West."

"He did. He loved it. I'm sure you'll be hearing from him soon."

"Ah, good, good. At our age, any birthday is preferable to none, and we all need our toys."

"I'm sure it is. Sir, I have a request. A friend has asked to speak with you. Can you make a call?"

"I'm all tucked in for the night. Tell him to call me at the office tomorrow."

"He's an American. FBI. I trust him. If he needs you, it's important. I'm assuming that he must speak to you outside of your *official* capacity."

There was silence on the other end of the line. Memphis decided to sweeten the pill. "Fancy a bit of sport? I'll let you have the run of the estate, whenever you're next north of the border." Sir Nigel was as rabid about hunting as he was terrorists and other threats to Queen and country.

Sir Nigel chuckled. "Not above a bribe, are you?"

"Now that's not a nice term."

"All right, James. For you. Tell your father hullo and I intend to help him break that Benelli in. I'd best be going if I have any hope of finishing my game."

Memphis imparted Baldwin's information and hung up, pleased. A shoot on the estate was a small price to pay for a favor from Ainsley. He wondered if Ainsley suspected something was up already, and that's why he agreed to talk with the strange American so easily. Ah, well. He'd find out about that in the morning.

He had a lovely outing planned for Taylor tomorrow. He forced away the waves of sorrow that had enveloped him since their postprandial chat. Told Evan's ghost to leave.

Thought about Taylor's glossy blond hair, and her eyes, the two mismatched grays competing for his attention. He didn't know if he could win her or not, but he'd damn well enjoy trying.

CHAPTER TWENTY-ONE

She walked the corridor, the familiar length of the hall leading to Memphis's office, the warm, crackly fire beckoning her in. She was barefoot, dressed in a long, silk nightgown with a richly embroidered robe atop it, her hair pulled into a braid that spilled down her back. Her stomach was distended, full of the child they'd created.

She was worried. Would he be there? The note said to meet him before dawn, before the house awoke. But the house never truly slept. Watchers were everywhere. She knew what foolishness this was, but couldn't help herself. Just the thought of him, his eyes, deeper blue than any loch, the sharpness of his jaw, the gentleness of his hands. She needed him.

Her hand was on the door now. He was inside. She could smell him. The scent made her careless, and her heart pulsed between her thighs. She pushed open the door.

Blood. Blood everywhere. The room was drenched. The walls dripped with the scent of sex, of lust dampened by the coppery tinge. She tasted it on her tongue, turned to vomit. Once she finished retching, she forced herself inside the room, shut the door behind her. She knew what had caused this. She was to blame. She'd pushed and cajoled.

His body, upright in the chair.

Her lover.

She went to him, careful not to drag the trails of her nightgown in the blood. Her arms skimmed the walls; so much blood. Seeping, all around her. The floor was getting deeper, the tide rushing in, covering her feet now. She moved forward until she could touch his arm. One last time.

Memphis turned, his face a compilation of holes, empty. "Leave here," he moaned. "Leave before it's too late."

She began to scream, louder and louder, until he raised up a bloody hand to quiet her, a hand with a gun, and she saw the muzzle flash as she yanked herself from his grasp, backed away quickly, heedless of the mess.

The bump of her body against something jarred her.

Taylor could feel her spine against the wooden paneling, her arms raised as if she were warding off an attack. She was drenched in sweat, her T-shirt sticking to her body like she'd been swimming in it.

Red, everywhere. Blood.

Her breath came short. She was dying. She could feel her body slipping away into nothingness. Feel the pain in her head grow larger, stronger, until the red was replaced by black.

She couldn't breathe. She had to breathe.

She forced her eyes open.

The room was empty.

She let her hands drop to her side, realized her heart

was pounding against her chest wall so hard it hurt. She breathed in several times, square breaths, trying to get her heart rate to slow.

Her eyes adjusted, the darkened space coming into focus. She was in her bedroom in the castle. Against the wall across from her bed. Not Memphis's office. And not in the attic of the Snow White's house facing the Pretender, stepping in the blood of her best friend's child.

It took a few minutes until she felt like she had herself back under control. She edged to the side table and turned on a lamp. The room leapt from the darkness as if it too was disturbed.

There was nothing sinister about it anymore. It was just a bedroom.

Her breath came more normally now.

Jesus. That was a whopper of a dream. She was used to having crazy nightmares, but Memphis's wild stories must have really landed in her subconscious. She'd actually felt like the scene was real. She touched her stomach, flat and taut. Crazy. She had felt the child inside her, moving.

And sleepwalking. My God, she hadn't done that since she was a child.

Her mind reached into the tendrils of the dream. The blood felt so familiar. Her blood. The floor of the attic rising up to meet her, the primal scream the Pretender made as he raised his arm. Stupid, stupid girl, letting him get a gun on her.

She'd gotten herself into this mess. And now look at her. Locked away from everyone, unable to cry for help. She should have never tried to take him down alone.

Taylor knew she wouldn't sleep the rest of the night. She went into the sitting area, snapping lights on as she went.

Heineken. Second half of Ativan. Another Percocet. Stood at the window until she started feeling a bit fuzzy around the edges.

That was better.

Her legs were feeling a bit wobbly. She sat down at the desk, hard, and opened her laptop. The castle had a strong wireless signal. Memphis had mentioned that they had a T1 line running directly into the castle, lightning-quick. She assumed that the room was also wired. How else would it penetrate those thick stone walls?

Seeking something mundane, she checked her email, deleting three from the various television stations around Nashville wanting interviews—my God, they were relentless—then sent Sam a note. That made her feel better, more grounded.

She closed the computer, helped herself to another beer, and parked in front of the television. She started surfing the channels idly, wishing for her pool table. Surely the castle had a billiards room? She'd have to ask Memphis, though to be honest, she didn't particularly want to go roaming around this place alone at night.

She settled on a crazy reality show where the contestants were made to strip down so the audience could assess their bodies in an attempt to bolster their flagging self-esteem. That would be a hit in America.

There was a soft knock on her chamber door.

"It's me," a low voice said. Memphis.

She was wearing a T-shirt and boxers. Not decent.

She grabbed her sweater from the chair and tossed it on. Grabbed her notepad. Went to the door. Opened it.

Memphis stood in the hall, hair sticking up, a blue-and-cream-striped robe half pulled on his shoulders.

She smiled.

"Are you okay?"

She nodded.

Of course. Why?

He looked at her like she was an idiot. "You were screaming."

I was? Funny. I don't have my voice back. Maybe you heard something else.

"No, Taylor, it was definitely you."

She didn't know whether to be happy that things were functional, or embarrassed.

I'm fine. Truly.

He leaned against the door frame.

"I would have come sooner… Honestly, I debated whether coming to you was the best idea."

At least he was aware of that.

Cold air was leaking in from the hall. She could see him shiver a bit. She pulled the door open wider, gestured for him to come in. Latched it behind him. He went straight to the fire and stirred it up, then turned back to her, the glow from the flames outlining his broad shoulders.

"Bad dreams?" he asked.

No more reason to pretend. He was here now. She wondered if she'd brought him subconsciously. Summoned him.

She sat at the desk and crossed her legs, prim and proper.

You could say that. It was bizarre. You told me to leave.

He stayed statue still in front of the fire. "I'd never tell you that. It's the last thing I want. I want you to stay. To be here."

He paused. His face was jagged in the firelight.

"I will never lie to you, Taylor. I've been as open and up front about my feelings as I can. I respect that you're with Baldwin. Hate it, but respect it. I promise, I will never do anything that you don't want. But right now, I'm going to ask a favor. Can I stay here tonight?"

She was taken aback. It was a great speech, completely controverted by the last statement. But he looked like a very frightened child.

I don't know if that's such a great idea, Memphis.

He tipped his head. "Your virtue is safe with me, my lady. I'd just like the company. We can sleep, or talk. If you think about it, we've been talking every night for the past several weeks. I missed it tonight. And seeing as you're having bad dreams, maybe we can help keep each other entertained for a bit. At least until you're ready to go back to sleep."

What if I want to go back to sleep right now?

Careful, Taylor. Careful.

He watched her warily, trying to ascertain any hidden meaning, or openings. Apparently sensing she was sincerely interested in sleep, or at least too drunk to stand up properly, he waved a hand toward the bed.

"Then by all means, do so. I'll watch over you in case you have any more bad dreams."

She broke eye contact, fiddled with the TV remote. He was right. They *had* been talking every night. He'd been the one she turned to when Baldwin had shut her out. Could she blame him for treasuring that intimacy? She'd been the one letting it happen, after all. Encouraging it, if she were being honest with herself. It felt good to have a friend she could count on.

All right. But just sleeping, Memphis. I am tired, and I'd like to try to get some rest.

He gave her that wicked smile that made her feel funny inside. "Of course."

She hesitated for another moment, then powered down the TV. Picked up her pen.

Turn off the lights.

He did.

The darkness felt different. Not as foreboding. Safer.

She went into the bedroom, pulled off her sweater and climbed back into the bed. Memphis lay down next to her, careful to point out that he was on top of the covers. She plumped up her pillow and stared at the ceiling.

They were quiet for a few minutes, then Memphis started to sing. It was a soft tune, quiet, and she got the sense that it was a lullaby of sorts. She let the words roll over her, her eyes shutting, all the fight gone out of her.

Maybe she could sleep again after all. With Memphis there to protect her.

CHAPTER TWENTY-TWO

Sam washed the blood off her knives and disinfected them, saw that the autopsy suite had been cleaned to her satisfaction, everything gleaming and sparkling, then headed to her office to do some paperwork.

She woke her computer and checked her email, was happy to see a note from Taylor. That girl. Foolhardy and headstrong, running off to Scotland without a thought to Memphis Highsmythe's "estate." Sam knew it was more than that; she'd Googled the man months ago, when he popped onto the scene and made a play for Taylor's affections. There was tons of information about Memphis online. About his family, and his wife's sad death. The castle itself had its own web page.

She knew Taylor would have never bothered to look that deeply into Memphis. It would have felt like a betrayal to her. She was committed to Baldwin, wouldn't waste time wondering what might have been with another man. Like looking up an old boyfriend on Facebook, just to see what he was up to. That wasn't the kind of thing Taylor did. She lived in the now, not in the past.

Sam knew her girl might walk a thin line with Memphis, but she'd never cross over. Whether *Memphis* could be trusted not to try and force her into it was another matter.

She clicked the email open.

Dear Sam,

I've landed safely. Memphis met me at the airport and spirited me away early, so I'm writing you from Dulsie Castle. I guess I never really thought about what Memphis's life might be like over here, but trust me, this place is unbelievable. It's huge. All stone and fireplaces and gorgeous furniture. And the food, Lord, the food. Cook did a seven-course meal for us tonight, with ridiculously expensive wine. I know, I know, I'm not supposed to be drinking, but a little bit of wine won't hurt.

Memphis has been very kind, and very good. No hanky-panky. Which is nice. I was a little worried he'd be pushy, and he's not. We talked after dinner, and he told me some of the castle's history, including this gruesome ghost story about the Lady in Red. I promptly fell asleep and had a terrible nightmare. Which is why I'm awake and writing you.

I still can't speak more than a couple of words at a time, but I'm meeting with Memphis's therapist friend in the morning. We'll see how that goes.

Any word on our hit-and-run?

Love you, so much.

Taylor

Sam shook her head. Taylor was a bright woman, but sometimes she could be so hopelessly obtuse. Of course Memphis was behaving himself. Like the spider to the fly. Make the web look safe, attack when weakness appears.

She didn't know why she disliked him so much. Outside of the fact that Taylor was finally, after all these years, settled and happy, and the first thing that happened was this interloper.

Oh, well. Taylor was a big girl. She'd have to make her own mistakes.

Sam typed quickly. She wanted to go home, see the twins. See Simon. She'd make a nice dinner, open a bottle of wine. She'd been married long enough to recognize that she was being too concerned with Taylor's relationship, and not enough with her own.

Hi, Taylor,

Glad to hear that you're in safe. Everything is fine here. We're getting more snow tonight—can you imagine? So much for global warming.

Remember when we were girls, and it used to snow all winter long? We'd go sledding on the big hill in Percy Warner Park, or ice-skate on the pond behind my folks' place. We'd come in frozen to the bone, our hands so cold we could barely move our fingers, and your mom used to have Mrs. Mize make us hot chocolate. She'd pretend not to listen to us giggle. I don't know if you ever noticed her, standing at the edge of the kitchen, watching us have fun. Kitty always seemed so sad, even back then. Before she grew bitter.

Wow, that was a step into the way-back machine.

I'm hoping to have some time to take the twins sledding tomorrow.

Our hit-and-run got more interesting today. Her name is Marias González. She had a marked bill in her pocket. Blue dye. Your brilliant young detective Marcus thinks she's involved in the Regretful Robber case somehow. It's a good thought. He's really coming along.

I'll let you know more when I find it out.

In the meantime, young lady, you continue to behave yourself. Beware of Viscounts bearing gifts, and all that. Or is that Greeks?

Love you too,

Sam

CHAPTER TWENTY-THREE

When Taylor woke, the sun was already high. She glanced at the clock. Almost eight. There was no Memphis, nothing to show that he'd even been there the night before.

She was surprised by her disappointment.

But she didn't have time for thinking, not now, at least. She needed to get moving. She was supposed to meet Dr. James at nine.

She showered and dressed, was brushing out her wet hair when she heard knocking on her chamber door. That would be breakfast. Memphis had mentioned they'd bring it to her room.

She went to the door and opened it. A small maid who couldn't be more than fourteen bustled in with a tray. Tea and toast, rashers of bacon and sausage, softly scrambled eggs, a bottle of water—"for yer hydration, lady"—a carafe of apple juice and a matching one with cranberry. The girl bobbed and disappeared as quickly as she'd come, leaving Taylor with the huge tray of food—more than enough for two.

Before the door was completely closed, she heard

whistling. She stuck her head in the hall and saw Memphis coming her way. He looked rested and happy, all the haunting sadness of the night before gone.

"Morning. Sleep well?" he asked.

He knew exactly how she slept, but she saw the maid lingering at the end of the hall, realized he needed to put on a show for his people as well. As modern as the castle was, spending the night in his unmarried lady friend's chambers was apparently frowned upon, or, more likely, fodder for gossip among the Highland staff.

She made a show of writing in her notebook. Felt strangely defensive, whether toward Memphis or his servants, she didn't know.

Mostly. Bad dreams.

"Oh, no. Well, let's feed you up and see you off to the doctor then."

Join me?

Memphis nodded in agreement, and she let the door close behind him.

The tray had been deceptive. There were two of everything, plates, cups, glasses, cutlery. Taylor realized Memphis hadn't just happened by, this was all planned. But she was too hungry to worry about it. Never one to pass up a meal, she sat at the little table and tucked in.

Memphis wandered around the suite with a glass of apple juice in one hand and a piece of toast in the other, distracted.

You're dropping crumbs on the floor.

Taylor pointed to the small piles of toast that trailed in Memphis's circumnavigated wake.

"The mice need to eat, too, you know. This saves them from having to leave this floor to tend to their meals." He dropped a bit of toast on the floor then, purposefully.

This place is too clean for mice.

"Oh, ho, not at all. The castle cats are fat with their plunder. There's enough to keep the circle of life in play. I made a pet of one of the mice when I was a boy. Named him Bilbo. I was besotted with Tolkien in those days. I fed Bilbo from my breakfast every morning. My mother caught me at it once. She didn't say a word, sent me on my way. I had to go hunting that day, I was nervous anyway. When I came back that evening, freshly blooded, flush with success—I'd bagged my first fox and my father had allowed me to ride home with the Master of Hounds—a gray tabby was curled up asleep on the bed. I never saw Bilbo again."

Poor mouse. Poor fox, too.

His eyes flashed in amusement. "Poor fox? Poor mouse? Poor *me*. I'd lost my boon companion. We had adventures, Bilbo and I. We sailed the high seas. He made an excellent first mate."

He must have been a lonely boy, to live in such a make-believe world.

"I know what you're thinking. God, you have a glass face. I *was* a bit lonely. I was older than my brothers, and my sister hadn't come along yet. There were few boys my age around the estate that summer, but it all changed in the autumn. I was sent off to school, and I've not been lonely since. Now, are you almost finished? Maddee will wonder what's become of us."

Taylor finished the last of her tea and stood up.

Ready. Just let me grab my sweater. What's freshly blooded mean?

Memphis escorted Taylor down to the first floor through a separate stairwell, explaining the intricate etiquette of a first kill. When he got to the part about having a bit of the fox's blood smeared on his face, she held up a hand and stopped him. She didn't need to know any more.

They ended up in the southernmost part of the castle, close to the public banquet hall, before trailing back around to a room done up in burgundy and cream. Taylor would never find her way back alone.

A woman sat in front of the fire, staring into its depths. When she heard them arrive, she stood and came to Taylor, hand outstretched. Her hair was dark and long, straight as an arrow, her smile friendly, her eyes brown and warm. She was Taylor's age, no more than thirty-five or so.

"You must be Taylor. I'm Dr. Madeira James, *à votre service*. But please, call me Maddee." Her accent was a shock, much more New York than Scotland. Taylor's face must have showed her surprise, because Maddee said, "Long Island, born and bred. I fit in so nicely amongst the locals."

Taylor laughed. She felt a bit like that herself.

Good to meet you.

"And you. Memphis has told me so much about you. Though he didn't do you justice. You're right, Memphis, she's stunning."

Taylor squirmed. She hated those kinds of accolades. She was much more than the sum of her exterior parts.

"And humble as pie, Maddee. Look at her blush." He was grinning, loving her annoyance.

"Stop teasing her, Memphis. It's not nice. You run along and we'll see you in an hour."

"As you wish, Dr. James." Memphis bowed and with a smile at Taylor, turned tail and left the room, leaving the two women alone.

Maddee took Taylor's arm and linked hers through it. She smelled good, like the fire, and vanilla, and an earthier, underlying scent, like she'd gotten some outdoor exercise this morning, the wind in her hair leaving the scent of the Highlands behind.

"We're going to get along just fine. Ignore him, he loves to poke."

No kidding, Taylor thought.

"Come, sit down. I've got tea for us already, unless you'd like something else?"

Tea is fine. Thank you.

They took their places, Taylor on the leather sofa, Maddee on an upright Victorian chair that looked to be an original, reupholstered in Brunschwig & Fils gray silk brocade. Probably worth a fortune.

When she saw Taylor was settled, she dove right in. "So. I'm sorry for teasing you earlier. Memphis fancies you, and I'm wildly jealous. He's the most eligible bachelor in five counties."

Taylor wasn't sure what to make of that.

Well, you're welcome to him. I'm engaged.

"And I'm married." Maddee burst out laughing, a genuine and infectious sound. "I adore him though. Evan's death has changed him. He used to be completely carefree, wicked good at his job, on top of the world. Sorrow isn't an emotion he wears well, I'm afraid. He's the kind of man who should have a woman."

She drifted off for a moment, then smiled brightly again. "Enough of that for now. So your voice hasn't made a full comeback yet. I spoke to Dr. Willig at length yesterday. Lovely woman. She said you saw some progress after EMDR. Would you like to continue that therapy?"

Yes. I need to get rid of these memories.

"Are they memories? Or are you having flashbacks?"

Taylor didn't respond.

"You know that EMDR won't banish the past. It's just going to make the memories less painful to deal with, and help you manage your emotions during the flashbacks. Besides, you don't really want to forget, not entirely. It keeps you sharp, remembering the bad stuff. You really should be journaling. Writing down all your thoughts, emotions. It's truly the best therapy you can engage in. By revisiting the memories, putting them down on paper, you're desensitizing yourself to them. I've been journaling since I was a teenager. Daily. Religiously. Thank goodness for computers, my stack of notebooks was threatening to topple me." She laughed, and Taylor smiled.

I've never had that kind of discipline, to be honest. And if I'm being frank, I'd like to exorcise it all.

"Would it be easier for you to type? I have a laptop here you can use."

Taylor nodded.

Maddee got out her laptop, a sleek eleven-inch Mac-Book Air, booted it up and opened it to a blank page for Taylor. They settled into their seats.

"Let's talk about what you find most objectionable to remember. Then we'll do some EMDR." She waved her hand, and Taylor saw the familiar implements on the table next to her.

My friend, Sam, was hurt very badly. I need to get the look of pain and anger on Sam's face out of my head. I don't want to live with that as a part of me. I failed her, and she let down her guard and allowed me to know it. It's haunting me.

"Sam was your friend who was kidnapped, right? I've read the notes from Dr. Willig. It seems she covered many of those issues at your first visit, correct?"

"Yes."

"Well then. Let's get started. I do things a little different. I want to lead you through a series of exercises that will help you relax before we get the EMDR underway."

I am relaxed.

Maddee smiled gently at her. "I beg to differ, my dear. You're obviously under a great deal of stress. You've got dark circles under your eyes. You didn't sleep. Your neck hurts too, doesn't it? You're holding it funny."

Her neck *was* sore, and her shoulders needed a good massage, but she wasn't going to admit that.

Strange pillows.

"Mmm-hmm. Right. Do you get any sort of regular sleep? I see here that you have a long history of insomnia. Why don't they give you something for that?"

We tried, once. Ambien. I had a terrible reaction to it. I'd rather not sleep than take medication for it.

"There are other really excellent drugs we could try. Sleep is vital for your recovery. It helps your brain to reset. When we're working on the neural pathways, it's essential that we get you at least six hours a night."

Taylor shook her head in protest, but Maddee held up a hand to stop her.

"Just hold on a second. There are all kinds of pharmaceuticals out there for sleep, but I prefer to go all-natural. Melatonin. Helps regulate your system, and you will find it helps with the jet lag as well. I want you to start taking it tonight." She handed Taylor an amber bottle.

I hate to take more pills. It's like admitting defeat.

"But you're willingly taking the Fioricet and the Ativan. And don't you have a prescription for Percocet, too? Your pupils are pinpoint, I assume you've been availing yourself of that one at least. So this isn't really different. Trust me, Taylor. This will help you. And that's all I want to do here, is help."

Busted.

All right. I'll try it.

"Thank you. Let's do a little relaxation exercise, too, just to humor me."

Taylor settled into the sofa, her hands folded loosely in her lap. Maddee's voice was low and soft, caressing.

"Good. Just listen to my voice. Think about your toes. They are all stretched and comfortable, like they're sitting in a pool of sunlight. Let them relax in the pool. It's so warm, so soft. It's a perfect complement to your feet. Can you feel the warmth?"

Taylor nodded.

"Good. Now think about your calves. That pool of light is moving up your legs, bringing with it the most delicious warmth and relaxation. You feel relaxed. You feel light as air. All your worries, all your problems, are being lifted from your body. Feel it get light."

Maddee worked her way up Taylor's body with her voice until she was at the top of her head, the pool of light shining all over her, keeping her warm and supple. She did feel more relaxed. That was an amazing exercise. She started to open her eyes, but Maddee told her not to.

"In your mind's eye, I want you to look at your wrist.

There's a string attached to it. The string goes high up in the sky. Do you see it rising?"

Taylor nodded.

"There's a blue balloon tied to the top of that string. See it floating in the air?"

Taylor nodded again.

"Good. Now let that balloon move toward the sky, and take your arm with it. You arm is feeling lighter and lighter."

Her arm did feel light. It raised of its own accord, up into the sky.

"You're a pro at this, Taylor. You can let your arm drop slowly back to your side now. Good. I want you to think back to your fear. Think about Sam. About the look on her face. What emotions are you feeling right now? Tell me aloud, don't just think them."

She shook her head. She couldn't talk. Maddee knew that.

"Come on, Taylor. Just give it a try. You can speak. There's nothing holding you back now. You're safe with me. Tell me what you're feeling."

"Sadness. Horror. Fury. Embarrassment."

Had she said that aloud?

"Look at the blue balloon, Taylor. Your arm is so light. Good girl. Why are you embarrassed?"

"Because I've come to kill. Sam knows that, and she's disappointed in me. I can't disappoint her. She counts on me too much."

It was so easy to talk to Maddee. Taylor didn't feel bad about telling the truth. Not now, not when she was so comfortable and warm, sunlight splashing down on her.

"You came to kill? You were planning to kill Ewan Copeland before you came into the room?"

"Yes. He deserved it. He hurt too many people. He hurt Fitz, and Sam."

"He didn't hurt you directly though, did he? You weren't in any physical danger from him until the very end, correct?"

"That didn't matter. I had to put him down."

"Tell me, Taylor. Tell me what you did."

"The birds were singing. They were calling me to him. And then they quit...."

Taylor remembered now. Sheer, unadulterated rage filled her. The Pretender was torturing her friends, and she had to end his reign of terror. She'd designed her own personal plan of revenge, one designed to take out the chess piece that had disrupted her life so completely for the previous year. She wasn't proud of the fact that she'd set out to kill the Pretender. And she'd failed, anyway, in the end. Sam was still hurt. She'd never heal properly.

She'd always blame Taylor for the loss of the baby.

Taylor was crying. She felt the tears on her face.

She hadn't told anyone what she was really doing at the house, Baldwin included. Though she was pretty sure he knew what she'd been up to. But there were plenty of other moments leading up to the shooting that she'd like to forget as well.

Oh, God. Had she just shared all that with Maddee James?

Her heartbeat began to race. She wanted to wipe her face, but her arm was still tied to that fucking blue balloon.

"Help," she said.

"Okay, Taylor. Hold it together now. I want you to let the pool of sun go away. When we're together, anytime you get frightened or upset, all you need to do is think about that pool of sunlight, and you'll feel better immediately. It gives you control over your emotions. I'm going to count backward from three. When I get to one, you will open your eyes. Three. Two. One."

Taylor opened her eyes. Maddee was looking at her with an unfathomable expression on her face, somewhere between contemplation and...was that happiness? It was fleeting; Maddee's face closed and became cool and professional again.

Taylor sat up. She had been crying. Maddee silently handed her a tissue. Taylor swiped it under her eyes and grabbed the laptop.

What just happened?

"Try speaking aloud."

"What..." Oh God, it was like swallowing razor blades. She shook her head.

Maddee reached across and took Taylor's hand. She smiled widely.

"There's nothing wrong with your voice. You spoke just fine for the past fifteen minutes."

"I... No."

"Yes." Maddee nodded, still grinning.

Oh, my God. She *had* said those things.

What did you do to me?

"Hypnotherapy. It worked, too. You were an excellent candidate. As you can see, you could speak just fine when you were under."

You hypnotized me?

"Yes. I'm surprised Dr. Willig didn't try that before EMDR. Sometimes you'll come out of it speaking just fine. Or, you'll be stubborn and still insist that you can't. But at least we know you're not damaged."

Hypnosis. Shit. She didn't know whether to be happy that Maddee had proved she could speak normally, or furious that Maddee had tricked her. Never mind that, she couldn't believe she'd been so open, either. She'd admitted the one thing she needed to keep from everyone. Not that it mattered; Maddee was bound by doctor-patient privilege. And Taylor hadn't killed Copeland. Baldwin had taken care of that for her. But still, admitting her intention was exactly the opposite of what she'd intended. She could get herself in more than moral trouble if she weren't careful.

She chalked the mental lapse up to jet lag, and terrible dreams. And she couldn't help herself—Maddee seemed like she could be a friend.

She smiled wanly.

So, that was fun.

"But you're feeling more relaxed, right? What we just did, it's just your basic biofeedback. A really great technique. You look like you're familiar with yoga. Are you?"

A bit. I'm not very good at the poses, but I rock the breathing.

Maddee laughed. "Good. It's the same thing when you're doing therapy. You set an intention, and allow your breath to regulate your thoughts. You did great.

You were much more relaxed than most first timers. I'm going to make you a tape. I want you to listen to it before you go to bed every night. It's the same kind of exercise we've just done, and it will help your mind let go. The more you relax, the easier it will be to talk. And I'll put in some suggestions to allow you to sleep. Insomnia is treatable, and I've had great success with this method."

All right. So now what?

"If you're up to doing some more, we can try some EMDR. See if we can help your feelings about Sam. A friend's disappointment is a huge burden to carry. Let's fix it."

They worked for another half an hour before Maddee turned the EMDR unit off and poured on a smile.

"How do you feel now?" she asked.

Taylor had to admit, she was exhausted. But she felt freer, lighter than when they started. Between thoughts of her happy place at the camp, and the warm pool of sunlight she'd immersed herself in twice now when things got too tough, they'd taken the worst of the memories down a notch.

Taylor was starting to understand why people went into therapy. It was incredibly liberating to get all the worry and fear off your chest, to give it to someone else to hold.

"Don't forget to take your melatonin tonight—probably around seven or so to give it time to get into your system. If you get a headache, take your pills and try to relax. Do the sunlight trick, thinking about the pain and watching it dissipate. The headache should leave.

Then listen to the tape. I'll make sure it's waiting on you tonight. You should sleep like a baby."

You're wonderful, Maddee. Thank you so much.

The woman smiled. "Of course. I'm glad that you're so responsive, we should have you back to normal very soon." She patted her on the hand. "Now go enjoy this beautiful country. Memphis told me he's taking you out for a drive. You'll have fun—he knows all the great vistas. I'll see you tomorrow."

Taylor watched Maddee gather her things and leave the room. She was pleased. Maddee certainly seemed to know what she was doing.

She felt unencumbered and happy, realized that for the first time since the shooting, she didn't have that sense of doom hanging over her head. Well, that was worth the trip overseas in and of itself.

Baldwin would be worrying about her. She sent him a quick text. She decided not to go into detail, said things were fine, sent him love. No sense telling him Memphis had sung her to sleep, or that she'd just opened her heart to a stranger. That wouldn't be productive.

She poured a fresh cup of tea and waited. Sure enough, within five minutes, Memphis came to get her, smiling widely.

"Head properly shrunk?" he asked.

She missed the ease of the laptop. Her notebook communication seemed so much slower.

You put it so nicely. Yes, we had a good session. You're right, Maddee's very good.

"Told you. Now, grab your coat and your boots. I'm taking you on a little excursion. You got to show me your Nashville, now it's high time I give you a taste of my roots in return."

CHAPTER TWENTY-FOUR

Taylor waited patiently at the back door for Memphis to retrieve his vehicle. The day was brisk, clouds scuttering through a grayish-blue sky, the threat of precipitation imminent. Rain first, then as the temperature dropped and the air turned colder, snow. Memphis wanted to be back before three, sunset was at three-thirty this far north, and the snow was going to kick in by then.

She heard the engine of the car roar, and wondered what sort of surprise Memphis had in store for her now. She loved cars. It was one of the few things she and her father had in common. Though she chose to drive a truck at home, a good engine could get her heart racing just as much as Baldwin's touch. She took a second to send him another text, telling him she'd be out of range for the rest of the day. He would touch base when he had the time. She'd tried twice, which was all that mattered.

The roar of the engine grew louder, accompanied by the tires crunching on the soft, loose stone gravel that made up the parking lot surrounding the castle. She almost gasped when the car came into view. Memphis was driving a pristine dark gray Aston Martin DB9. She knew off the top of her head that it retailed for over $180,000.

She didn't care about the driver, she just wanted to get in and let that car take her wherever it wanted to go.

Memphis pulled to a stop, then got out and grinned. "Like her?"

You know I do. A bit flashy for you though, isn't she?

"My one indulgence. And I can hardly drive around London with her. It wouldn't send the right message to the people I work with. I have to leave her here. Are you ready to take a drive?"

He walked around to the passenger side and opened the door.

She didn't hesitate.

You bet.

She took three steps down the stairs, put her hands in the pocket of her jacket to warm them. As she reached the last step, a sharp pain in her middle finger made her gasp. She whipped her left hand out of the jacket pocket, shocked to see she was bleeding.

"Ouch!" She'd blurted it out without thinking.

Memphis was at her side immediately. "Whoa, what happened?"

She stared at the cut on her finger. It looked like something was stuck in the wound. Memphis grabbed her hand, twisting it to and fro, then handed her a handkerchief.

"I must need bins, I don't see anything in there."

She tried dotting the blood but felt another searing pain. At a loss for what to do, she shrugged and stuck the offended digit into her mouth. She used her tongue to feel the cut. There was a hard chunk of something in it. Gently, lightly biting and sucking, she maneuvered it free. She pulled it from her mouth with her fingers, relieved that the sharp pain diminished.

"What is that?" Memphis asked.

Thank goodness it was her left hand: writing would be a pain with an open wound.

Glass, I think. In the pocket of my jacket.

Concern prominent on his face, Memphis bustled her back inside, made her take off the jacket. Trixie was in the next room; Taylor could hear her dressing down one of the serving maids. Memphis called for her. When she arrived, he sent her to the medicine kit for a plaster. Then he took Taylor's coat and turned the pocket inside out.

There was a fine layer of shiny grit lining the pocket. In the hall light it was easy to see the miniature shards of glass.

"What in the hell?" he said. "How could that have happened? This is a brand-new coat. It was just delivered yesterday. Damn, I can't get all this out."

Taylor was still sucking on her finger.

Some sort of mistake in the factory, probably.

"Look at this. There's actually a cut in the lining. They're going to have a very unhappy call from me this afternoon. I'll just be a moment."

He hurried into another room, was gone for a few minutes. He and Trixie arrived back at the same time, she holding a plaster and bottle of antiseptic cream, Memphis carrying a tattered brown canvas jacket with a thick flannel lining.

"Here you go. This is one of mine. You can wear it today, it should keep you warm enough."

They got Taylor all fixed up, making much too big a deal out of the tiny cut. Trixie seemed especially upset by the matter, as if she'd had control of the coat arriving from the store ruined. She told Memphis she'd handle getting a replacement straightaway, then disappeared with the offending garment tucked under her arm like a dead duck. Taylor realized she hadn't made eye contact, and thought that was strange. Maybe Trixie knew Memphis had made a late-night visit to her room and disapproved. Maybe she'd put the ground glass in Taylor's pocket to warn her off.

Oh, that was crazy. It was obviously just a mistake at the factory, or the shipping company. Some glass broke near the box, that was all.

Bandaged and redressed, they tried again. Taylor was less flustered about it all than Memphis, who was growling as loudly as his car's engine.

The seats of the Aston Martin were soft dove-gray leather, and she angled herself in, feeling foolish for causing such a stir. It was bizarre, the glass, but hardly a capital offense.

Their second attempt was more successful than the first. Ten minutes later, Memphis turned onto the A9, heading toward Inverness.

Memphis chatted, desultorily, of the land around them. Taylor was struck by the stark beauty, the ever-changing landscape that snuck from hills to mountains to lochs to forests at a dizzying rate. The road signs made her laugh. They were so very helpful. Her favorite read Tiredness Kills, Take A Break. There was an area of ruined trees, akin to what she was used to seeing at home when a tornado moved through. Memphis explained that they'd recently had a century storm, with gale force winds and drifting snow.

As they drove higher, the clouds came down and kissed the tops of the mountains. A falcon perched on the lay-by sign, gloomily watching the cars pass. His dejected look made Taylor sad. Something just didn't feel right about all of this. It was beautiful, and a treat, but she really should be in Nashville, dealing with her life instead of running away from it. Maybe coming here wasn't such a great idea after all. Though her morning with Maddee had been full of revelations, making herself so available to Memphis, leading him into thinking that she was here for more than just a rest, was going to get her in trouble.

Oh, stop it already, Taylor. Getting a little cut on your finger isn't worth ruining your mood. You haven't done a single thing wrong. It is high time you stop punishing yourself.

Memphis doled out bits of history to her as they passed by various landmarks. After twenty minutes, he took a roundabout and exited off to the north, toward a place called Grantown-on-Spey. She loved the name. So very Scottish. That cheered her up. The town itself came into view, a lovely resort village. She could smell smoke and peat from the fireplaces. It was obviously an affluent area; the architecture was some of the finest she'd seen. The roads were well paved, and the whole

town was done up for Christmas. It looked quite elegant.
Memphis explained that this was a prime water sports
and caravanning spot. But in the winter, it curled in on
itself like a dead leaf, waiting for the warmer weather
to break it free.

"Do you need to stop?" he asked. "We can get some
tea."

She shook her head. If she saw any more tea this
morning she may float away.

Memphis left the town behind, driving into the
forest. The road got narrower, the pavement breaking
in parts. It got continually worse for several miles.

Where are we going?

"To the family seat."

The family seat?

"Yes. This is my history. We're not all ghosts and
castles, you know."

She couldn't get her bearings. The trees were so thick
that the sun didn't shine through, and the cloud cover
made it impossible to tell which direction was north.
Memphis seemed like he was making turns at random,
taking her deeper and deeper into the woods. The road
narrowed to one lane. There was nothing out here, no
villages, no signs. Just the extensive flora and fauna of
the Highlands. She was hopelessly lost.

She finally saw a sign, tiny, brown, with an arrow
pointing to a church. Memphis said, "Nearly there,"
and turned left. She didn't think it was possible for the
road to get any narrower, but it did.

"In the summer I can't bring this car out here. The branches hang over the road and scratch the paint."

She could see how it would be more suited to an off-road vehicle. They were practically on a dirt track.

The road twisted, and the church advertised on the sign came into view. It was stone, collapsed, untended. A ruin. She felt suddenly sorry. No sacred place should go unloved. Memphis drove by it without a glance, then slowed to a stop.

"We go on foot the rest of the way," he said.

She followed him from the vehicle, glad to have his coat for warmth. The air was crisp and she heard water running. They walked for about a hundred yards, around the bend, and she caught her breath when the scene unfolded in front of her. A quaint but substantial stone bridge, bordered by a huge waterfall.

It was beautiful.

Memphis gave her a moment to take in the scene. "You can only truly see the waterfall during the winter. In the summer, it's in full leaf here and hidden from view unless you're under it, in the river. Great fishing in some of the pools that filter off of it."

She was reluctant to take her hands out of her pockets to write; the chill was sneaking under the edges of her coat already.

Wow. It's stunning.

"This is Dulsie Bridge."
She turned to look at him, puzzled.

Wait a minute. Your family is named for a bridge?

"Yes. It's a very important bridge."

But a bridge? You don't have a town or a village or a county, or...something?

"That old church back there. But it fell down two centuries ago."

Ah, I see. Okay then.

Memphis laughed. "No, you don't. But that's all right. If an army needed to cross this land, there was no way across the river. They built this in 1255 to allow English troops to move across the land. You'll know that Highsmythe is a British name, not Scottish, yes?"

She nodded.

"We were granted the lands early, and left them untended for many years. But when the fourth earl came north to view his properties and collect rents, he immediately saw the advantages to be had. A way to get even richer than he already was. He built onto the castle with the proceeds from the deal, then settled into his life in the Highlands, far away from England's rule. Married young Isabella and gained even more land. And the rest, as they say, is history."

That's some story.

"And more importantly, Robert Burns stayed here once, too, while he was visiting Strathspey. He took a liking to Mrs. Grant."

Ah. 'My love is like a red, red rose.'

"You know him?"

She smiled at him.

Everyone knows who Robert Burns is, Memphis.

He took her hand and put it to his heart. *"'So fair art thou, my bonnie lass, So deep in love am I, And I will love thee still, my dear, Till a' the seas gang dry.'"*

His face was hopeful, smiling lightly. Taylor bit her lip. She knew he was just quoting from the poem, that it was another's words. But did he?

She didn't know what to say.

"Taylor, I—"

She held up her hand. God, not being able to talk to him right now was killing her.

Stop, Memphis. Please. Before you say something you might regret.

He turned back to the river. She could see he was fighting with himself. There was more he wanted to say, more that he wanted to do. She could feel the frustration coming off him in waves.

She was frustrated as well. She didn't know what she wanted. She'd always thought she did, but the past few weeks, with Baldwin pushing her away and Memphis pulling her in… She kicked at a rock, watched it spill over the edge and down into the torrent of water below. Her head hurt.

Memphis turned to her, his eyes dark. "I won't say it, then. But I will do it."

He took two steps toward her, so quickly that she didn't have a chance to back away, put his arms around her, and pulled her to him. Without hesitating, he lowered his face to hers.

Their lips met urgently. She exhaled into him, getting lost in the kiss. The last time this had happened, she'd pulled away. But right now, with no one watching, no one to see, she didn't want to.

He put one hand behind her neck and the other around her waist, pulling her closer, deeper. She couldn't breathe, didn't want to breathe, didn't want to think, didn't want the kiss to end. It was perfect, hard and soft at all the right moments, the rhythm moving in a way that told her they would be good together in more ways than just this.

A little voice spoke out from the back of her head— *Taylor, you are losing yourself....*

She told it to shut up. She'd been lying to herself, to Baldwin, to Sam. She'd come to Scotland, for better or for worse, to figure out what sort of glamour Memphis had put on her, whether it was something real, or something destined for failure. Now, standing on his family's lands, at the very heart of his history, was as good a time as any to find out.

She was pinned against the stone wall. Without breaking the kiss, he put his hands under her bottom and picked her up, rocking her body against his as he did, forcing her to grab hold of his arms for balance. He set her carefully on the wall. He was as hard as he looked from the outside, muscles tense, like granite under his clothes. She pulled his shirt from his pants, got her hands under the fabric. Felt his chest, his smooth stomach. He yanked up her sweater, unsnapped her bra with one hand. Her breasts spilled out into the cold air. He caught them in his hands, brought them to his mouth. He moaned, low in his throat, and she felt the answering cry start deep within her.

Oh, no. She had to stop now. Before it was too late. But his hands were going lower, expertly moving down her ribs, unbuttoning her jeans, plunging into her panties. It felt so good. So amazingly hot… *No, no, no, no,* she had to stop. *Stop. Stop, stop, stop, stop.*

"Stop." There, she'd said it aloud.

And Memphis froze.

Two heartbeats passed. He had her at quite a disadvantage, and knew it. He flicked his forefinger and she nearly came undone. She forced her mouth closed, gently removed his hand, pulled down her sweater, and slid off the wall.

She could hear the ragged breaths that escaped from his mouth. She was panting as well. She put her hand over her mouth to try and calm herself.

He whispered the words. *"'Till a' the seas gang dry, my dear, and the rocks melt wi' the sun! And I will love thee still, my dear, while the sands of life shall run.'"*

When she didn't respond, he put on his Scottish brogue for her. "Aye, Burns is a bonny poet."

"Aye," she whispered. The moment was gone. Over. Her lips were raw, her skin felt like she'd been brushed from head to toe with sandpaper.

Hand still over her mouth, she met his eyes. They were deeply blue. She realized his changed colors when he was aroused. And he was most mightily aroused. The outline in his pants was hard to miss.

She'd owed him more than this. She just didn't know how much of herself she had to give.

"I'm… It's… I can't… I don't…"

Shit. She took a deep breath, still staring into his bottomless eyes, and forced the words out.

"I'm sorry."

CHAPTER TWENTY-FIVE

Memphis looked out over the rushing water. "These lands were important. You needed to cross through here to get to Inverness. My family controlled the land. Simple as that. They didn't live here, they just owned it. They owned a lot of it. From here all the way back down to the estate. But as the years passed, and allegiances changed, the lands were stolen, or taken legally, or traded for women. We still own about five thousand acres up here."

Neutral territory. He had the decency to turn and look away. She took advantage of the moment to hook up her bra. She wasn't quite sure what to say, decided to stick with his lead. Her notebook had fallen in the dirt by the wall. She retrieved it, brushing it off before writing.

So this is Highsmythe country. You should put up a sign.

"Stop your teasing. I just thought you'd think it was pretty."

I do. God, Memphis, if you only knew. It's lovely.

He pushed off the wall, held out a hand as if nothing had happened, as if that very hand hadn't just been making rather indecent proposals against her body.

"Excellent. Let's go see if we can find Nessie, shall we?"

We're going to Loch Ness?

She couldn't help herself; she knew her smile went from ear to ear. It seemed wrong to be so excited to leave this place, but she couldn't wait to get away.

"What, did you think I drove you all the way up here to look at a bridge?"

She had to make this better.

I think you drove me up here to take advantage of me, that's what I think. Lovely area, pretty bridge, private waterfall, love poems. You're a naughty boy, Memphis.

He smiled at her again, showing his teeth this time. They walked back to the car. It was as if nothing had happened. He was back to his normal tone of voice, and her heartbeat had finally slowed.

Memphis turned the engine over and slid the shifter into gear. "We should have just enough time to have luncheon at the Dores Inn before we take a drive down the loch. Fish and chips suit you? They have some of the best in the Highlands."

"Mmm."

They drove back out to the main road in silence. She was starting to sense Memphis's moods, and noticed that they were mercurial, at best. There was something bothering him. The joking, jovial, sensitive man from the bridge was gone. Not that she was surprised. It was probably her fault. She'd given in to temptation, then yanked it away. Maybe that wasn't fair, but had he any right to be upset about it? He'd taken advantage, too.

The silence grew too loud for her to bear.

Are you mad?

"At you? No. Of course not." There was no sarcasm in his tone, but he didn't look at her, kept his blue eyes firmly forward on the road.

You're awfully quiet.

He sighed deeply, both hands gripping the steering wheel of the Aston. "I don't know if I should tell you this."

Tell me what, Memphis?

He didn't answer right away. When he did, his voice was strained, and he wouldn't look at her.

"Taylor. I am hopelessly, desperately in love with you. Everything about you. And I know you feel something for me as well. You can't deny that."

She didn't bother. Her body had given away all her secrets when they kissed. Yes, she did want him. But love? No. Not that. Not ever that.

She shook her head. He took that as a sign that she was agreeing with him, reached over and took her hand. Damn Brit, misinterpreting everything.

"If this was a mistake, I'm very sorry. I hadn't planned it at all, to be honest. We had tickets for the noon ferry tour around Loch Ness. I was driving by the roundabout and stopping at the bridge seemed like… the right thing to do."

She sensed he was telling the truth, that he hadn't planned to make a move on her. She didn't care what he said, he wasn't over Evan, not by a long shot. And she was afraid he was going to try to make her a substitute. She'd be a poor one, at that, but safe. And very much alive, as she'd proven less than a quarter hour ago.

You're forgiven. But Memphis, I'm engaged. We can't do this.

God, she was going to have to burn these pages as soon as she got back to the castle.

"You're wrong, Taylor. We most certainly can. But it's not right for me to take advantage of your situation, either. So you'll accept my apology, my lady. Please."

Of course.

She touched him on the back of the hand, briefly, amazed at the shock that ran through her body.

You stupid, stupid girl.

Memphis changed the subject as they drew closer to Inverness, talking of the history of the land they were driving through. The Jacobites had fought and died here, on Culloden field, which appeared on her left. Taylor knew the sad history of that battle. The last stand of Bonnie Prince Charlie's men, ragged, wounded, starving. They fought for their freedom on the moor, died there, nearly all of them, and were buried where they lay. She saw the blue and the red flags from the road—the lines demarking where the British and Scots had stood, facing one another across Drumossie Moor in the cold dawn, before the final charge that would end so many lives.

She felt her skin crawl, goose bumps parading up and down her arms. She was surrounded by death. All she wanted to do was get back to the castle, away from this sadness.

But Memphis was determined, and fifteen minutes later, they pulled into the parking lot of the Dores Inn, on the northernmost tip of Loch Ness. It was eerily beautiful, mist rising off the water, the gray skies lending themselves to her introspection. A rosebush outside the door still sported the remnants of heavy pink roses.

The building was warm and cozy, a fireplace pouring out heat. The staff was obviously happy to see them; it was certainly too chilly to be doing much besides staying inside, warm by a fire. This wasn't exactly high tourist season, though there were people out sailing the loch—Taylor could see the tour boats powering down the murky water. It must be freezing out there, especially with the breeze.

Taylor needed a little something to take the edge off, so she ordered a Guinness. Took a Percocet. Let the edges blur. Tried to stop watching his hands. Tried to forget the bridge.

Memphis made an effort to be cheerful, but he too was distracted. They ate in silence, a strange veil of discomfort surrounding them. The food was delicious, though she couldn't finish it all. After an interminable thirty minutes, they bundled up and went back into the cold to drive down the loch a bit then head home. Taylor was more than ready for this side trip to be over.

Memphis turned the car south, pointed out a few landmarks, then grew quiet. After a few moments, he said, "I'm sorry. I should never have taken you to the bridge. I'm not quite sure what I was thinking."

She didn't know what she was thinking, either. Or what she'd been thinking when she succumbed to his charms. She rubbed her forehead, feeling the small scar on her temple. Her headache was worsening. She slipped another Percocet into her hand, and a Fioricet. There was a bottle of Highland Spring in her bag. She downed the pills and grabbed her notebook.

Memphis, I'm getting tired. Why don't we just head back?

He smiled in relief, as if he'd needed her permission to abort their journey.

"Of course. Let's go home."

They were down near Fort Augustus. It took over an hour to make it back to Dulsie Castle.

They passed the time on a much safer topic. The case Memphis was working on, the enigmatic Urq, and the three missing girls. Crime was the one place Memphis and Taylor truly had common ground.

When he pulled through the gate that led to the castle grounds, it was three o'clock. The snow had held off, and pink streaks of sunset were burgeoning through the clouds to the west.

"Let me make it up to you," Memphis said suddenly.

Taylor just wanted to go lie down and let the aching

stop. She wasn't all that sure she wanted to indulge him anymore, but good manners and a bit of curiosity won out.

All right· What do you have in mind?

"Follow me." He jumped out of the car, rushed around to her side and got the door open. "Button up your coat, it's getting cold now."

Cold was an understatement. It was downright frigid, and damp to boot. She felt it through the coat, carefully put her hands in the pockets, gun-shy after the morning's adventure. In answer, her finger gave a dull throb.

"We're heading up here," he said, then strolled across the gravel forecourt onto a small path. Fifteen feet in, there was a large arched wooden gate, over eight feet tall. Memphis unlocked it and beckoned for her to step inside so he could lock it behind them. The path widened and started up a slight incline. Taylor could see a statue ahead, probably a football field length away. She looked back at the house, realized that there was a straight shot from the front door up this rise.

What's that?

"You'll see," Memphis replied.

She was a little tired of surprises, but followed dutifully anyhow. There was a seven-foot-high stone wall to her left. She couldn't figure out what was inside. A graveyard, maybe? That uneasy feeling she had from the afternoon returned with a vengeance.

A few minutes later they were at the top of the hill. The statue was of a woman, holding a bow and arrow in one hand. A small owl perched on her right shoulder. It only took Taylor a moment to place her; the plaque at the woman's feet gave it away.

Athena?

"Yes. She is my father's favorite. And mine, of course. The sixth earl had this statue commissioned from a minor sculptor, Rama Nardi, in Florence back in the 1500s. He apprenticed with Niccolò di Piero Lamberti, but never lived up to his initial promise. He had a problem with scale that he couldn't overcome. Look at her feet. They're much too large for her body. Nardi died before his twenty-fifth birthday, sadly. This is only one of ten pieces of his known to exist in the world. There are four more inside the wall."

The statue was old, weathered. Small cracks at the base had been repaired.

Doesn't that make it valuable?

"Certainly. But Nardi wasn't terribly famous, or good, for that matter. And we're in a private area of the estate. It would be hard to walk off with her. She weighs quite a bit."

What is all this?

"Come see," Memphis said, and steered her around the statue, back to the stone wall.

She was able to see over the edge now. Extensive, beautiful gardens, bordering a small lake in the center.

A secret garden.

It's lovely·

She could tell he was pleased to surprise her with something good this time.

"Isn't it? There are several sections, tiers, really. The public is allowed to enter at the bottom but can only come up halfway. There is a small house on the grounds, back over here, where the gardeners live. They're a couple. Suited to it. It's been in his family for a couple of centuries. He's a Dulsie legacy— Oh, see the swans?"

She could, three of them. Two white and one gray, all three big.

"Mute swans. That's William and Harry. Harry's short for Harriet, of course. And the gray one, that's their cygnet, Charles. He's not quite full-grown, he's just starting to turn. They've been here for years. I like to visit them while I'm home, though Harry tried to bite me once when I went in the water."

He was trying to distract her. She smiled at him, nodded. She understood. She wasn't comfortable, either.

The sun was setting now, nearly gone, and the first flakes of snow started to fall. He turned her around and pointed out the view from the other side of Athena, a glorious spill into the valley below. Taylor took a deep breath, and felt the flakes hit her tongue.

I love it·

Memphis pressed something into her hand. It was an iron skeleton key, big and old-fashioned. "Then you must come here anytime you'd like. As you've no doubt realized, your rooms face the mountains, not the gardens, which is why you hadn't seen them yet. But it's yours to explore. Taylor, I think it's best… I'm afraid I need to head back to London tomorrow. I have work to do. Will you be all right here on your own?"

Her emotions split in two. She didn't want him to go, yet she didn't want him to stay. It would be easier without him around, she was sure of it. She shoved the key in her back pocket and wrote quickly, heedless of her degenerating scrawl. Got it on paper before she changed her mind.

Of course. That's why I came, isn't it? To work with Maddee and heal. This is perfect. I can't tell you how much I appreciate everything you've done, Memphis. I'm sorry today was so…difficult.

He shook his head. "That was my fault. I don't know what possessed me to take you to the bridge." He brushed a piece of snow from her hair. "It wasn't all bad. No sense in pretending it didn't happen. Are you sorry?"

She looked at the ground. *Am I?*

We stopped. Nothing to be sorry for.

Was that true? Would Baldwin feel that way if he knew? The thought of him, his disappointment in her—another person disappointed in her—stabbed her heart. *He will never know, Taylor. You will not hurt him like that. This is between you and Memphis.*

They were at the bottom of the path now, and the snow was picking up. Memphis borrowed the key from Taylor, let them out and locked the gate behind them.

The castle lights were dimmed, only a few private quarters lit up. Saving electricity, Taylor supposed. They both stopped and looked at it, so forlorn, so alone, so stoic. Just like the family contained inside.

Memphis broke the spell. "You're just not the kind of woman people get over easily," he said, shrugging. "So, let's see what Cook has prepared for dinner."

CHAPTER TWENTY-SIX

Dear Sam,
I am a fool.

I know what you're thinking. I can hear you in my head right now, giving me what for. And I've always been able to count on you for sound advice.

Memphis kissed me today, on Dulsie Bridge. It's part of his family lands. Beautiful place. I can't say that it took me by surprise. We've been dancing around the attraction for a while now.

Sam, I'm lost. I don't know what to do. I don't love him. Not in the way he wants me to. Or needs me to. That's the thing, he needs me, so much. It's so different from Baldwin. Baldwin has never needed me. He adores me—that I have no doubt about. But if something happened to me, he could go on, and be happy with another woman.

Memphis has already experienced that loss. And I know I'm just a substitute for Evan. But when he kissed me, I felt something I'd never felt before. And I don't know what to make of it.

Write me back. Say something wise.

Love,
Taylor

CHAPTER TWENTY-SEVEN

Baldwin liked Sir Nigel. He was down-to-earth, pragmatic, and not a bit of help.

"I checked all of our files. We don't have a record of ever using Julius, anywhere. Granted, that's not much of a surprise. These kind of men are best left off paper."

"Isn't that the truth. Well, I appreciate your help."

"There is someone who might know, though. I've got a call in to him. As soon as I hear back, I'll ring."

"Thank you. I owe you one."

"Certainly. Till then."

Julius. Where the hell are you, man?

Atlantic insisted Julius had simply gone off the reservation, but Baldwin wasn't so sure. Julius had always been so reluctant. Terribly good at his job, a world-class sniper, but with a code. He wasn't like many of the guns for hire. Julius was a thinking man's assassin. Baldwin actually liked the man.

If anything, Julius had decided enough was enough and had dropped off the grid because he was tired of the job. He'd done this before. Baldwin had talked him into coming back.

That time, he'd tracked him to a cozy hidey-hole in Amsterdam, but so far he hadn't shown up there.

Baldwin closed his laptop and sat back in the chair. The house was too quiet without Taylor. He missed her. God, he missed her.

If he found Julius, he was going to have to go talk him off the ledge and bring him back home, make sure he wasn't going to lose his edge. But all he really wanted to do was catch the next plane to Edinburgh.

The texts had arrived in the middle of the night, polite and noncommittal. And he, not wanting to look like he was desperately awaiting word, had waited to respond. He got out his BlackBerry and read them again.

Tried to imagine where she was right now, what she was doing. What ridiculously charming event Memphis had planned for her.

He was being petty. He knew Taylor wouldn't do anything to jeopardize their relationship. He understood her desire to get away. Hell, if it had been him, he'd have collapsed long ago. She'd find her way back to him. Didn't they always say that if you loved someone to set them free?

The phone rang. He hoped to see the 615 area code, but no luck. It was Ainsley again.

He answered on the second ring.

"That was fast."

Ainsley didn't waste any time. "He went to Argentina."

"Are you kidding? What's in Argentina?"

"Wine and alpacas. Probably a woman, too. Who knows why they choose these places. I'll send you the specifics. With any luck, you'll catch up to him."

"With any luck. Thank you, again. I appreciate the information."

"Be well, Dr. Baldwin."

"And you."

He hung up the phone. *Fuck. Argentina? Julius, you asshole.*

His email dinged. The information from Ainsley. He read it, forwarded it to Atlantic.

The reply came back almost immediately.

Just received the same information. He's not there anymore. We got a hit on one of his identities. He took a flight from Buenos Aires to Amsterdam last night. Hope your passport's ready.

Perfect. Amsterdam he could handle. It would get him closer to Taylor, anyway.

Atlantic's people would arrange his flights. With any luck, he could be in Europe by nightfall. He'd be met by someone from Angelmaker; they'd grab up Julius and he'd be finished before Christmas.

Then he could get his focus back. On his missing son. On Taylor.

He banged out a text before he went to pack.

Taylor, that's good news. I'm glad your meeting went so well. I am leaving shortly for the airport. I'll do my best to be in touch, but if you don't hear from me, don't worry. I'll call as soon as I can. Be good. I love you.

He just hoped she'd be willing to have him when he got back.

CHAPTER TWENTY-EIGHT

Dinner was another elegant affair. Taylor knew she was going to gain at least five pounds on this trip if she didn't watch it. Memphis was cheerful, vigilantly avoiding talk of their indiscretions on the bridge. Instead he regaled her with talk of his escapades as a young boy, of his brother's wine-making venture in South Africa, and Jacobite lore. She was thoroughly entertained.

After dinner, she loaded up on meds and explored the castle with him. He showed her all the little bits and pieces that strangers paid hard-earned cash to see. He told stories in each room as if he were a tour director. She was relieved when they visited the billiards room, at last. It turned out the room was only three doors down the hall from her bedroom, so she would be able to sneak in to play a game here and there if she got bored or couldn't sleep.

There were two snooker tables and one for regular pool. The table was grand, traditional green baize, heavy wooden lion legs, the pockets made of excellent well-broken-in leather. They assembled their cues, flipped a coin, and Memphis won. Ever the gentleman, he ceded his turn to Taylor, who, feeling frisky, ran the table.

The next game, Memphis got serious. He was a competitive man by nature, and Taylor wasn't one to shy away from a challenge. They began laying bets, a pound a game. They played late into the night, the score moving back and forth, until Taylor got on a major roll and won seven pounds off him. Not a bad night's work.

The pallor from earlier in the day was lifted. When Taylor finally excused herself to head to bed, Memphis didn't fight it. He walked her to the door again, gave her a warm hug and a kiss on the cheek. He told her to call him if she needed anything, and to meet him in the dining room for breakfast at eight.

He lingered a moment.

"Do you want me to come in?" he finally asked.

Did she? Her body said yes, her mind said absolutely not. Her heart, well, she was learning to ignore the bitch.

Memphis. I think what happened this afternoon shouldn't happen again.

He was quiet for a minute. "Whatever you want, Taylor. I'd never make you do anything you didn't want to do. Good night, then."

He headed off down the hall without looking back.

Great. Now he was pissed at her.

But it was better this way. With him gone, she could focus on the real reason she was here—getting back to normal. She was tired of feeling vulnerable. It wasn't in her nature.

Her room was warmed by a fire, the flames dancing merrily, casting shadows on the walls. There was a tape next to the player with handwriting on it—Maddee's biofeedback lessons. Taylor just wasn't in the mood. She didn't want to work right now. She wanted to forget. She wanted to disappear.

She noticed a new decanter on her bar, this one filled with a ruby-red liquid. She went to the bar, pulled the stopper out and sniffed, delighted to find the vintage port from last night. Thoughtful man. She poured herself a glass and sat in the chair opposite the fire.

She wondered how Baldwin was faring, wondered why he hadn't called her back. She knew he was busy, that that bastard Atlantic would have him jumping through hoops on some top-secret project. She thought that maybe hearing his voice would help her center, get her grounded again. She grabbed her phone from her purse and saw the text. He'd be gone by now. She called anyway. Got his voice mail. It was better than nothing, but it didn't help. Damn.

The port was warm and delicious. She finished the first glass and started in on another. Her head was still hurting, so she set the drink aside and took all her medicine, including the melatonin Maddee had given her.

She sat at her computer and saw Sam had written her back. She didn't want to deal with that, either, but she sucked it up. Like tearing off a Band-Aid, it was better to get the worst over as quickly as possible.

She opened the email.

Dear Taylor,
Yes, you are a total fool. I told you this would happen.
     I don't know what to say about the kiss. You're a big girl, and you'll make the right decision.

But there is something I want to make sure you know.

Dulsie Bridge was the place where Evan died. Did he tell you that while he was kissing you? Did he tell you his wife plunged to her death over the side of that same bridge as he was making a move on you?

I know you haven't spent a lot of time looking into Memphis's background, so I've done it for you. Here's a few links to the story, so you can see for yourself. Make sure you read all the way through them, honey. He is not the knight in shining armor he makes himself out to be.

I can't tell you what to do, but if I were in your shoes, I'd make sure he stayed very far away.

Take care, Taylor. You don't want to ruin everything you've fought so hard to get.

Love,

Sam

"Son of a bitch," Taylor said without thinking about it. Her voice sounded foreign, thick and deep, her usual huskiness masked by disuse.

"Shit."

Okay then. Cursing was good. Could she do any more?

"Memphis, what were you thinking?"

She breathed in deeply, a huge sigh of relief. She wasn't completely broken. A little drunk, a little stoned, and terribly distraught, but not broken. Not anymore. Maddee and her hypnosis had proven that. And now Taylor had proven it to herself.

Finally.

Memphis *had* promised to heal her.

She shoved that thought away and clicked on the first link Sam had sent. It was a newspaper article, in the *Scotsman,* from December of 2008. She read it quickly, her stomach roiling.

Sam was right. Evan had died at Dulsie Bridge.

Oh, God. He'd been kissing her where his wife died?

Jesus. Jesus H. Christ on a Popsicle stick. What the hell was all that, then? What sort of strange compulsion had led him to take her to the very spot his wife died to try and kick-start their relationship?

Taylor hit Delete, then went into her trash folder and deleted the past two emails from Sam.

She didn't want to know any more.

No wonder he'd gotten quiet as they left the bridge. He was thinking about Evan.

Taylor recognized a long dormant feeling springing up in her chest. For God's sake. She was jealous. Jealous of a dead woman.

Memphis leaving was definitely the best thing. This little crush would be extinguished and she could go back to focusing on her health.

She tried to read a little bit more, but she couldn't pay attention to the story anyway. Not after Sam's little bombshell. And her eyes were crossing. She was amazed at how quickly she'd gotten tired. It had been a long, emotional, weird day. She decided to chuck it all and start fresh in the morning. Ten minutes later, brushed and washed, she collapsed in the bed, lids heavy. The wonderfully unfamiliar sense of being tired and able to sleep carried her off quickly.

* * *

She was in a car, the engine revving as she took the hairpin curves faster and faster. Away. She just needed to get away.

The bridge was up ahead. She swung the car to a stop. Memphis stood on the stone wall, beckoning to her. He smiled, and she smiled back. Went to him. He took her in his arms, kissed her deeply.

"Evan. I love you."

"I love you, too."

With a deep laugh, he hurled her over the edge.

The water was so cold. It rushed over her lap. She couldn't feel her legs. The water was rising, rising. Her chest was underwater now, then her jaw. She was drowning. As the water streamed over her head, she screamed.

CHAPTER TWENTY-NINE

It was half past two when she jerked awake, bladder full and insistent. The fire had died down and the air in the room was chilled. The floor was freezing on her bare feet. She went to the bathroom, cursing not sleeping in socks. She hurried back to the bed, gathered the blankets to her chin, then snaked a hand out into the cold air to turn on the electric warmer.

She lay quietly, listening to the house creak and moan around her. There was something about the place after nightfall that was disconcerting. It was like being the only guest in a very large hotel, and the entire staff has gone home for the evening. There were unfamiliar noises, and what sounded like footsteps in the hall that she could only imagine was one of the servants creeping around. Maybe she needed to back off the Percocets? The dreams were getting crazier and crazier.

She turned and faced the window, and let her eyes close. She still felt tired. Sleep might come back to her.

She was thinking about the bridge, about Evan going through the windshield, imagining what Memphis would have done if she hadn't stopped him, and why in the world he'd take her to the spot his wife died and not share that information, when she felt something touch her back.

She jumped straight out of the side of the bed closest to the window, whirled back around to see who was there. The room was empty, the air black and thick. She reached for the lamp, clicked the light. It didn't come on. The bulb must have blown. She inched back toward the window, hoping to pull open the drapes and let some light spill in from the outside. She got a hand on the thick velvet and started to pull it aside when the light by the bed turned on with a crack.

The bulb lit up the room. It was empty. And here she was, crouched against the window, looking like a complete fool. She was letting the ghost stories get too far in her head.

She marched back to the bed, took the cord of the offending lamp in hand, and clicked the button. The light extinguished. She clicked it again and it came on. Obviously there was a short in the cord somewhere; that's why it hadn't turned on immediately. Or the bulb itself was affected by the temperature, needed to warm up before illuminating.

She felt like a right idiot. She went to the fire and stirred it, put on another couple of logs so it would heat the room again. Then she climbed back into the bed and turned off the light.

She lay on her back, staring at the ceiling, watching the light from the fire tango through the shadows. The furniture felt like it was moving. She wished Memphis would come and lie next to her. She'd slept better with him near. It wasn't like her to be nervous in strange places. She had to admit, it would be nice to have a warm body next to her.

She was just starting to drift back to sleep when she felt the feathery light touch, cold as ice, on her forehead. Right on the healing bullet wound. Her eyes flew open and she tried to move, to get out of the bed, to turn on the light—something, anything—but she was stuck, arms at her sides as if bound there. She couldn't raise her head, couldn't turn it. Something was on her chest—a weight holding her down. She started to scream, fought to rise, and the thing put its arms around her and hugged. She felt the cold tendrils shimmying up and down her back.

She screamed again, her cries echoing through the room, and felt an answering laugh. She stopped, and the hold around her body loosened.

I'm dreaming. I'm having another nightmare. I'm asleep. I do not believe in ghosts. Go away.

She felt the nimble touch again, more familiar this time, then it stopped and she was able to breathe and then sit up. She turned on the light, hands at her throat, gasping for air. Her heart was pounding out of control. What in the hell had just happened?

You had a bad dream. Get up, get a book—not a ghost story, fool—and get your mind off of it.

She couldn't believe she was nervous about getting out of the bed again. There was no safety within; she'd already proven that. Should she ring the bell? Call Memphis and have him come sit with her? She didn't want to be alone.

She heard footsteps in the hall again. Okay. She was tired of this. She pulled her sweater on and went to the door, flung it open.

Trixie was standing in the corridor, four feet from the door. She was slightly turned away, like she was about to leave.

"All right, mum?" she asked, eyes full of concern. Fake concern, Taylor knew. Trixie had no love for her.

"I'm fine," Taylor answered, her voice barely above a whisper, but working.

"Forgive me, mum. I heard you screaming fit to wake the dead. I came to see if you were sick."

Great. If she'd awakened the servants, had Memphis heard too? He'd come to her last night after she'd cried out, but not tonight. She didn't know how to feel about that.

"Is Memphis awake?"

"I don't rightly know, mum. Shall I fetch himself to you?"

"No, no. There's no reason to bother him."

"Aye. I have some tea for you, should you be needing it. Will help you sleep."

Over Trixie's shoulder, Taylor saw the tray on a linen-covered rolling cart. It was a singularly kind gesture on the older woman's part. Maybe Memphis was right. Once she saw Taylor wasn't going to try and take Evan's place, she'd warm up.

"Thank you."

Trixie brought the tray in, got the tea arranged and poured. "'Tis chamomile, from the gardens. Will knock out a horse if needs be. Drink up your cuppa, and you'll have nae more bad dreams t'night."

Taylor sat in the chair and put the porcelain to her lips. The tea was very hot. She blew on it and took a tiny sip, then set the cup in its saucer.

"Trixie?"

"Yes, mum?"

"You were Memphis's nurse when he was growing up, right?"

"Aye, mum."

"So you've been in the castle for many years."

"Aye. Seen it all from this lot. Drink your tea now, that's good."

Taylor took another sip, surprised at how relaxed she felt. The tea was good. She didn't normally care for chamomile, but this one was lightly sweetened and went down easily.

"Trixie, have you ever seen a ghost in the castle?"

The housekeeper laid a finger on her mouth for a moment, then answered with a nod. "Och, aye. The castle's full of 'em. Is that what happened then, one of the wee beasties came to visit? Can put you right off your sleep, they can." Her voice had softened. Taylor could see that she might make a good nursemaid to the children after all.

"I don't believe in ghosts," Taylor said.

"Of course you don't. You're American. Lacking in imagination." She said it without rancor, just a statement of fact. "We Scots are surrounded, always have been. We know there's more to life than work and death. Our people stay with us, guide us through, so we don't make too much of a hash of things. Now, you must be feeling better. Get yourself into bed and get back to sleep."

"Let's not mention this to Memphis, all right?"

"No, dear. I won't breathe a word."

Taylor allowed herself to be talked to like a small child and, ushered back into the bedroom. She, climbed into the bed. But after Trixie left, she went to the door and double locked it, tilting a chair against the handle.

No one would be able to get in without making a racket and waking her.

She went to the window, looked out onto the blackened landscape. The snow had stopped. Quiet as death, the night outside. She started to turn away but saw a light, off in the distance. Bobbing, as if someone were walking with a flashlight.

She extinguished her lights so her silhouette wouldn't be seen against the window and watched. The light grew closer, and she recognized the powerful beam of a Maglite. The shape of the figure came into view as it passed beneath the huge Douglas fir trees. A man. It was Memphis. What was he doing, out wandering around in the middle of the cold, dark night?

He looked up at her window then. She pulled back a bit—there was no way he could see her, it was dark in the room except for the firelight, and she was back far enough away from the window as to be out of the line of sight, but he watched for a few minutes. She watched him back, wondering what in the world he was up to.

He finally turned away, toward the doors of the castle. She let the curtain fall across the sash and crept back to her bed. She was feeling strange. Hot. Dizzy. Yes, she'd definitely taken too many pain pills today.

She lay down, her body tired but her mind whirling. Memphis was up and about. Could he have gotten into her room? Could he have been the one touching her, wrapping his arms around her, holding her down, and she was simply so groggy from sleep and medicine as to not recognize it was him? The housekeeper had been lurking right outside her door. Had she been aware of her master's intent?

A chill went down her body. Surely not. She was

being ridiculous. Her imagination was getting away with her.

Just in case, she checked herself for wetness or tell-tale soreness. She felt nothing unusual, then felt insane for even entertaining the thought. As if Memphis would drug her, then sneak into her room and force her to have sex? That was ludicrous.

Wasn't it?

CHAPTER THIRTY

It could have been minutes, or hours. Taylor stared at the ceiling until her eyelids drooped shut. The headache began to dissipate, and her body relaxed into the sheets. She heard a noise, like fingers scratching at her door. Not again. She couldn't open her eyes, wouldn't open her eyes. If she ignored it, it would go away.

The door opened. Her lids colored from the dim light of the hallway sconces. Then everything was dark again. Her heart began to race.

"Taylor." The voice **was** deep, and strong.

Not a ghost.

Memphis.

He'd brought the chill in from the night sky. She could feel him shivering. She kept her eyes tightly shut. She didn't want to see.

"I'm afraid," she whispered.

"Don't be. I'll keep you safe."

His hand cupped her cheek, the flesh cold, but warming as it touched hers. She didn't move, didn't dare. Soft, light touches on her face, her neck, followed by his lips. He kissed her scars, flicked his tongue against her earlobe, slid his mouth slowly down her neck to her collarbone. She began to squirm, and he said, "Be still." She forced herself to stop moving. The exquisite agony continued, her breasts, her stomach. She was suddenly unclothed, naked in the bed, the crisp sheets cool against her bare skin. The heat from his body was enough to warm her.

He ducked his head between her legs and worked her into a frenzy. She couldn't help herself. She arched to meet his mouth, dug her fingers in his hair. At the moment she was about to lose herself, as if he knew, he pulled back, left her panting, dying for more. He rose up above her, slid his hands up her rib cage, around to her back, down under her ass, and let his body move up the length of her, his mouth finding her lips as he lifted her slightly off the bed and entered her, fast and hard, with one thrust.

She moaned into his mouth. He didn't move. They were touching from head to toe, connected, joined, him deep inside of her, and the thought, the feeling was too much. She felt the waves of her orgasm begin. He let her finish before he started to move, slowly, barely a whisper, pulling nearly all the way out before sliding back inside her, so deep, deeper than anything she'd ever felt, faster now, the rhythm she'd sensed in their earlier kiss building, and he was whispering to her, words she couldn't understand, didn't want to understand, she just wanted more of him, wanted him to go faster, and the orgasm built again.

The whispering grew louder, he was telling her how much he loved her, how special she was, how he'd never felt anything like this before, and as he finally reached the end, losing all of himself into her, his mouth sought hers again for a last kiss, and she felt like their souls were on fire.

She was lost.

Lost in the sensations—of being loved, of being touched, of the newness, of feeling his hard, tight body in her arms. She didn't want him to stop. She wanted this to go on forever.

He rose, the weight of his body no longer pinning her to the bed.

"Sleep now. I must go. I love you."

She rolled, catching the pillow, pulled it to her as if it were her lover. Drew her legs up until she was fetal, the pulsing of her desire still coursing through her veins, making her muscles twitch.

Dear God, she had no idea it would be like that with him.

She was so tired.

"Why were you outside?"

He didn't answer, and the words died on her lips.

Sleep took her.

CHAPTER THIRTY-ONE

Sam's day in the autopsy suite was finally over. Things had gone relatively smoothly, considering how short-handed she was. There had been eight guests today, which meant they'd had to rotate the bodies in and out in shifts.

There'd been a small mishap when one of the techs had nicked an aorta, and the chest cavity of the man he was working on had filled with blood, sending Sam and another tech rushing for a ladle and a plastic pint container so they could save the aortic blood for the samples, but, overall, nothing terribly out of the ordinary.

Toxicology had come back on Marias González. Sadly, the final autopsy findings showed the woman had been in very good health. She would have lived many more fruitful years had she not been mown down in the middle of the street.

Untimely death always saddened Sam. Lord knows she saw enough of it in this town. Drugs and gangs and prostitutes; the natural but unattended deaths of an aging society; accidents; suicides and murders. There was nothing that didn't cross her table. She certainly knew she hadn't seen it all, but she'd seen enough. Having children of her own had changed her perspective, given her more compassion for the families who came to Forensic Medical to identify their loved ones. She still had a great deal of detachment, but being best friends with Taylor, seeing the insanity that seemed to follow *her,* Sam had an appreciation for life that she wasn't sure she'd had before.

Almost dying did that to a girl.

Which brought her full circle. She was still so mad at Taylor. What was she thinking, kissing Memphis? That was going to lead someplace very bad. And then Sam would be caught in the middle. Damn it, she had her own problems to deal with.

She had a stack of paperwork to attend to before she left for the day. She settled in—signing orders, signing off on yesterday's autopsies, finding a good rhythm. The stack grew smaller. She might make beef stew for dinner, something warm and hearty. She used to have time to make bread, but with the kids being so little, that was always hard.

Bam. The loss hit her like a hammer to the temple.

She took a deep breath in and closed her eyes, waited for the wave of intense longing to pass.

It was amazing how the mind worked. She didn't need to see a child on the street, or think of a baby. Something as mundane as the idea of not being able to make bread brought it all back.

The knife sliding into her flesh, the cramping, the sheer horror of knowledge.

She was a doctor. She knew exactly what that knife had done. She'd winced when she dissected Marias

González's womb, knowing that's what hers looked like, so small and inconsequential, so vastly empty.

The blade had sliced the anterior edge away, just there.

God, she was going to have to go see Taylor's shrink if she couldn't get her head wrapped around this.

Keri McGee appeared in her doorway, knocked softly on the wood. "Did you hear? About the standoff?"

Sam was grateful for the distraction. "What standoff?" she asked.

"Turn on your television."

Sam grabbed the remote from the coffee cup she usually left it in and powered up her TV.

"Hit WSMV, they've got the best camera angle," Keri said. "But it's on everywhere."

Sam inputted channel four and sat back in her chair. A breaking news banner was on the bottom of the screen, it read: Serial Bank Robber Suspect in Standoff with Metro Police. A raven-haired reporter was speaking into the microphone. Sam recognized the backdrop. They were in Belle Meade, by the country club. It looked like they were on Chickering Road, right near where she grew up.

"Shit." Sam pulled the phone toward her and dialed Marcus Wade. He answered on the third ring. She could hear a ton of noise in the background.

"What's happened? You've only been gone for three hours."

"Hey. Had a break. Marias's husband decided to talk. She's a house cleaner, works for Executive Cleaners. Long story short, Marias found the money and a wig while she was cleaning, completely by accident. She took some cash with her as proof to report the man to us, but she didn't think we'd believe her. She's been sitting on that money for two weeks. Finally decided to come forward, but from what I can piece together, she decided to tell the robber herself first, plead for him to turn himself in. He refused."

"That wasn't smart."

"No, it wasn't. He must have been watching her, hoping she didn't turn him in. When he saw that she was, he had no choice but to stop her. Marias wouldn't tell her husband the man's name, so we cross-checked all the clients of the cleaning service with DMV and found the Jaguar. It's registered to a Douglas Bowerman. He's a freaking lawyer, of all things. Nice house. But he's going under, the bank foreclosed on him. He got desperate. We got paper, went to arrest him, but he had other plans. Barricaded himself. He's got a wife and kids in there. I take it you're watching?"

"Yeah. Think Keller will be able to talk him out?" Joe Keller, their hostage negotiator, was a tough, nononsense cop, and a great favorite of Taylor's. She had trained for SWAT and had worked with Keller many times. Sam didn't know him as well, but had faith that if anyone could end this peacefully, Keller was the man.

"Honestly? I don't know. He's been volatile so far. It was just a matter of time before someone got hurt."

"You're sure it was him driving the Jaguar, not his wife?"

"I'd like a chance to ask. But I don't know if I'm going to get that. Hey, I gotta go. They're going to toss in some flash bangs, see if they can't roust him."

"Good luck. Stay safe."

Marcus hung up and Sam dangled the phone between

her fingers for a few minutes. Keri watched her, rolling her hands together.

Sam put the phone back on the hook and viewed the television for a minute. There was a flurry of activity, and the reporter looked scared.

So much for things ending well.

"You geared up?" Sam asked Keri.

"You think we'll be needed? I'm supposed to be off in twenty minutes."

"I wouldn't be surprised. These things don't usually work out, not when it's a criminal with nothing to lose. He's most likely already killed one person. There's no good way out."

"Dr. Loughley, I know I'm on duty tonight…but I was hoping… I sort of have a Christmas party I'm sup-posed to attend. My boyfriend's company get-together. Though if you need me, I'm happy to stay."

Of course she did.

"Go on, then," Sam said. "Have fun."

Keri rewarded her with a wide smile. Sam remembered what it was like to be excited about a date. She'd like to recapture some of that for herself. Karma…

More action on the television screen, and the reporter started yelling, "Oh my God, were those gunshots?" She turned to the camera, realized the cameras were still running, and became suddenly grave. "There has been gunplay tonight in Belle Meade, where we're standing in front of a home…"

The phone rang. Sam caught the caller ID. Marcus. So much for the beef stew.

CHAPTER THIRTY-TWO

Taylor woke flushed and lazy, and as she came to, horrified. Oh, God. What had she done?

She had a wicked headache, different than usual—harder, more insistent—almost like she was hungover. She hadn't had *that* much to drink. Maybe she was coming down with something. Yes, maybe. In any event, she was glad Memphis wasn't there. Facing him in her bed in the morning felt too familiar for where they stood in their relationship.

God. Baldwin would never forgive her.

Could she forgive herself?

She got showered and dressed. Avoided looking herself in the eye. She wasn't proud of what happened last night. But at least now she knew. Things could be good with Memphis. Very, very good. She checked her phone, and saw that she still hadn't gotten a call from Baldwin.

She couldn't fit both of them in her brain right now. Maybe she could ring the bell, and ask for breakfast to be served in her room instead. She didn't know if she could face Memphis just yet.

Grow up, Taylor, she told herself. *You're a big girl.*

You did it, and now you have to pay the price. Go have breakfast with the man and get it over with.

She went to the door, surprised to see the chair still leaning against it. She wondered how he could have pulled that off.

As she touched the wooden arm, it fell over with a crash. It hadn't been wedged in at all, just leaned delicately. He must have set it there as he left, snuck out of her room before the servants were the wiser. Now that was a fancy trick.

The hallway seemed much longer than ever before. Eyes followed her. She could swear she saw the Pretender standing in the doorway of the billiards room, leaning back against the frame, one ankle hooked over the other, a toothpick in the corner of his mouth.

Blood streaming from the bullet hole in his forehead, a dark gape in his perfectly white skin.

She shook her head and looked back. The doorway was empty.

She scurried into the dining room. Memphis was alone, waiting for her.

"Morning. Everything okay?"

She nodded. Made no mention of the strange sense from the hallway, her bizarre dreams the night before, or Trixie's late-night visit, or his follow-up. Now, in the light of day, she felt rather foolish about the whole thing—she hadn't had a morning-after walk of shame in a long, long time.

She sat down quickly, knocking a fork onto the floor.

Good grief, girl. Get it together.

Memphis was downright cheerful. Of course he was. His nocturnal sojourn didn't show in the least. Instead, he seemed rested and comfortable in tan cords, a white button-down and a shaggy green sweater under a dark gray fleece vest. It seemed he was back to himself. There were no shadows from yesterday's misfire at the bridge, nor any inkling that he'd been directly responsible for Taylor's disturbed night's rest.

"How are you this fine day?" he asked.

She opened her mouth to answer and stopped herself. She didn't want to share that she had her voice back. Not just yet. That was something she needed to keep inside. And to be honest, she didn't know exactly what to say.

She had stashed her notebook in her back pocket when she left the room, a cop's habit as much as anything, so she pulled it out.

Cat apparently has my tongue.

He laughed. "Are you sure you're okay? You look like you were up all night."

She shot him a look. There was no one around; he could talk about it.

Well, that's because I was. Having the most terrible thoughts.

He didn't rise to the bait.

"Take it easy today, okay? Jet lag can be a monster. Plan your day so you can have a nap. It will make you feel better."

Um, yeah. Okay. He really wasn't going to say anything. What the hell? She wasn't even good enough for a mention? She buried her face in her teacup. This was beyond embarrassing.

She just wanted him to leave. Then she could go back to bed and sleep. Sleep would be good. She was exhausted. She'd gotten maybe a full two hours last night, in spurts. The melatonin was working; she'd have to let Maddee know. She was more tired than she'd been in years. If only it worked on headaches. And heartbreak.

She wanted to ask about the bridge. About Evan. She just didn't know how to bring it up.

They settled into breakfast, the usual Scottish fare— this time with porridge on the side, which Taylor was surprised to find she loved, since she wasn't a huge oatmeal fan.

Memphis finally pushed away his plate and smiled. Not the lazy, come-hither grin he was so good at, but a tight, perfunctory smile.

"You'll be okay while I'm gone?"

She flipped to a fresh page.

Of course. Too much on my plate already. All this healing and resting to do, it's going to be exhausting. What about you?

"I'll be fine. Don't let Maddee push you around. If you're not comfortable, you just tell her to stop, okay? Same goes for anyone here on the estate. You're to treat this as your own home, and everyone has been instructed to give you anything your heart desires."

Don't need anything. Planning to rest, read, work with Maddee, take a few walks. That's all.

"Be sure you have Jacques take you ferreting for rabbits, though. That's great fun."

*Ferreting for rabbits· Check· On the list· Any-
thing else?*

"I think you'll do. Just make sure to stay in touch—
email or text me and let me know you're okay. I won't
be gone more than a couple of days. I'll be back at the
weekend. I'll take you to Ben Nevis, we'll hike up the
mountain."

Ben Nevis?

"The highest peak in Scotland. Beautiful views of
the great glens."

Sounds lovely·

"It will be. I promise. I've got to run now, my train
is at ten. I'll see you in a couple of days. Will you be
able to find your way to your rooms?"

It's like second nature·

He laughed, then kissed her lightly on the forehead. He let his hand linger on the top of her head for
a moment. She didn't know whether to raise her chin
and invite him to kiss her lips, or pull away and cower
under the table. She was no better than a schoolgirl.

She did neither, just sat there, frozen and immobile.

"Bye, Taylor."

He was gone. She heard him banter for a few moments with Trixie, then things went silent.

Well.

She knew the Brits were a bit buttoned-down, but
really. Last night deserved at least some sort of mention.

Unless he hadn't enjoyed it—no, he had. There wasn't much mistaking that.

Maybe he wanted her to make the next move. No pressure. She couldn't remember all the details, had she told him to never mention it again? Because that's how he was acting. He was sometimes good at following her directions. Or maybe he was embarrassed, too?

Her range of emotions finally settled on relief. She needed to get her head on straight about this. Decide what it was she really wanted. She'd made a mistake. A big one. One that she'd felt in her bones she might make. And now that she had, well, she regretted it. Fully.

After the strangeness last night, having him gone seemed preferable. The idea of him creeping around outside at night freaked her out anyway. And that he could get into her room anytime he wanted... Yes, him leaving was for the best. She'd broach the subject of Evan and the bridge on a chat, where she could really express herself.

She stowed her embarrassment at him not bothering to mention their liaison. He was leaving it all up to her.

The day stretched before her. It was cold outside, but she definitely wanted a walk. Maddee would be here at ten to have her session. She had an hour to herself—maybe now would be the perfect time to stretch her legs. Or curl up and relax. She was awfully tired.

She glanced in the hall before she left the dining room. It was empty. Nothing lingering. Maddee's hypnosis had helped her find a way back to her voice, but it seemed like she'd tapped into something else too, something darker. Maybe today they could exorcise those thoughts completely as well.

Taylor left the dining room, took a moment in the hall

to orient herself, then set off for her stairs. It didn't take long for her to get turned around. She backtracked and took the right staircase, found her hallway. But the door was in the wrong place. She realized she was standing in front of Memphis's office.

Any port in a storm, she thought, and tried the knob. It was locked.

She debated for half a second, then remembered the key in her back pocket. The door had an old-fashioned locking mechanism; it looked similar to the gate to the gardens.

Glancing over her shoulder one more time, she slid the key into the lock. Turned it. Was only half-surprised when it opened.

The skeleton key must be the master. For the whole castle.

He wouldn't have given it to her if he didn't want her to use it, right?

Rationalization was the most useful skill of all.

She slipped inside and shut the door behind her.

The office was strangely empty. There was no fire in the grate, and thankfully, unlike her dream, no blood dripping from the walls. Just Memphis's elegant roll-top desk, left open, with stacks of paper on it. He was a horizontal filer. That was interesting. Baldwin was just the opposite. Everything had its place. His desk was always clean.

Now you're going to compare their filing systems?

She shook her head. Comparing them, anything about them, was a path to sure destruction.

A discarded newspaper sat on top of the pile. Obviously the cleaning elves hadn't made it to this room yet. She wondered what the newspaper held. She'd take it back to her room, cozy up to the fire for an hour, and read it before she met with Maddee. A normal morning thing to do.

A framed picture of Evan sat on the corner of Memphis's desk. She hadn't noticed it yesterday, but that didn't mean anything. She hadn't been snooping yesterday. She picked up the silver frame and looked at her host's dead wife.

There was a resemblance between herself and Evan, without a doubt. She'd noted it in other photos before. But Evan looked so much more carefree in this photo than Taylor ever felt. Perhaps it was the weight of her job, what she saw, what she'd done, but Taylor didn't ever remember feeling as light as Evan looked. She was a simpler woman. An easier woman. But of course, she was dead. Memphis must see something of a replacement in Taylor.

She set the photo down. No sense going there. Memphis had been clear about what he wanted, had shown her the possibilities. Regardless, he was her friend, nothing more.

So what was she doing in his office, looking through his desk?

She sat heavily in his desk chair. The scent of him, all leather and wood smoke, lingered in the room. He smelled different here than in America, where he'd been subjected to hotel soaps. Here, he smelled real. Maybe he was right not to mention anything. Maybe they could forget it ever happened. She wished to God it hadn't. And she was going to have to bear that knowledge for the rest of her life.

Annoyed, she grabbed the newspaper. There was

a file underneath it, sitting on the top of his desk. She read the tab. It was labeled *Evan*.

Evan?

She glanced over her shoulder. Listened carefully. No one was around to see her sneak a peek.

The file was about an inch thick. She used a pencil to open it.

There was a picture of Evan on the top, and a pile of newspaper clippings underneath. Taylor set the pencil down and leafed through them. As she already knew, the story of Evan's death had made the front page of all of the U.K. papers. *The Scotsman* had done the most intensive stories, with deep background on Evan, her family, and her life.

Taylor realized it would take her hours to go through all the material. She didn't know why this file was left out, practically in the open, for anyone to see. Anyone who had a key to his office, that is...

But Memphis was gone, and would be for a few days, at least. She might as well take it with her, read at her leisure. She needed to get going if she was going to make her meeting with Maddee anyway.

She tucked the file inside the newspaper, just in case one of the servants came along. If it were private, Memphis would have locked it up—heck, maybe he'd left it for her, knowing she was interested. Maybe it had answers to questions she didn't know to ask.

As she turned to go, she saw a glimpse of red, just a quick flash out of the corner of her eye. Her heart rate sped up, and the hair on her arms stood on end. She forced herself to look into her peripheral vision. There was nothing.

Get a grip, Taylor. You're being an absolute idiot.

She folded the newspaper around the file and stuck it under her arm. She started to stroll out the door, going for nonchalant. Two steps in, she tripped. The newspaper and the file flew out like a flushed quail. She reached to catch herself on the doorjamb. She tried to curse but nothing came out, which frustrated her even more. She looked at the floor and saw a small needle-point-covered footstool. She kicked it over, then, feeling guilty, uprighted it and moved it out of the path to the desk. Stupid footstool.

The file's contents were spread out in a five-foot radius. There was no way to cover up that she'd been looking through it now. She gathered all the paper up and managed to get out of Memphis's office without further mishap. She hurried to her room, barred the door behind her and sighed in relief.

The fire was cozy, fresh tea had been laid out by the chair. She sat down, poured herself a cup, put the file with Evan's stories in the top desk drawer and covered it with stationery. She'd read through it all later, try to get it back in order.

She opened the paper instead.

The front page focused on the latest tragedy on the A9 near Inverness, deemed one of the most dangerous roads in Scotland. They'd driven right past that spot yesterday. Creepy.

A fisherman had gone missing off the Hebrides. And there was a small story about the missing London girls. Memphis's case.

She skipped the rest of the news and read about it with interest. Memphis had mentioned he wasn't completely convinced that they were on the right path. Maybe she could help.

The paper had seized on the one thing the girls had in common—the church that Urq built.

Urq, as he called himself, was an interesting character. His real name was Roger Waterstone. He was the son of the famous British financier, Stephen Waterstone, and heir to the family fortune. He'd been educated at the finest schools, dated the finest women. For fun, he'd pursued a career as an architect.

Four years ago, he'd disappeared. Went to Bali for vacation and never came back. She remembered reading about the case; it was rather high-profile at the time.

Then his father died, and Roger reappeared, a changed man. He'd found God. He used some of his inheritance to start a church. Brought together people from all walks of life. Stopped short of saying he was the messiah, but Taylor couldn't help but think this was a cult. It had all the markers.

If he wasn't above murder to get his point across... How did his father die again?

"Yoo-hoo! Earth to Taylor...."

She jumped a mile. Maddee was shouting and knocking on her door.

She went to the door and pulled it open. Maddee looked genuinely relieved to see her. Goodness, she must have everyone in the house and surrounds worried about her. Or Memphis told them she was terribly delicate and needed looking after. Most likely the latter.

"Finally. I've been knocking for five minutes. When you didn't show up downstairs I decided to fetch you myself. That old bat Trixie is off in the kitchens, but she let me in so I could come by. Are you ready?"

Taylor nodded.

"Okay. Let's go then."

She let Taylor out the door in front of her, but glanced back over her shoulder. "I've stayed in this room before. One of those nights when they had a party and we couldn't make it home. It's changed a bit since last time. I don't remember all the books."

A gift from Memphis·

Taylor wondered if it was her imagination, but she could have sworn Maddee's smile grew tight. Hmm. Maybe Dr. James had a bit of a thing for her friend Memphis.

It was understandable. Memphis *was* handsome, obviously witty and fun, and heir to a massive fortune. He was certainly a catch. But Maddee was married to his best friend, and supposed to be a close friend to Memphis's dead wife. Perhaps that hadn't been the case after all.

Taylor made a mental note and let the thought go. Women were strange creatures when it came to attraction, that much she knew. They got territorial, even with their male friends that they had no amorous intentions toward. She didn't plan to get involved in the dynamics of their relationship any more than she had to.

"Our Memphis was always one for grand gestures. You'd best be careful, he'll sweep you right off your feet and you won't want to leave."

Taylor let that one go. God, if Maddee had any idea of what had transpired in here last night...

She followed Maddee down the stairs. Her long hair was in a bun today, drawn back from her face sharply. It looked uncomfortable, pulled so tight, like a ballerina about to go on stage. Taylor's omnipresent headache throbbed in camaraderie. She hated wearing her hair down. But she didn't have a choice; the pressure of her ponytail was too much to take.

The drawing room was set up just as before—the EMDR equipment on the table, a fresh and full tea cart at the ready. Taylor gladly accepted a cup. Her throat was terribly sore and the warmth helped. She wondered how many pounds of tea the estate went through in a year.

"How are you sleeping?" Maddee asked, handing Taylor her laptop to write with. Taylor didn't know why, but she didn't want Maddee to know she had her voice back yet, either. She was being foolish, she knew that. The minute Maddee did the hypnosis, she'd be yakking up a storm. It just felt…private, somehow.

Sleeping is okay. Bad dreams, but I'm actually tired. That's new.

"So the melatonin helped you sleep?"

Helped me GET to sleep, yes.

"That's wonderful. You can take up to two capsules at night. That will really knock you out. How's the headache?"

Bad in the evening, but if I take the meds early it simmers down to a dull roar. The Percocet does a good job taking away the worst of the pain. Either that, or I'm getting used to it.

"Any dreams? Good ones, bad ones?"

Some. A couple of bad nightmares. Creepy stuff.

Maddee laughed. "It's this castle. Plays tricks on the mind. They claim it's haunted. I think that's wishful thinking. Drives the tourists in. Personally, I don't believe in ghosts."

Me either.

Truly, Taylor didn't believe in ghosts. But she did believe in the power of suggestion to kick-start her imagination. That's why she hated ghost stories, and horror movies. She'd seen enough bad things in real life. She didn't need someone else's overactive imagination horning in on her.

"All right then. Anything else you want me to know?"

Maddee seemed a bit distracted this morning, but Taylor didn't think it was necessary to point that out.

Maybe just one thing. I… How to put this without sounding completely nutty? I've been seeing things. Just flashes, really, of things and people who aren't there.

Maddee sat back in her chair. She played with an oversize ring on her right hand, heavy gold with an onyx stone. "You know, there are many accounts of people with head trauma who are left with echoes of things that happened before the accident. Seen it a few times myself, too. This is normal, Taylor. It means you're healing. Your brain is rewiring itself after a severe shock.

Even a bad concussion can cause these echoes. It's perfectly natural to be unnerved by it. Anyone would."

A sigh escaped Taylor's lips. That's what it was, then. She wasn't being haunted. It was all in her head.

Though the Pretender standing in a doorway wasn't an echo, or a remembrance. It was a new image, and felt more like a message. A threat.

She didn't tell Maddee that.

"Anything else I need to know about?"

Taylor shook her head.

"Then let's get started. Lay back for me now, and think about that warm sunlight hitting your toes. That should be a nice change from the chilly weather we're having."

Maddee took five minutes to get Taylor into her relaxed state, watching the blue balloon lift into the sky before asking her to revisit the hour before the shooting. Taylor felt her blood pressure rise immediately. She didn't really want to go there. But Maddee was insistent, and her voice was so gentle and soft, so comforting, that Taylor allowed herself to be pulled under. Maddee talked for a few more minutes, then dove in.

"We're going to talk about Sam now. You knew she'd been kidnapped, correct? And answer me aloud, Taylor."

"Yes."

"And you knew where the Pretender had taken her, correct?"

"Yes."

"When did you know that?"

"I'd always known that it would end there. That's what he wanted. He liked the idea of a show, of continuity. But when we realized Sam was missing, that's when I knew we were coming to the end."

"And how long did it take you to get to the house?"

Taylor squirmed. The balloon started to fade.

"Taylor, look at the balloon. Let your arm rise in the air, light and carefree. It's okay. You're safe here."

The balloon reappeared, pale and translucent against a cartoon-blue sky, though it was fighting to float away.

"Good job. Now, tell me. How long did it take you to get to Sam?"

"No more than an hour. I had to find a way into the house. I couldn't just go bang on the front door."

"But if you'd called for backup, you could have done that."

"No. I couldn't. I had to go myself. I had to finish it."

"But in that hour, what happened? Isn't that when the Pretender was torturing Sam? If you had gone straight to the house the moment you knew she was there, could you have saved her baby?"

"I don't... I—"

"Taylor, think about the moment just before you entered the house. You wanted to kill the Pretender, didn't you? You wanted to make him go away, to stop hurting you and your friends. That's good, Taylor. It's good to want to eradicate evil. That's what your job is, to find and kill the people who hurt innocents. That's why you've been put on this earth, to eliminate those kinds of people."

Taylor shook her head. No. No—she wasn't supposed to kill them. She respected the law, even though it didn't always work perfectly. This case, the Pretender, that wasn't how things were. It was a one-time thing.

She wasn't like her father, bending the rules when they didn't suit him.

Was she?

"It wasn't like that."

"You say that now. But when you're faced with another adversary, another killer who gets in your way, your first inclination will be to kill them. To eliminate them. To assassinate them. To, what did you say, 'put him down'? That's what you do. That's what you're good at. Look at your record. So many police officers never fire their weapon, yet you've killed four people. Tried to make that five. You are a weapon, Taylor. And if you're honest with yourself, you like it. You like killing. It makes you feel good. You could have saved Sam, and instead, you followed your own path so you could see what it felt like to murder someone."

"*No!*"

The balloon was gone. The calming pool of light disappeared, leaving her chilled and shaking on the couch. She didn't want to open her eyes.

Was that true? If faced with the situation again, would she choose to kill? Was it the easy way out? Had she lost her moral compass entirely?

Dr. James surely seemed to think she had. And her own actions last night certainly pointed in that direction. Was a moral compass key to getting her job back? Would her team think she was trigger-happy? No, they didn't know. They couldn't know. *No one* knew that she'd planned to take out the Pretender herself. No one knew that. Until she'd spilled her guts to Maddee James.

She opened her eyes. Maddee was standing over her, watching, a small smile on her face. Taylor jerked back and upset her teacup with a clatter. It spilled to the carpet unheeded.

Maddee stepped back and shook her head. "Sorry, I was just trying to see if you were still under."

"Not very—what the hell, Maddee? I am not some blunt instrument that kills for fun. I've only ever killed when I had no other choice, in self-defense. I hate that I had to, every moment of every day."

"Wow. Your voice, Taylor. You're back. And you aren't under hypnosis. You're speaking again. Well done."

Maddee sat back on her chair, quietly contemplating Taylor. She steepled her fingers under her chin.

"Now. Let's talk about what just happened. Do you really believe that's true, Taylor? Be honest with me. Hell, be honest with yourself. If you look inside your soul, to your very core, can't you admit that a part of you liked it? Liked planning to kill him?"

"No. Are you out of your mind? Absolutely not. It haunts me, Maddee. That's why I'm here, trying to get away from it."

Maddee shook her head slowly. She wasn't smiling anymore.

"Oh, but Taylor, it's all inside of *you*. *You* have free will. *You* have a choice. Even when your life, or lives around you, were in danger, you *chose* to kill. To end a life. What does that make you, hmm? How is that any better than doing it instinctually?"

Taylor didn't like this at all. She wasn't here to answer for her past sins. She was here to exorcise the demon of what she'd almost allowed herself to do. To regain control over herself, not go deeper into the abyss.

"Taylor, you're not in therapy to regain your voice.

That was a surface issue, a symptom. You're here be-cause the people around you don't trust you anymore. Whether you realize it or not."

"No. That's not true."

"You're here alone, aren't you? My God, you're on an entirely different continent. Your boss wouldn't let you go back to work. Your best friend is back in the States, letting you go through this alone. Your fiancé is off doing his own work. Even Memphis has left you behind. You're here, all alone, because even you rec-ognize that you've lost control. You've lost your edge. You've become the people you hunt. And everyone but you seems to know it."

Taylor stood up, teeth gritted. Frustration made her cry, and she refused to let that happen now.

Don't you dare do it, Taylor. Don't you even think about it. You've shown her enough weakness. Walk away. Walk away now.

"I think we're done here."

"Don't go, Taylor. Don't run away now. We're just starting to get somewhere." Maddee sat contritely on the chair, her hand extended. "Please, sit down."

Taylor shook her head. No. She was done.

CHAPTER THIRTY-THREE

Taylor grabbed her boots and Memphis's jacket and took off out onto the grounds of the estate. It was freezing cold, about to snow, but she didn't care. She just needed to get away. Away from Maddee and her accusations, away from herself.

She heard a car engine revving and looked over her shoulder. Maddee's Mercedes. She was leaving. Good. Taylor didn't want to be anywhere near the woman. She didn't want to see Dr. Madeira James ever again.

She turned and headed off into the woods. Memphis said she could have anything she wanted. And right now, she wanted that *therapist* to go directly to hell.

She shoved her hands in the pockets of the coat to find her gloves. Instead, she found a pill bottle. Her Percocet. She didn't remember putting it in there, but she was glad she had—her head was splitting. The demons from the past hour were close about. She popped the bottle open and shook two pills into her hand. Swallowed them dry, forcing them past the lump in her throat.

Leaves lay thick on the path, reds and oranges and golds, as if it were a gaudy New England fall. The seasons here were not distinct. She knew the temperatures were relatively consistent, a range that normally covered no more than thirty degrees between winter and summer.

The dogs were barking, chasing each other around in circles down the path toward the gardens. She avoided them, cut north, going up the hill. She didn't know where she was going, just that she wanted to be away.

She could feel the storm brewing. There was a displacement to the air that she recognized from big weather at home. She hadn't been paying too much attention to the forecast, just assumed it would be cold and rainy, with a few flakes of snow thrown in for good measure. She'd have to check it when she got back. She'd bet her life it was going to snow, and snow hard.

The path went steeply up a hill, and she followed it blindly, seething, angry with herself for rising to the bait, and wondering just what Maddee intended. Some sort of reverse psychology perhaps, or something meant to break her down, like they do in the military?

Taylor wasn't familiar with therapy, per se. She'd done her scheduled meetings with the department shrink as required for her fitness reports over the years, but she hadn't spent any time on the couch herself outside of this recent…situation. Despite her earlier thoughts, she had changed her mind. She hated therapy. Hated it with a passion.

The path straightened and she realized she was out of breath. She stopped for a moment, laid a cold hand on the moss-covered stone wall to her right, and looked around her. There was forest on three sides, and a smallish village in front of her. She assumed that was where the original town would have been, housing the support staff for the estate—a smith, a distillery and the like. In front of her was a small stone bridge arching over the road, and to her left, barely shielded by the large stone fence and the heavy tree cover, she could see a pile of stones.

She set off in that direction. After twenty feet, the path opened into a clearing, and she realized she'd stumbled onto the back way into the estate's kirk. The church was missing its roof. The windows were caved in as if the eyes of the building had gone blind, and the doorway resembled a mouth crying out in agony. Another ruin, the second she'd seen on Highsmythe land. It pissed her off even more. Did these people care nothing for their past? Were they so busy with their ghosts that they didn't bother with their souls' shelters?

She picked her way closer, through the moss and lichen-covered gravestones. There was a clear path here, the leaves brushed out of the way. Someone had been here recently.

There was a large gravestone, not weathered and covered in lichen like the others, but still shining with the moist green mold that coated most everything inanimate in the Highlands—fences, stones, roofs, trees. Graves.

There was a small bundle of heather intertwined with roses, still fresh, at the base of the grave. She looked at the names, and everything clicked.

EVANELLE FRASER HIGHSMYTHE
BELOVED WIFE
MAY 8, 1974 – DECEMBER 21, 2008
JAMES FRASER HIGHSMYTHE
DARLING SON
DECEMBER 21, 2008
TAKEN TOO SOON. YOU WILL NEVER BE FORGOTTEN.

She was standing on Evan's grave, and the grave of Memphis's unborn son.

Her mind whirled. Memphis had been visiting Evan's grave last night, right before he came to her room and made love to her.

Not twelve hours after he kissed Taylor right on the spot where his wife died.

My God. What kind of man was he?

She wondered if he visited his wife's grave often; she knew he wasn't in the Highlands much anymore. Surely he was just tending to her grave. But in the middle of the night?

Looking around to her right and left, she saw the detritus that answered the question for her—small candles, broken stems, pieces of paper. A proper vigil had been kept here.

She looked at the date again and realized it was the anniversary of Evan's death.

Jesus. Today was December 21. She'd never thought to ask Memphis when she died. She knew it had been recent, but she'd never asked the actual date. And here she was, at his mercy, a pseudo-surrogate, on the death's anniversary.

She whispered a prayer, of forgiveness, of apology, to Evan's spirit, then backed away and headed back to the castle. She needed to get away from here.

She started down the path and saw a flash of red. She tried to ignore it, turned her head away, picked up her pace until she was almost running. But it followed, growing closer, larger, and she finally stopped and collapsed in the middle of the path, arms over her head, silently crying out, willing it, whatever it was, to go away.

She was shaking, not from the cold, but from fear. She didn't want to open her eyes, but when nothing happened, she finally screwed up her courage and looked.

There was nothing. Just the ever-present forest of trees, the thin blanket of leaves on the ground, and the chilled air.

She got up and turned slowly in a three-hundred-and-sixty-degree circle.

Nothing but the gulls, soaring into the gray sky.

She knew she hadn't imagined the red wave. It was almost like a cloth that had been draped in a breeze, flowing and rippling in the air, but luminous, more gossamer than thick. A disturbance in the air. Didn't Memphis mention the ghost seemed borne of synesthesia to him? Was it possible that she was seeing the same thing?

Was Evan haunting her? Following her around the grounds of the estate? Coming to her in the night? Memphis had said the Lady in Red didn't appear to anyone but the male heir to the title. Perhaps he was wrong. Perhaps all dead Highsmythe brides became the Lady in Red, and haunted whomever they damn well pleased.

She set off down the path, determined to gather herself once and for all. She was overly tired—a nap, her anxiety medicine and something stronger than tea was in order. She felt like an invalid, worthless to herself. She needed to get it together.

The first flakes of snow began to fall as she got to the back entrance, dancing lightly in the air. She stopped to watch their intricate ballet. Now this, this was real. Abundant water vapor causing small particles of ice, too heavy to be contained in the clouds, to fall to the earth. Science. Incontrovertible evidence. But at one time, it must have seemed like magic.

She opened her mouth and let one settle on her tongue, a cold pill that melted immediately. She took comfort in the fact that all things had an explanation, and headed inside.

The castle corridors were quiet. Deathly so. She hurried to her room, stripped off her outdoor gear, and grabbed her phone. There was a missed call from Baldwin. She took a deep breath. She pushed all thoughts of Memphis and last night out of her head. The two men were mutually exclusive in her mind. They had to be.

She dialed him back, and sank in the chair across from the fire as the phone began to ring.

"Hey," he answered. "I've been trying to reach you."

"I'm sorry. I went for a walk. It's starting to snow." Calm. Banal. Perfect.

"Whoa! When did your voice come back?"

"During a hypnosis session with Maddee James. But I'm finished with her. She's not very nice."

She dropped another log on the fire.

"Well, I'm glad it's back. It sounds wonderful, darling. You'll be ready to go home in no time. Now you can just have a little vacation and relax. Right?"

"Yeah. So long as I don't have any more bad dreams."

"Why are you having bad dreams?"

What to tell him about that? That she was being visited by otherworldly creatures? That she thought Memphis's dead wife was shadowing her? Hardly.

"Overactive imagination. They've been telling me ghost stories. I have nothing to occupy my brain."

"That's what happens on vacation. I saw on the news there's a big storm heading your way."

"Where are you? Can you say?"

"Trust me, you don't want to know. But everything is fine. Case closed. The question is, will you be all right there by yourself?"

Oh, Baldwin. Will I? I hope so.

"Wait. How do you know that I'm going to be alone? Do you have someone watching me?" Her voice ratcheted up an octave. "What the hell, Baldwin?"

"Honey, that's not what's going on. Don't be paranoid. Of course you'll be fine. I know there are plenty of people around there. I know Memphis isn't there, that's all I meant."

"I'm not being paranoid. I hate it when you say that. How did you know Memphis was gone?"

"He called me from London. He said you suggested he ask me for help."

Memphis. You son of a bitch.

He better keep his fool mouth shut. God, if he made some sort of sly comment and tipped Baldwin off, she'd never forgive him.

"That's a change of circumstance."

Baldwin laughed lightly. "Sweetie. Please, let's not fight. It's just so good to hear your voice again. That means you're getting better."

Baldwin kept chattering, seeking to connect with her. Damn, this was insane. His voice brought up all kinds of crazy emotions in her. She missed him. She was afraid to see him. She wanted his arms around her. She wanted him to stay away.

What had she done?

She loved him. She did. More than anything. And she didn't feel like she could even tell him that, not without him getting suspicious. She needed him, not Memphis.

She knew that. She'd always known that. God, she was so upset she was feeling dizzy. She took a few deep breaths for good measure.

"Honey? What's happening up there? You sound really upset."

"Just…give me a second," she managed to say.

Get it together, fool. She swallowed hard, cleared her throat, and started again.

"I miss you."

His voice warmed. "I miss you, too. No pressure, but if you want, I could come over for Christmas."

"You'd do that?"

"I'll do whatever you want, sweetie."

She couldn't help herself, she had to ask.

"Why are you helping Memphis?"

"Because I owed him a favor. It's a long story. I'll tell you about it when I see you, okay?"

"I should let you go. I'm getting sleepy."

"In the middle of the day? Aren't you leading the life of Riley? Lazybones."

"It's the talking. Head hurts, throat hurts."

As she said it, she realized it was true. She really wasn't feeling all that great.

"Oh, of course. I love you, honey. I'll see you in a couple of days, okay?"

"Okay."

She closed the phone and stared at it for a moment. She never felt quite so alone as she did when they disconnected—physically, emotionally, it didn't matter. When she wasn't with him, she didn't feel whole. She knew he felt the same.

A wave of guilt overwhelmed her.

He could never know about yesterday.

She'd have to find some way to explain to Memphis, to make him understand that she didn't love him. Not the way he wanted. Though his coldness this morning meant he might have already figured it out.

She was so tired. She just wanted to escape. Some oblivion. She found her medicine bottles, took her pills. Chased them with a beer.

Pill.

Beer.

Pill.

Bccr.

Anything that let her avoid thinking about Baldwin and Memphis. About Sam, and Evan, and the ghosts of dead babies.

The hours passed. She was so very tired. She decided to go ahead and take a quick nap. Maybe some sleep would sort her system out and her voice would be back when she awoke.

She drew the curtains and bolted the door. The room wasn't as dark as at night, but it was dim enough that the outside light wouldn't interfere in her sleep.

The bed was soft and inviting, and she curled up under the blanket, cozy and warm. She realized she'd forgotten to mention to Baldwin that today was the anniversary of Evan's death, to go easy on Memphis. She debated texting him, but sleep was dragging her under. She'd do it when she woke up.

She closed her eyes, and was asleep within minutes.

CHAPTER THIRTY-FOUR

Taylor woke from her nap feeling groggier than ever. She rose from the bed and stretched, then checked the clock. It was nearly four. She went to the window and pulled back the curtains. The estate had transformed while she'd been asleep. Baldwin was right about the storm. Snow gathered in piles; there was at least six inches on the ground. It was falling fast.

She went to the television and turned it on, surfed around until she found the BBC. After five minutes the weather update came on. The storm was getting worse by the minute—there could be up to three feet of snow overnight. Airports and railways were closing throughout Scotland. Which meant neither Memphis nor Baldwin would be getting up to the estate anytime soon.

Lovely.

She turned the television back off and pulled out her laptop. It was early back in the States. Sam would be in her office, prepping for the day's autopsies. Maybe she could catch her before she got lost in the land of the dead.

But Sam didn't come back right away on the chat, which meant Taylor had already missed her.

Oh, this was for the birds. All she had wanted was to get away, and now look at her. She was alone in a castle in Scotland, locked up in a snowstorm, desperately trying to reach the people in her life who'd apparently gotten on with things. Like she couldn't handle herself alone.

Maddee's voice rang in her ears: *you're here because the people around you don't trust you anymore.*

God, that hurt. She didn't know whether to believe it was true, either. She knew people had been talking about her. About her actions. Asking questions. Maybe she was deluding herself. Maybe they all knew.

The truth of the matter was she'd taken things into her own hands and gotten Sam's baby killed. There was no escaping it anymore.

There was a knock at her door.

She crossed the room and opened it. Trixie stood there, the ever-present tea cart to hand.

"Dr. James said as you may be feeling poorly. I brought ye tea to help. Will you be having dinner outside the room tonight, then?"

"Hello, Trixie."

Taylor stepped aside and let her bring in the tea. It was a job for the serving maid. Taylor wasn't sure why Trixie was continuing to handle it. But tea sounded good. It would wash the pills down just as easy as beer.

"You're not looking well, lady, if I may be so bold."

"I'm not feeling so well, Trixie. I think I'll go back to bed. Thank you for the tea. I'm going to skip dinner."

"Aye. I'll have a maid fetch your breakfast. Just ring if you need anything."

She lingered by the tea cart.

"Can I help you, Trixie?"

"Will you be needing me to draw a bath, or help ye with the tea?"

"No, Trixie, I'm fine."

The woman was nervous and jumpy. What was going on?

"All right then. You sleep well. Make sure you drink your tea."

God, this place and their tea.

"Good evening, Trixie."

She saw Trixie to the door. The corridor was cold as ice. Tendrils of freezing air reached into her room, winding around her wrists as if it wanted to drag her outside. Taylor felt the ghost before she saw it. The cold became a wall between her and the hallway, then she blinked and it appeared.

The Pretender. Standing across the way from her.

She jerked back into the room and slammed the door. The red wave coming on. Taylor latched the door behind her, breath coming short. Trixie was calling out. Oh God, it was happening again. She was allowing another innocent to be tortured, when all he wanted was her.

She breathed deeply through her nose and flung open the door, ready to charge.

But the corridor was empty.

And Trixie was nowhere to be seen.

CHAPTER THIRTY-FIVE

Memphis tucked his chin lower into his jacket to avoid the wind that was blowing down the back of his neck. Visiting Frankland Prison wasn't his favorite thing to do on a good day, much less one with lousy weather. But this was all a part of the job. Standing in line, awaiting his turn to move through the security gates into the relative warmth of the prison proper. No special preferences for a viscount here.

His detective constable, Penelope Micklebury, was obviously miserable, her nose bright red and her teeth chattering. The day was raw, the snow building rapidly. The weather forecaster said this could be a huge storm before nightfall. He was worried about Taylor, all alone back in Scotland. He could fly back up there if needs be, but if the airports closed, the train was the only option, and in heavy weather, they too could stop running. She'd be lonely, and isolated, and probably mad at him for leaving her. At least, he hoped she would be.

The thought made him feel terrible. He shouldn't be thinking of Taylor today. This was Evan's day. He'd visited her last night, knelt on her grave, begged for her forgiveness. He hated that he was in love with another woman, hated that he was sullying his wife's memory. But it had been three years. When would be the right time to move on? His heart already had. It was his head that was giving him problems.

And right now, he had to get his head in the game. They were going to interview a former associate of Roger Waterstone, now known as the prophet Urq. He'd offered to give information in exchange for consideration on his extensive sentence.

The queue began to move.

"Finally. Do me a favor, Pen. You talk. This fine young gentleman might open up to you more than me."

"Of course," she answered, cool and collected. He pretended not to see her smile. Letting her take the lead on the interview was a first for them. But she'd earned it. Pen was turning into an excellent investigator.

"Shall we?" he asked, pointing toward the gated guardhouse.

They moved past the gates and were admitted to the outer ring of the prison. They showed their identifications, signed forms. After five more checkpoints and innumerable corridors, they were led to a small room with a steel door.

A young redheaded guard unlocked it for them.

"He's all yours," the man-child said. "If he gives you any guff, just give a holler. We'll get you out of there straightaway."

Wonderful. Brilliant.

They went into the room. A young man dressed in gray was led in. His head was shaved. He looked cold.

He sat at the table and lit a cigarette.

Memphis and Pen sat across. Pen made a show of taking out her notebook, setting up her pen, before she cleared her throat and dove in.

"Mr. Madison. Thank you for volunteering to talk with us. You know why we're here. Tell us about your friend Roger."

The man—no, he was just a boy, really—had wide blue eyes. He smoked the cigarette as if he'd just learned, not inhaling, but pulling the smoke into his mouth, holding it and blowing a stream that dissipated the moment it hit the chilled prison air.

"You have to promise me that I'll get out of here. I don't belong here. All I did was steal some oranges from the takeaway. There's people in here done much worse."

"We will make a recommendation. You have our word. Now, tell us about Roger Waterstone."

"Not Roger. Urq. He's batshit. He seems all fine, but once you're in, he drops the mask. But by then, you're on the pipe, and it's too hard to walk away. Nothing's free, you know. Nothing's ever free. I wanted to get straight, so he kicked me out."

Puff. Blow. Puff. Blow.

"Kicked you out of the church?"

"Out of the house, innit. The house on Baker Street. The one no one's supposed to know about."

Memphis's cell phone rang. He cursed. He wasn't supposed to have it in here. Pen shot him a look. He jumped up, apologizing, and stepped out of the room.

The phone number was instantly recognizable. It was the house phone at Dulsie.

Ignoring the guard's steely glare, he answered. It was Trixie.

"I think you'd best come back, my lord. Something is terrible wrong with Miss Jackson."

CHAPTER THIRTY-SIX

Taylor paced the sitting room, back and forth, back and forth. She couldn't get his face out of her head. His eyes, empty and unseeing, looking right into her soul.

Taylor didn't know what else to do. She called Sam's cell phone, not caring that she was interrupting her work.

Sam answered on the fourth ring.

"Sorry, I was gloved. What's wrong?"

"How did you know something was wrong?"

"You've got your voice back. Sounds like it hurts to talk, but that's wonderful!"

"He's coming for me, Sam."

"Who is?"

"The Pretender. He's here. He's been following me around the castle."

"Taylor, honey, you're imagining things. You're just overtired. Overwrought. You need rest. You need sleep. Drink your tea and go to bed. Maybe back off the Percocets. They can make you a little goofy."

"I'm not being *goofy,* Sam. I know it can't be real. But it's happening all the time now. It's getting worse."

There was a brief pause.

"What's happening all the time? What are you talking about, Taylor?"

"It was my fault, Sam. It was all my fault. If it weren't for me, you'd still be pregnant."

"Taylor, honey, stop saying that."

She did a lap around the room, stopping at the fireplace. She pulled her notebook from her back pocket and threw it in. The evidence needed to be destroyed. She had to destroy it all before it was too late.

"No, really. Maddee made me see, Sam. If I'd come straight to you, if I hadn't waited, I could have stopped him. I could have saved you."

Tears started down her face. She needed to confess. To be shriven. To have Sam chase all the ghosts away.

There was silence, then Sam sighed.

"Taylor. You need to listen to me. The very first thing he did was stab me. It happened hours before you knew I was missing. There's nothing you could have done. Did you hear me? *He* stabbed me. Not you. You are not to blame for this. He was a sick man who chose to do what he did. Do you understand me?"

Taylor heard the words but they didn't sink in. She couldn't get her feet under her. She couldn't erase the image of Sam, her eyes brimming with tears, the pool of blood at her feet.

"Taylor, I've got open bodies. I have to go back to work now. But listen to me. You have to stop internalizing all this. You have to let it go. You aren't the only one having problems. The sooner you see that, the sooner you'll be back to normal."

The phone was a snake with bared fangs. She shut her eyes then opened them. It became a phone again.

Sam was right. This wasn't all about her. She just needed to find a way to make everyone else understand that.

* * *

Sam hung up the phone, worried. Taylor had been drinking, without a doubt. She always got paranoid when she had too much to drink.

It was my fault.

Oh, God. A wave of despair crashed over Sam. In her darker moments, she'd said the very same thing about her girl, her *best friend*.

But she knew, in her heart, that she couldn't blame Taylor. The Pretender was the one who'd made the choice. He'd kidnapped her. He'd knifed her in the abdomen. He was responsible. Not Taylor.

But something felt wrong about this. She'd sounded… scared, for lack of a better term. And that wasn't something Sam ever saw in Taylor. Fear wasn't an option for her.

She picked up the phone and let it dangle between her fingers. Taylor would kill her if she went behind her back.

Some things couldn't be helped.

Sam dialed Baldwin's cell. The voice mail kicked in immediately. She debated, then hung up without leaving a message.

She was being irrational. This was Taylor. Probably on a bender. And off on her own, with no support system to tell her things were fine and to put down the bottle.

Sam wrote her a note, encouraging her to lay off the alcohol and pills for a couple of days, see if her headache wasn't some sort of rebound from the opiates, and went back to work.

She couldn't face it anymore. Not now.

CHAPTER THIRTY-SEVEN

Taylor couldn't sleep.

She'd taken all the meds, dutifully, one by one. Laid in bed, fretting. Worried she shouldn't have called Sam. Knowing she'd just dragged all the bad stuff back to the surface.

Her unique gift—shitting on the parade.

What was wrong with her? She was supposed to be getting better. Yes, she had her voice back, but Maddee's words rang through her head over and over until they became mantra.

They don't trust you.
> *They don't trust you.*
>> *They don't trust you.*

She got out of the bed. The snow fell in graceful piles outside her window. The fresh green landscape was gone, covered in a blanket of white.

She knew that feeling. She was being smothered.

There was nothing else to do.

She closed the drapes and sat on the chair by the bookcase. The only light came from the fire.

She invited the ghost, and let the memories take her. When it came for her, she didn't even flinch.

Four in the afternoon. She had no idea what day it was. She was freezing cold in the chair, the fire gutted. Her head was splitting. The detritus of her pity party lay scattered around the room. Yikes. It looked like a rock star's hotel room, minus the furniture damage. She'd had a little too much to drink.

Chagrined, Taylor straightened up, then showered and dressed. She was sick of sitting in her room, sick of letting things happen to her. She'd never get it together like this.

She decided to go for a prowl around the castle. If she couldn't go outside, at least she could stretch her legs inside.

When she reached her door, she saw a piece of paper had been shoved under it. It must have been delivered while she slept. The note was handwritten, and Taylor didn't recognize the handwriting. She scanned to the bottom and saw the name Maddee signed in a flourish.

She was tempted to rip the thing to pieces, but decided to be a grown-up about it. The note was simple, straightforward.

Dear Taylor,
I am so sorry for the way yesterday's session ended.
Please accept my apologies. I was trying to get you
to vocalize. I thought if you got mad enough, you'd
forget that your voice wasn't working. While it did
work, I was wrong to handle it that way.

*Can we try again? I'm here in the castle. I came
back to apologize in person and the snow has ham-
pered my escape. I didn't want to wake you. My husband will be along to fetch me in his four-wheel drive
after dinner.*
   Friends?
Yours truly,
Maddee

Taylor's first thought was *Bitch*. Her second was
Fine. It *had* worked. She did have her voice back.

She needed to get out of this room anyway, so she
didn't just sit and pout for the rest of the day. It would
be good to have some company for dinner, at least. Provided they stayed on safe topics.

She gathered her sweater and headed downstairs.

Maddee was sitting in the drawing room, right where
Taylor had left her yesterday. If she hadn't actually seen
her drive off after their aborted session, she would have
assumed she'd never left. Her hair was still skinned
back from her face. She was reading a magazine. Taylor
caught the cover as she turned the page—the glossy
Hello! So the woman wasn't above a little gossip.

Taylor cleared her throat and Maddee jumped.

"Wow, you're quiet. Hey, I'm so glad you came
down." She put the magazine on the couch and came
to Taylor. "I'm so sorry. I thought, well, you read the
note. You know what I thought. No chance it helped?"

She looked genuinely remorseful and hopeful at the
same time. Taylor forgave her. She was just trying to
help.

"Yes. It did. I don't condone what you said, that really

hurt. But I can talk. So I guess in one way I owe you a debt of gratitude."

"What about some tea?"

Taylor saw that the ubiquitous tea cart was sitting against the wall. She shook her head, she was getting sick of tea.

"What about a little whisky, then? That might help things along."

She shook her head, vehemently. She hated whisky. But some hair of the dog wouldn't go amiss. Her head was pounding, and it wasn't from the aftereffects of the shooting.

"I'll have some, if you don't mind. I don't want to drink alone, though. What will you have?"

There was a small bar off to the right of the tea cart that Taylor hadn't noticed before. Maddee bustled up to it, picked out a decanter and poured some amber liquid into a cut-crystal glass. The scent of… Good grief, that was Jack Daniel's. Her stomach turned. Ugh.

Taylor picked through the other decanters until she found one that was red. She took the stopper out and sniffed. Yes, the vintage port. She poured some for herself.

They sat opposite one another on the sofa, clinked glasses and drank.

Maddee took a slow sip, savoring, then, with a wink at Taylor, tossed the rest of the drink back.

"What the hell, right? We're stuck here for a bit, and I'm not driving. Roland might get lucky—if he's a good boy. What do you say, Taylor. Shall we tie one on?"

She went to the bar and poured herself a bigger shot this time, mixed in some Coke, dropped in a couple of square ice cubes.

Taylor debated for a second. It wouldn't take much to get her back over the edge. But a beer wouldn't hurt.

She set the wine down on the table and rummaged in the small refrigerator under the bar until she found a Heineken.

"Oh, no. Not that swill. You need to drink a real beer." Maddee dipped down and looked in the fridge, pulled out a Tennant's lager.

Maddee handed her the bottle, then turned to the bar and found a glass. She held up it critically to the light, then apparently decided it would do. She took the Tennant's back from Taylor and poured it into the glass ceremoniously.

"We *are* in a castle. Drinking out of the bottle is a bit gauche, don't you think?"

Taylor smiled and nodded. She'd had Tennant's before. She liked it well enough. She took the proffered glass and took a sip. They settled into the chairs.

Maddee turned out to be good fun. She regaled Taylor with stories, tidbits about the estate, about Memphis and his foibles, of which there were many, and gossip about the servants. She knew everyone, it seemed. She assiduously avoided the topic of Evan, which suited Taylor just fine.

Trixie came for them at seven, to announce that dinner was ready, and found them both quite tipsy. They made their way up the stairs to the second dining room. Taylor sat heavily at the table. She was suddenly feeling the beer, was light-headed and silly. Her hands moved clumsily as they tried to secure her napkin.

Dinner was a somewhat simple affair, with only soup, Highland steaks, carrots, peas and a side of boiled potatoes, but Maddee insisted they have a bottle of champagne to toast their newfound friendship. The bell was rung, the serving girl sent off to the cellars. She returned five minutes later with a bottle of Dom Perignon, 1987. Taylor had to admit, there was something nice about having a massive wine cellar of excellent vintages at your disposal.

Maddee popped the cork and poured. She held the crystal flute high and slurred, "To friends."

"To Scotland," Taylor said.

They clinked glasses again, buddies, and tucked into dinner.

The food was good, a bit undersalted for Taylor's taste tonight, but she guessed that had to do with her throat being sore. Three bites into the steak, her stomach started to get upset. She set her fork down and licked her lips. Surely she wasn't going to get sick. She hadn't had *that* much to drink.

It was quickly apparent that she was most definitely wrong.

"Where's the bathroom?"

Though drunk, Maddee's face creased in concern.

"Over there, through the cream-colored door. Do you need me?"

Taylor shook her head and bolted for the door. There was a long hall that ended in a bath. Thanking whichever earl had decided to install modern plumbing, she ran down the hall and made it just in time.

She vomited up all the drink and food. Even had some dry heaves for good measure. That wasn't going to help her throat.

After fifteen minutes, she cleaned herself up and was able to make her way back to the dining room. Maddee was still there, but her head was on the table, cradled in her arms. She'd passed out before the pudding.

Good grief. Taylor made a note to check the alcohol content of the beer she'd had. Even after being sick, getting all the alcohol out of her system, she still felt woozy and unsteady on her feet.

There was a bit of a commotion from the hall, and with effort, Taylor turned her head toward the main dining room door. A stocky brown-haired man came through. He took in the scene, shaking his head.

"Och, Maddee, lassie, what have ye done?" He turned to Taylor. "Ye must be Memphis's friend. I'm Roland MacDonald, Maddee's husband. Ye'll no be better off than she, I see. Trixie," he called. "Trixie!"

Trixie appeared through the same door.

Roland was smiling good-naturedly, though Taylor could tell he was annoyed. "These lassies have drank themselves to sleep. See to the lass there. I'll get Maddee home."

"Och, Miss Taylor, are you all right?" Trixie's concern was nice. Taylor allowed herself to be led from the room. She heard Maddee come to a bit as she left.

"Hiya, honey," she said to Roland, then started to laugh. She hardly sounded drunk, just exceptionally happy.

But Taylor definitely was intoxicated. Her feet weren't moving the right way. She had to lean heavily on Trixie's arm, and listen to the older woman muttering under her breath.

"Not right for women to act like that. What was she thinking?"

Taylor wished she could tell Trixie that she really hadn't had much, just the beer and a few sips of champagne, not enough to be sick, for Christ's sake, but she settled for an agreeable mmm-hmm and let herself be led into her rooms.

"Ye'll be needing some ginger tea, that will help with the digestion. And the headache, I daresay. Sit ye down and let me call for it."

Taylor needed some water, that's what she needed. She weaved her way to the bar, found a liter bottle of Highland Springs, and brought it back to her chair. She couldn't get the lid off. Her hands weren't working right. Her head wasn't working right either. Jesus, she was bleeding drunk.

Deciding discretion was the better part of valor, she dropped the water, swayed upright and managed to get to the bed. She sat on the edge, hoping Trixie would come back soon and lift her feet off the floor. Her eyes just wouldn't stay open.

She dimly heard Trixie return, heard the clinks of teacups, then the world turned dark and swallowed her.

When Taylor woke, she was alone. The room was pitch-black. The fire had gone out again, or she'd gone blind. The thought made her want to throw up, so she lay quietly in the bed until the urge passed.

Her head was pounding. She'd passed out without taking the Fioricet or Percocet. She'd be a mess until she got that in her.

Bolstering her courage, she sat up. The headache made her sway in place. She'd never felt the pain this bad, not even when she'd woken from the coma after the shooting and the halo held her head steady, the four points of the metal biting into her flesh. Thank God it was dark in the room; she couldn't imagine dealing with light.

Her feet touched the cold floor. Good. Upright. She managed to get into the bathroom, using the walls for guidance. The pill containers were out. She didn't know which was which, so she opened all four and extracted a pill from each of them. Fioricet, Ativan, Percocet, melatonin. Got water flowing, into a cup, into her mouth.

It took all of her effort to make it back to the bed. She got horizontal, the searing pain making her nauseous again.

Don't be sick. Don't be sick. Don't be sick.

There was a voice on the radio, or television. She didn't know which. She didn't know how to shut it up. How could she shut off that damn voice?

She listened. It hurt. Then she realized what it was. Maddee's biofeedback tape.

Trixie must have put it on thinking it would help her.

She listened for a moment. The blue balloon rose to her mind's eye. There was a knife. Her wrists. The pill bottles.

So easy. So easy. So easy.

She had to say goodbye first.

She needed to talk to Sam. Needed to apologize again. The laptop wouldn't stay still. She fought with the headache as she typed. It didn't all make sense to her, but the idea was there. How many times could she apologize?

The medicine started to work quickly. The pain began to fade. She began to drift, floating, feeling lighter. She put a foot out of the bed onto the floor.

The world stopped revolving so quickly.

That was better.

Time passed.

She realized she wasn't alone.

She was afraid to open her eyes.

A hand cupped her face. Just like Memphis from the night before. But this was freezing cold, almost like ice. It felt good. It helped the pain go away.

But then it moved, to her forehead, touching her scars. And she knew it wasn't Memphis, wasn't anything real. The panic began in earnest, the feeling that she was tied down, couldn't move. Flashes from the night before invaded her mind, the long thrusts, the gentle sucking, the icy touches. It was Memphis, and Baldwin, and Roland now, all three of them crowding around her, touching her, making her gasp with pleasure, then with pain. Somehow her shirt was off, and her own hands found her breasts. She was feverish, burning up, and the icy fingers moved around her body, between her legs, through her hair. Something in her spoke, deep, insistent. *This is wrong.*

A voice, neither man, nor woman, not human, began to whine in her ear. "Leave now, Taylor. Leave now…"

And then it stopped.

She knew she couldn't scream. Her voice wasn't working. But she could cry. Tears ran down her face. She was losing her mind. She couldn't open her eyes for the pain in her head. It was eating her alive.

In her last moment of consciousness, she leaned over and vomited again, then passed out with her head hanging over the side of the bed, an icy vein boring through her skull.

CHAPTER THIRTY-EIGHT

Sam was driving the Forensic Medical van alone. Keri wasn't the only 'gator with plans tonight. Such was life. Sam didn't see any need for her team to suffer just because she hadn't had a chance to straighten out all their lives. And this was a straightforward situation. She could handle it herself.

Damn, but it was cold. Sam loved Nashville, and loved winter, but not when she had to venture out in the freezing dark to attend a crime scene. A messy one, at that. The Regretful Robber had been so regretful that he'd shot himself. In the head. Sam wasn't surprised. Honestly, she was just relieved that the rest of the family had made it out of the house unscathed.

Nashville done up for Christmas was a beautiful sight to behold. Sam and Simon had taken the twins to the Christmas tree lighting this year. They'd giggled and cooed and talked to each other in their bizarre twin babble. This would be the first time the kids had a real sense of the season, that is if their mother could pull her shit together.

There was no easy way to the scene from the highway. She opted for White Bridge to Post Road, then turned left at Dunham Springs Road and took the street directly onto Belle Meade Boulevard.

If Nashville's Christmas could be categorized as beautiful, Belle Meade's was more like a fairy tale. The owners of the stately mansions spent a lot to have their yards and houses professionally decorated, and the vast majority of them chose to go with Greta's Custom Christmas. Sam knew this because both she and Taylor had gone to school with the owner, Greta Torhild. Sam also knew that she was raking in the dough; some of the custom designs went for upwards of $25,000. How people could spend that much on Christmas decorations, Sam would never be able to fathom. But they did.

She parked the van two driveways away and walked in on foot.

Douglas Bowerman's house was decorated, but not by professionals. The place was an original Belle Meade bungalow, just off the country club golf course. A nicely made up evergreen wreath with fake fruit and gold bows hung on the door. Sam could see directly into the house; the door was splintered open and there was a lit Christmas tree. The tree had to have been on a timer. She couldn't imagine the family taking time out from their benefactor's suicide to turn it on.

It was moments like this that she missed Taylor dreadfully. Taylor would have cleared the scene already, had a spot carved out for the ME's van to pull in. Instead, Sam was going to have to go back out, get the gurney, move it all herself. It was going to be a long night.

She mounted the stairs. Marcus was just inside the door.

"Hey. I thought Keri was on tonight."

"She had a party. You're stuck with me. Where's the body?"

"Living room. He let his family leave, then locked the door and shot himself. Seems pretty cut-and-dried."

"Shouldn't you turn off the tree?"

"I don't know. I thought it made things look kind of festive. Though I don't think I'd want to wake up to this scene Christmas morning."

Marcus was right. There was never anything nice about suicide, especially by gunshot. Bowerman had used the .40 Glock. Sam could see it lying right next to his hand. He only had half a face.

"Ugh."

"Yep. You need any help?"

"I'll yell if I do. Thanks."

She just wanted to get this over with.

She set up by the body, gathering his effects. She flipped open his wallet, doing a standard double check of the man's identity. The driver's license said Douglas Bowerman, but the photo showed a blond. This man, what was left of him, was brown-haired. Remembering the wig hairs found in Marias González's pocket, she reached down and pulled. No, the hair was real. The height was off, too—the license said six feet, and this man was infinitely shorter than that. They were going to have to go through a full identification process in order to figure out if this was Bowerman, or if the Reluctant Robber had murdered yet another innocent in his bid for freedom.

"Marcus?" she called.

He wasn't far away, was by her side in seconds.

"What's up?"

"Who is this?" She pointed at the body on the floor.

"Bowerman."

"No, it's not." She stood and handed him the driver's license. He looked at it, then down at the body.

"Son of a bitch."

"Yeah, that's what I thought."

"Keller!" Marcus took off like a shot. Sam backed away from the body. Suicide was one thing—especially one attended by so many people. But if this wasn't the suspect, then who had been shot? And why?

She stepped to the kitchen, took off her gloves and retrieved her BlackBerry from her back pocket. Sent Simon a message that she'd be later than planned. Called Keri McGee and told her to apologize to her boyfriend and get her butt over to the crime scene.

Marcus was still talking to Keller, who was gesticulating wildly. They were having a doozy of an argument. She left them to it, sat down at the abandoned kitchen table and checked her email. They'd call her when they were ready for her to get the body. They'd need a crime scene tech to take a different set of pictures and video first.

There was a new note from Taylor. She'd sent it in the middle of the night. Up all hours, just like at home. Some things never change. Poor thing. Nothing would fix her insomnia; it was a part of her being.

Sam opened the mail and started to read.

Dear Sam,
There is a moment in every life that defines, shapes, transcends your previous spirit, molding you as if from newborn clay. It's come for me. I have changed, and that change is irreversible.

Sam, there's no doubt anymore. I'm losing my mind. The shooting is haunting me. The horror of your loss, of who I've become, all of it is too much. I'm not sure how much longer I can stand to go on like this, trapped under glass, trapped away from everyone. I'm lost.

Oh, no.

This was not good. Taylor was completely going around the bend. Ghosts and hauntings were one thing, but she was coming unhinged. Damn it. She should have listened harder yesterday. Taylor was trying to tell her she was in trouble.

Sam knew her best friend very well. Better than she knew herself, in many ways. Something was wrong, and it wasn't with Taylor's mind. She was probably having a bad reaction to the meds Dr. Benedict had given her. She didn't want to be an alarmist, but the more she read of the note, the more she felt like something was terribly wrong.

She finished reading the email quickly and immediately speed-dialed Taylor's number, not caring about the international rates. It went to voice mail. Damn it. She tried again. Nothing.

She didn't hesitate this time. Taylor would be pissed at her, but what did that matter? She was in trouble, and Sam wouldn't forgive herself if she didn't at least try to help.

She forwarded the email to Baldwin, then followed up with a call. He, unlike Taylor, answered on the first ring.

"Sam. Are you okay?"

"Hi, Baldwin. Yes, I'm fine. I'm sorry to bother you

I know you're working. I was calling about Taylor. I just forwarded an email she sent me—something is obviously wrong. I think she may be having a bad reaction to the meds. I think she needs you. She's certainly too proud to ask for your help."

"Well, hold on and let me read it."

"Sure." Marcus was gesturing for her. "Actually, can you call me back when you're finished reading it? I'm at a scene."

"No rest for the wicked. Of course. I'll call you right back."

She hung up and went into the living room. Marcus was fuming.

"Hey, Sam. Holding pattern. We have to all stop and treat this as a homicide. I need to go talk to the wife, find out if she knows who this is."

"This guy likes the chase—no one robs banks for their health. There's a huge rush to it. Now he's guaranteed you have to come looking for him."

Marcus shook his head mournfully. "We were set up. Marias González has cleaned here. They have a Jaguar. The wife said her husband wrecked it and it's in the shop for repairs. Bowerman's our guy, I'm sure of it. The real Bowerman, that is. But where the hell is he?"

"Think he used her as an escape hatch? Y'all didn't know this guy was in here. Bowerman sends his family out, shoots this one and takes off. We think it's a suicide and don't go looking any further, at least for the time being. Gives him time to flee. He'd have to know we'd figure it out eventually."

"I don't know, Sam. I hope his wife isn't in on it."

"Anything's possible."

"You know it. I've got a BOLO on him. He can't have gone too far."

Her phone rang. Baldwin. "I gotta take this, Marcus. Hang on."

Baldwin's voice was strained. "I can't raise her. You're right, that letter is over the top. I'll keep trying. If you hear from her, you let me know, okay?"

"Can't you just go get her?"

"I don't think I can." His voice was bleak. She hadn't heard him sound this upset before. "There's a huge storm, all the transportation services are out. There are no flights getting into or out of Great Britain. I'm in Amsterdam, if you can believe that. I'll be stuck here, at least for another day."

"Where's the illustrious Memphis?"

"I don't know."

"Great. So we can both worry about her from afar. Let me know if you hear anything."

"You too." He hung up. She tried Taylor's phone again, got her voice mail.

She had to get back to work. Sam typed a quick message then, frustrated, turned back to Marcus.

"Sorry. You were saying?"

His forehead creased. "What's wrong with Taylor?"

"Nothing. She's fine." *I hope,* she added silently.

CHAPTER THIRTY-NINE

Please, God. Not again.

Memphis had been stuck in the car for over an hour, trying to get onto the A1. The trains were stopped. The planes were grounded. The only hope he had was driving, and he was still nearly three hours away. He couldn't believe the snow. It was coming down harder than he'd seen in years.

All he knew was he had to get to Taylor, as quickly as possible.

Damn that woman. She hadn't seemed that bad to him. Delicate, certainly. Not being able to speak, being forced away from hearth and work, into the clutches of the big bad wolf…yes, she'd been a bit vulnerable. But not crazy. But she was used to acting strong, to keeping people at arm's length. But from what Trixie said, she was well past that. She'd gone straight to hallucinations and crying in her room. Acting decidedly unlike the Taylor Jackson he knew.

Acting like Evan, before she died.

Please, God. Not again.

The car in front of him inched forward. He thought he would scream if they didn't start to move.

How could this be happening again?

Evan was never a strong woman. And he'd been attracted to her like a moth to the flame, his chivalrous streak overwhelmed. He remembered the night he met her. At Oxford, at the Playhouse. Tryouts for *Hamlet*. They'd sat together and shared a cigarette, then a finger of scotch, for courage. He was shocked at how nervous he felt. He went on and did his lines, was well received. But Evan—Evan *became* her role. She captivated. Drew a standing ovation from the group of drama students who were casting the roles.

She'd been humoring him. She was a fine actress. It was only on the stage that she left behind her fears, her concerns.

He'd been cast as Laertes. Evan was, of course, Ophelia.

If he'd only known then. If he'd seen it in her eyes. That terrible foreshadowing of her eventual end.

They'd kept the truth within the family. The media had been held at bay.

He still had the note she'd left. He wanted to burn it, but it had been Trixie who stopped him.

"Someday, you'll need this. Put it away and forget about it until then."

He thought they'd arrested Evan's psychosis. Maddee had worked with her. They brought in a specialist, one trained to deal with nervous disorders. But nothing worked.

And then she'd fallen pregnant.

And they'd all been so very thrilled.

And she improved, dramatically. Became the old Evan.

He'd coddled her. They'd had an idyllic few months in London, nesting in the Chelsea flat.

Then he'd taken her to the castle to let his parents dote on her. He'd gone back to London to work. That had been the mistake, in the end. Her isolation brought the old fears back to the surface. She started seeing things. Losing weight. Accusing him of the most despicable acts. She was beyond his reach.

He hadn't known what else to do. They'd been considering committal when she snuck the keys to his car and crept away, found her way to Dulsie Bridge.

And drove the car off the edge.

The idea of her screams invaded his head. He couldn't see this happen again.

Traffic was moving. Slowly. But moving.

Taylor might feel it was a disloyalty, but he'd deal with that later. It was time for him to call Maddee.

He looked at his mobile, saw the red light flashing. A message. He put it on speaker.

Speak of the devil.

"Memphis, it's Maddee. Your girl here has had quite a psychotic break. I'm trying to find a way to sedate her, but she's locked in her room. I'll—"

The phone cut off. His battery, damn it all.

It was happening again.

What had he done?

CHAPTER FORTY

Baldwin paced through Amsterdam's Schiphol airport. His flight to London had been cancelled. Everything into the U.K. was grounded for the foreseeable future.

He alternated trying Taylor's cell with calls to Memphis. Neither one was picking up, and he was ready to pull his hair out.

He had to get to Scotland. It didn't matter that the airports were closed. Taylor needed him.

He couldn't drive, obviously.

It was time to call in the big guns.

He called Atlantic.

"Good job on Julius. Is there something else you need?"

"I need to get to Scotland. Just outside of Edinburgh."

"Impossible. The airports are closed."

"Atlantic, it's an emergency. So help me God, if you don't get me there, I will go public with your little operation."

Atlantic chuckled, his laughter cold.

"You'd be dead before you uttered a word, Baldwin. But let's not go there. I think of you like a son. And since it's so vital that you reach your destination, get yourself to the following coordinates. And be prepared for a bumpy ride."

CHAPTER FORTY-ONE

It took Sam hours to clear the crime scene. Marcus, diligent, talented detective that he was, had pinned the wife down in a lie, and was back at Metro, interrogating her. It wasn't his fault; they were all terribly distracted.

All they knew was that Bowerman planned to run all along, get settled somewhere, then bring his wife and kids. She swore she had no idea who the dead man in her living room was.

They didn't believe her.

The dead man's fingerprints registered back to a man named Joseph Trimble. Trimble was homeless, and according to a quick check with the folks at the mission, Trimble had a benefactor, someone he claimed was "helping him back on his feet." Proving it was Bowerman was a different story.

On the surface, it seemed he'd been setting him up to be the fall guy for the bank robberies. But Marias González had ruined the plan, and Bowerman had been forced to stop her.

It was far from a tidy little scheme. It was unfortunate that they didn't know where Bowerman was truly headed. The Regretful Robber, at least for the time being, had gotten away.

Sam finally got home at eleven-thirty, only six hours later than she'd been expected. Simon had put the twins down and was waiting for her with an open bottle of wine. Honestly, all she wanted to do was fall into the bed and sleep forever, but she accepted the offering and sat at the kitchen table with him for a few minutes.

"We need a vacation," he said.

"I couldn't agree more." She accepted a glass of wine from him. "Where do you want to go?"

"Somewhere warm."

"Can you leave the lab?" Simon ran Private Match, which specialized in running DNA samples for a variety of clients, some public, some private. He usually accepted the overload from Metro if they got too bogged down and needed results ASAP.

"Yes. I think you and I need to find ourselves again. Maybe think about getting pregnant?"

He looked so hopeful. She didn't know how to tell him she wasn't ready.

That she didn't know if she'd be ready ever again.

She was saved from answering by the ringing of her cell phone. She glanced at the ID: Taylor. Finally.

"Baby, I need to take this. We'll talk more later, okay?"

Simon was not happy with her. "Can't you put this conversation first? Really, Sam. This is important."

"It's Taylor. Baldwin and I have both been trying to reach her for hours. Just give me a few minutes, okay?"

Simon stalked off toward their bedroom. *Shit.*

But this was something that couldn't be helped. Taylor needed her.

She answered the phone. "Taylor Bethany Jackson, I have been worried *sick* about you."

CHAPTER FORTY-TWO

Birds were pecking at her head.

For a moment she thought she was back in Nashville, at the entrance to the Snow White's house, with those damn birds chirping. She'd felt that way when she woke up in the hospital too, that incessant beeping crowding its way into her head. But this, this wasn't the same.

She felt empty. Her throat, her head, her arms, everything hurt.

Taylor was afraid to move. She knew she'd been sick last night, very, very sick, that she'd gotten a violent migraine that had left her unable to move. Seeing things. Hearing things. Feeling things.

She cracked an eyelid.

The world didn't explode.

She cracked the other. Dragged herself upright. It was morning. There was brightness streaming through the window. It didn't burn, so that was a good sign.

What happened last night?

She got out of the bed, avoiding a small puddle of what looked like water on the floor between the bed and the window. She went to the bathroom. The pill vials were scattered on the counter. She remembered having the worst migraine of her life and barely managing to get the medicine in her.

She remembered thinking how much better off everyone would be if she'd just end it all.

Then passing back out.

Memphis had come to her again. As had Baldwin. That much she remembered. Her cheeks flamed. It had felt so real. But neither man was here. It was impossible.

Something was not right. Something was very much not right. She felt like she was sick, but didn't feel ill, not like the flu or a cold. She felt…shattered.

The bathroom window showed her a magical world, a snowstorm that was blowing flakes by the window so hard that it looked like a white sheet had been spread across the glass.

Taylor stripped and got under the shower. Let the hot water work its magic on her sore muscles. Goodness, she hurt from head to toe.

She stayed under the double heads until she was getting wrinkled, then toweled herself off, wrapped her hair in the damp towel and went to the computer.

She needed to talk to someone about all of this. Opened her email. There was a message from Sam. Perfect.

Taylor clicked on the message, shocked to see Sam writing in all caps, like she was yelling at her. The message was abundantly clear:

STOP TAKING THE PILLS!

Out of habit, Taylor looked at the note below it that Sam was responding to. She read a long, rambling diatribe that she'd apparently written in the middle of the night. It was more cogent than she'd felt. She didn't remember writing it, just the vaguest sense of moving about her room and getting her laptop out. She checked the time stamp. Good grief, she *had* written it last night, in the middle of her hallucinations.

Great. Now she was imagining things and writing letters she couldn't recall sending. She had gotten sick last night, that much she was sure of. She could taste it in her throat.

She reread the email. It made little sense, but was clear on one thing. She had felt she was losing her mind.

And maybe last night, she was.

But now, in the cold light of day, her body so wretchedly empty, she didn't think that was the case. She thought Sam had a very good point.

The pills.

Oh, hell. The tea.

Trixie.

Taylor grabbed her phone. She'd turned the ringer off somehow. There were eight missed calls from Sam and four from Baldwin.

She didn't even bother listening to the messages. If Sam had sent her something wild and crazy in the middle of the night, Taylor would have immediately tried to touch base, and, failing, would have moved on to Sam's husband, Simon. Since Sam hadn't reached her, she'd obviously checked with Baldwin, who'd started his own campaign.

No calls from Memphis. Hmm. He obviously hadn't been pulled into the red alert.

She looked at the clock. It was six in the morning in Scotland, which meant midnight in Nashville. She'd be forgiven if she woke the twins. She dialed Sam's number. Sam answered on the first ring, her voice ringing with concern.

"Taylor Bethany Jackson, I have been worried *sick* about you. Why did you turn your phone off? Don't answer that. You better have a damn good reason for freaking me out like this. You scared the living daylights out of me. Losing your mind? You? Where the hell have you been?"

"I…"

"Your voice is gone again? Open a chat right now. And don't you dare hang up. I'll wait. Are you okay?"

"No. Give me a minute." God, it felt like she was swallowing glass. She must have been screaming in her sleep. She drank some water and tried again.

"I'm fine. You said no more pills. How did you know?"

"It's hardly a secret. Dr. Benedict prescribed you the Percocet and Ativan, plus the Fioricet. After your bad response to the Ambien, I thought maybe you were having a reaction to one of them. You always react backward to meds, remember? And if I know you, you may have been taking too much of the Percocet. Why, what pills are you talking about?"

"Maddee, Dr. James. Memphis's friend? Gave me melatonin. I was thinking that might be causing a reaction. But Sam, I think I know what's happening. I think Trixie is poisoning me."

She heard Sam take a deep breath. "Now, honey—"

"Don't honey me. I'm dead serious. And very, very sober right now. Trust me. Something is wrong with that woman. She's always lurking around my door. She's fed me tea fourteen times a day since I got here. That has to be what's happening. I bet she thinks I'm trying to replace Evan. She probably loved Evan. Everyone seemed to."

"Taylor. Listen to yourself. Sweetie, I think we need to get you home."

"I don't disagree. I've had quite enough of this place."

"Are you still having hallucinations?"

Taylor looked around the room, waiting for the telltale red wave to start. Nothing. Maybe she'd gotten it all out of her system when she threw up. She pulled the towel off her hair and shook her head. Still nothing, outside of the pounding headache.

"No. I feel better right now. Clearer. The…visions come at weird intervals. I keep seeing red flashes out of the corner of my eye, and get the sense someone's watching me. Then I see the Pretender, just standing there. Like he's waiting for me."

"God, Taylor, I'm sorry. You tried to tell me, and I just assumed…"

"I don't remember typing that letter."

"That was one seriously fucked-up email, girl."

"It's been a seriously fucked-up few days. Sam? I need to tell you something. Please don't yell at me, okay?"

Sam answered carefully. "What is it?"

"I think I slept with Memphis."

The screech that was heard around the world rang through the phone. "What? When?"

In for a penny, in for a pound.

"The night before he left. The night we kissed on the bridge. I thought I had the door barred. There's always someone creeping around this place. I don't like the access they have. Hell, they probably have some sort of secret passageway or something. It seems like people can get in my room even if the door's locked. I hate feeling like I'm not totally alone. At least that I could handle. Anyway, after I went to bed, I had a bad nightmare. Trixie brought me tea, then he came in my room. Things got pretty out of hand."

"When did you start feeling strange, Taylor?"

"The second night I was here."

"You said you *think* you slept with him. You mean there's some doubt in your mind about it?"

Doubt. Yes. She was starting to doubt everything.

"There wasn't until last night. At the time, it felt awfully real. But it was totally weird. He wasn't there when I woke up, which felt really odd. Then he acted like nothing had happened at breakfast. Actually left for London without a single word about it, no flirting, no innuendo. Definitely no kiss goodbye. No setting me up for the next time…which doesn't seem like him, you know?"

"No, it doesn't."

"I'll admit, I was hurt. And embarrassed. But, Sam, what if it didn't happen at all? What if I hallucinated the whole thing? It would explain the way he was behaving."

Sam was quiet for a minute. When she spoke again, her voice was gentler, not as angry. "Taylor, that might be wishful thinking. Are you sure you're not feeling remorseful and just wishing you hadn't slept with him? 'Cause it's kind of hard not to know if you've had sex."

"I know that. And yes, I've regretted it, every minute of it. It was wrong. If I did it, I shouldn't have."

"True."

"Sam, come on."

"What do you want me to say, Taylor? I'm not going to condone it. You know he's not high on my list of favorite people."

"Trust me, you've made that abundantly clear. But listen to the rest before you make up your mind. This is going to sound crazy, all right? Last night, Memphis was here. With me. Again. We were… But so was Baldwin. And Maddee's husband."

Sam chuckled. "Jeez, Taylor. Only *you* get to hallucinate a threesome."

"Foursome, if you're being accurate," Taylor mumbled.

"Was it good?"

"The foursome? No, it was creepy."

"I mean with Memphis."

Taylor stopped and thought back. Good was an understatement. She knew she needed to tell Sam the whole story if she was going to figure out what was real, and what wasn't.

"It felt very real, but Sam, I never opened my eyes. I never actually saw him. And after what I dreamed, or hallucinated, last night…parts of it were very familiar. There's no way we did it, because he's in London, or was, at any rate. He's not physically here in the castle."

"Honey, if you aren't sure, then yes, you might have hallucinated being with him in the first place. It's possible to have an erotic fantasy fueled by certain types of drugs—LSD, for example. Maybe you didn't even kiss him that other time. I think you need to ask him."

"No, I'm sure about the kiss. But the rest… There's an embarrassing question. 'Hullo, Memphis, how are you? Did we sleep together the other night, or did I just imagine the whole thing?'"

Sam had the decency not to laugh. "It's gotta be done, sugar. For your peace of mind as much as anything. Listen, I have to go, the twins are crying, and Simon is less than pleased with me, and you sound way more coherent. But don't take any more pills. Stop taking everything. I'm sure you have some Advil. Take eight hundred milligrams if the headache starts, repeat that every six hours. You might have some shakes after a day or so—that's the Percocet talking. Just gut it out. I know you can. And if there is any way to have blood drawn, so you can see what's in your system, do it."

"All right."

"And Taylor? For God's sake, watch your back."

CHAPTER FORTY-THREE

Taylor hung up with Sam and sighed deeply. She didn't know how to get a blood sample, outside of cutting herself and putting the blood in a glass from the bathroom. Maybe one of the discarded water bottles?

They wouldn't need much, would they?

She didn't have a knife. She cast about the room, looking for something that might work. Glass.

She took one of the crystal lowballs to the bathroom and threw it into the tub, and immediately was reminded of Baldwin shattering his wineglass in their kitchen. God, he'd been right. He'd been right the whole time. She should have listened to him.

She picked up a thick shard of glass that looked sharp enough to do the job and cut her forearm before she could change her mind. Blood welled to the surface. She caught it in an empty Highland Springs bottle. She had no idea if that would be enough, or the right kind of blood to test, but it was better than doing nothing.

She bandaged herself up and put the bottle in the bottom of her suitcase.

Her phone was ringing but she ignored it.

She took the dregs of her last pot of tea and filled another bottle with it. There. She felt more in control now.

Time to bite the bullet. She needed to lay all the ghosts to rest.

Her next call was to Baldwin. He was even more upset with her than Sam had been.

"*Where have you been?* Sam forwarded me that email you wrote her. What in the world is going on?"

"It's kind of a long, messed-up story."

She gave him the gist of what was going on, leaving out any erotic details about the nocturnal escapades.

"So you think you've been drugged?" he asked, incredulous. "Are you sure you haven't just overdone the pain meds? They're strong pills."

"Yes, I'm sure. I can't believe you'd say that."

"Don't get defensive. I'm asking as a doctor, not your fiancé."

She took a deep breath. She needed him on her side right now. "It has to be external, Baldwin. Either that or I'm in big trouble mentally."

"Did you mention this to Memphis?"

"No, I haven't talked to him." Her voice sounded queer. She kicked herself. She sounded guilty. Baldwin was kind enough not to mention it.

Baldwin made an excellent point. Where was Memphis? He hadn't gotten in touch since he left. At first she'd been glad, but then... Could he be in on this? She hadn't wanted to think that Memphis would have anything to do with a plot against her. But if he'd helped Trixie drug her, then come to her room and had sex with her, knowing her to be compromised... No. No.

She couldn't think that about him. She couldn't think

that he'd basically date-raped her. And from what she recalled, she'd been willing enough, at the time.

And she couldn't share that part with Baldwin, either. She steeled her voice.

"I can't imagine he'd be so callous. Memphis may be many things, but he's a cop, a man of integrity. He's like us."

"He's just a man, Taylor. And he's in love with you. God, I knew this was a horrible idea, letting you go up there unsupervised."

"Whoa, there, Baldwin. *Unsupervised?* I'm not fourteen."

"No, but you are hopelessly naive when it comes to Memphis. You've never been able to see him for who he is. For what he is willing to do."

"What's that supposed to mean?"

"Taylor. Take the blinders off. You can't tell me that he didn't make a move on you."

She got quiet. Deception was one thing, sins of omission. He'd been doing that to her for years. But openly lying to Baldwin? She couldn't do it. She hoped he never asked again.

"I figured," he said bitterly.

"It's not what you think," she said finally.

"Oh, I'm sure it's ten times worse than I could possibly imagine. He can't be trusted, Taylor. My instincts are rarely wrong about people. I don't know what he's capable of."

"What, you think I'm in danger from him now? That's insane."

"Is it? Did he tell you why his wife and child died, Taylor?"

"It was an accident. He took me there. To the bridge. Dulsie Bridge. Sam told me that's where Evan died."

"She was running away from him."

"Where in the hell do you get that from? Why would he lie?"

He heaved a great, knowing sigh.

"I got it from my contacts. His family managed to keep things relatively quiet—it wasn't seemly. But word on the street was they were breaking up."

"No way. He adored Evan."

"Again with the naïveté. You've consistently taken Memphis at face value since you met him."

"Baldwin, I—"

"They'd been fighting, Taylor. Evan wanted to leave him, was considering divorce. He was in London, working all the time. Some sources say he had an affair and she found out. They had a huge row and she took off, then drove her car off the bridge. He was the reason she died. It was ruled a suicide. They didn't even do an autopsy. The family kept everything completely hush-hush. But what if it wasn't, Taylor? What if he killed her?"

Now that pissed her off. "Oh please. He was in London when she died. You're just trying to turn me off him. No, Baldwin. That's not possible. Memphis wouldn't do that. That's not what happened. No one knew why Evan was up there. He told me."

"He's supposedly in London right now, too, Taylor. And another of 'his women' is spinning out of control. Who are you going to believe, Taylor? Me? Or him?"

The file. She had the file from Memphis's office. She scrambled to the desk and found it, hidden right where she'd left it.

"I'll call you back," she said. He started to disagree, but she repeated herself. "I will call you back. Bye."

The file was a mess, full of articles cut from newspapers, handwritten notes, pictures. She took a deep breath. How best to do this? It was much too late to pretend she hadn't had her hands on it. And in light of everything, she hardly felt guilty for snooping.

She got down on the floor and spread everything out before her. Took all the newspaper articles and put them in a pile. She put the handwritten notes in their own stack. She'd come back to them. She didn't want to be any more biased than she already was before reading the newspaper clippings.

She sorted the clippings by date, then started to read.

Baldwin was right. News of Evan's untimely death had been splashed across multiple U.K. newspapers, the stories sad and sober. But there was one little article, from an obscure U.K. gossip rag, that tore Evan and Memphis's relationship to pieces. Memphis was treated with disdain, frank curiosity and downright nastiness. The woman he supposedly had the affair with was never named, but "sources" claimed she was a coworker.

She couldn't believe Baldwin had fallen for all of this. Lies. It was clear as day. Anyone who heard Memphis talk about his wife could see he'd been madly in love with her. Couldn't they?

Paparazzi photos of Memphis with a cute brunette triggered a memory—was that Penelope Micklebury, his DC? She grabbed her laptop and went to the Metropolitan Police website. A quick search through his division scored her a photograph. Yes, the mystery woman in the gossip magazines was his detective constable, then just an up-and-coming officer. Taylor knew that they certainly hadn't had an affair. Pen was a lesbian.

Taylor was well acquainted with how gossip and innuendo worked. She'd been the victim of it herself not six months prior. She'd even been suspended, and had to fight to get her command back over the mess. She was more than happy to side with Memphis on this one. The papers were in business to sell papers, and sensationalism did the trick. She knew for a fact that smoke didn't always equate to fire.

She wondered if Evan had heard the rumors and gotten upset, then rushed off. If that was the case, no wonder Memphis blamed himself.

She sat back on her heels on the floor. She was being quick to defend Memphis. *Did* she really know him? She thought she did; he'd shown her his heart, after all. But he'd always kept secrets from her. Never fully let her in. And knowing she was engaged to marry Baldwin, he was still more than happy to compromise her and her relationship to get what he wanted.

No, Memphis wasn't a saint. Far from it. But she wasn't entirely convinced he was such a sinner either.

Until she moved to the pile of handwritten notes. They told a different, more lurid story.

She realized she'd never seen his writing before. It was an elegant scrawl, masculine; he'd used a fountain pen on most of the sheets.

Some of the notes were letters to Evan. Those were the hardest to read. They were all dated, some before, and some after Evan's death. They told a clear story of pain and desire, with Memphis trying to tell his wife that, no, he wasn't doing any of the things she was being told, that he loved her, loved their baby. He even offered to quit working for the Met and come home for good. She was reading a purely one-sided conversation, but Taylor got the idea. Evan had someone she trusted implicitly giving her the information about his exploits. Evan believed that single tabloid story over her own husband.

What a blow that must have been.

The letters from after her death were the worst. She skimmed these only, seeing his pain, watching him bleed on the page. Reading them thoroughly didn't feel right. It was voyeuristic at best. She set them aside. She just couldn't go there.

Why had he left this file out in the open for anyone to stumble upon? Had he wanted her to find them? She wondered where Evan's letters back to Memphis were.

Okay, he hadn't exactly left it out in the open. She'd used the key he gave her and broken into his office. But Memphis was a cop, used to compartmentalizing, aware of consequences if private material got out in the open. It just didn't make sense. Unless he trusted that she wouldn't invade his privacy by going in his office, sitting at his desk, picking up the newspaper and finding the file underneath. Why would he expect that she would do any of that? He wouldn't.

But he had very purposefully given her the key.

She started to put the file away, saw one last piece of paper sticking out from the bottom of the stack. She pulled it out just to straighten it before she put it back with the others, couldn't help but see the opening words:

I'm so, so sorry.

What was this now?

The paper was different than the letters, thick and white, with a ragged edge, like it had been ripped from a sewn or bound notebook. A journal, maybe? The ink was brighter, fresher, more recent. She read the words, felt her heart begin to flutter.

The letter was dated December 21.

It was Evan's suicide note.

CHAPTER FORTY-FOUR

21 December, 2008

Dear James,

I am so, so sorry to do this to you. But I can't face another moment with these creatures in my head. They claw at me. They tear me to shreds. Their eyes follow me everywhere. I can't escape. They make me want to die. So that is where I am going. To death. He will welcome me.

I will make sure he takes care of the baby. I do love you.

Evanelle

CHAPTER FORTY-FIVE

Taylor felt like she was going to throw up again. Baldwin was right. Evan had committed suicide. Why hadn't Memphis told her? Why hadn't he trusted her? And why had he taken her to the spot where his wife took her own life if not to share in some sick, demented fantasy about the two of them?

And why did she completely understand how Evan felt? Last night, she would have welcomed death with open arms. It seemed like the best solution to her problems.

Taylor put the rest together. She was right in her earlier assumption. Trixie. Trixie was the common denominator.

She grabbed her computer. Maybe there was something in the woman's past that would explain why she wanted to drive the women around Memphis crazy. Though finding details about a Scottish housekeeper on the internet was probably pointless. Family documents, other servants: that's where she'd get the whole story. But why would they trust Taylor?

She opened her computer, the home page glowing

in mundane comfort. There were several new emails in her inbox. One caught her eye.

It was from Memphis. Dated yesterday. So he had been in touch.

She clicked on the message.

Taylor, you are my heart's desire. I will do anything to keep you. If you knew what I've been doing, you'd never forgive me. But I must have you. I must keep you. Taylor, I am so, so sorry for what I have to do. For what I have done. You will never know that I was responsible for her death. That I drove her over that precipice. And you won't know what I've done to him, either.

You will be so sad, my love, but I will heal you. I will fix you. You will be happy again. I promise.

I love you.

Jesus, what was this?

A confession? For killing Evan. For killing his son? Or for what he planned to do?

Maybe it wasn't Trixie who was making her ill after all. Maybe it *was* Memphis.

Keeping her off balance, keeping her sick…

He could have easily put medicine in her pill bottles that made her hallucinate. He'd been in her room—hell, he'd slept there, the very first night she'd been at the castle. She'd drunk plenty in his presence: wine, tea, juice. He could have easily spiked any of it.

God, the port. Every time she drank his port, she had a horrifying hallucination. And him, planting the idea of the ghost they called the Lady in Red in her head. Telling her that ghastly story. And she, falling for it all like a teenage girl at a campfire who didn't know any better.

She read the email again, heart racing.

Him. Did Memphis mean his son, or someone closer? Someone still alive?

Could he mean harm to Baldwin?

She needed to talk to Baldwin. She needed to warn him.

She put the file back together, set it on the desk and grabbed her phone. His voice mail answered. Before she could leave a message, there was a knock at her door.

"Miss Taylor? Are you feeling all right this morn? I've brought ye some tea."

Fuck. Trixie. They had to be working together. Trixie was the lynchpin, plying Taylor with tea all the time. She'd been the one to soothe Taylor after the very first nightmare. She should have trusted her instincts when she suspected her before.

Things came crashing together. The coat with the glass in it. Trixie had been the one to set the boots and coat in Taylor's room. And she was always hanging around, always lurking. Doing her master's bidding.

Memphis, you sodding bastard.

"Miss Jackson?" Trixie called again.

Act like nothing's wrong. Answer the door.

Taylor shoved the file back in the desk and strode to the door. She swung it open, saw Trixie's anxious face and wondered if perhaps she was wrong. She looked... frightened. And then relieved.

"Oh, so you are all right then. Good. I was worried. I've got fresh ginger tea and some ginger biscuits. That should settle your system. The storm is very bad. Do you have enough wood by your fire? I'm afraid it will be days before we can get out."

Taylor let her wheel the tea tray in. She'd be damned if she ate or drank anything that she didn't prepare herself for the rest of the time at the castle. But for now, she didn't need to let them know that she was onto them.

She pointed at her throat so Trixie would assume she couldn't speak. Being known as functionally mute was going to have its advantages after all.

"Och, lassie, I'm not surprised. Made a mess downstairs, yes you did."

Taylor pointed to the side of the bed, mimed throwing up.

"There, too? I'll send along one of the cleaning lassies. Can I be getting you anything else now? Would you like Cook to make you a breakfast?"

Was that a hopeful note in the hateful old besom's voice?

Taylor shook her head, held her hand over her stomach. Pointed at the tea cart. Forced herself to smile. She was stuck in a fucking blizzard with a woman who may or may not be a part of a plot to derail her mind. Super.

"Perhaps ye'll be feeling well enough to join Maddee and Roland for luncheon, then."

This was said without guile, just a making-conversation-with-the-inmates tone. But it was critical information. Maddee was still here. There were witnesses. She would be safe.

Taylor shrugged and signaled to the door. She needed to be alone. Needed to figure out her next steps.

Trixie, long adapted to clues from her employers, nodded once and excused herself. Taylor locked the door behind her.

The first thing she did was add some of the tea to

the bottle she was keeping, then she tossed the rest of the cookies into the toilet and flushed them.

Itching for an evidence bag, she set the pot of tea back on the cart and fetched a fresh bottle of Highland Springs water from the bar. The cap was secure, the seal hadn't been broken. She felt reasonably sure she could drink it without repercussions.

She drank straight from the bottle in case there was something in the glasses. Thirst slaked, she rummaged in her carry-on for the bag of trail mix she'd stashed there in case the plane's food was awful. It was still factory sealed. She could live on water and trail mix for a day or two, no problem. It would tide her over until Baldwin could get her the hell out of here and back to Nashville.

With her feast now laid before her, she tried Baldwin's phone. Voice mail again. God, of all the times to miss her call. He'd been frothing at the mouth to find out what was going on, now he didn't answer her?

She looked at the email from Memphis again.

He was a sick, sick man.

Her phone rang. She grabbed it, hoping for Baldwin. It was Sam.

"You won't believe the email I just got from Memphis."

"Taylor, wait. I need to tell you something. You said Maddee James gave you melatonin, right?"

"Right. She said I really needed to sleep, and thought I'd do better on something all-natural."

"What does it look like?"

"Long clear capsule with tan grains. Horse pills."

"That could be anything, Taylor. You can't take anything else she gives you."

"God, you think Maddee's in on this, too? Why

would she want to hurt me? That makes no sense. She's supposed to be helping me."

"Some help. What's the last thing you remember from yesterday?"

"I don't remember sending you that note, that's for sure. The last really solid thing I remember was having a beer with Maddee. And I got horrifically ill shortly afterward. She did pour my beer for me, I think… You don't think all three of them are trying to kill me?"

"I don't know, Taylor. But at least one of them is. You have to get out of there."

"I can't."

"Why not?"

Taylor pulled back the curtain. The world was white, the wind whirling the snow around.

"Because I'm in the middle of a whiteout blizzard."

"Where is the illustrious Dr. James?"

"Somewhere in the house. Trixie just came to bring me more tea, and dropped that Maddee and Roland wanted me to join them for a late lunch."

Taylor could hear tapping. Sam was on her computer.

"What are you looking for?"

"Just checking on Dr. James's license. Which, from what I can see here, doesn't exist. Where did you say she's from?"

No license? "Long Island."

A few more taps. "Sorry, sugar. Bad news. There is no one named Madeira James with a license to practice psychology, psychotherapy, nothing."

"But do you need one to practice in the U.K.?"

Tapping again. "Absolutely. She's not a part of the British Psychological Society, the governing body there. She's not listed anywhere that I can find. It doesn't mean she wasn't trained, but she can't hang out a legitimate shingle."

"That's just great news. Wouldn't Willig have picked up on this?"

"Why would she? You told her the woman was qualified in EMDR. She sent the files."

"Memphis told me she was."

"Another strike. Do you still have internet access, with the storm?"

"Yeah."

"Check her out."

"Sam…"

"Seriously. None of this smells right, Taylor. You're still not thinking completely clearly, or else you'd have already put this together."

"I'm finding it hard to believe that the whole lot of them are in on a conspiracy together."

"I don't know, Taylor. But we don't know these people."

"I *know* Memphis."

"No. You don't. You can't know him. It takes more than a few emails and chat sessions to get to the heart of a person. And I know *you* well enough to know that you haven't let him in yet. Not all the way. So Taylor?"

"Yes?"

"If you did sleep with Memphis, which I'm starting to doubt you did, it's okay. The world won't end. You and Baldwin aren't married. Just…don't do it again, okay?"

That was as close to forgiveness as she was likely to get, from anyone.

"Yes, Mom. Talk to you later. And Sam? Thanks."

"Love you, honey."

"Love you, too."

CHAPTER FORTY-SIX

Madeira James didn't exist. She was a ghost.

Taylor looked everywhere she could think. Criminal records first, but no one with that name had run afoul of the law. She moved on to all the regular databases she had access to—credit card companies, tax rolls, real estate. Nothing.

Maddee was from Long Island. She hadn't come to Scotland until she was twenty-one or so; Memphis had told her that. There had to be something, some record. But there was nothing.

Taylor had friends in New York who could look deeper into the files there, but that would take too long. She felt like time was running out.

But she knew someone who could break through all the barriers, seen and unseen. If there was information to be found, he could access it.

She grabbed her phone and dialed up Lincoln Ross.

He answered in a quiet mumble. She'd woken him, but he would understand.

"It's Taylor."

"I know. What's up?"

"I need your help." She outlined the story for him. Again with the barest of essentials, skipping many of the finer points. If she were wrong, she didn't want her team around her to think she'd gone off the deep end.

Lincoln, ever the adventurist when it came to tracking people through the internet, was game for some action. She heard him start typing away.

"Good. I owe you one, Linc."

"Always good to need a favor. I'll get back to you. This number is secure?"

"It's the best I've got. Keep it quiet and cover your tracks. If she's hiding something, and there are alarms set up, I don't want her to know we're into her world."

"Will do. Talk to you shortly."

Home.

A wave of longing for the normalcy of Nashville crashed over her. She'd even face her father if she got through this one unscathed. He was nothing, comparatively.

Taylor sat at the desk for a few minutes to plan her next steps. Phase one was in play. Now to deal with the bigger issue.

She was here in the house with Maddee and Trixie. Maddee's husband was present. She couldn't imagine that she was in any kind of real danger from the women, not with so many witnesses around. That would be insanity.

What if this whole escapade, if you will, was designed for her to see the good in Memphis? That the plan was for her to be mortified, scared and sick and alone, and him to come charging in on the white horse to save her? Yet it had backfired something terrible.

She opened her email and read the note he'd addressed to her again. It was so desperate, so intense. She'd felt those emotions coming off Memphis in Nashville, and again in Italy. He'd tamped them down a bit since her arrival in the U.K., though they'd flared again at the bridge, and of course, their overnights. If those were real.

In novels, they called it burning desire.

She may not know exactly how she felt about him, but one thing was for sure. Being possessed, by any man, wasn't going to happen. Taylor may make mistakes—doozies, too. But she was well past the point of letting a man—letting anyone, for that matter—control her.

The fire was dying out. She went ahead and tossed on another couple of logs. Surely the storm must be breaking. A quick check of the radar showed it was as intense as ever. For the moment. The blizzard should last through the evening, start tapering off after dark. Thank goodness. She'd be gone in twenty-four hours, no more, even if she had to shovel her way to the road and hitch a ride.

She tried to call Baldwin back again.

As she dialed his number, the case for the tape Maddee had given her caught her eye. She'd forgotten all about it. Curiosity got the better of her. She'd left the tape in the Bose sound system on the bookshelf to the right of the desk. She hit Play and listened for a few seconds while Baldwin's phone connected.

Maddee's voice was soft and soothing. Taylor couldn't help herself; she started to think about the pool of light enveloping her toes, of the warm, soft breezes…

"Taylor!"

Wow, she'd drifted off. Baldwin was shouting in her ear.

"Whoa. Sorry. I put in the biofeedback session Maddee had taped for me and I must have dozed off." She hit Stop on the disc.

"*What* were you listening to?"

"Maddee said it was biofeedback. She wanted me to play it before I went to sleep. It was supposed to help me relax."

"Let me hear it. But I want you to go to the bathroom and run the water, I don't want you listening to it. Okay?"

"Why—"

"Just do what I ask, Taylor. Please."

"Okay."

She set the phone by the stereo and hit Play again, then went to the bathroom, shut the door and started the water, singing "La la la la la" out loud for good measure. She could still hear a bit, but not the words. She gave it a few minutes, then went back out. Clicked the tape off and picked up **the** phone.

"So?" she asked Baldwin.

"That's not biofeedback. That's hypnosis. They're similar in nature, of course, but... In any of your sessions, did you say things you didn't mean to say? Share secrets?"

"Well, yes. She did hypnosis. It's how we knew my voice was working. I could speak fine when I was under. Why? What's on that tape?"

"Did you feel suicidal at all after you listened to it?"

She swallowed hard. This was not exactly the conversation she wanted to have. But hiding her thoughts from Baldwin wasn't the right thing to do. She knew that now.

"Last night. I may have had a few thoughts about ending things. But I don't feel that way now, Baldwin. I promise."

"Don't listen to that tape, okay? You'll go back under. And be very careful if you talk to her. She's put suggestions into your mind that will allow her to manipulate your thoughts."

"Suggestions to do what?"

"Harm yourself."

Evan.

"Baldwin. Evan. Her suicide. Could it have been Maddee? Could she have planted suggestions in head her, too?"

"Taylor, that is a distinct possibility."

"What the hell is going on here, Baldwin?"

"I don't know. Either they're all working together, and she's meant to get your walls down so Memphis can look like a hero, or she's working alone, and has a serious grudge. You need to be doubly on your guard. You can't trust either of them."

"I met the woman three days ago. I'm not that abrasive, I don't think."

"But think about it. Maybe she has feelings for Memphis. And if that's the case, and she isn't the most healthy individual, she sees you as a rival. And rivals are unwelcome."

"She's welcome to him. This is all a bit much for me to process."

"Well, keep processing, because if that's the case, you're in serious danger."

"I've been doing some research. I have a file from

Memphis's office, his private file on Evan's death. I think you're wrong about him cheating, though the tabloids certainly made sure he looked guilty."

"Regardless of the circumstances, Taylor, there is a controversy about her death. We don't know the truth. Whether you believe it all or not is your business, obviously."

"Don't take that tone with me, Baldwin. I'm the one stuck up here trying to make sense of all of this." God, should she tell him? She might have to if she wanted him to take her seriously.

"Okay. I'm sorry."

"You're forgiven. Listen. Memphis emailed me earlier. It gave me pause. Creeped me out, actually. You're sure Memphis is nowhere around, right?"

"I haven't heard word one from him. Why?"

"The note makes it sound like he might harm you."

"What?"

She pulled the words from memory, recited them to him. "'You won't know what I've done to him, either.' At first I thought he was talking about his unborn child. But I think he's talking about you, Baldwin."

"Taylor, listen to me. I'm at one of Atlantic's offices in Amsterdam. I'll be there in two hours, three at the outside."

"You're in Amsterdam? I thought you were in Nashville."

"The case, Taylor. It worked perfectly for me to get there over Christmas. Don't worry about that now. There's no way he's getting to me. Besides, I'm armed."

"Well, I'm not."

"Which you need to fix immediately. It's a working castle, correct? Surely there's something less than ceremonial around there. Check with the gamekeeper. He should have something you can handle."

Have Jacques take you ferreting for rabbits. That's great fun.

Jacques, the driver, the bodyguard, and his blatantly visible shoulder holster. She would go to him. And hopefully, he would help her.

"Yes, I know who to talk to. Okay, that's one thing settled. I have Lincoln doing some searching for Madeira James's past. Sam couldn't find any record of her having a license to practice, in the States or the U.K."

Her other line beeped. She glanced at the caller ID. It was Lincoln.

"Let me take this, it's Linc. He may have found something."

"I'm going to look at some mode of egress for you. See what we can do to get you out of that castle. Or at the very least, get someone in who can protect you until I can get there."

"I can protect myself, Baldwin. I can handle this bitch."

"You're compromised, Taylor. Just remember that. If you have to be around her, and she starts trying to get you to relax, leave the room. Sing. Do anything to interrupt her flow of words. Okay? Just promise me you'll be vigilant. Last night you were saying your goodbyes. I'm not ready to lose you."

"I'm on my guard now, Baldwin, I have it back together. Don't worry."

She clicked End and the line automatically switched over to Lincoln.

Lincoln's voice was breathless. "Thank God I got you. Taylor, you've got a problem. A very big problem."

ENDS

"Rue not my death. Rejoice at my repose,
It was no death to me but to my woes.
The bud was opened to let out the rose.
The chain was loosed to let the captive go."
—ROBERT SOUTHWELL
ON MARY, QUEEN OF SCOTS

CHAPTER FORTY-SEVEN

Memphis was getting closer. He was exhausted. He'd been stuck in the car for hours, crawling up the A1. Seventeen hours to make a two-hour drive. He nearly cheered when he saw the signs for the A9. He was almost home.

His cell phone had died after the message from Maddee. He'd turned it off for a bit, let it build up a tiny charge. Then he'd put in a call to Pen, heard just enough about what had happened after he rushed out of the prison.

She was going to be the toast of London tonight— she'd used the information Madison gave them about the house on Baker Street to solve the case. She'd stormed it with a team. All three girls were found, in various states of disarray, held against their will by the enigmatic Urq. But alive. Roger Waterstone had been arrested.

Pen was jubilant. He'd been right to let her take over the case. She needed a few wins under her kilt to get the right attention from the commanders. He was happy for her, and happy his gut had been wrong for once.

He just hoped it was still wrong now.

CHAPTER FORTY-EIGHT

Taylor sat in the chair in front of the fireplace. Lincoln's nimble fingers had gotten the information they needed. This was bigger than Taylor and Memphis, bigger than a petty jealousy. Bigger than they could possibly imagine.

As she suspected, Dr. Madeira James wasn't who she said she was.

Taylor had taken fifteen minutes, laid out everything that had happened, and emailed the summary to Sam for safekeeping. If something went south, Sam was to use the information to make sure Maddee was taken down.

But Taylor didn't think it was going to get that far. She had every intention of dealing with the doctor herself.

She had a fresh notepad in her lap, was mapping the castle corridors and stairwells. She couldn't stay in her room, locked away, pretending she was sick. She had no choice. She had to venture out.

She needed two things, and needed some stealth to gain them.

A gun.

And Maddee's laptop.

She sketched the rooms she knew from memory, filling in staircases, locked doors, rooms she'd been in, rooms she'd walked past. This place was so damn big. Maddee could be anywhere. Waiting. Watching.

A soft knock at her chamber door broke her concentration. It was followed by a high-pitched, girlish voice.

"I'm here to clean your room."

Ah. One of Trixie's elves. Perfect.

Taylor went to the door. She wasn't taking chances. She opened the peephole and double-checked. Breathed a sigh of relief. The girl was alone.

She unlocked the door and let her in, then shut and latched the door behind her. It was the serving maid who'd brought Taylor's breakfast on her first morning in the castle. That felt like weeks ago.

She had a pail and mop, started over to the bed. Taylor stopped her. This was an opportunity she couldn't pass up.

"What's your name?"

"Maisrie, mum."

"That's a beautiful name. This has to be between you and me. We need to keep this a secret from everyone, Maisrie. Can you promise me that?"

The girl looked surprised, her forehead creasing momentarily. "Yes, mum?"

"Good. I need you to do something for me. I need to see Jacques. Is he here, on the estate?"

"Why, yes, mum, he surely is. But he's probably down wi' the sheep. All the stock was brought in, but there was some sheep as he couldn't find."

"So where would he be?"

"In the barns, maybe?"

"Can you take me there?"

She hesitated. "Well, yes, mum. I can take you to him. But it's snowing something fierce out of doors now. Ye may want to wait until the storm's passed."

Oh that I could.

"I need to see him now, Maisrie. And we need to go the back way. I don't want anyone knowing that I've seen him. It needs to be a secret. Okay?"

The poor child. She would probably promise most anything to the wild-eyed woman towering over her if she would loosen the grip on her arm.

"I must tell Trixie though. She'll skin me alive if I disappear."

Taylor dropped to her knees. The girl was only about five feet tall; this brought her to eye level. She looked her dead on, imploring.

"Listen to me. This is a matter of life and death. No one can know. Not Trixie. Not Dr. James. This will be between you and me."

"Och." The girl shook her head in disgust. "I'd never be telling her anything. I don't like her."

She slapped her hand over her mouth then. Talking poorly of her betters was surely discouraged.

Taylor suppressed a smile. For better or for worse, she had an ally.

Taylor wound her hair back from her face and secured it with a ponytail holder. She'd need her jacket if they were going to the barns, and her boots. She grabbed these items while Maisrie fretted by the door, waiting for her.

She wasn't about to go into the corridor with just her bare hands to defend herself. The glass shards from the lowball wouldn't work, she would cut herself trying to use it.

But the bar had a corkscrew, a professional sommelier version. She didn't know why she hadn't thought of it before. When extended, the Teflon-coated worm sat perpendicular to its base. Awkward unless you led with it, like a dagger among brass knuckles. But the foil cutter was a two-and-a-half-inch-long serrated knife. It faced the opposite direction of the screw, which was too bad, but it was better than nothing.

Taylor opened it like a blade, turned it over in her hands to ascertain its best defensive use, thrust into the air a couple of times to judge its weight, then folded it back up and stuck it into her pocket. It would be a formidable weapon if anyone got close.

Maisrie saw her do it, turned four shades paler.

"Ready?" Taylor asked.

The girl nodded, head bobbing quickly.

Taylor followed her to the door. Unlatched it, then gestured for the girl to proceed.

Maisrie had obviously seen her share of spy movies. She darted her head out for a quick look, then flattened herself against the doorjamb with a breathless "Eep."

Obviously there was someone in the hall. Taylor bit back a laugh. This was serious, and she was glad the girl was taking it so, but cloak-and-dagger was obviously not her strong suit. Taylor counted to ten, put her finger to her lips, then motioned for the girl to keep moving.

This time the coast was clear. Following a path Taylor didn't recognize, Maisrie led her the back way down the servants' stairs to the kitchen. Taylor could hear the familiar noises of pots banging and water being run—lunch was being prepared. Maisrie was getting

better at being circumspect. She dodged around the
entrance of the kitchen, took Taylor to a large pile of
firewood, probably three cords' worth, stacked floor to
ceiling against the wall. There was a small bench that
housed coats and Wellies, as humble and normal as any
cold-weather house. Maisrie availed herself of a coat,
gloves and boots, then looked to Taylor, her face serious.

"Ready?" Maisrie asked.

Taylor nodded.

"Hold on to me. I don't want to lose ye in the storm."

Taylor grabbed the girl's collar, whispered, "Come
on, then."

Maisrie opened the door.

The world became a swirling mass of white. Bitter
cold snapped at Taylor's skin. God, it was still coming
down.

Maisrie started off then, sure-footed, her steps
guided by years of following this path, from kitchens to
barn back to kitchens. It only took them seven minutes
to make the trek. In good weather, it would probably
only be three or four. Taylor hadn't seen the building
they were entering before; it was on the opposite side
of the estate from the tennis courts and the run-down
kirk, back toward the road. Toward civilization.

She was overcome with the urge to just grab the first
vehicle she saw and take off, but chided herself. That
would be the height of stupidity. She didn't know where
she was going, and her foray out with Memphis the
other day had proved only one thing—the Scots weren't
terribly concerned with getting people from point A to
point B by the quickest, easiest route. She could slide

off the road in the storm, freeze to death in the car and no one would be the wiser until things thawed out.

That made her think of Evan, crashing over the edge of the bridge into the icy water below. No, setting off alone wasn't an option.

She could just hide in the barn until the storm was over; that would work, too.

But Taylor wasn't the hiding type. And truth be told, she was pissed off. She didn't like being manipulated, liked not knowing who was behind it even less. No, she needed to see this through. A few tools, that's all she required.

They burst through the barn doors, breathless, covered in snow, shaking themselves like chickens shedding feathers.

It was warm inside, full of bleats and moos and clucks and the occasional whinny, the estate's stock crammed into a space that wasn't quite large enough to hold them all at once. Taylor wondered about the deer. Where had they been put? Or were they still out there, breathless and white, partially frozen, huddled together for warmth under some prickly gorse?

Maisrie was holding on to Taylor's hand like the frightened child she was. Taylor gently untangled herself from the girl.

"Stay here."

Maisrie shook her head, eyes wide. She was scared to pieces, of what she'd done, perhaps, of the repercussions if she were found out. She allowed Taylor to drop her hand, but followed when Taylor started to step away.

"Fine. Come on then. Let's find Jacques."

The groundsman wasn't hard to find. There was a small office off the main entry. He must have heard the barn doors open and close, because he wandered out, a toothpick stuck in his teeth. Taylor had a moment's flash of the Pretender, standing in the corridor outside her room, the same toothpick jutting out of his rotted mouth, but she was able to force it away.

Jacques took one look at the two women and his eyes grew large.

"What are you doing here?" he asked in French.

"English?" Taylor asked. Her high school French, while adequate for getting herself to the bathroom, wasn't going to work here.

Jacques sized her up, then answered in slow, accented English.

"Yes, some. What is the matter? Why are you out in the storm? Not fit for man nor beast."

Some English my ass. If he had idioms, he spoke the language.

"Maisrie, wait right here. Jacques, in your office, if you don't mind."

He cast a glance at Maisrie, then shrugged and walked back the way he came. Taylor followed him. Maisrie stood looking forlorn, but didn't seem inclined to bolt. Good. She'd need her to guide them back to the house.

Jacques stopped by his desk, turned to Taylor, a quizzical expression on his face. The desk looked like a bomb had gone off. Taylor got the sense that he was the estate manager, dealing with all the paperwork that went with running a farm. A factor. Handy to have, especially if he was good at his job.

"The first day we met, you said that if I needed anything, to come to you. I need your help. I need a weapon."

"Why? You plan to shoot something?"

"Self-defense."

"Against the sheep? Or the snow?" He leaned against the desk and crossed his arms.

"I don't have time to go into details."

"Perhaps we should call Lord Dulsie and ask him first."

She didn't know if he was bluffing. And she couldn't have Memphis finding out she was on to the game, not until she knew for sure he didn't have anything to do with it.

She decided to gamble. The thought had crossed her mind several days ago. With any luck, she could appeal to him like this. Professional to professional.

"The weapon you were carrying when you picked me up from Waverly, in Edinburgh. A Sig Sauer P226 in a single harness shoulder holster. Standard issue for Security Service."

The veil of vague indifference lifted. Jacques, if that's what his name was, went on alert. His shoulders squared, lips tightened.

Yahtzee.

"I assume you're in place to safeguard the earl? Someone to watch over him and the family when he's away from the centers of power? Protecting the family seat?"

"I'm hardly the standard." The French accent was gone, the English unmistakably British. "And you're wrong. The family's been getting death threats. After the viscount's wife died under less than crystal clear circumstances, the earl wanted someone on the estate full-time to keep an eye on things."

"Death threats? So you think Evan Highsmythe was murdered?"

"I can't discuss that with you."

"You just did."

He narrowed his eyes at her. The dentures made more sense now. Jacques the Brit had the look of a brawler about him now that he wasn't trying to be charming.

"No one from the family is here, yet here you are, snug as a bug in your *office,* playing the role of factor."

"They call it undercover for a reason, sweetheart."

"Well, you're not that good, if I can pick you out at fifty paces. So why are you here and not in South Africa with the earl?"

He blushed. Ah. Someone was in trouble and had been left behind on the scut detail.

"Oh, like that, is it? Okay then. I get it."

"You don't get anything. These are serious threats. They found… That's neither here nor there. From what I hear, *you're* supposed to be a trained professional. I was doing you a courtesy, letting you see the harness. So you'd know you could come to me if anything went south. Which I assume it already has. When's the bloody viscount coming back, anyway?"

"I haven't a clue. He went to London and I haven't heard from him since." No sense going into that creepy email with the help. It wouldn't give them anything to work with.

That got his attention. He snapped to, grabbed a cell phone from his pocket. It was GPS-enabled, a satellite phone. He extended the antenna, dialed a number.

"Rook calling in for Bishop."

"Who are you calling?" Taylor asked.

"Shut up," he said to her, then turned his attention to the phone. "Where's Bumblebee?"

Taylor bit down hard on her lip. *Bumblebee*? *That* was Memphis's code name? Did he know?

The answer Jacques got must have satisfied him, because he thanked the bishop and hung up.

"He's on the A9. My people are right behind him. They are following a snow plow. He's headed this way."

She didn't know whether to be relieved or scared.

"How long?" she asked.

"An hour. Maybe more, depending on how the roads do. He's apparently been on the road for hours, trying to come home. What got up his nose, eh?"

She didn't appreciate the innuendo.

"I haven't a clue. I still need that weapon."

"You don't need a weapon. You have me."

"And you're so subtle. You're the factor, remember? You can't go crashing into the house for no reason. Just hook me up. I'm only covering my bases."

"What's in the house that you need a weapon to protect yourself against?"

She hesitated.

"Better to let me go in with you. Professional or not, you can't carry on our soil. If they found out, I could be made redundant quite quickly."

Taylor held up both hands. "No. You can't go in there. I'll lose her if you do. She's not stupid, she'll know something's up immediately."

"You'll lose who?"

Time to gamble. If the family was getting death threats, if there was a chance Evan had been murdered, and Taylor had been poisoned, perhaps one person was responsible for all that. And knowing what she knew about Madeira James's background, Taylor wasn't all that surprised.

"Dr. James. Madeira James. She's up at the house, got stuck there last night with her husband Roland Mac-Donald."

"That nut? She's a headshrinker. Crazy, but harmless. We've checked her out. The only thing we have on her is a name change. She went to James a few years back, when she stopped practicing. No one knows why."

Stopped practicing after she changed her name. That's why Sam hadn't seen her listed with the licensing boards. And I know why. She's in love with Memphis and wants part of him. What better way to share a person than by taking his name? God, the woman was sick.

"Did your investigation find her extensive juvenile record?"

His forehead creased. "No. Tell me."

"You're Security Service. Look it up."

She was pissing him off now, she could tell. But she needed to get back to the house and get that laptop, and they were wasting time.

"If you think it's her, let's just go get her. My people are on the road. We'll hold her until they arrive."

"It's not that simple. You go barging in there, she'll clam up and we'll get nothing. Let me do this my way. Then y'all are welcome to her."

"'Y'all.' I like that."

She had him.

"What the hell is your name?"

He gave her another of those pretty Chiclet smiles. "It actually is Jacques. My mum's French."

"All right then, Jacques. I still need that weapon."

He stared at her for a few moments. "If you tell anyone I provided this to you, I'll deny it. I'll claim you forced your way into my desk and stole it. You got me?"

"Your name will never come up."

He opened the desk drawer and withdrew a key. The bottom drawer on the right had a lock. He used the key to open it. Handed her a Glock 26 and a full magazine of ammunition.

She loaded the weapon, felt the familiar comfort of it in her hand, and smiled. She was starting to feel like normal.

Jacques locked the drawer back up, tossed the key into the drawer, then stood.

"I'm going in with you. I don't care what you say. If she's dangerous, you need protection. You're a guest of the family. They'd have my head if something happened to you on my watch."

"Too late for that."

She filled him in about thinking she'd been drugged.

"You know, that's weird. Before the wife died, there were reports that she was acting abnormally. Seeing things. That does fit, then."

Oh, poor Evan. Poor, poor Evan. Driven off the edge, literally, by her best friend.

Jacques press-checked his weapon. "Don't worry about me. I can be circumspect. I'll stay around the staff, that's what I normally do. Here's my number. You ring if you need me. I'm a damn sight closer to you up there than down here."

A small, soft voice rang out.

"Erm, mum? I'm needing to get back to the house."

Shit. Maisrie. She'd completely forgotten.

Taylor turned and expertly stashed the weapon in the back of her jeans, pulled her sweater over it. No sense spooking the girl further.

"Okay, Maisrie. We're all set. Jacques is coming back with us. Again, honey, let me stress, don't tell anyone about this, okay?"

The girl nodded her head. Taylor turned back to Jacques. "Ready?"

"As I'll ever be," he said.

He sounded confident. She hoped she could say the same.

CHAPTER FORTY-NINE

They got back to the house undetected.

Maisrie led the way, through the kitchens, where Jacques, seeking to distract the crew of servants about to exit into the hallway to bring food to the dining room, made a show of entering, shaking snow off his thick hair, jovially tossing French compliments out to disarm the cook. Taylor and her small companion snuck on alone now.

Taylor heard noises coming from the hallway, a familiar voice. Maisrie stopped full, her face showing alarm. It was Trixie. Well, there'd be no helping it. With a smile, Taylor pushed Maisrie out in front of her, hoping the girl would be enterprising enough to improvise, at least long enough for Taylor to get into the drawing room.

She was hoping that Maddee would be set up in the drawing room like she had been the past two days, waiting for her, unaware of Taylor's suspicions.

Yeah, that was probably too much to wish for.

Taylor looked at her watch. It was past two. Surely Trixie had told Maddee that she was up and about, and that Taylor knew she and Roland were in the castle.

She got to the drawing room, listening carefully for signs of someone nearby. Hearing nothing, she stuck her head in. No one was there. What luck. Perfect. She that asketh, getteth.

She slipped in. For their sessions, Maddee had kept her laptop out on the table for Taylor to use while her voice wasn't working. When they finished the sessions, Maddee put the laptop into her bag.

Oh, this was too lucky for words. The bag was there. Now, was the laptop inside?

A flash of silver caught Taylor's eye.

Score one for the good guys.

Taylor dove into the bag and grabbed the little laptop. She didn't waste any more time. She needed to get back to her room. The drawing room only had one exit. Taylor went back to that door, listened, heard nothing, and slipped out into the hallway. Her heart was beating double time in her chest.

Just keep them occupied, Maisrie.

Taking Maddee's laptop was dangerous, but there might be something on there that gave some answers to her past. And Taylor needed to delete their session notes. There was just too much personal information in them, words she'd said under hypnosis that could come back to haunt her. And God knew what sort of notes Maddee had inserted herself to make Taylor's actions look even worse.

Up the stairs now, to the keypadded door leading to the family's private quarters. Taylor had no idea if Maddee knew the combination. Now she understood the newly enhanced security measures: the castle being closed for the season, electronically locked doors. Jacques had started to share something that had alarmed

Special Branch, something they'd found. She could only imagine what that might be. Personal protection from the government wasn't cheap. The threat must have been very real for them to cover a continuous protection detail.

She was in the hallway now. Her room was two doors away. One door. There. She breathed a huge sigh of relief and went inside, locking it behind her. Nice to know she had a future in cat burgling, if she wanted it.

She set Maddee's laptop on the desk. She knew it was password protected. She was going to need Lincoln's help. But she needed to talk to Baldwin first. She dialed his number. It went to voice mail.

"Come on, Baldwin. Pick up your phone."

She didn't know what to think. It could be the storm had killed cellular service. Or it could be something much, much worse. She was starting to get completely freaked out by all of this. And there was no place she could go. She was stuck at the castle. If he were in trouble, she couldn't help him. He was a capable man. He said he was in Atlantic's offices in Amsterdam, was going to be here soon. She didn't know how he would manage with the storm. She would have to fend for herself. He was safe, for now at least. She had her own issues she needed to deal with.

She left a message—"Call me"—then clicked off and dialed Lincoln's phone. She wasn't surprised when he answered immediately.

"Did you get it?" he asked.

"Yeah. Right here. I don't know how much time I have."

"I've been thinking about possible passwords. If you

were using an alias, and no one knew your real name, what would you use?"

"You're clever, Lincoln. It's worth a try."

Taylor typed the letters, holding her breath.

R-A-C-H-A-E-L-M-A-C-K

The screen saver disappeared, and the desktop background appeared. A beautiful shot of Loch Ness at sunset. Taylor remembered it from their first session.

"We're in. And you're amazing."

"Okay. I emailed you the list of places to look and steps to take if there are barriers. Get to it. Call me if you need any help."

"Will do, Linc. Thank you so much."

She hung up with him, set the phone on the desk next to Maddee's MacBook Air. Opened her own laptop, read through Lincoln's instructions. Started combing through the doctor's computer files.

Taylor quickly found the session notes from their two meetings. Taylor scanned through them, deleted the most egregious bits, then emailed them to herself and to Lincoln. Best-case scenario, she would have opened a file-sharing folder on Dropbox and uploaded all the files, but that would take more time than she had. Email wasn't as secure, but it worked quicker.

She trekked her way through the past few days of files, opening, perusing, sending, then found what she was looking for.

Maddee's online journal. Surely this would provide them with some answers.

She mailed the folder to Lincoln for him to look through as well, then went to most recent entries, the ones that had been made since she arrived at Dulsie Castle.

What she read turned her cold.

Like a child, Maddee, or Rachael, as Taylor needed to start thinking of her, started each entry the same way. *Dear Diary.*

Dear Diary—The bitch has arrived…

Dear Diary—That stupid cunt thinks he actually loves her. She's here to find out if she loves him, too…

Dear Diary—I can tell Memphis still has feelings for me. I saw the way he looked at me when he introduced his newest slut. All I can remember is the feel of him under me, my hands so full of him…

Dear Diary—There's no help for it. She has to go. She wants him, and he wants her. I can't go through that again. Not again.

Taylor's phone rang, startling her. It was Lincoln.

"Are you reading this?" she asked.

"Go to December 21, 2008," he said.

"That's the day Evan died." She clicked back onto the dates, happy to get out of the woman's psychotic head, even if only for a moment.

She read the entry, her mouth dropping open in shock.

Dec. 21, 2008
Dear Diary,
Everyone thinks she's dead. Now she's going to feel what it's like to be in my shoes for a while. The bitch

deserves every horrible thing that's going to happen to her. She should have never doubted me. I tried to help her. Everything we did, hypnosis, medications, it was all working. And then she had to grow a spine, decide to tell Memphis about our sessions. I couldn't take the chance that he'd find out.

"Lincoln, what the hell?"

"If what I'm reading is right, and not the ravings of a complete lunatic, Evan Highsmythe isn't dead. She is very much alive."

CHAPTER FIFTY

"Lincoln, that's absurd. Evan Highsmythe died in a car accident. The earl identified her body."

"They didn't do an autopsy. Why didn't Memphis identify her?"

Taylor thought back to the conversation she and Memphis had right after she arrived, that night in his study, before everything had spun so far out of control.

I never got to see her, you know. After the accident. Father wouldn't let me. He said it would be a very bad idea indeed. She'd gone through the windscreen, was cut to ribbons. He thought I would carry the image with me forever, what she looked like."

"No, he didn't. The earl wouldn't let him. She had extensive facial lacerations."

"That's doubt enough for me."

"But if it wasn't Evan in the car, who was it?"

"I don't know. They'll have to exhume the body, run DNA. Probably some transient passing through. Rachael got her hands on them and used them to her own end. She's good at that."

"Christ. That seems awfully risky."

"You're dealing with a stone-cold psychopath, Taylor. Risks are her specialty."

"Okay. Assume that you're right, that this is all a huge cover-up. That Rachael managed to wreck the car with someone else in it, spirit Evan away. So where is Evan now? Her death was splashed across the covers of every newspaper in the country. It would be difficult to hide her. Her face would be recognized."

"Look at what she says in the entry. 'Now Evan is going to feel what it's like to be in my shoes for a while.' Rachael was locked away for seven years."

"Committed. So you think Evan has been committed somewhere?"

"In an insane asylum. That would be the perfect punishment."

"Oh, my God, Lincoln. I can't believe Rachael would be able to manage it."

"Look at her past, Taylor. Rachael succeeded by manipulating others to do her work for her. It's possible. And with a doctor's license, she could fake the papers. She's a master forger, family signatures would be nothing to her. We just need to find out where she put her."

Evan's suicide note. Could Maddee have written it? Could she have sent the email from Memphis's account, too?

A voice rang out from the hallway. "Taylor? You should come to lunch. We've been waiting for you."

Rachael.

She had the electronic code to the family's private quarters after all.

The Highsmythes had let the wolf into the chicken coop.

Taylor's voice was mouse quiet. "Lincoln. She's at my door."

"Did you send me all the files?"

"Yes."

"Then find a way to get her computer back into her bag, and don't let her know we're on to her. I'll get looking for places Evan might be."

"You know what name to look under, right?"

"Yes. Rachael Mack."

"Right. Do me a favor and get Baldwin. I've been trying to reach him without luck. He's supposed to be heading here, so he may be en route. Find him and let him know what's happening. Talk to you in a bit."

"Taylor. Watch yourself."

"I will."

Rachael was knocking on the door now. Hard. Taylor slapped the laptop shut. Looked at it critically. It was so thin... She stood and put the computer down the front of her jeans, sending a mental thank-you to Steve Jobs's design team. The heavy wool sweater she wore covered both the laptop and the gun at the small of her back perfectly.

She went to the door and opened it. Rachael had a huge, winning smile on her face. If she knew something was up, she was one hell of an actress.

"Hiya. Hey there. How you feeling? Trixie said you were up and about. Want to come down and have lunch? You can meet Roland—properly, this time. I'm afraid he was a bit put out that I was so trashed last night. Then we couldn't get down the drive. The truck kept sliding off to the side of the road. He'd forgotten the chains. So we gave up, hiked back up to the house. We had to stay here last night. He wasn't all that thrilled, let me tell you. The kids are home with the nanny, and God knows what sort of trouble they've managed to get into."

Taylor forced her voice to stay in a normal range. "That's quite an adventure. Lunch sounds great. I'm actually starved, and I'd love to meet Roland."

But I don't plan to eat a bite with you anywhere around, you psycho bitch.

Dr. Maddee James, née Rachael Mack, didn't seem to have a clue that Taylor was on to her. Which was helpful. Taylor shut the door to her suite and the two started off down the hall together.

"I was hoping you'd come down for our session this morning. Did you at least do the exercises I gave you?"

Taylor gave her own winning smile. She wasn't too bad of an actress herself.

"Yeah. We maybe hit it too hard last night. Getting up this morning wasn't exactly easy. Despite the hangover from hell, I did do the exercises. And I listened to the biofeedback tape. I kind of passed out last night after our party—haven't done *that* in a while—woke up in the middle of the night with a horrid headache. I took all my meds, got back in bed and slept through till Trixie woke me. That melatonin is amazing. I need to get some back in the States. I owe you—no doctor has ever been able to cure my insomnia."

Rachael touched Taylor's back with the palm of her hand, between her shoulder blades. A reassuring pat. Taylor did her best not to cringe.

"You are so welcome. I'm glad it helped. So you listened to the tape. How did it make you feel?"

"So relaxed. I am feeling so much better. You're doing wonders for me. I really don't know how to thank you."

"You just did," Rachael said. The cold snap in her

voice was hard to miss. She didn't want Taylor getting better. She wanted her dead. The tape proved it.

They were at the door to the second dining room now. This would be Taylor's only shot. She patted her front pocket.

"Oh, crap. I forgot my phone. I'm waiting for my fiancé to call. Listen, you go on in and sit down. I'll be right back, okay?"

"Oh, sure. No problem. See you in a minute." Rachael went into the dining room without a backward glance.

The moment Rachael was inside the door, Taylor reversed course. She ran down the stairs, down the hall, back to the drawing room. All the while, the same three words ran through her head.

Evan's not dead.

Evan's not dead.

Evan's not dead.

CHAPTER FIFTY-ONE

The door to the drawing room was closed. She didn't think about it, just turned the handle and went inside. Crossed the room.

Rachael's bag was gone.

Shit. She looked around a bit, thinking maybe one of the maids had moved it, but no, it was nowhere to be seen. What were the odds that Rachael hadn't looked into the bag and noticed her laptop missing? It was a light little thing, it wouldn't change the weight of the bag if she'd picked it up hastily.

"Looking for this?"

Taylor froze. Son of a bitch.

She turned slowly. Rachael was standing there, dangling her leather bag off two fingers, swinging it lightly back and forth.

"I can explain," Taylor stammered.

Rachael's sweet, disarming smile didn't match her tone.

"Oh, I'm sure you can. May I have my laptop back? I assume you're finished digging through my private life."

Think fast, Taylor. Think fast.

"I was borrowing it to send my guy an email. My laptop's been acting weird. I think it has a virus. I was down here getting some tea, saw it in your bag, and borrowed it. I'm sorry. I should have asked permission first."

Rachael moved into the room, still swinging the bag in front of her. Tick, tock. Tick, tock.

"I've heard that about you. You like to break the rules, and you only ever apologize if you get caught. That's not a very noble way to live your life."

Remember what Baldwin said, Taylor. Don't listen. She's planted suggestions in her hypnosis sessions. She's trying to get you to listen so she can trigger you.

"I said I was sorry. Here, take your laptop. I'm going to lunch."

Taylor set the laptop on the end table and started edging toward the door.

"I don't think so. We still have so much work to do."

Rachael set her briefcase down on the couch. Every move was deliberate. Calculated. She never looked away from Taylor's eyes.

"I think you need to relax, Taylor. You've had a very big week."

She inched closer.

"Stop now, Rachael."

Her eyes flew wide in surprise, then she collected herself. "You poor girl. You're completely deranged. My name is Madeira. Madeira James."

"Your name is Rachael Mack. I know all about you. I know what you've done. It's over. You need serious help, and I'm sure the American authorities will be more than happy to provide that for you. Skipping out on probation is rather frowned upon. There's a warrant out for your arrest. Now stop moving, and stop talking."

"Taylor. Think about that warm—"

"No. Stop, right now. You say another word, and I won't be responsible for my actions. *You* hypnotized *me,* remember? All I have to do is show that biofeedback tape to a judge and I'll be off the hook. You've been messing with the wrong woman's mind this time, Rachael."

Her face contorted. "I said my name is Maddee!" She started toward Taylor.

That was the last straw. With a lightning-quick draw, Taylor removed the weapon from her waistband and sighted down on Rachael.

"Stop," she said.

Rachael kept moving, edging sideways.

"I'm not going to warn you again, Rachael. You take one more step and I *will* shoot you."

Rachael stopped. Calculated.

"Ah, Taylor. Ever the avenging angel. Doing what you do best. You can't use your wits to get out of the situation, so you resort to brute force. Murder. You don't scare me. I've seen inside of you. I know how much you enjoy this part. In fact, I'll let you prolong it for a bit."

"You are out of your mind, Rachael. I feel sorry for you. Here you served your time, had a chance at a normal life. You have a husband and children of your own. You've thrown it all away, and for what? Trying to gain the favors of a man who doesn't want you? Who will never want you?"

Rachael smiled, an eerily cold grin. She started to move again, edging left, and left, and left again. Taylor kept the gun pointed at center mass, moved in concert. They danced through the drawing room, inch by inch, a centrifuge of anger and wariness.

"Where did you stash Evan? Tell me where she is, and I won't shoot you."

Rachael showed her teeth. "You don't frighten me, Taylor. You aren't going to shoot me. You can't stand the thought of yet another life weighing down your conscience. You've hit your limit. I was right about you. You enjoyed killing your *Pretender*, but you know your soul will fracture into too many pieces if you kill again."

"You are so very wrong. I don't need to kill you to shoot you, you bitch. You of all people know how that works. You disabled them beforehand. Made it easier. But you couldn't do it all yourself. You needed a helper. Tell me, what did it feel like when they put your Robert to death? When they shoved a needle in his veins and pumped him full of drugs? When his heart stopped beating? Did that make you happy? Your secret died with him, or so you thought."

Rachael stopped moving. She was perpendicular to the entrance. Taylor was directly opposite. The room's furniture spread between them.

"You don't know anything about me." Rachael's voice was a hiss, each word enunciated. "You have no idea what my life was like. I had no choice."

"Oh, but you did. Remember what you said to me, you loathsome piece of crap? *You have free will. You have a choice.* I certainly believe that. I've never killed without knowing it would shatter me inside, without knowing that if I didn't, innocent people would lose their lives. But you, you killed for your own gain. Things weren't going the way you wanted, so you murdered your family. Manipulated your boyfriend. Told him you were being mistreated, abused. That your daddy had sex with you, and your mommy knew it and didn't care. How much convincing did it take to get Robert to kill them for you?"

Rachael's tone changed, became soft, cajoling.

"You've suffered a great trauma, Taylor. Seeing your friends hurt, it was too much for you. You've been in a fragile state. Everyone knows it. You've told enough people about the things you've seen, heard and done. We are all very concerned about you. We're just trying to help you. Please, Taylor, you need to put down the gun. This won't solve anything."

"What the fuck are you talking about? This isn't about me. This is about you. What *you've* done."

A deep voice. "Taylor, listen to Maddee. She's only trying to help."

Memphis edged into the room.

Taylor didn't dare take her eyes off Rachael. Memphis started to come toward her, right arm outstretched, like he was planning to take the gun. Taylor backed away a few paces.

"Don't even think about it, Memphis."

He stopped.

"Taylor. You're okay. It's all okay. Just put the gun away. No one needs to get hurt."

She glanced at him, a fraction of a second's look. He wasn't smiling.

"I came as quick as I could, Maddee. I'm so glad you called. Looks like I got here in just the nick of time."

Taylor met Rachael's eye. "*You* called him. That's why he set off in the middle of the storm. What did you say, Rachael? What sort of lie did you sell him this time?"

"Who the hell is *Rachael?* Taylor, you're acting insane. Please, give me the gun."

"I'm sorry, Memphis. But I can't. I don't know that you're not in on this with her."

Rachael turned to him. "I told you, Memphis. She's had a psychotic break. We need to get her sedated as quickly as possible. I have some injectable Haldol in my bag. I was trying to get to it to give her a shot, and she pulled a gun on me. I'm frightened, Memphis. She's out of control."

Memphis looked from Taylor to Rachael, completely confused.

"Oh, for God's sake. Memphis, her real name is Rachael Mack. She had her whole family murdered when she was just sixteen. Spent seven years in an asylum in upstate New York. Her boyfriend, Robert Deaver, was executed for the killings. They used an ax to cut them to pieces, then burned the house down. Her mother, her father and her baby sister. All because they said she couldn't date him. She's the one who's insane, not me."

"She's delusional, Memphis. You've known me for years. Does that sound right?"

"Ask Rachael about Evan, Memphis—*ask her where Evan is.*"

That got his attention. His face creased with worry, but he was facing her, not Rachael. Taylor caught it out of the corner of her eye, and knew she needed to move quickly. He was choosing Rachael's story over hers.

"Oh, Taylor. Honey. I'm so sorry. This has obviously gone further than we can all handle. Let me get you some real help. The storm is breaking. The snow had all but stopped when I arrived. I can have Baldwin brought here. We'll get you straightened out. I'm so sorry. I should have never left you alone up here."

Rachael went to Memphis's side. "Listen to him, Taylor. We just want what's best for you."

Taylor was getting furious. How could Memphis not listen to her? Why wouldn't he hear what she was saying? She took two steps toward Rachael, who muffled a scream behind her hand and clutched on to Memphis's sleeve.

"Like you wanted what was best for Evan?" She looked at Memphis. "Seriously, Memphis. You have to listen to me. Evan isn't dead. Rachael couldn't stand the fact that she had you. She wanted you for herself. She started with a smear campaign on your name. *She* 'leaked' your 'affair' to the press. Hell, she even changed her last name to your given name, to feel closer to you. Didn't you ever wonder why she picked James? Then she started drugging Evan, feeding her the same shit she's been feeding me. Remember how sick Evan was, and the doctors had no explanation? She was losing weight in her third trimester. When that didn't do the trick, she staged Evan's death and stashed her away in an insane asylum. Lincoln is scouring hundreds of records, looking for your wife right now."

He still didn't believe her. She could see it. He thought she was crazy.

Memphis and Rachael kept up the soothing dialogue, like they were trying to calm a seriously pissed-off bee.

They'd take a step to the left, Taylor would respond with one to her left. She was getting closer and closer to the door. Maybe she could bolt for it. Lock herself in her room and wait them out. Memphis had said the storm was breaking. That meant Baldwin would be on his way.

Another step. Another. Memphis was using the tone

he'd used on the bridge, that charming, you-know-you-love-me voice. Rachael was simply watching her, wary and distrustful. Taylor was the one with the gun, after all, though she'd truly prefer not having to use it.

A quick glance over her shoulder—the door was two feet away. She edged one step closer, took a quick peep at Rachael, then saw Memphis's eyes slide over her shoulder.

Taylor whipped her head around in time to see Jacques lunge at her. He grabbed her in a bear hug, wrestled the gun from her grip, and everyone exploded into motion. Memphis bolted toward her to help Jacques. Rachael leapt for her bag.

She'd been flanked.

Taylor started to scream. "Don't you let her do that, Memphis! She's trying to kill me. She's going to kill you too. Please, Memphis. Jacques, tell him! Tell him!"

Jacques just held her tightly. He had her in a half nelson. Normally she could get out of it, but he had a bad angle on her. She continued to struggle, but slowed a bit, as if she were giving up. She'd need the element of surprise if she were to get out of this.

Memphis reached down to grab her legs, and she booted him in the face. Her Wellies weren't as solid as cowboy boots, but he hadn't been expecting it, and his neck snapped back. Blood spurted from his nose.

She took advantage of the shock to slam her head back into Jacques's nose. She felt the cartilage give way. He stumbled back against the doorjamb, only one hand on her now. She whirled fast to her right, all the way around and kicked him in the knee, hard enough to break the bone. His leg doubled in on itself and he went down.

Memphis came back at her again, yelling expletives. "For Christ's sake, Taylor. You broke my nose. What the hell?"

"Just get her, Memphis," Rachael yelled.

He dove back in. She felt horrible. She didn't want to do this. She didn't want to fight him.

He didn't want to fight her, either. He came at her with his arms outstretched, like he could snare her. Rachael darted in from the left, trying to distract her.

Taylor let her. Jacques was trying to rise aided by the doorjamb, a ferocious scowl on his face. He hadn't drawn his gun yet, that was a plus. He might still be on her side. Or he might shoot her in the back. She had to take the chance. She kicked at him, knocked him off balance. He crumpled to the floor again with a moan.

Memphis had one hand on her now. She let them come in, made like she was about to hit Memphis again. She feinted with her elbow, he ducked. She used her leg to sweep him off his feet. He landed on his back with a grunt, then started to scramble up. Taylor paused for a second as if she were winded, then as he rose, she punched him, hard, on the cheek. He went down again, and she turned, just in time to see Rachael a foot away, the hypodermic needle poised to jam into Taylor's thigh.

She dodged to the left, too quick for Rachael to follow. She swept her left hand out and caught Rachael's upturned hand, while chopping her arm with the right. Taylor had been trained, and was in the grip of a Valkyrie fury. Rachael only had the will to survive on her side, plus two very broken men.

Taylor wrenched the syringe free, twisted the woman around to face Memphis and plunged the needle directly into Rachael's neck.

CHAPTER FIFTY-TWO

Rachael froze, all fight in her suspended.

"Tell them," Taylor growled at her. "Tell them right now, or so help me God I will shoot you full of whatever is in this syringe and send you straight to hell."

The whites of Rachael's eyes shone. She was genuinely scared, panicked. Taylor's instincts were dead-on. The contents of the syringe were deadly.

Taylor saw the plan. It was ingenious, devious. With all of Taylor's strange medication allergies, it would have been a no-brainer for Rachael to inject her with something, then claim Taylor had suffered anaphylactic shock and died from a bad drug interaction. Memphis would have been there to corroborate the story that Taylor was acting crazy, that "Maddee" was just trying to help.

Too close for comfort.

Memphis was struggling to his feet. She glanced at him and immediately felt horrible. She'd done a number on him. His nose was broken, his cheekbone probably, too. Jacques was back on the ground, groaning. Knee shots were so effective.

"Tell. Him." She moved her thumb to the plunger. Her

teeth were gritted, her own voice so raspy, so broken. She didn't even recognize herself. But that wasn't going to stop her.

Rachael began to cry.

"Stop that. Tell him the truth. Rachael."

"Maddee? Taylor? Tell me what's really going on. Right now."

Finally. Memphis was starting to realize the situation wasn't as it first appeared. Taylor held herself back from openly rolling her eyes.

"She's insane. I told you."

"You poor, stupid girl," Taylor said. Her thumb moved, and the tiniest bit of the contents of the syringe went into Rachael's neck. She hissed in pain.

"That stings, huh? Good to know." Taylor pressed harder.

"Stop," Rachael screamed. "It's true. It's true, okay? Evan isn't dead. I didn't want to kill her—she's my friend. I just needed her out of the way."

The transformation on Memphis's face was impossible to watch, but Taylor forced herself. Disbelief, followed by crushing pain, and then, with the tiniest of movements that settled in his eyes and forehead, hope.

Followed immediately by rage.

CHAPTER FIFTY-THREE

Taylor quickly realized that while she was out of danger, Rachael was not. She pulled the needle from the woman's neck, tossed the syringe across the room toward the fireplace. She shoved Rachael upright and back against the wall, then stood in front to cover her. They were smashed together, Rachael's front against Taylor's back. She pushed back against the wall as hard as she could, so Rachael couldn't wiggle away. Or stab her in the back.

Memphis had taken on the look of an enraged bull. Another couple of steps and he'd be right on top of her. His voice was thick with pain and anger.

"Let. Me. Have. Her."

"No," Taylor said. "We need to let the police sort this out."

"I *am* the *fucking* police."

"No, you're the victim's husband. Rachael will tell us where she is. Won't you, Rachael?"

Rachael was whimpering, in pain, in fear. Taylor didn't care which.

"*Won't you,* Rachael?" she said again, whirling around

and planting both hands against the wall on either side of Rachael's face. "Where is she? Where is Evan?"

Rachael was going to try defiance again. Taylor was going to have to hit her. She might enjoy that a bit too much. Without turning her head, she said to Memphis, "May I have your handcuffs, please?"

That did it. Taylor congratulated herself on being a keen judge of character. Death didn't frighten Rachael as much as the idea of incarceration.

"She's in Moldavia. A place up in the Carpathian mountains. If she's still alive. That's why I chose it. Most don't survive the first winter. You already had the papers signed. You were going to commit her anyway. I just took care of it for you."

Taylor punched the bitch in the stomach for adding that last bit of torture.

Chatty Rachael collapsed onto her hands and knees, vomited on the drawing room floor.

"Nice shot," Memphis said.

"Thanks. What are we going to do with her?"

"I don't know. String her up on the grand staircase?"

"Tempting. But perhaps we can lock her in one of the rooms until the constable arrives, instead."

Memphis was still red in the face, upset and furious. She didn't blame him. "I suppose that would be all right. Why is she wearing my mother's ring?"

"What are you talking about?" Taylor asked.

"The onyx ring. It's my mother's. She used to bring it out as a novelty at parties. Another one of the Highsmythe family legends—that ring has a hatch in it for poison."

Taylor went to Rachael and wrenched it from her hand.

"So that's how she did it. I knew she put something in my beer."

She handed the ring to Memphis, watched him turn it over and over in his hands. He could barely meet her eye.

"Oh, Taylor, I am so sorry."

"Me, too."

"We should probably have to have someone watch her. She's tried to commit suicide before. She told me that's why she became a psychologist, to help combat the demons. I want to make sure she's never able to do this to anyone again."

"She had me considering it. She tried to drive your wife to it. I can't say she deserves any less."

Taylor stood straight, flexing her fingers. Punching people hurt; she had abrasions on all her knuckles.

"Um, Memphis? Trixie has been helping Rachael poison me. Giving me something hallucinogenic. I've been seeing ghosts, having rather vivid dreams."

"Trixie wouldn't do that. Would you, old girl?"

Drawn by the shouts and screams, the entire staff of the castle had gathered in the hallway. Trixie was standing in the drawing room door, hands folded in front of her.

"No, sir. I did all I could to keep the lady safe. Dr. James was acting strangely, and the lady was obviously getting ill. I kept an eye on them as much as possible."

"Taylor, Trixie was the first one who called me. She thought something was wrong, asked me to come home. Then Madd… I mean, Rachael, called and said you were delusional, that you'd had a break. I knew I needed to get back straightaway. The trains and planes weren't an option, so I drove. Took me all bloody night, too."

"I'm glad you got back in time, Memphis," Taylor said.

"Me, too."

Rachael didn't fight them when they handcuffed her to the fire grate. It was as safe a place as any to hold her. Trixie stood guard, five feet away, her back ramrod-straight, a heavy fireplace poker in her hands. She looked quite menacing. Rachael had retreated within herself, to some catatonic place where she could live out her vivid, sick fantasies alone. A red welt surrounded the spot where the needle had been inserted in her neck. She'd reach up to scratch it every few minutes.

Taylor and Memphis were on the other side of the drawing room, watching.

"Why didn't you tell me about Jacques?" Taylor asked.

"I did."

"About the threats to the family, Memphis."

He ran his hands over his face, wincing as he touched the damaged flesh.

"Because I had no idea they were directed at anyone but my father. With him away, I felt this place was as safe as any other. I had no idea that the threat was from within. Could it be true, Taylor? Is it possible? Is Evan alive? And my son?"

His son. She didn't know the answer to that. She shook her head and shrugged.

Taylor's phone rang. The caller ID was from Nashville. Lincoln.

"Hold on." She clicked the answer button. "Linc.

What do you have for me? Rachael just mentioned Moldavia."

"That's a possibility. I've scoured the U.K., France and Italy. Nothing yet. Let me expand the search parameters. How would she get her there?"

"Friends. She grew up on Long Island, that much was true. Look at the Russian community, see if she did time with anyone. She probably met them inside."

"God, you're good. I'm ready for you to get back to work. Come home soon, okay? I'll get back to you as soon as I have something." He clicked off.

"We're working on it," she said to Memphis. "Let's deal with one thing at a time, okay?"

Trixie had brought Memphis an ice pack. He was gingerly trying to put it on his cheek.

"Here, let me." Taylor took the bag of ice and laid it gently against his cheek. She took the opportunity to assess the damage. His nose was definitely broken, but that cheekbone would need an X-ray to know for sure.

"Why, pray tell, did you feel the need to hit me? That wasn't very nice."

"Like you gave me a choice? You were going to hold me down while she shot me full of God knows what. I can't believe you believed her over me."

"I've known her longer. And she's been insinuating herself into my world for a very long time."

His face was wrecked. The emotions from the past hour coupled with the swelling wasn't doing him any favors.

Aside from Rachael and Trixie, they were alone in the room. Jacques had been tended to by the kitchen staff, carefully carried into the kitchens, where he was now lying on the servant's table awaiting the local emergency services, who were coming with the police. The constable had just called; he was due in ten minutes. They had time.

"Memphis? I need to ask you something."

"Anything."

"The night after we went to the bridge, did you come to my room?"

He didn't answer for a moment, then said, "Would you like me to say yes, or no?"

"I just want the truth. The medicine Rachael gave me made me have very strange dreams, strange thoughts. I did a lot of hallucinating. I need to know if you were there or not."

"You mean, whether making love with me was real? I'm glad it was that memorable."

Oh, shit. She had slept with him.

She handed him the ice pack, avoided his eyes, and turned away.

It was wishful thinking that she could blame a hallucination for her actions. Stupid, stupid girl. Letting your hormones make decisions for you. Rachael was right. We all have a choice.

She took a deep breath. She would get through this. She and Baldwin, together, would get through this.

"Taylor," Memphis said softly. "It doesn't matter. None of that matters. If Evan's alive… If…if there's any chance that she's actually alive, that she'll forgive me, I must take that chance. She is my wife."

"I know that. I wouldn't want it any other way. I adore you, Memphis, but I don't love you. I love Baldwin."

"Well, that's good to hear."

Baldwin strode into the room, took in the scene. She felt all her air leave her. How much had he heard?

But he was smiling at her, a wide, happy, welcoming smile. He'd only just arrived, heard her pledging her love to him.

She went to him, a magnet drawn north. Let him envelop her in his arms. A huge sigh escaped her. She was safe. She could let down her guard now.

"Memphis," Baldwin said. "Someone did a number on your face, brother."

"Talk to your woman. She's got a fierce right hook."

Baldwin coughed out a laugh, looked down at Taylor, nestled in his arms. "You did this to him?"

"I didn't have a choice. He didn't believe me."

"Remind me never to disagree with you," he said lightly.

"How did you get here so quickly? I thought the airports were closed?"

"Atlantic made a call to Special Branch, pulled a favor, and I got a ride on a Lynx that was headed up here. That was fun. The British military do have some cool toys."

Memphis wasn't enjoying the byplay. He gave Baldwin a mock salute. "Baldwin. Thank you for all your help. I'll leave you two to catch up."

He stood, shakily at first, then made to leave the room. As he walked past them, he glanced over his shoulder.

"Taylor?"

She turned from her shelter, looked at Memphis.

"I wasn't there," he said, then smiled, sadly, and left the room.

CHAPTER FIFTY-FOUR

Baldwin leaned down to give Taylor a kiss. She welcomed it. When he'd walked through the door, she couldn't help herself, she'd wanted to leap into his arms and be held forever. She just couldn't face this world without him. If anything, this trip, her time in Scotland, had solidified that for her.

She was just happy she'd escaped with her life.

"God, I missed you. Are you okay?" he asked.

"I am. And I am so happy to see you. You have no idea."

He gestured at the door, where Memphis had just walked out.

"What was all that about?" Baldwin asked. "Where wasn't Memphis?"

She debated for half a second. No, she didn't want to go any further without getting this off her chest. Memphis had just given her the answer she needed. He'd never said he'd been in her room, but he had said that he hadn't. She would take that. It was all a hallucination.

"Taylor? What's up?"

"I... How to explain this?"

Baldwin released her. Crossed his arms on his chest. "You need to be honest with me. Did you sleep with him?"

"No."

"Did you want to sleep with him?"

"I don't know."

The pain on his face made her cringe. He wanted honesty from her, and while she agreed that she owed him that much, what was the point? Hearing that she'd had doubts, that she was attracted to another man, was going to do nothing but hurt him.

And she was tired of hurting him. God, she was tired of so much. She just wanted to be sure again, of herself, of her life, her purpose, her trajectory. She was like a shooting star that had looked down at Earth, gotten distracted and subsequently became lost in the dark of the night's sky.

"I was so mad at you, Baldwin. You kept so much from me. Memphis gave me friendship when I needed it most, when you were pulling away from me. Since I've been here... I was being drugged. I had some pretty intense dreams. But that's all they were. Just dreams."

"That's an awful lot, Taylor."

"Can you forgive me?"

His deep green eyes met hers. "Can *you* forgive me?"

"Yes. I can."

"Then you know my answer."

He pulled her close again, settled his lips on hers. His beard scratched her chin, and felt her heart pounding.

This was so right.

She was sorry when he stopped.

"Taylor, are you really okay?"

Not entirely. But she was getting better. She squeezed his hand.

"I'm okay. At least, I will be. Right now, we have more important issues to deal with. We need to get Memphis and Evan together. Can you help?"

He smiled.

"I think I can. Let me make a call."

EPILOGUE

Taylor had a chance to see Rachael one last time.

The British government wanted to prosecute her, but the United States wanted to extradite her as well. She'd broken parole and stolen the identity of a woman named Madeira Hudson. Started a new life. Went to school. Got her degree. Met and married Roland MacDonald, moved to Scotland and bore him three sons. Had a normal life, for a while. Then became overwhelmingly obsessed with Memphis. Changed her name to James and started her second downward spiral.

God knew how many other crimes she'd committed. Her initial release from the state mental institution had been predicated on compliance with her probation. Since she'd broken that, and fled the country, she was going back inside.

But there were bigger issues concerning her case in the States. The parole officer assigned to her case was dead, and Rachael was the prime suspect. The New York police would be able to clear a homicide if they got her back. The Brits had her on too many charges to count—kidnapping, two counts of attempted murder, drug possession. Whoever got to have first crack at her, Rachael Mack was going away for a very long time.

Taylor didn't know whether an asylum or jail was the right place for a person like Rachael. She was obviously a psychopath. The syringe had been loaded with penicillin, which Taylor was deathly allergic to. Coincidentally, so was Rachael, and that's why she'd flinched when Taylor put the needle in her neck.

Taylor thought it telling that the woman would gamble that way. Or maybe, just maybe, it was her own personal suicide bomb, like a cyanide capsule, just waiting for her to be caught. Maybe she was simply crazy after all.

Rachael had stolen Evan away from her comfortable life, stashed her in an asylum in Russia, and effectively killed the child she carried. The tiny boy had been born early, in freezing conditions; with no neonatal support, he had died within hours.

That news alone had been heartbreaking for Memphis, but it was tempered by the fact that his wife had been found. She was alive. No one knew for sure what her mental state would be, but the finest doctors were lined up to take care of her.

After extensive questioning, Rachael broke and explained her crimes. The intimidation. The forgeries. The illusions. How she'd broken into Memphis's world, his email, his office, and pretended to be him. The physical intimidation, passive-aggressive at first, when she put the cut glass in Taylor's new coat, then more direct. The hypnosis. Then the hallucinogens, her own prescription for Seroquel tinged with LSD. How over two years ago, she'd taken the young woman she'd recently hired to nanny her sons, a woman who wouldn't be missed, to Dulsie Bridge and murdered her, hitting her in the chest with a rock to imitate the blunt force trauma of a steering wheel. Then she cut her face to shreds with a knife and stashed her body in the truck before inviting Evan on a drive. Compromised by the drugs she'd been taking, trusting Maddee as a friend, Evan suspected nothing.

Rachael told Evan she was Memphis's mistress, that he hated her, that he didn't want her or the child, then knocked her out. She put the nanny in the driver's seat, spread her blood throughout the car, and shouldered it off the edge of the road. Time and gravity managed the rest. And since it seemed Evan had been suicidal—they had that suicide note, expertly forged by Rachael—Memphis and his family had quietly hushed things up and let it be known that she'd been in a bad accident. Their influence assured nothing more was done to investigate.

Rachael had taken Evan to the coast, off Inverness, and put her on a boat. She'd made many friends while incarcerated. And the Russian mafia in Long Island possessed a legendary cruelty. They already had the signed committal papers. A few favors, a few strings pulled, and Rachael had Evan out of the way.

The story was astounding in its simplicity and duplicity. Evan's grave up at the kirk was exhumed, the body inside tested for DNA, matched to a woman named Patricia Cantrell, who'd been missing for over two years.

The Inverness airport was situated on a strip of land between the city of Inverness and Fort George, an English garrison built to house the English troops left in country after the Jacobite uprising of 1746. There was no more fighting on Scottish soil between the Brits and the Scots after that. Their enemies were larger, from without, not within. Like the Highsmythes and Rachael Mack. They'd never seen her coming.

They were coming now. Rachael was shackled, head bent, shuffling along like a crippled dog. Taylor refused to feel anything for her. Compassion was best reserved for creatures who could be saved.

Rachael was being transported to London for holding while the various governments decided what to do with her. It seemed to Taylor that she had shrunk, and she doubted Rachael would see the inside of a prison. She'd kill herself before she went back inside for long, Taylor was sure of it. And she was certain that she wasn't sorry about that, either.

As if she knew Taylor was there watching, she lifted her head and stared right at her. A small smile played on her lips. She awkwardly turned her hands around within their metal braces and raised her middle finger.

Such a classy girl.

Taylor resisted the urge to return the gesture, settled for watching Rachael get loaded into a British Airways 767. She hoped she'd have a very uncomfortable flight, then dismissed her. She'd have to testify, come back to England to let them know what Rachael had done to her, but that was probably a while away.

As the plane with Rachael inside left, another pulled up. This one was a private plane, a Bombardier Learjet, specially procured by Baldwin's covert friends.

Evan had been found, desolate and alone, fighting to keep her sanity. While she wasn't directly mistreated, the Russian government was more than happy to keep the news of a British citizen's unlawful incarceration on their soil quiet, and were willing to do most anything requested of them.

Memphis stood five feet away from Taylor, watching the plane arrive with breathless anticipation. He'd lobbied to go directly to Russia to get Evan himself, but was denied. Instead, he'd had to wait for her to return to U.K. soil, just like everyone else.

The Lear pulled to a stop. The door swung open and the stairs unfolded. A man Taylor didn't recognize stood in the door, then reached behind him to give a hand to someone else.

Taylor heard Memphis suck in his breath.

Evan looked nothing like Taylor in person. Her hair was shorn. She was obscenely thin. But she gave Memphis a wavering smile, and he bolted for the stairs of the plane. She met him halfway down the steps, and they embraced, two drowning souls who'd just found a bit of flotsam in a very wide sea.

Taylor felt tears prick her eyes. This was right. This was good. The universe was realigned.

She watched Memphis, his arms around Evan, the joy on his face. She was so happy for him. Having Evan taken from him so abruptly, and to have her restored, brought back from death, was too much. She couldn't help but feel a small gnawing at her heart. Memphis would never look at her in the same way again, not now that he had his Evan back. She wasn't jealous, not at all, but felt the sadness of the inexplicable shift that happens in every relationship, the moments of before and after that change the color and complexity of life.

No child, but the chance at redemption. They had time to create another life. They had a future.

And so did she.

To her left, there was movement. Baldwin, dressed for the weather, stood stoically watching the reunion. He looked over at Taylor. Things weren't right between them, not all the way, not yet. But she could hope.

Baldwin held out his hand to her.

"Come home, Taylor. Please, just come home with me. We can figure everything out there."

That's what she wanted, more than anything.

"I need you to promise that from here on out, if we've got any hope of surviving, you will be honest with me. No more secrets. No more lies. I can't take any more deception from you."

He nodded. "Taylor, you know everything. Everything that I know. I promise. I'll never hold back from sharing with you again."

She looked at the man who'd fought for her so hard, through everything, through bullets and transgressions and serial killers and false starts, the man she knew in her soul she would spend the rest of her life with. He stood so still, his face hopeful, the hand he extended more than just a chance for succor, but the opportunity of a lifetime.

With a last glance over her shoulder at Memphis and Evan, she turned to Baldwin, resolute, and took his hand, smiling.

"Let's go home."

* * * * *

ACKNOWLEDGMENTS

Thanks first to my outstanding team: my dear agent Scott Miller and his trusty sidekick Alex Slater at Trident Media, my wonderful editor Adam Wilson, my awesome publicists Megan Lorius and Melanie Dulos from MIRA Books and Deborah Kohan and Anna Ko at Planned Television Arts, and all the booksellers and librarians who've played such a role in making these books a success.

The rest of the MIRA/Harlequin team all have my enduring thanks: Donna Hayes, Alex Osuszek, Loriana Sacilotto, Craig Swinwood, Valerie Gray, Margaret Marbury, Diane Moggy, Don Lucey, Adrienne Macintosh, Maureen Stead, Nick Ursino, Tracey Langmuir, Kathy Lodge, Emily Ohanjanians, Karen Queme, Alana Burke, Jayne Hoogenberk, Tara Kelly and Gigi Lau. I would be remiss not to thank Sheryl Zajechowski and Natalie Fedewa from Brilliance Audio for all their hard work, and the amazing Joyce Bean, who brings these stories to life so artfully and effortlessly.

Thanks also to my tribe: Laura Benedict, Jeff Abbott, Erica Spindler, Allison Brennan, Toni McGee Causey,

Alex Kava, Jeanne Bowerman, Jill Thompson, Del Tinsley, Paige Crutcher, Cecelia Tichi, Jason Pinter and Andy Levy. *Molto grazie* to the wonderful writers and readers of Murderati, who keep me honest. Joan Huston's gimlet eye did a great job, as always. And thanks to Zoë Sharp, who read for Britishisms and Scottishisms and helped me make Memphis a proper lord.

Many thanks to Sherrie Saint and Dr. Sandra Thomas—you know what for. Dr. D.P. Lyle answered questions on aphonia and dysphonia. Bill Sites and Jan Schweitzer, from Ward-Potts Jewelers in Nashville, turned me on to the concept of the poison ring. My Twitter Chickadees and Facebook friends kept me going when the going got tough.

Madeira "Maddee" James, BG "Trixie Gardner" Ritts and Penelope Micklebury all gave money to charity to become characters in this book. Bless you all—I can't thank you enough for your generosity and courage. Note that these three woman are all heroes, regardless of what license I took with their names.

Research for this book was extensive, including two trips to Scotland. The folks at Blair Castle in Scotland were a huge help, as were the McBeans, proprietors of the Lochardil House in Inverness and distant relations of my husband. The Glasshouse in Edinburgh got me turned onto Laphroaig, so many thanks for that. Every place we visited in Scotland was stellar—we were welcomed with perfectly Scottish weather, open arms, ready stories and delicious food. I can't wait to set another book there.

I had a lot of cheerleaders while writing this book, but none so vociferous as my parents, who commiserated with every moan and congratulated every milestone. I couldn't do this without you.

And my darling husband, who doesn't need to read this one because I read practically every word and thought aloud as we went. Love you more, sweetie.

REQUEST YOUR FREE BOOKS!

2 FREE NOVELS
FROM THE SUSPENSE COLLECTION
PLUS 2 FREE GIFTS!

YES! Please send me 2 FREE novels from the Suspense Collection and my 2 FREE gifts (gifts are worth about $10). After receiving them, if I don't wish to receive any more books, I can return the shipping statement marked "cancel." If I don't cancel, I will receive 4 brand-new novels every month and be billed just $5.99 per book in the U.S. or $6.49 per book in Canada. That's a saving of at least 25% off the cover price. It's quite a bargain! Shipping and handling is just 50¢ per book in the U.S. and 75¢ per book in Canada.* I understand that accepting the 2 free books and gifts places me under no obligation to buy anything. I can always return a shipment and cancel at any time. Even if I never buy another book, the two free books and gifts are mine to keep forever.

191/391 MDN FEME

Name	(PLEASE PRINT)

Address	Apt. #

City	State/Prov.	Zip/Postal Code

Signature (if under 18, a parent or guardian must sign)

Mail to the **Reader Service**:
IN U.S.A.: P.O. Box 1867, Buffalo, NY 14240-1867
IN CANADA: P.O. Box 609, Fort Erie, Ontario L2A 5X3

Not valid for current subscribers to the Suspense Collection
or the Romance/Suspense Collection.

Want to try two free books from another line?
Call 1-800-873-8635 or visit www.ReaderService.com.

* Terms and prices subject to change without notice. Prices do not include applicable taxes. Sales tax applicable in N.Y. Canadian residents will be charged applicable taxes. Offer not valid in Quebec. This offer is limited to one order per household. All orders subject to credit approval. Credit or debit balances in a customer's account(s) may be offset by any other outstanding balance owed by or to the customer. Please allow 4 to 6 weeks for delivery. Offer available while quantities last.

Your Privacy—The Reader Service is committed to protecting your privacy. Our Privacy Policy is available online at www.ReaderService.com or upon request from the Reader Service.

We make a portion of our mailing list available to reputable third parties that offer products we believe may interest you. If you prefer that we not exchange your name with third parties, or if you wish to clarify or modify your communication preferences, please visit us at www.ReaderService.com/consumerschoice or write to us at Reader Service Preference Service, P.O. Box 9062, Buffalo, NY 14269. Include your complete name and address.